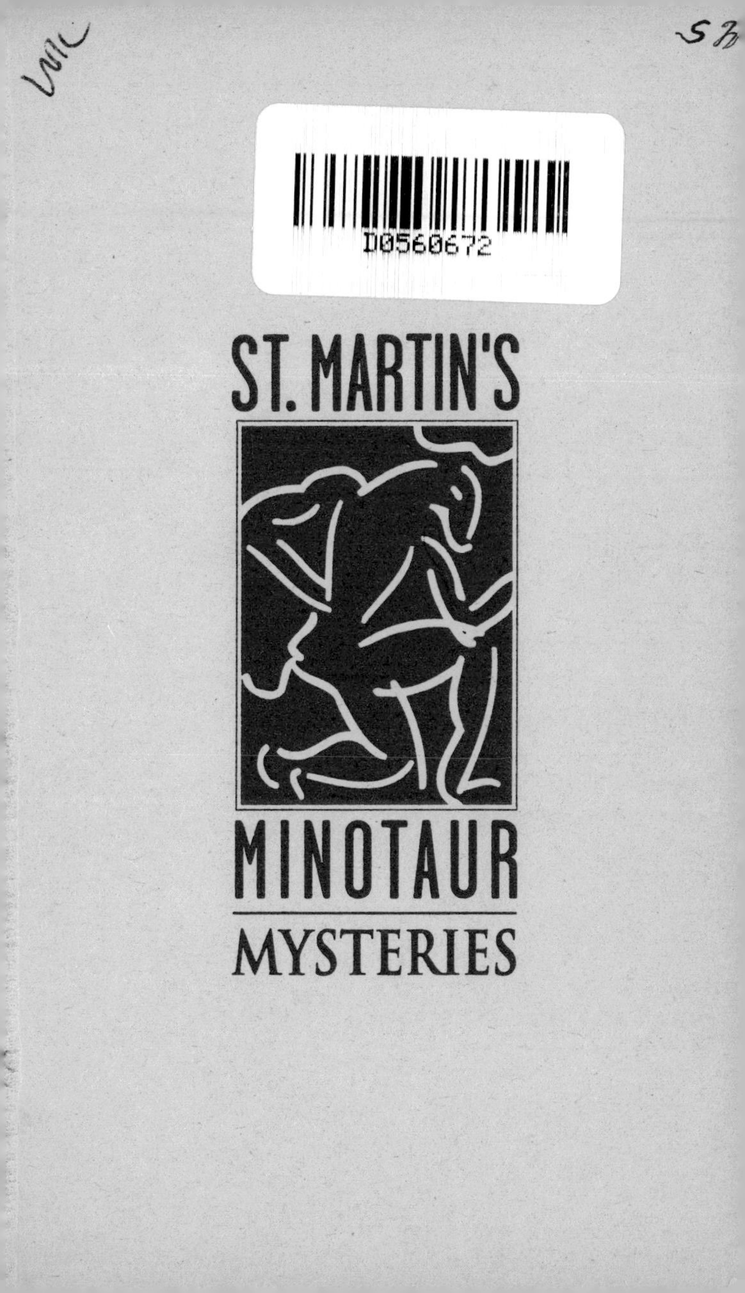
D0560672
ST. MARTIN'S
MINOTAUR
MYSTERIES

Praise for . . . THE BARBED-WIRE KISS

"Stroby does wonders with his blue-collar characters."

—*New York Times Book Review*

"A scorching first novel that mixes the melancholic heart of tough-guy fiction with a fierce and violent gangster plot."

—*Washington Post*

"Every so often a debut novel comes along that is so arresting and powerful you just know the author will go on to a fine career. Such is *The Barbed-Wire Kiss*."

—*Cleveland Plain Dealer*

"A fast-paced debut . . . prepare to have your V.Q. (violence-quotient) challenged to the max."

—*Kirkus Reviews*

"*The Barbed-Wire Kiss* is as gritty and tough as its Soprano-land New Jersey setting, and Wallace Stroby is a no-nonsense guide and a fine writer."

—C. J. Box, author of *Savage Run*

More acclaim follows . . .

"A new member has been added to the Michael Connelly-Robert Crais-Harlan Coben club of crime fiction. This work marks the debut of a novelist of great promise."

—Gerald Petievich, author of *To Live and Die in L.A.*

"Drawing on his career as a journalist living on the Jersey Shore, Stroby has written a novel that is part Sopranos, part Springsteen, but in all a unique and stunning debut."

—Bartholomew Gill, author of *The Death of an Irish Sinner*

"*The Barbed-Wire Kiss* is one of those books that gut-hooks on the first page and never lets you go."

—John Gilstrap, author of *Scott Free* and *Nathan's Run*

"Intense and gritty, *The Barbed-Wire Kiss* weaves a melancholy path through the decaying skeletons of the Jersey Shore's dead resort towns, a dark, brooding landscape strobed by lightning strikes of passion and mayhem. If James Lee Burke had grown up in Asbury Park, he might have written *The Barbed-Wire Kiss*."

—F. Paul Wilson, creator of *Repairman Jack*

THE BARBED-WIRE KISS

Wallace Stroby

THE BARBED-WIRE KISS

ISBN: 0-312-99547-4

Printed in the United States of America

St. Martin's Press hardcover edition / February 2003
St. Martin's Paperbacks edition / March 2004

St. Martin's Paperbacks are published by St. Martin's Press, 175 Fifth Avenue, New York, NY 10010.

10 9 8 7 6 5 4 3 2 1

For my family

In memory of
Mark McGarrity
1943–2002
Friend, colleague, mentor
I'm with ya

Slán go fóill

When the bells justle in the tower
The hollow night amid
Then on my tongue the taste is sour
Of all I ever did.

—A. E. HOUSMAN

Great coolness is necessary with the drowning if you would bring them help without peril to yourself.

—BALTASAR GRACIÁN

Sometimes, at night, he drove. He had no route, no reason. He never planned it. Alone in the big, empty house, the wind rattling the windows, he would suddenly find himself with car keys in his hand.

He'd take the old Mustang out on the county road, head west to the Turnpike or east to the ocean. Some nights he drove for hours, stopping only at all-night gas stations, not turning back until dawn lightened the sky and brought with it the hope of sleep.

He told this to a therapist once, in those first months after Melissa died.

"On the scale of things we've talked about," the therapist said, "that's an easy one."

"What do you mean?"

"You're trying to go back. To fix the things you loved that got away from you."

"Maybe."

"And you know something else, Harry?"

"What?"

"You can't."

He knew that. He'd always known it.

Still, he drove.

ONE

When Harry walked in the door, Bobby was sitting at the end of the bar, watching a redhead take off her clothes.

Barely dark outside, but in here the night was in full swing. Cigarette smoke hung in the air like cotton, and the music was loud enough that Harry could feel the bass through the soles of his boots. Years since he'd been in here, but the clientele hadn't changed much. Fishermen mostly, drinking their dinners, hard faces chiseled by sun and wind. He had grown up around men like these.

Bobby's eyes were on the dancer. Harry came up behind him unseen.

"Hey, slick," he said. "Put your tongue back in your mouth."

Bobby froze, a cigarette halfway to his lips. He swiveled slowly, the hard look on his face twisting into a smile. "Son of a bitch. You made it."

He put out his hand and Harry took it, felt the calloused palm, the strength there. Bobby wore his work clothes: a red flannel shirt with the sleeves rolled up, jeans, tan work boots. The black snake tattoo that circled his left forearm was faded from years in the sun.

Harry slid onto the stool beside him. Bobby stubbed out his cigarette in a tin ashtray, signaled to the barmaid. She was a hard-eyed blonde in a halter top, with a blue butterfly tattoo above her left breast. He pointed at his empty shot glass, and she took a bottle of tequila from the speed rack, poured, looked at Harry.

"Whatever's on tap," he said.

"Just bottles now."

"Corona."

She came back with the open beer, the sides slick with condensation, a slice of lime wedged into the top. Bobby slid a wet twenty toward her, and she took it away without a word.

"There used to be a girl tended bar here," Harry said. "A tall blonde . . ."

"Lisa."

"Whatever happened to her?"

"Moved on, I guess. Just like everybody."

He pushed the lime through, clamped his thumb over the mouth of the bottle and upturned it. The slice rose toward the bottom in a thin stream of bubbles.

Bobby lifted his shot glass. "You know what this shit always reminds me of?"

"What's that?"

"When we snuck that bottle of Cuervo into the dance, junior year? And got busted by Sister Francis? My old man beat my ass over that. Not that he ever needed a reason."

He righted the beer, let the carbonation hiss out under his thumb. He scanned the faces on the other side of the bar. Some looked back, held his gaze, eyes shining with alcohol.

"You still driving that old Ford?" Bobby said.

"Got it outside."

"Still pouring money into it?"

"Put in a new clutch plate last week." He raised his right hand to show the pink spots on his knuckles.

"I do that shit because I have to," Bobby said. "What's your excuse? Hire a mechanic, for Christ's sake."

"Keeps me busy."

He held his bottle out. Bobby touched it with his shot glass.

"It's good to see you," Bobby said. "We shouldn't have let it go this long."

They drank. Harry's beer was sharp and cold.

The redhead was down to just a thong and bra. She finished her routine, stepped gingerly from the stage.

"Nice view," Harry said. "But not a great place to talk."

"Better than the house. I had to get out of there for a while. And here at least, if you didn't show up, the night wouldn't be a total loss."

"Got a point there. How's Janine?"

"Fine, I guess. But there's some shit going on, isn't exactly making life easy. That's what I wanted to talk to you about."

A Prince song began to blast from hidden speakers and another dancer took the stage. She had short blonde hair and wore a sheer white teddy over bikini panties, her nipples and pubic area dark patches beneath the material. He watched her move, wondered if she was married, if she had small children whose clothes and food she bought with the money she made here.

"Tell the truth, I can't remember the last time we actually sat down, had a drink together," Bobby said. He thumbed open a box of Marlboros, took out a cigarette, slid the box toward Harry. He shook his head.

"Quit."

"Forgot. How long now?"

"Almost two years. I stopped in the hospital. Just never picked it up again."

"Good man."

Bobby lit the cigarette with a plastic lighter.

"Sometimes I think about what you went through," he said. "First Melissa, then that other thing. I don't know if I could have handled it."

"Sometimes you don't have a choice."

Harry sipped beer, watched the dancer. She was on all fours now, tiger-crawling across the mirrored floor, her movements jerky in the strobe lights. She reached the edge of the stage and swung down.

Bobby separated a five-dollar bill from his change, folded it lengthwise, held it out. She noticed it from the corner of her eye, moved toward them. Harry saw she was younger than she looked on stage, twenty-five tops, her skin taut and firm, filmed with perspiration.

She smiled at them, leaned over the bar and shrugged the straps of the teddy halfway down her shoulders, pushed her small, pale breasts together. Bobby folded the five again, tucked it into her cleavage.

She kissed him quickly on the mouth, smiled at Harry, and drew away. When she got back on stage, she tugged the teddy into place, dropped the five into an open gym bag, and fell instantly back into her routine.

"Pretty good," Harry said. "What do you get for a twenty?"

"She gives you a handjob in the back room and then a bouncer beats the shit out of you and throws you out."

"Not a bad deal." He swiveled on his stool. "They still have that deck out back?"

"Yeah."

"Let's go. We can talk better there."

Bobby emptied the shot glass, gathered his cigarettes and change. Harry picked up his beer, and they walked down a short corridor, past bathrooms and pay phones, and out onto a small wooden deck overlooking the inlet.

The night was warm, the smell of the tide thick in the air. Bobby leaned on the railing, flicked away his cigarette. They looked down at the red and green lights of charter boats heading out to sea.

"Bluefish," Bobby said. "They're running now. Night's best time for it. Guys pay fifty dollars a head, go out there and drink beer, catch fish all night long."

Harry stood beside him, waited. In the distance, he could see a long line of brake lights on the Route 35 drawbridge heading into Belmar. Across the inlet, a car nosed into the weeds near the water's edge. The headlights went out and, after a few minutes, they heard teenage laughter, the sound of a bottle breaking.

"It was Janine's idea I talk to you," Bobby said. "At first I told her, nah, you don't need to hear this shit. But the more I thought about it . . ."

"What's the problem?" He set the bottle on the railing.

Bobby opened the pack of Marlboros, shook one loose.

"Business deal," he said. "I should know better, right?"

He lit the cigarette, tucked the pack and lighter in his shirt pocket.

"There's this guy I know from the boatyard. He had a shot at something, but he needed a partner. It was a sweet deal."

"What kind of deal?"

"What do you think?"

Harry said nothing. The boats were moving under the open drawbridge now. The lead vessel saluted the bridge tender with a bleat of its horn.

"I used to sell a little weed years back," Bobby said. "You knew that. It was no big deal. Everybody was doing it. Except you, of course. You remember Jimmy Cortez?"

"Should I?"

"You'd know him if you saw him. He used to tend bar at a couple places around here. Lives in Bradley Beach. Skinny guy, dark skin, looked like that actor . . . what's his name? Andy Garcia?"

Harry shook his head, shrugged.

"I used to go out with his older sister, Andrea. You might have known her, she was a couple years behind us at Red Bank Catholic. We hooked up for a little while after I quit school. She lives in Denver now. Got the fuck out of New Jersey while she could. Can't blame her."

"Tell me about Jimmy."

"He used to deal a little on the side when he was bartending. Nothing big. Six, seven years ago, he cut me in on a couple small things. He made it worth my while."

"How small?"

"I probably got five hundred back each time. Not much. We were a little strapped for cash, so it made a difference. I never handled the product, just helped him with the front money. About six months ago he came to work at the boatyard. I hadn't seen him for a while. He sounded me out a couple times, asked if I wanted to pick up where we left off.

I told him no, I didn't think so. It wasn't worth the trouble anymore. He understood."

"And then?"

"Two months ago he came to me again, told me he was putting something together, something good, bigger than before. But he needed a partner to make it fly, someone he could trust."

"And this time you said yes."

"Some things had changed. I decided to reconsider."

"You sure you want to tell me all this?"

"Who else can I tell? I'm not pissing and moaning. I knew what I was getting into. It was my decision."

"What happened?"

"It was a little scary at first. It was like playing in a different league, you know? I had to scrape a little to come up with my end. For a while, I didn't know if I could. Would have been better if I hadn't, I guess."

"How much money?"

"Up front? Twenty grand."

"You had that much lying around?"

"We were equal partners, so we only had to come up with ten each. Even then it wasn't easy. But we got it together. Jimmy gave it to this guy and he fronted us a package. I went along for the ride."

"Why?"

"He knew Jimmy couldn't come up with that kind of money himself. He wanted to meet me, check me out, I guess. What we gave him wasn't a third of what it was worth, so he had a lot coming back. It was a big investment on his part."

"How much did you owe on the balance?"

"Enough."

"How much?"

"Fifty grand."

"That's a long way from selling loose joints."

"Tell me about it."

"That's felony weight."

"That what they called it when you were with the state police?"

"That's what they call it in the courtroom when they're sending people to Rahway for fifty years."

Bobby nodded, blew out smoke. "Thing of it is, Jimmy already knew guys who were willing to take the whole package, couldn't wait to get their hands on it. All we had to do was buy it and pass it on to them, more than double our money. We were looking to clear about forty-five grand apiece. It would have been a nice nest egg."

"So what happened?"

"He's gone."

"Jimmy?"

Bobby nodded, dropped the cigarette on the deck, and ground it out with a boot heel.

"He took off on you?"

"Maybe. Hard to believe it if he did. But put enough money in front of someone, there's no telling what he'll do. I'm living proof of that, right?"

"How long has it been since you've seen him?"

"Three weeks yesterday."

"He have the whole package?"

"Every ounce. He was keeping it until he could close the deal on the other end. That was fine with me. I didn't want it around."

"Do you know who his buyers were?"

"Some bikers in South Jersey. He'd dealt with them before."

"Where does this leave you?"

"In the shit. And feeling like an idiot. This was going to be it, you know? A one-time thing. I'd finally found the balls to put the chips down and let it ride."

"Your supplier, he know about this, about Jimmy?"

"I had to tell him."

"How soon did he expect the rest of his money?"

"A month, maybe a little longer. He wasn't sweating it."

"Now the month is up."

"You got it."

"What was his reaction when you told him?"

"I gave him the whole thing, straight up. But the way he looks at it, he fronted us something for a down payment, with an agreed-on balance due. And all I've given him so far is a story about my partner dropping out of sight and my not being able to find him. Sure, he's pissed, who wouldn't be? He doesn't want to hear about my problems. He wants his money or his stuff back."

"And?"

"And I haven't got either."

"He putting heat on you?"

"It's coming. He sent somebody around to the house looking for me the other night, guy that works for him."

"What happened?"

"I wasn't there. Janine wouldn't let him in. She said she told him to leave or she'd call the police. It scared her, though. That's what pisses me off. I mean, business is business. But coming to the house, that's not right."

"Did he make any threats?"

Bobby shook his head, took out the cigarettes again.

"He was there and that's enough. I guess they felt it was time to make some sort of gesture."

"Your friend Jimmy. You must have trusted him a lot."

"What do you mean?"

"Why did he need you?"

Bobby got a cigarette going.

"Like I said, the front money. He couldn't come up with the whole twenty himself. And he knew he could trust me."

"Maybe he thought he deserved more because he was taking more of the risk. Maybe he thought he deserved it all."

"You mean make the exchange, keep the money, say, 'Adios, motherfucker'?"

"Why not? What would have stopped him?"

"I've thought about that. I guess I just didn't want to believe it."

"Janine know about all this?"

"Most of it. She thinks it's pot. I didn't tell her otherwise. Like I said, it was her idea I talk to you."

Harry watched the drawbridge slowly close, the cars start to move. Beyond he could see the boats leaving the inlet, heading out into the darkness.

There were footsteps behind them, and they turned to see a gray-haired, unshaven man come unsteadily out onto the deck. He looked from Harry to Bobby, his eyes unfocused, then went over to the far corner, unzipped his pants, and began to urinate loudly through the railing into the weeds below.

Bobby looked at Harry. "Do you believe this shit?"

He turned to the old man. "Hey, pal."

The man looked back over his shoulder, urine drops spattering the planks of the deck.

"Why don't you go do that somewhere else?"

He looked blankly at Bobby, then at Harry. "Fuck you," he said finally, his voice slurred.

Bobby took a step toward him, and Harry caught his arm. The old man turned his back on them, carefully shook off and zipped up, then went back into the bar without a word.

Bobby shook his head, turned back to the water. Harry picked up his beer bottle, swished it, drank some. He put it back down, rested his elbows on the railing.

"You never told me," he said. "Who was the supplier?"

"A guy named Eddie Fallon."

Harry pushed away from the railing, looked at him.

Bobby felt the silence, turned.

"What?"

"Eddie Fallon?"

"You know him?"

"I know who he is—and what he is. I know his reputation."

"Hard to blame him in this case. He gave us an opportunity. He and I both got fucked."

"If you feel that way, you're not thinking straight. People like Eddie Fallon don't get fucked. They spend their whole lives making sure someone else's ass is on the line when it comes down to it."

"Maybe, but isn't that what all businessmen do?"

"Most businessmen don't sell cocaine."

Bobby turned away, blew smoke out.

"Cocaine's passé," he said.

Harry watched the side of his face.

"Let's go back inside," Bobby said. "I think I need another drink."

"Hold on. What happened when you told him?"

"Not much. I called him when I realized Jimmy was gone. He had me come by this restaurant he owns in Manasquan, the Sand Castle."

"I know it."

"He didn't even show up. He sent this guy Wiley, the same one that came by the house. Big, bald-headed bastard, used to bounce at one of his clubs. I told him everything, but he didn't react at all. Just told me he'd pass on the message, generally treated me like a piece of shit. I wanted to hit him. I need that drink."

They went back inside. There was another dancer on stage now, a brunette in a mesh top and zippered leather pants. Their stools were still empty.

The barmaid came over, lifted the tequila bottle. Bobby shook his head, pointed at Harry's half-empty beer.

"So," Harry said when she was gone. "You try and look for this Jimmy?"

"As much as I could. He's got two paychecks waiting for him at work. No one's picked them up, and no one I've talked to has seen him. He hasn't been at his apartment in a while, either. I went by a couple of times. His car's gone. Whether his clothes and things are still there, I don't know. I didn't go inside."

"You talk to the sister?"

"And say what? 'Hey, it's Bobby Fox, remember me? Your brother and I were doing a dope deal together and he ran out on me. Have you seen him recently?' No, I didn't talk to her. Maybe I should have, but I didn't."

The barmaid brought two Coronas, no limes this time. Bobby gave her a ten.

"He have any other family around here?" Harry said.

"Not anymore. At least none that I know of."

Bobby lifted his bottle, drank.

"I've got a friend," Harry said. "We were with the state police together. He has connections with the state AG's office."

"What do you mean?"

"Think about it."

"Go to the police? Testify against Fallon? It's not like I'm an innocent in all this, is it?"

"You have to consider your options. There aren't a lot."

"Maybe so, but there have to be more than that. Like I said, I got myself into this. No one else."

Harry looked around, felt a vague depression creeping over him, a feeling of backsliding. He wanted to be out of there.

"You want my advice?"

"That's why I called you."

"Pay him."

"If I could do that . . ."

"How much could you put together? Right now, in the next week. How much money could you get your hands on?"

"I don't know. Four, maybe five thousand tops. And that's stretching it."

"Round up whatever you can, even if it's only a few thousand. Give it to him as a gesture of good faith, tell him there's more to come."

"A few thousand? He'd fucking laugh at me."

"Maybe not. You give him four, five grand, tell him you'll pay him the rest as soon as you can. This way at least he doesn't think you're trying to make a fool out of him. He'll take it, I guarantee you. And it'll buy us some time to think this thing through."

Bobby turned to him and Harry saw a flash of wetness in his eyes. Bobby looked away quickly, raised his beer.

"Janine was right," he said.

"About what?"

"About talking with you. But I was worried."

"Worried?"

"That things had changed. We haven't seen each other much lately. I wasn't sure what you'd think about all this."

"You want me to tell you that you fucked up? You already know that."

"Yeah, I do. And up until this moment, the only light I've seen at the end of the tunnel has been one big goddamn train."

Harry slid off the stool.

"I'll give you a call at the house tomorrow. We'll talk more about this."

He put his hand out. Bobby took it.

"Nothing's changed," Harry said.

Bobby squeezed his hand, let it go. He turned his face away, lifted his beer.

Harry started for the door. Halfway there, he saw the blonde dancer sitting at the bar. She was dressed now, T-shirt and jeans, her gym bag at her feet, her bangs still damp and dark with sweat. She was sipping a Coke, nodding while the old man from the deck leaned close to her, pantomimed catching some phantom fish. She caught Harry's glance, smiled without hesitation. *Save me.*

He started toward her and a bouncer moved in front of him, shouldering a case of beer. He put it on the bar, ducked below the flap, came up on the other side, and began shoving bottles into the ice chest.

"Hit the road, Pops," he said to the drunk. "Leave the lady alone."

The old man drew himself up, his eyes narrowing into slits. The bouncer looked into his face, pushed beer into ice. Mumbling, the old man turned away, started back down the bar. The blonde put her hand on the bouncer's arm, said something close to his ear. He laughed.

Harry walked past them to the door and pushed out into the night.

TWO

Ten in the morning and the air was already thick with humidity. He threw back the single sheet, lay naked and sweat-slick on the bed, watching the ceiling fan turn above him.

After a while, he made his way into the bathroom and showered, washed the bar smells and cigarette smoke out of his hair. Standing in front of the mirror afterward, he touched the ugly quarter-sized scar two inches to the left of his navel. The tissue there was thick, like melted wax left to harden, dimpled slightly where the bullet had gone in. He dried off as best he could in the heavy air, put on a sleeveless gray T-shirt and cutoff jeans.

He made instant coffee in the kitchen, carried the mug out onto the front porch. The sky was a hard, bright, cloudless blue. He sat in the ladderback rocker and looked down the long willow-lined slope of his driveway to where it joined the county road. Traffic was sparse now, but it would be bumper-to-bumper this afternoon, as people headed east to the Shore for the weekend.

He had spent childhood summers in this house, staying with his grandparents, and he remembered a time when there were few vehicles on that road besides pickup trucks and tractors. Colts Neck then was nothing but farms and apple orchards. Now every year there were more cars, more people, fewer farms.

Across the road, he could see yellow surveyor's tape

strung through the woods. Before November, he knew, the bulldozers and backhoes would arrive. They would clear the trees and drive the wildlife out onto the highways to become road kill. Then the houses would spring up, indistinguishable from all the other subdivisions that now lined this stretch of Route 537.

They'd drive him out too, one day. He was the only Rane in the county now, and though he still referred to the place as the farm, the seventy adjacent acres his grandparents had once used for corn lay fallow. His grandmother had sold the acreage a year before her death, willed him the money and the house. The amount was more than he'd expected, nearly $300,000, and he had planned to put the house up for sale as well, but something had stopped him. Then, after Melissa was gone, he'd decided to sell the house in Metuchen instead, move in here. In the meantime, the developer who'd bought the seventy acres had gone bankrupt. The land remained untouched.

It wouldn't stay that way, he knew. The title would someday be cleared, someone else would buy the land and build on it—it was worth too much. The farmhouse would be an island in a sea of development, an anachronism. Eventually the lawyers would come to him with the right numbers, and then one day the machines would roll up his driveway. Then the farm, and everything it meant, would live only in his memory.

The coffee was bitter, acidic. He drank half, then leaned over the railing and poured out the rest.

He took the mug back inside, rinsed it in the sink, and used the kitchen phone to call Ray Washington's office. The receptionist put him through.

"This must be a wrong number," Ray said when he came on the line.

"Why's that?"

"I have only one friend named Harry, but he would never call me. Can't figure out how to use those new phones. The kind with the buttons instead of the dial."

"Sorry, Ray. Long time, I know."

"How are you doing?"

"I'd say I've been busy, but that would be a lie."

"Edda was just asking about you. She wants to know when you're going to come work for me."

"Someday you'll ask me and the answer will be yes."

"I hope so. Man offers you a job, you should think about it before you say no. What can I do for you?"

"I'm looking for some information."

"Let's hear it."

"What do you know about a guy named Eddie Fallon?"

"Fellow used to own all those clubs?"

"That's him."

"Not much. He lives in Spring Lake now, I think, but he's kept himself out of the news the last few years. Owns some racehorses too, but he's not quite the mover and shaker he thinks he is."

"Any arrests, indictments?"

"I'd have to check. The most serious thing I can remember him being involved in is that business at that club up in Wayne, where that kid got killed. That had to be ten, twelve years ago now, though."

"I remember that. Anything else?"

"Nothing comes to mind. I know he still owns some places up here. He had one or two down in Florida for a while, I think."

"You recall his name coming up at all when we were at Major Crimes?"

"Not especially. Everyone knew he was dirty and wondered where he got his money from. But nothing beyond that. Why the sudden interest?"

"It's for a friend of mine."

"Anybody I know?"

"Maybe."

"In other words, mind my own business?"

"I didn't mean it like that."

"What's the trouble?"

"He got involved in a business deal with Fallon. Things went sour and now Fallon's getting ready to put the screws to him."

"This a real business deal or an Eddie Fallon business deal?"

"The latter."

"And why are you involved?"

"I thought I'd look into it, see if I could find a way to help him out. But I wanted to talk to you first. I've been out of the loop for a while."

"Let me reach out to some people, see what I can turn up. What sort of information you looking for?"

"Anything and everything."

"Might be nothing you haven't heard."

"I'll take the chance. One other thing. He's got someone who works for him, was a bouncer at one of his clubs, I think. Name's Wiley. Don't know if that's a first name, last name, or what. Not sure how it's spelled."

"You're making me curious. I'll ask around, but that's not much to go on."

"Anything will help. I'm just trying to put together as much information as I can right now. Like they say, knowledge is power."

"Or something like that. You be home later?"

"All day."

"Give me a few hours. I'll see what I can do."

Later, he got a plastic bottle of water from the refrigerator and a towel from the bathroom. He went out to the old barn he used as a garage, pulled open the doors, felt the heat surge out around him.

A month after Harry had gotten out of the hospital, when he was still so weak that he couldn't walk to the end of his driveway and back, Bobby had hung a heavy bag from the rafters of the barn. In those first weeks home, Harry had gone out there every day, thrown punches until he was exhausted. His stomach was healing, but the six weeks in the hospital had left him weak and depressed. Hitting the bag helped.

Bobby eventually brought weights and a weight bench, and he and Harry had spent long hours in the barn, Bobby spotting him while he worked the dumbbells and then the bar. Gradually his strength returned, and the endorphins and oxygenated blood helped chase some of the darkness from his mind. Even now, on the nights when he couldn't sleep and was too tired to drive, he would go out and hit the bag until his arms felt like lead.

He set the water bottle on the hard-packed dirt floor, pulled off his T-shirt, and got the leather bag gloves from the workbench. He pulled them on and stretched, touched the floor, limbering up, feeling the gentle pull of torn and reconstructed abdominal muscles. He began to work the bag, half speed at first, left jabs followed by right reverse punches.

It was Bobby who had first taught him how to fight. They'd met in the seventh-grade class at Star of the Sea in Long Branch, Bobby a transfer, his own house just two streets from Harry's. They'd been altar boys together, and once, walking home from the rectory on a Sunday after Mass, they'd been caught by four older kids from the nearby public school. The kids had peppered them with stones and gravel, chased them. But after a block of running, Bobby had turned to face them and Harry was forced to do the same. In the fight that followed, Harry got the worst of it—a black eye and a chipped tooth—but Bobby had fought with a fierceness that Harry had never seen in him before. The four were all at least five years older and thirty pounds heavier, but Bobby had knocked two of them down, sent the others running. He'd helped Harry from the ground, walked him home.

Harry told his mother he'd fallen off a swing, and she'd believed him. That same week, he'd started meeting Bobby after school in a field near his house. Bobby had two pairs of boxing gloves his older brother had given him before going into the Army. They had to double-tie the strings to keep the gloves from flying off, but they worked well enough. Bobby taught him what he'd learned from his brother—how to punch and block, how to cover up—and they'd beat each other silly for weeks, Harry eventually learning to hit hard and fast, to pick his targets.

The bag swung, chains creaking. He built the combinations, turned up the speed, careful to keep his wrists straight, the impact rippling up his arms every time his fists thumped into the canvas. He felt the dull pain begin to grow in his stomach.

They'd gone on to high school together at Red Bank Catholic, outcasts again among the rich teenagers from Little Silver and Fair Haven. One day sophomore year Bobby had come to homeroom with his left eye blackened, his jaw swollen. The sister called the principal, who took him out of class.

By the time Harry got home that afternoon, his parents already knew about it. A neighbor had called them. They weren't surprised. They'd heard the stories.

"It's the drinking," his mother said that night at the dinner table. "That's what makes him do it. Why else would someone treat a boy like that?"

There had been more days like that over the next few months. Then, midway through their junior year, Bobby's father was dead, the cirrhosis in his liver kicking into sudden overdrive. They smoked a joint out behind the funeral home, Bobby dry-eyed, straight-shouldered. "Fuck him," he said.

Four months later, Harry's own father was gone, his clam boat capsized and broken by an early nor'easter. He and Bobby grew into adulthood without fathers, stronger for it. The summer before their senior year, Bobby got a job at a Sunoco station, pumping gas and doing basic mechanical work. He kept the job when September came, dropped out of school and never went back. On graduation day, Harry spotted him at the rear of the crowded gym, standing near the far doors. That night, Harry blew off the postgraduation party and they drove around in Bobby's primer-gray Dodge Charger, sharing a six-pack of Tuborg in cans, tossing out the empties, blasting the eight-track. Harry felt like he was waiting for his life to begin. And then it had and nothing was ever the same again.

The pain in his stomach was blooming now, sharpening. He pushed away the bag and stepped back, kicked, caught it on its return swing, the ball of his right foot sinking deep. He stepped forward, followed the kick with a combination at face height, pushed away the bag with a shoulder, and fired shots to the body. The sweat was rolling off him now, spattering the dirt.

He threw combinations until he couldn't raise his arms, then slowed, stopped, leaving the bag spinning. He pulled off the clammy gloves, got the bottle and twisted off the cap, took a mouthful of water, swirled it around and spit it out. He wiped the sweat from his eyes with the towel, leaned against the fender of the Mustang until his breath was back to normal. Then he gathered up the T-shirt and bottle and walked slowly back to the house.

He was sprawled on the couch, half asleep in the heat, when Ray called back. He sat at the kitchen table and talked for ten minutes, taking notes on a yellow legal pad. When the conversation was over, he thanked him, promised to keep in touch, and hung up. He looked over the notes, turning the situation around in his mind, fitting it all together. Wondering how things had come to this.

THREE

Driving to Bobby's house, he found himself taking the long way there. Heading east on Route 36 to the ocean, he turned right onto Broadway and detoured into Long Branch.

It had been years since he'd driven these streets—he never had any reason to come back. He passed the gray stone mass of Star of the Sea Grammar School, closed for a decade now, the windows boarded over. He made a left and turned down the street where he'd grown up. The old house was gone, bulldozed years ago to make room for a methadone clinic. Graffiti marked the white cinder-block walls.

He drove on, past abandoned businesses and the occasional Spanish storefront church. In the 1940s and 50s, when Long Branch was still one of the predominant resort towns on the Shore, these streets had been the heart of its downtown. But the years had been hard, and riots in the late 60s had accelerated a process already begun. When he was growing up, Long Branch was a blue-collar, hardscrabble town, black and white, Italian and Spanish, all living in the same cluster of lower-middle-class neighborhoods. Even after white flight had begun in earnest in the early 70s, his family had stayed on. They had nowhere else to go.

He drove by Bobby's old house, saw a half dozen people gathered on the porch, beers in hand, salsa music blaring through open windows. They watched him as he drove by.

He turned back onto Broadway, headed east again. When he hit the wide stretch of Ocean Avenue, high-rises sprang up along the beach side, all but fencing off the ocean from view. When he was a kid, the beachfront had been arcades and boardwalks, an amusement pier with a Ferris wheel. All of it was gone now, replaced by ocean-view condos, each claiming its own stretch of private beach. There was no middle ground anymore. Long Branch went from poverty and despair to wealth and insulation in less than a half mile. The people who lived in these high-rises would never know the real town, would never even consider going west into its neighborhoods. He couldn't blame them. There was nothing there for them.

He turned north, the seawall on his right, and crossed into Monmouth Beach, a one-mile-square town bordered by the ocean on one side and the Shrewsbury River on the other. He passed the Marine Police station and turned left off Ocean Avenue into the center of town, a small compact business district surrounded by middle-class homes.

Only white faces on the streets here. The town had been founded by fishermen, and the sea had been its only industry until development and rising real estate prices had driven the fishermen out. It was an old story, relived at a hundred seaside towns along this stretch of the coast.

Bobby's house was one of a cluster of old homes on a spit of land extending out into the river. The reeds a hundred yards beyond the house were already flooded. During the strongest nor'easters, when the river and the ocean rose to meet each other, this part of town was always the first evacuated.

Bobby's old Chevy pickup was parked on the cul-de-sac that marked the end of their street. He pulled in behind it, saw the shiny new FOR SALE sign with the realtor's logo on it stuck into the lawn. He got out of the car, mosquitoes whining around him. The sun was dying in the west.

He went up the concrete walk and onto the sagging porch, rapped his knuckles on the door, and waited. He slapped at a mosquito on his neck, rolled it into a wet ball, and flicked it away. After a moment there was a flash of movement behind a curtained window to his left. He knocked again.

"Hold on."

There was the click of a dead bolt being drawn, the door swung open, and Bobby was standing there. He wore jeans and a white pocket T-shirt. In his right hand, half hidden behind his leg, he held a gun.

"Hey," Harry said.

"Christ, come on in, man." Bobby stepped aside. "I was expecting you to call."

"I felt like going for a drive. Things that bad?"

Bobby raised the pistol as if he'd forgotten he was holding it. It was a nine-millimeter Glock 26, black plastic and steel. "Getting a little paranoid these days, I guess. I'm sorry. It's probably the last thing you want to see. Come on in, sit down."

Bobby closed and locked the door behind him. They were in a small living room, furnished with a couch, a coffee table, and a single chair facing the television. An acoustic guitar rested against the wall.

"Janine's taking a shower," Bobby said. "She'll be down in a minute. Have a seat."

"Are you moving?"

"You mean the sign? Landlord sent us a letter last month, said he was selling. Then two days ago the realtors show up and put that sign there. We have a lease, though, so he can't kick us out until at least October."

Bobby sank onto the couch, set the gun on the coffee table atop a *TV Guide*. Harry took the chair, turned it, and sat down. He picked up the Glock, checked the rear safety, pointed the muzzle at the floor, and ejected the thick clip. The gun felt alien in his hand. It occurred to him that it was the first time he'd held one since the night he'd been shot.

"You have a license for this?"

"You kidding? In this state? Not a chance. I bought that in Florida last year through a buddy. That's a five-hundred-dollar gun."

Harry pulled the slide back to clear it, looked into the breech, sniffed.

"You've been doing some shooting."

"Out at the range in Englishtown. That thing kicks pretty solid. Not much weight to it."

"You have a spare clip?"

"Yeah, why?"

"Move the shells from clip to clip every once in a while. It keeps the springs from wearing out. Automatics jam like crazy if you don't take care of them. You always bring it with you when you answer the door?"

"Lately, yeah."

Harry slid the clip home again, set the gun back down.

"Can I get you something to eat?" Bobby said. "We had dinner a little while ago, but I think there's some pasta left."

Harry shook his head. Behind him, from the other room, he heard footsteps on the stairs. Bobby opened a drawer in the table, slid the Glock in.

"She doesn't like to see it around," he said.

Harry stood, turned as Janine came into the living room. She was a full head shorter than Bobby, her long brown hair wet and dark from the shower. She wore jeans and a gray Monmouth University sweatshirt, was barefoot on the carpet.

"Harry, is that really you?"

"Hey, girl."

They met halfway, hugged. She smelled of soap and henna.

"How are you?" she said. "How do you feel?"

"Fine," he said. "Things are fine. You look great."

"We talked last night," Bobby said to her. "I took your advice."

Her smile faded briefly, as if she'd been reminded of something unpleasant.

"Come on," she said. "Sit down."

He went back to the chair and Bobby made room for her on the couch. She sat beside him, pulled her feet up under her.

"I see Bobby hasn't been a very good host," she said. "Would you like a beer, a glass of wine?"

"No, thanks. You go ahead."

"Not for me," she said. "Not anymore."

He looked at her.

"Bobby didn't tell you, did he?"

He shook his head.

Bobby laid a hand on her knee, squeezed.

"Janine's pregnant," he said.

She was smiling again.

"You look shocked. It's hard to believe, I know, especially after all this time. I'm not sure I'm used to it myself."

"How long?" he asked.

"Almost four months. And I'm already starting to get fat. You didn't notice?"

He shook his head, found himself smiling.

"That's great," he said. "I'm happy for you." Meaning it.

"We'd been talking about it for a while," Bobby said. "Even so, it was kind of a surprise when it happened. But the doctor says everything's fine so far."

"What do you mean?"

"I'm not twenty-four anymore, Harry," she said. "These things get more complicated when you're my age. In a year or two, we might not have the option at all. So we decided, if we were going to do it, now was the time."

"That's terrific," he said.

"The idea of being a father still scares the hell out of me," Bobby said. "But I'm starting to get used to it, I think."

"For him, that's a bold statement of commitment," she said.

"Hey," Bobby said, getting up, "I want to show you something out back." He kissed the top of Janine's head. "We'll be back in a couple minutes."

"That bike's staying right where it is," she said.

"Whatever you say, Mom. You're the boss."

Harry followed him through the kitchen and out onto a weathered deck. It was almost full dark now. Bobby closed the sliding glass door behind them.

"It was her idea I talk to you," he said. "But I think she's still pissed at me about this whole thing. Not that she doesn't have a right to be."

They went down the steps into the yard. There was a corrugated tin toolshed on the side of the house, the door open. Bobby went in, pulled the chain to illuminate the single bare bulb that hung from the ceiling. The shed was about six feet wide and ten feet long, a homemade workbench running along one side. It was full of car and boat parts, some in oil-stained cardboard boxes, others left out on the workbench. A grass-encrusted lawn mower was pushed into one corner. The shed smelled of newly mown grass and gasoline.

"Look at this," Bobby said. Leaning against the far wall was the frame of an old motorcycle, the front wheel missing, brown paint chipped off the tank and body. It was low-slung with dual pipes, both pitted with rust.

"It's an old Harley Panhead," he said. "A 'fifty-nine. I bought it from some guy for a hundred bucks. Tough getting parts for it, though. Engine's totally shot."

He pulled it away from the wall, straddled it, the front forks digging into the dirt. He gripped the handlebars, settled back on the cracked and worn leather seat.

"Restored, these things go for about fifteen grand," he said. "I always wanted one when I was a kid. Janine's convinced if I ever get it running, I'll kill myself on it." He swung off the bike, set it back against the wall. "Maybe she's got a point."

"I was unsure what to say back there. I didn't know if you wanted to get into it with Janine there or not."

"She knows most of it. But, no, I don't want her worrying more about it than she already has. Especially now."

Mosquitoes were flitting through the shed, drawn by the light. Bobby opened a shallow drawer in the workbench, took out an El Producto cigar box.

"Can't do this in the house anymore," he said.

He set the box on the bench, took out a rolled baggie of marijuana and a packet of E–Z Widers. He pulled one of the papers free.

"I talked to a friend about your situation," Harry said.

Bobby looked at him.

"No specifics. I just wanted to try to find out some more about Fallon."

"Did you?"

"Not a lot, but enough. It could be this situation isn't as bad as it seems."

"That's the closest thing to good news I've heard in weeks. What makes you say it?"

"Fallon's a businessman. He's no heavy hitter. He's looking for his money, not trouble."

"Let's hope you're right," Bobby said. He rolled and sealed the joint, twisted the ends shut.

"How long have you known him?" Harry said.

"Like I said, about two months. I never met him before that time Jimmy introduced us, the night we made the deal."

He took a disposable lighter from the box, got the joint going. He puffed deep on it, the paper crisping as it burned. He held out the joint, blew smoke to the side, the acrid smell of it filling the air.

Harry took the joint, drew on it, felt the harshness fill his lungs. He restrained the urge to cough, blew the smoke out in a thin cloud, waved it away from his face.

"He doesn't have much in the way of an arrest record," he said. He handed the joint back. "About fifteen years ago he was indicted for attempted bribery while trying to buy a bar in North Jersey. The case never went to trial and the charges were eventually dropped. The councilman he had supposedly bribed resigned, so that ended it."

Bobby drew on the joint, turned his head, and blew smoke at a hovering mosquito.

"Right now, he owns five places. Two nightclubs in Florida, two clubs and a restaurant up here."

Bobby offered the joint. Harry hit on it briefly, couldn't control the cough this time. He handed it back, his eyes watering.

"He owns all the places himself, outright. But some

people think he borrowed the seed money on a couple of them from some OC guys in North Jersey."

"OC?"

"Organized crime."

"Fuck."

Bobby set the joint on the edge of the workbench.

"Keep in mind, though, the fact he borrowed money from them—if he actually did—doesn't mean he's one of them. Chances are, any loans he took out would have been paid back long ago. In fact, it looks like the biggest trouble he's been in was that Empire East thing."

"What was that?"

"Happened about twelve years ago. It was a dance club he owned up in Wayne. A real meat market—deejays, strobe lights, coke in the back room, the whole deal. One Saturday night, this woman—a regular customer—complained to the bartender that some kid was trying to pick her up, wouldn't leave her alone. The kid was nineteen, drunk, shouldn't even have been there."

"I think I remember this."

"The bartender tells him to take off, but the kid's drunk—or just stupid—enough to put up a fight and, while the bouncers are throwing him out, he takes a swing at one of them. So they bring him into a back room and take turns knocking him around—five of them. The kid's unconscious when they finally toss him out the side door. Come closing time, he's still lying there. So one of the bouncers calls an ambulance and tells them the kid was drunk, went outside, tripped and fell. But he never woke up. He died in the hospital two days later. Multiple skull fractures."

A thin line of blue smoke spiraled up from the unattended joint, hung in the air between them.

"I remember reading about that," Bobby said. "I didn't know it was one of Fallon's places. I never made the connection. What happened to them, the ones who beat him?"

"Not much. At first they denied everything. Fallon claimed he wasn't even there. But once the prosecutor's office started talking to witnesses, the whole story fell apart.

Finally, they managed to squeeze one of the bouncers into testifying against the other four as part of a plea agreement. They all eventually pleaded out, involuntary manslaughter and assault charges. Only three of them did time, one of them nine months, and that was the longest sentence. Alcoholic Beverage Control came down pretty hard on Fallon, since the kid was underage to start with. It cost him a few grand in fines and he ended up paying a settlement to the kid's family. He shut the place down for good shortly afterward."

"And that was it?"

"After the bouncers did their time, Fallon hired them all back to work in his other places. All except the one that turned, of course. One of the ones who went to jail was Lester Wiley."

"Why am I not surprised?"

"Wiley was the one who did the nine months. He testified Fallon wasn't there that night and didn't know anything about what had happened."

"*Was* Fallon there?"

"Depends who you ask. The bouncer who turned said it was Fallon told them to bring the kid in the back, then stood by while they beat him. But no other witnesses could put him there and the other four all stuck to their stories. Eventually there was no way they could prove anything. Fallon said he was home that entire day and night, had a birthday party for his daughter in the afternoon and never left the house after that. If he was at the club when the kid died, he covered his tracks pretty well."

Bobby picked up the joint, pinched it out.

"When does the good news start?" he said.

"I just wanted to let you know who you were dealing with here. But the point is, Fallon doesn't need any more trouble. If he can find a way to work this out without any, I'm sure he'll take it. That's why you should give him some money as soon as possible. A preemptive strike."

Bobby picked a fleck of cigarette paper from his lip.

"I guess in the back of my mind I was thinking there might be some other solution," he said.

Harry shook his head. "Like I said, I think you're facing some limited options here."

They heard footsteps outside. Janine stepped into the light wash from the shed.

"Am I invading the boys' club meeting out here?"

"No," Bobby said. "It's only when we're in the tree house that you can't come in."

She moved to stand beside him.

"It reeks in here," she said. "I should have guessed."

"Just kicking," Bobby said.

She looked at Harry. "So what do you think about this situation?"

"Like I was just telling Bobby, it might not be as bad as it seems."

"Thank God if that's true," she said.

"I have some ideas. A couple things to look into. We'll work this out."

She looked at Bobby. "See? What did I tell you?"

He smiled at her. Harry slapped him lightly on the shoulder.

"I have to get going," he said. "There's someplace I need to be."

"Thanks for stopping by," Bobby said.

Harry hugged Janine again.

"You should come by more often, Harry," she said. "It's no good, spending so much time alone."

"I'll be around," he said.

He left them there in the light of the shed, walked out to the street. At the car, he turned to see them outlined in the doorway, talking low. He couldn't hear their words.

A soft breeze blew from the west, riffling the reeds, bringing with it the smells of the river. He started the Mustang, U-turned in the cul-de-sac. As he drove away, he looked back a final time at the house, its windows throwing squares of light onto the dark yard, and wondered why he felt so suddenly and completely alone.

• • •

On the way home, he stopped at a liquor store and bought a bottle of red wine. He opened it in the kitchen, got a glass from the cabinet, and went into the living room. He sat on the couch, poured wine into the glass, set the bottle on the coffee table.

He drank, looked across the room at the empty fireplace and the bookcase beside it, feeling the pull. After the second glass, he got up and took the photo album down from the top shelf.

He carried it back to the couch, filled the glass again. Months since he'd looked at it, but he knew each page by heart.

First were childhood shots, color Polaroids, the hues already faded. Melissa had put these pages together. On the first was a photo of Harry on the day of his first Holy Communion, wearing a jacket and bow tie, standing between his father and mother in the living room of the old house. On the same page, Harry and Bobby at thirteen, wearing shirts and ties, shoulder to shoulder on the steps outside Star of the Sea Church after their Confirmation, squinting in the sun.

He flipped the page. More shots from the old house. In one, Harry's father stood behind him, hands on Harry's shoulders. He was smiling, a cigarette tucked into the corner of his mouth. In the background, almost out of frame, Bobby on the living room floor, opening a gift. "Christmas 1974" was written in ballpoint pen in the white lower margin of the photo. It was his mother's handwriting.

He stopped, knowing what was next. A few minutes later, when the glass was half empty, he turned the page.

At the top was a photo of Melissa as a little girl, dressed as a witch for Halloween. Then, beneath it, a few years older, in a Girl Scout uniform, hugging a collie. For weeks after her death, he had tortured himself with these photos, touching the pain as if prodding an open wound.

On the next page: Melissa in high school; her graduation portrait. Already a woman at seventeen, already beautiful, her black hair shining. She had looked no older when they met five years later at Rutgers, Harry gathering credits before applying to the state police academy, Melissa a teaching assistant in his social science class.

Next were the wedding photos. Melissa in white, bridesmaids spread out behind her; he in his dress uniform, three weeks out of the academy. He remembered how he'd felt that day, his career stretching before him, the woman he loved at his side. For their first dance together, the song they'd chosen, he'd whispered along with the words as he held her:

We said we'd walk together, come what may
That come the twilight should we lose our way
If as we're walking a hand should slip free
I'll wait for you
And should I fall behind
Wait for me . . .

He turned pages. Melissa on their honeymoon in Grenada, laughing, perched on the gunwale of a sailboat, holding on to a line while the boat dipped steeply toward the bright blue water. Then on the beach outside the hotel, picking shells from the surf, the sun low behind her.

Almost the end of the album now. An eight-by-ten of Melissa in the yard of their house in Metuchen, wearing a T-shirt and shorts, not smiling, her dark hair catching the light. Then a final photo, taken on the day she came home from the hospital, her head shaved, her arm around the oversized stuffed dog he'd bought her. The last page was her funeral card, centered in the plastic sheet.

He turned back to the shot of her in the yard, touched it, felt the sad and sudden tang of desire that always came to him when he looked at it. He traced her body with a fingertip, thought of her in those last days at home, shrunken and sick, a different person. Not this woman at all.

He thumped the album shut.

FOUR

The road up to the Shore Line Country Club was lined with dogwood trees, their bloom already fading in the midsummer heat. White petals covered the ground like snow.

He downshifted as he neared the main building. To the left, the golf course stretched out perfect green to a far line of trees. To the right was a fenced-in pasture and, beyond it, a barn. In the pasture, two figures rode horses side by side at a canter.

He felt tired, irritable. Too much wine and too little sleep had given him a headache that aspirin couldn't touch.

The road ended in a circular parking area in front of the porticoed entrance. He pulled up under the green-and-white awning, and a teenager wearing a blazer in the same colors got up slowly from a chair beside the front door. Harry waited for him to come up to the car.

"I'll park it myself," Harry said. "Just show me where."

The kid looked the Mustang over. He had long blond hair gathered in a neat ponytail.

"Phat wheels. What year?"

"Sixty-seven."

"What you got under there?"

"Two eighty-nine. Four-speed."

"Rockin'. You can pull up on the grass over there, under the tree."

He parked under a spreading oak, alongside a midnight

blue BMW convertible. There were only a half dozen cars in the lot, two of them Mercedeses, one a gleaming black Lexus.

The kid was back in his chair by the time Harry got to the door.

"Which way's the bar?"

"Straight through to the right. You can't miss it."

"Thanks."

He pulled open the heavy smoked glass door, stepped through into air-conditioning. There was a small fountain tinkling quietly in the center of the lobby, chairs evenly spaced on the marble floor. Beyond the fountain was a reception desk, unmanned, and beyond that two sliding oak doors opened onto an empty dining room.

He took off his sunglasses, slipped them into the pocket of his shirt. To the right of the desk was a glass door with a carved wooden sign above it that read THE PADDOCK ROOM. He went through. Inside was a small lounge with a short bar, a half dozen tables, and open double doors that led out onto a roofed porch.

The lounge was empty except for the bartender, a man in his sixties with snow-white hair and a tough Irish face. He was smoking a cigarette and watching a baseball game on the TV above the bar, the sound turned low. From outside, Harry could hear the steady *thwops* of a tennis game in progress.

The bartender looked at him, nodded.

"What's the score?" Harry asked.

"Five–two, Yanks. Baltimore's choking. What can I get you?"

"I'm here to see Mr. Fallon."

The bartender nodded at the double doors. "Out there. I think he's expecting you."

He walked out into bright sunshine. The porch stretched the length of the rear of the building, curving around on both sides. There was another door to the left, the outside entrance to the dining room, closed now to keep the air-conditioning in. There were tables out here on the porch as well, wrought-iron with glass tops, chairs with cushioned seats. Steps led down to a flagstone path that ran past a fenced-in pool area and tennis courts. Flowers in stone planters lined the walkway, and on either side of the steps were small, stone-lined ponds, their surfaces choked with water lilies.

"You Rane?"

He turned. At a table behind him sat a big man in his early thirties, his head shaved like a wrestler's. Acne scars pitted his thick neck and a neatly trimmed goatee surrounded his mouth. He was wearing a too-tight sport jacket over a shirt unbuttoned halfway down his chest, exposing a thin silver chain. On the table was a newspaper open to the sports page.

"Yeah," Harry said.

"About time."

Harry didn't respond. The big man looked him over, got slowly to his feet.

"Wait here," he said. As he turned away, Harry saw the telltale bulge on his right hip beneath the jacket. Clip holster, he thought. Likely an automatic. Something small and flat.

The big man went down the steps and out toward the pasture. There was a man leaning against the split-rail fence there, talking to one of the riders, a woman on a white horse. She wore jeans, a denim shirt, and a riding helmet with the bill pulled low. The other rider, a man, had moved his horse away as if to be out of earshot, waiting for the conversation to end.

The man at the fence raised his voice, slapped the rail in anger. Harry couldn't make out what he was saying. The woman listened without speaking, then wheeled the horse away, started toward the barn. The other rider moved to follow her.

The man at the fence was shaking his head, still talking to her receding back, when the big man came up behind him and spoke. The man turned, looked back at Harry on the porch. After a moment, they started toward him across the lawn.

Eddie Fallon was in his early fifties, with wide shoulders and the beginnings of a paunch. He wore a thin gray jacket that might have been silk over a black linen pullover. His slacks were the same color as the jacket. His hair—an unnatural glossy black—was combed straight back from his forehead, every strand in place.

Harry waited. They came up the porch steps, eyeing him. Harry put out his hand.

Fallon ignored it.

"I'll be out in a minute," he said. "I have to take a piss."

He walked past Harry, went into the bar.

The big man smiled, cocked his head at a table on the far side of the porch, facing the pasture.

"Have a seat," he said.

Harry went over to the table. On the glass top were a cell phone, a pack of Kools, and small, compact binoculars. The big man took his paper and moved to another table a few feet away.

He picked up the binoculars, looked out at the pasture. The two riders had dismounted, were walking their horses back to the barn, the woman looking at the ground. The other rider had a hand on her shoulder as if consoling her. From their body language, he read teacher and student. At the entrance to the barn, the woman swept off her helmet, and he caught a flash of red hair and the glimpse of a profile. But she turned before he could focus on her, entered the dimness of the barn.

"My wife," Fallon said behind him.

He put down the binoculars. Fallon was looking beyond him to the barn.

"All the money I'm spending for private lessons, and she just never learns," he said. "Did you see what she was doing out there?"

"I don't know much about horses."

"You don't need to know when someone's not paying attention. She's scattered. Can't keep her mind on what she's doing." He pointed at a chair. "Go on, sit down."

Fallon sat across from him. His leathery skin had the nutbrownness of the year-round tan, and his upper body showed the definition of regular workouts. Fifties and fighting it, Harry thought. He wore gold on both wrists, a Rolex on the left, a thick-braided ID bracelet on the right. Harry caught a waft of musky cologne.

"I appreciate your seeing me like this," Harry said. "I know you're busy."

Fallon took a cigarette from the pack, tapped it against the tabletop.

"So talk."

He fished a silver lighter from his pants pocket, got the cigarette going, clicked the lighter shut.

Harry said, "First of all . . ."

The phone trilled on the table between them. Fallon picked it up, unfolded it. "Yeah?"

Harry looked off toward the pasture. There was the faintest scent of manure in the air, mixed with the smell of freshly cut grass. He could hear the whirring of sprinklers on the lawn, the buzz of insects, and the sounds from the tennis game.

Fallon had the phone to his ear, listening.

"Tell him no," he said finally. "How complicated is that? What the fuck do I pay you for?" He listened some more, then looked at Harry as if seeing him for the first time. He covered the mouthpiece.

"Give me a minute here," he said. "I need to deal with something. Wait over there." He pointed at another table. "Lester, see if he wants a drink."

Harry turned. The big man looked up, smiled, and went back to his paper.

"How many times are we going to go over this?" Fallon was saying into the phone. "Twenty-two, tops. No higher."

Harry pushed back his chair, got up. He walked past the table Fallon had pointed to.

"Yo," Wiley said.

Harry ignored him, went into the coolness of the bar.

"Find him?" the bartender said.

"Yeah. I found him."

He slid onto a stool.

"What can I do you?"

"Corona if you have it. Amstel if you don't."

"Amstel it is."

The bartender made his cigarette disappear, got a glass from the overhead rack and a bottle from the cooler behind the bar. Harry took out his wallet, found a ten. The bartender opened the bottle, poured beer carefully into the tilted glass, keeping the head thin.

"Thanks," Harry said.

The bartender took his ten, rang it up, and put a five in front of him. Harry sipped beer. In the mirror behind the bar he saw Wiley come through the porch doors. He slid forward on the stool so that his boots were flat on the hardwood floor.

"Maybe you didn't hear him clearly," Wiley said. "He meant for you to wait."

The bartender looked at Harry, raised an eyebrow.

"You deaf or something?" Wiley said. Harry felt him come up close behind him. "I'm talking to you."

A hand closed lightly on his right arm, just above the elbow. He shook it off, half turned, raised his hand.

"Don't."

He turned back to the bar.

"Tough guy, huh?" Wiley said. He caught the arm again and Harry waited until he felt the tug, then went with it, swiveled, slipped free and off the stool. Wiley fell back a step, then came in fast, reaching for Harry with his left hand, the right already balled into a fist.

Harry drove a boot heel into Wiley's right knee. It stopped him, bent him in pain, and Harry stepped in close, caught the lapels of his jacket and twisted his torso to break his balance. His right leg swung out and back, caught Wiley behind the knees, and knocked both feet out from under him. Still holding on to the lapels, he turned him in midair, heard cloth rip, then brought him down hard onto the floor with a crash that shook the bottles behind the bar.

He dropped his left knee into Wiley's stomach, drove the breath out of him. Wiley clawed at the holster and Harry slapped his hand away, got the gun out. It was a small, silver automatic with rubber grips. He pushed the muzzle into Wiley's throat, his finger on the trigger.

Wiley froze. The room was silent except for the distant sound of the tennis game.

"Easy," the bartender said.

Harry tried to slow his breathing. The room seemed to swim in and out of focus around him. He felt a drop of sweat roll down the side of his face.

"Lie there," he said. "Don't move."

He moved the gun away, used his free hand to pat Wiley down for another weapon, didn't find one. With his knee still in Wiley's stomach, he looked at the gun. It was a Star 9, made in Spain, a street gun. He ejected the clip, worked the slide. A shiny brass shell sprang from the breech, clattered on the floor, and rolled away beneath a table.

Wiley looked up at him, not moving. Harry got to his feet, stuck the clip in the back pocket of his jeans. The bartender was watching him.

"Sorry about all this," Harry said to him. The stool had fallen over during their struggle. He righted it, his breathing under control now. He looked down at Wiley.

"Stay there," he said. "Don't follow me, or I'll put you down again."

He went back out onto the porch. Fallon was still on the phone. He watched as Harry approached.

Harry set the gun on the tabletop.

"Listen," Fallon said into the phone, "we'll go over this later. I've got a situation here." Harry could hear a tinny voice protest on the other end of the line. "I said later. I'll call you back." He folded the phone shut.

"Where's Lester?"

"In there. He fell."

"He pull that on you?"

"He tried to."

Fallon shook his head.

"That fucking guy. Come on. Let's take a walk."

As Fallon got up, he glanced toward the bar entrance.

Harry turned to see Wiley limp out onto the porch, still breathing heavily, his face red. Harry gripped the back of the wrought-iron chair, got ready to lift it.

Fallon looked at Wiley, shook his head.

"Go back inside," he said. "Wait for me there."

"But Eddie—"

"Go back inside."

Wiley looked at Harry, the anger bright in his eyes. He turned and went back into the bar.

"Let's go," Fallon said.

Harry pushed the gun into a pocket. He followed Fallon down the steps and toward the pasture.

"I got your message this morning," Fallon said. "I told them at the restaurant to go ahead and let you know where I was. I wouldn't normally do that."

"I know that. I appreciate this."

"Good." Fallon went to the rail, put his elbows up. "So let's hear it."

"Bobby Fox." Harry waited for a reaction, got none. "He's a friend of mine. He had some bad luck and he wants to straighten things out."

Fallon nodded, looked off toward the barn. "Keep talking."

"Bobby's sorry things worked out the way they did. It was beyond his control."

"So what's that got to do with you?"

"I'm doing him a favor. He doesn't know I'm here."

"You a cop?"

"No."

"You look like one."

"I used to be with the state police. I'm not anymore."

Fallon looked at him. "Trooper?"

"For a while. Then I was with the Major Crimes Unit."

"That why he sent you? Because you used to be with the state police? That supposed to have some sort of effect on me?"

"He didn't send me. I came on my own."

"Why'd you quit, young guy like you?"

"Does that matter?"

"I'm curious. I like to know something about the people I'm dealing with, their motivations."

"Like I said, we're friends. I'm just trying to help him out."

"That's noble."

"He owes you something. He accepts that. He's going to pay it back, he just needs more time."

"Don't we all. So you here to vouch for this guy, pay his debts?"

"Not at all. He's putting something together for you right now, but he needs a little time. You put more pressure on him or send your friend Wiley"—he nodded back toward the porch—"back to his house and you're in a blood-from-a-stone proposition. There's no need for it. Serves no purpose."

Fallon turned away again.

"So, you say you're a go-between. So far I haven't heard many specifics."

"He'll have some money for you within the week. It won't be a lot, but it'll be something."

"You wired?"

"What?"

"Are you getting all of this? Should I speak closer to the microphone?"

"There's no wire."

"Whether there is or not, here's the deal: If you have something for me, something owed to me, then fine. Give it to me. If not, then don't waste my time."

"Is that what you think I'm doing?"

Fallon turned to face him. "Let's not make a mistake here. Like you said, you're not a cop anymore. You're not anything. You came out here, I liked the way you looked, I liked the way you acted. Maybe we can work something out. But if you think you can threaten me or bullshit me, then you're just another stupid person who thought he was smart."

"Nobody's bullshitting you. Or threatening you."

"Good." He turned away. "Now, my wife's waiting for me. So if you've got anything else to say, say it."

"Just a time and a place. Let us know where to bring it and we'll get this started."

A golf cart with a canvas roof trundled out of the open barn, whirred slowly up the dirt path toward the tennis court area.

"There she is," Fallon said. "Call the restaurant. Leave a message. They'll get in touch with me. If we have some business to conduct at that time, we'll do it."

"You'll hear from me this week."

He took the automatic out, offered it to him butt first.

"Leave it on the table when you go," Fallon said.

Harry stuck it back in his pocket.

"I'll be in touch."

He put his hand out. Fallon looked at it.

"You know something, Rane?" There was a half smile on his face.

"What?"

"You're out of your league. It's all over your face. Go on, get out of here. Call me when you're ready to talk business."

Fallon turned back to the rail, and Harry felt the flush in his cheeks. He stood there for a moment, looking at the back of Fallon's head, then turned and started toward the porch. When he reached the steps, he dropped the gun into one of the ponds. The clip went into the other.

As he went up the steps, he heard the golf cart shut off, then boot heels on flagstones. The woman was coming up the path behind him. He turned, curious.

For an instant, he felt a strange sensation in his feet, as if the floor of the porch had shifted slightly. He blinked, frozen. She reached the middle step, looked up at him.

The hair was brighter, the color of freshly sheared copper, shorter now. The face was thinner, lined. But the eyes were the same. If he moved closer he would see the fleck of gold in her left iris, the island in a sea of green.

She stepped back, almost lost her balance, put a hand on the railing. He inhaled, opened his mouth, but nothing came out.

"Harry?" she said low.

He took a step toward her, her name forming on his lips.

"Cristina!" Fallon yelled. Harry turned, saw him coming across the grass toward them.

He looked back at her, knowing now there was no mistake, could never be any mistake.

"Cristina!" Fallon called again. "I want to talk to you."

She looked at Harry for a long moment, then cut around him, pulled open the door to the dining room. He found himself reaching for her arm, wanting to slow her, stop her, but she was past him and gone.

He turned, disoriented, saw Fallon come up onto the porch. He stopped, put his hands on his hips, looked at Harry.

"What's the problem?"

Harry shook his head.

"Then what are you still doing here?"

He didn't trust himself to speak. Fallon gave him a last glance, then went past him, into the dining room. Harry stood there, watched the door swing shut.

"You look lost."

He turned to see the bartender standing in the lounge doorway, cigarette in hand.

"I wouldn't come back in this way," he said.

"Why not?"

"That big boyo's out in the lobby. Might be he's waiting for you. No reason to force the issue."

Harry looked at the dining room door, but the smoked glass was too dark to see through. He turned back to the bartender.

"Thanks," he said. He went back down the porch steps and started around the side of the building, walking in a daze until he reached the Mustang.

Cristina.

He got behind the wheel and started the engine. In the rearview mirror he could see the front entrance, the valet sitting beside the door.

He backed away from the tree, K-turned in the parking circle, raising dust. He shifted into first, gave it gas, and drove away from there.

• • •

When he got home, he sat in the driveway for a long time, the Mustang cooling and ticking.

Eighteen years fallen away in a turn of the head, a glance from green eyes. Cristina.

FIVE

Did you know?" Harry said. Bobby leaned back against the transom, popped the pull top on a can of Budweiser.

"Know?" he said. "Hell, how would I? I never met his wife."

They were on Bobby's boat, an old eighteen-foot wooden cabin cruiser he'd rechristened the *Bitter End*. They were anchored about a mile off the beach in Sea Bright, a stiff wind blowing occasionally from the east, raising slow waves that rocked the boat and made them reach for support.

They had two lines out, the poles in plastic rod holders mounted on the gunwales. Two fluke lay gray and unmoving inside the red-and-white plastic cooler at Bobby's feet, beer cans shoved into the ice around them like headstones. It was all they had to show for their day.

Harry looked out across the water toward the tip of Sandy Hook, watched seagulls follow a party boat as it rounded the headland and started back into the bay. Dusk was still two hours away, but the wind was kicking up stronger now, the threat of it driving some of the smaller boats in.

"So what did she say to you?"

"Nothing. There was no time. She just looked at me, went past."

"And you're sure it was her?"

"Positive."

Bobby sipped beer. He was naked to the waist, his skin burned a deep red-brown.

"Who would have thought?" he said. "With that guy, no less. When was the last time you saw her?"

"That summer after high school. She left in September."

"She ever call? Write?"

"One letter early on. After that, no."

"So you haven't heard from her in, what, eighteen years?"

"About that."

Bobby drank beer.

"You know," he started. "I never pried . . ."

Harry gestured at the cooler. Bobby opened the lid, took out a beer. Harry caught it in midair.

"I knew something was going on, and I knew it fucked you up, but I never asked for details. I figured if you'd wanted me to know, you'd tell me."

Harry opened the beer and foam spilled over the lip of the can. He sipped it off.

"You probably know a lot of it already."

"Only that you met her senior year. And I took it for granted you were nailing her, though I didn't know that for sure. She was a transfer, wasn't she?"

"They'd moved out from Ohio. Just her, her mother and her stepfather. He was a corrections officer, worked county lockups. First Monmouth, then Middlesex."

The boat moved beneath Harry's feet, and he caught the edge of the cockpit to steady himself. He heard something fall inside the small, windowless cabin.

"And?" Bobby said.

"She was seventeen when we met, a junior, but her stepfather still wasn't letting her date. She had a friend who covered for us, so we snuck around, got together anywhere we could. After my mother started working again, we'd meet at my house. At that age, you feel like you've found the answer to all the questions, you know? We thought this was it. True love."

"She was nuts for you, I remember that much. So you saw this girl for what? Six months total?"

"More like eight. Then all hell broke loose."

"That's the part you never told me."

Harry took a pull of the thin, cold beer. There was a gray line out on the horizon, moving toward them. The boat dipped and rose.

"We were talking about getting married, heading down south. We knew there was no way her parents would let her, so we were planning to just take off, hole up somewhere until she was eighteen, and then get married. At least that was the plan."

"Must have been a pretty big secret if I didn't know about it."

"She was worried about what her old man would do if he found out. So we didn't tell anyone. I'd been putting my money away. I think I had about twelve hundred dollars saved up. I thought that was going to get us clear. I was nineteen and stupid."

"So what happened?"

"There was a complication."

"She got pregnant."

Harry nodded.

"I'm kind of surprised at you, slick," Bobby said. "You were always the careful type. How did that happen?"

"We were at my house one day. My mother was at work. I tried to pull out, she wouldn't let me. She told me she didn't care."

"She wanted it."

"Maybe."

"She wanted *you,*" Bobby said.

"She wanted to get away from her parents. I guess she thought that would make sure it happened."

"Hard to believe all this went down without my knowing it."

"I was lying a lot in those days. To myself as well. Once we knew for sure she was pregnant, I started thinking it wasn't such a bad thing. Get out of Jersey, start a new life. Build a family."

Harry looked toward the horizon.

"It's kicking up," he said. "We should probably start heading back in."

"We got time. You made me wait eighteen years to hear all this, you're not getting off that easy. Did she tell her parents?"

"We were planning to do that together. But she got into it with them one night when I wasn't there, told them everything. She thought we were free, you know? That nothing could stop us.

"That was the summer my cousin had gotten me a job in the public works department in Long Branch, landscaping, picking up trash. That next day I was out with a crew, down at Seven Presidents Park on the beach. We'd quit for lunch, were just sitting around, and I saw the old man's pickup pull up. I tried to put up a fight. It didn't help. He put a pretty good beating on me before the others pulled him off."

"That black eye you had. . . ."

"That was the least of it. I had two cracked ribs too."

"You told me you got it at some bar in Asbury."

"Like I said, I was lying a lot in those days."

"I guess you were. What happened then?"

"He took her back to Ohio with him. She finally managed to get a letter to me after a few weeks. There was a doctor he knew out there that he took her to, some hack. She said she was still bleeding from it three days later."

"Christ."

The wind began to whistle around the poles. The boat dipped, steadied.

"I never told anybody," Harry said. "Not you. Not Melissa."

"And you never saw her again?"

Harry shook his head.

"That's rough," Bobby said.

"For a while, I thought about heading out there, trying to track her down. I used to fantasize about kicking her old man's ass, bringing her back. But I never did. Three years later, I met Melissa."

"Eighteen years," Bobby said. "And all that time you never had any contact with her?"

"Not since that letter. Not until yesterday."

"Un-fucking-believable. You have any other long-lost secrets you want to share with me?"

Harry smiled, shook his head, sipped beer.

"It was a long time ago," he said.

Bobby set his beer on the transom, peered off at the horizon. Low thunder boomed in the distance and the wind began to snap around them, a coolness in it now.

"Getting gray out there," Bobby said. The boat pitched beneath them and Bobby's beer hit the deck, rolled, spewing foam. Harry scooped it up, lurched to the other side of the cockpit. Rain began to dimple the water and spot the salt-crusted windshield. He poured the dregs over the side, then shuffled back to the cooler, opened the lid, and dropped the empty can in.

"Looks like it's time to call it a day," Bobby said. "Haul these two sorry-ass fish home. I'll get the anchor."

He caught the handholds on the lip of the cockpit, hopped lightly onto the gunwale, and started toward the front of the boat, crouched over, holding the grab rails. Harry set his beer can on the port engine cover, reeled in the two lines, carefully stripped the squid pieces off the hooks and tossed them over the side. He secured the hooks and stowed the rods on the gunwale rack.

Bobby swung back onto the deck, went to the wheel. He looked back at the horizon and, almost on cue, there was a flicker of lightning in the clouds. He turned the key to start the engines, inched the throttles forward. The twin diesels chugged, smoked, and the wake began to churn up behind them. Harry held on to the gunwale as Bobby brought the boat around, aimed it at the headland.

"Just in time," Bobby said. With a crack of thunder, the rain began to sheet down around them. Harry moved under the cockpit for cover, listening to the heavy drops sound on the wood above him. Bobby turned on the wipers, pushed the throttles open. The engines coughed, roared throatily, and the boat plunged and bit into the water, spray lashing the side windows.

"Take the helm," he said.

Harry put his beer in a cupholder on the cockpit wall, gripped the smooth wooden spokes of the wheel. Bobby ducked down into the cabin and emerged a minute later, wearing a sweatshirt and carrying a windbreaker.

"Here," he said. Harry moved aside to let him take the wheel again. He pulled the thin jacket on over his T-shirt, zipped it.

"So tell me something," Bobby said.

"What?" Harry reclaimed his beer.

"You were with the state police what, ten years?"

"Twelve."

The houses on the shore were looming larger now. Bobby throttled back slightly, turned the wheel so they were running parallel to the beach. Rain washed the deck, ran out through the scuppers.

"You ever miss it?" Bobby said.

"Not much. Not lately."

"You never thought about going back?"

"No."

The bow rose and crashed back down. Harry spread his feet to keep his balance. They were cutting across the waves at an angle, Bobby steering for the channel markers. The long, bare beach of Sandy Hook stretched out to their left.

"They never found out who those people were, did they?" Bobby said. "The ones who shot you."

Harry shook his head. "They found the car in Virginia two days later. Abandoned. No sign of the driver. The only prints they managed to lift belonged to the owner. He'd reported it stolen earlier that week. It was a dead end."

Bobby shook his head slowly.

"It was my fault," Harry said.

Bobby looked at him.

"I wasn't thinking clearly. It was too soon after Melissa. I thought going back to work quickly would help. But it was a mistake. I was careless."

Bobby didn't respond. They were rounding the tip of the Hook now, steering clear of the shallows. Harry moved out onto the deck, the wind flapping the sides of his jacket, the rain whipping against him. He looked back the way they'd come. Out there the sky was a gun-metal gray, lit by distant flashes of lightning. He watched the storm for a while, feeling the coldness of the rain, the bite of the wind through the thin jacket.

When he finally moved back under the shelter of the cockpit, Bobby glanced at him but said nothing. They headed into the bay, the water calmer now, and Bobby slowed the engines, flipped on the running lights. The early night was on them.

They looked toward the land, the open ocean at their back, and headed home.

The storm blew through the night. In the bedroom, with the wind and rain rattling the windows, he lay sleepless in the tangled sheets. Whenever he closed his eyes, the memory came back to him unbidden.

It had been a gray December afternoon, nearly two months to the day after Melissa's death, the clouds heavy with the threat of snow. He'd spent the day at the federal building in Newark, meeting with an assistant Essex County prosecutor to compare notes on an extortion indictment that was headed nowhere fast. He'd felt distracted, restless. As he headed home on the Garden State Parkway, driving the unmarked Chevy Caprice he'd gotten from the pool, the first flakes of snow had begun to fall.

He'd been halfway home, just past Exit 135, when he saw the brown Nova. It was moving fast in the passing lane, doing seventy-five at least. He could see a man at the wheel, a woman beside him and, in the back, the unmistakable outline of a child's car seat.

It had been years since he'd made a motor vehicle stop, but the sight of the car seat made him angry. They were doing almost twenty miles an hour above the speed limit in bad weather with a small child in the backseat.

He'd stepped on the gas, felt the Caprice's big engine respond. He was on the Nova in seconds, saw the Jersey plates and the dented and gaping trunk held shut with an elastic cord. He switched on the red and blue flashers hidden inside the Caprice's grille, gave a two-second burst on the siren, saw their brake lights go on, then the blinker.

The snow was heavier now, the road slick, the overcast afternoon slipping into true dark. He watched the Nova glide onto the shoulder and come to a stop, blinker still flashing.

He'd slowed, felt gravel beneath the tires as he steered onto the shoulder. To the right was a guardrail, then a deep, wooded gully. He stopped twelve feet behind the Nova, the Caprice angled slightly to the left as a shield against passing traffic. He could see the couple facing each other, arguing. He took the heavy black aluminum flashlight from the seat beside him, opened the door.

Three steps from the Caprice, he'd realized he hadn't called in the plate. It was standard practice, never deviated from, the first thing they learned in road training. He stopped, considered going back. Instead, he lifted the flashlight, flicked it on, and let the beam play though the rear window of the Nova. Snow swirled in the light. The two stopped arguing, swiveled to look back at him. Light flashed from the woman's eyes. She was Hispanic, in her twenties, long black hair tied back. The driver was older, darker. Harry moved closer, saw that the car seat was empty. The angry expression on the woman's face grew into a faint, nervous smile that he couldn't help but return.

The driver rolled down his window, but Harry went up on the passenger side instead, saw the woman turning to face him. She was pretty, with high cheekbones, wearing a brown Western shirt with pearl snaps. He let the flashlight beam drop slightly so as not to blind her. When he reached the window, he saw the folded jacket on her lap, shined the light inside.

When the window exploded, he stepped back quickly, instinctively, and then he was falling, his breath gone. He sat down hard on wet gravel. The flashlight hit the ground, rolled, and ended up pointing at the Nova's right front tire. He tried to draw in breath, couldn't, and then the pain began to bloom in his stomach. He brought his right hand to his shirt, felt the warmth and wetness there, and then the realization came: *I've been shot. Mother of Christ, I've been shot.*

They were shouting at each other in the car now, their voices loud, panicked. Cubes of safety glass glittered like diamonds around him. He heard the passenger side door unlock, the latch pop.

Coming out, he thought, *to finish the job*.

His hand went to the Heckler & Koch in the belt holster beneath his overcoat. He drew it, his hand slick with blood, thumbed off the safety. A jolt of pain hit like a kick drum in his stomach, filled his body. *I'm dying*, he thought. *Whatever happens now doesn't matter, because I'm already dying*.

The door opened wide. A pair of booted feet swung out, touched gravel. He raised the H&K, but it seemed to weigh too much. It was like holding a cinder block at arm's length. The squat, square barrel wavered, swayed.

Broken glass crunched under the boots. The woman stepped out from behind the door. At first he couldn't see the weapon—her right hand was empty. Then he saw the short-barreled revolver in her left, the dull metal finish of it. A small gun, he thought, watching it come up. Almost a toy.

She thumbed the hammer back with her right hand—a solid metallic click—and then he was looking into the darkness of the muzzle. She was taking aim with both hands, a look of concentration on her face, but he felt no fear, no alarm. A great calmness had come over him. When the woman leveled the gun at him, he carefully shot her twice in the chest.

She stepped back abruptly, as if trying to climb into the

Nova butt first, without turning. Her gun went off and a bullet whined over his head into the trees. He fired again, saw the black spot blossom above her right eyebrow. She slumped back into the car, and then the tires squealed and her body jolted out, fell onto its side. The Nova lurched away, spraying gravel. He fired at it, heard the round puncture metal. The car fishtailed out onto the highway, the passenger door swinging wide and then thumping back shut. He watched the taillights grow smaller, the directional still flashing.

He lowered the H&K, looked at the woman. She was on her right side, facing him, brown eyes shining wetly. He looked into them, into the emptiness beyond, and then she rolled slowly, facedown onto the gravel.

He pressed the palm of his left hand over his wound, felt the warmth flowing out between his fingers. The crotch of his pants was soaked with it, as if he'd wet himself. Two cars flew past without slowing. The lights in the grille of the Caprice were still flashing, like some miniature carnival ride. He could hear the crackle of the radio inside.

The H&K was suddenly too heavy to hold, so he set it down. The snow blew around him, filled the air, but he couldn't feel it. Even the pain in his stomach was easing.

He tried to lower himself back slowly, felt hard ground beneath his head. He looked up into the gray sky, watched the snow spiraling down around him.

Melissa, he thought. *Look what I did. Look at how stupid I was. How did I let this happen?*

He felt her presence suddenly, like a warmth in the air beside him. The scent of her perfume. It made him smile. And then there was nothing but grayness and drifting snow, and all the pain was gone.

SIX

There was a framed photograph on the wall behind Ray Washington's desk. Harry moved closer to look at it.

It had been taken at the State Police Academy in Sea Girt during their training: two ranks of cadets in fatigue jackets and caps, standing at parade rest on a cold morning, the barracks looming behind them. He remembered the day. It had marked the midway point of their five months at the academy. They'd survived ten weeks of physical and mental abuse and were proud of it. Ray stood front and center, one of only six black faces in the group of ninety. Harry was in the second row, his cap partially obscuring his face. They both looked impossibly young.

"Hard to believe, isn't it?" Ray said as he came back into the room. "Young and stupid. Ready to eat up the world."

"It feels like another life."

"It was."

Harry turned to face him. Ray wore a tailored gray suit, but his tie was loose, the jacket unbuttoned. He looked like a lawyer at the end of a hard day in court. His head was shaved close and his scalp gleamed, and though he'd put on more than fifty pounds since the photo had been taken, his posture was still military erect, his arms and shoulders thick with muscle.

He dropped a wide manila envelope onto the desk. "Thought you'd want to see these right away," he said.

"They're just Xeroxes, but the guy who gave them to me would have his ass in a sling if anybody found out. He owed me a favor. Now I owe him one. Don't ask me his name, because I won't tell you."

"He with Major Crimes?"

"Yeah, what's left of it. I think he's looking to get out, though. Tired of the politics."

"That's a surprise."

"Bureaucracy is no friend to the steadfast and righteous. Verily, I say it unto thee. Pull up a chair."

They sat down. Ray opened the envelope, took out four sheets of paper, slid them across the desk.

"Now you're going to look at these," he said, "and then we're going to talk."

Harry spread out the sheets. They were black-and-white copies of eight-by-ten photos, taken from about a half block away.

"These came in as part of a regular surveillance detail," Ray said. "They were taken last week up in Bloomfield."

The photos were in sequence, all apparently shot within minutes of each other. Each showed an elderly man standing on the sidewalk outside a storefront restaurant. Eddie Fallon was in all of them. In the first two, he and the old man were deep in conversation, heads inches apart. In the third one, they were embracing. In the last, Fallon was getting into the passenger side of a dark Lexus.

"Some coincidence, eh?" Ray said. "I call him out of the blue to ask about somebody and a day later these photos come across his desk. I didn't tell him much, but I'm sure it aroused his curiosity. Recognize the goombah?"

"Just the type."

"That's Paolo Andelli. 'Paulie One-Eye' on account his left one is glass. Somebody put his real one out in a cell-block riot in Rahway in the fifties. He's running the Scarpettis now since the feds put Al and his brother away last year. Funny thing is, before that, Paulie was a loose cannon, nobody wanted to put him in charge of anything. He was too much of a hothead."

"Where is this place?"

"A restaurant where he holds court most of the time. That is, when he's not at home pretending to be a grandfather or in a hotel bed with his mistress, trying to get it up. MCU, the feds, practically everybody knows about that restaurant. They watch it all the time. Andelli always goes outside to talk business, because the inside's wired seven ways from Sunday. Everybody knows it. Makes you wonder why they bother."

"What else do you know about him?"

"When I was with the OC Strike Force he was never more than a minor player. He's been on the sidelines all these years, getting old, waiting for his turn to come. He runs a waste-hauling firm, a vending machine company, all the same shit you've heard a thousand times. He's got a house in Florham Park, another down in Brick. Until they let the brothers out, which is not ever gonna happen, he's the man."

"When exactly were these photos taken?"

"Thursday morning."

"Had Fallon ever shown up there before?"

"He was a new face, that's why he caught their eye at MCU. They figured out who he was quickly enough, but I don't think they'd placed him with Andelli before. Now, of course, they've taken an interest. Does all this mean anything to you?"

"Not really. Not yet, at least."

"Would you tell me if it did?"

"Yes. I'm not jerking your chain here, Ray. Where Andelli fits into this, if at all, I don't know."

"Well, let me just say this, then. These are serious people, Harry. They have their hands in a lot of things. If your friend is mixed up with them in any way, it may be time to get someone else involved."

"A little early for that. There might not be any connection at all."

"No connection? Out of nowhere you ask me about somebody, and two days later I get photos of him up close and personal with a top LCN guy. You call that coincidence?"

"Might be."

Ray frowned.

"Well, there's something else interesting about these photos, anyway," he said. "The last one, at least."

Harry looked at it. Only the front half of the Lexus was in the frame, but the driver's face was partially visible, his tinted window halfway down. Something about the profile jogged his memory.

Ray tapped the photo with the eraser end of a pencil. "Recognize him? You should."

He looked at the face again. The feeling was stronger now, but the connection still eluded him. He shook his head.

"That's Mickey Dunleavy," Ray said.

Harry looked at the hard features, the short dark hair.

"Yeah," he said. "It could be, I guess. I didn't know him well."

"It is. One of the MCU guys on the surveillance team had been with him in Troop D. That's Dunleavy, all right. Landed on his feet as usual. They should have put him away when they had the chance."

"I followed the trial in the papers. Hard to believe he got off."

"No one wants to send a state trooper to prison, no matter how bad a guy he is. Far as the jury was concerned, he was a brave soldier in the War on Drugs. Hard to tell what side he was on, though."

"What's he doing with Fallon?"

"Good question. Last anyone heard, he headed down to Florida after the trial was over. A lot of people were hoping he'd stay there."

Harry looked through the sheets again.

"I have to tell you that as far as our mutual benefactor at MCU is concerned, this is a quid pro quo arrangement," Ray said. "For giving me these photos, he'll be expecting something in return. Any information I get on Fallon or his friends that might pertain to an ongoing investigation, I'll have to pass on to him. So don't put me in the middle. You can tell these guys to go polish their knobs, but I'm a black man in a white man's business. I've got to live with them. And keeping good relations with them makes my job a hell of a lot easier."

"I'm not holding anything out on you. It's just that it's hard to see where this is going so far. If I find out anything that's relevant . . ."

". . . you'll let me know."

"Yes."

Ray sat back. "Don't forget me, Harry. And don't forget my offer. You still have a taste for the Life. If you didn't, you wouldn't be involved in this. You're a natural to it. Why piss those skills away?"

"That a compliment or an insult?"

"Both, I guess. You've got to go back to work eventually, you know, some kind of job, whether you need the money or not. It's not healthy, living out there by yourself, sitting on your ass all day, not doing a goddamn thing."

"I've worked on the house, the car."

"That's not the same. You know what I mean. You've had some rough times. A lot of things that probably seem like they all came down at once. And maybe you're a little bit scared. But you need to get out there again, Harry. You need to reconnect. Reengage."

"Maybe that's what I'm trying to do."

He stood up.

"I appreciate your calling me," he said. "If nothing else, I have a better idea who I'm dealing with."

"Still sticking to the five P's, eh? 'Proper Planning Prevents Poor Performance.' That was your mantra in the old days."

"Yeah, I guess it was."

"I hope it still is, partner. Watch yourself."

As soon as he pulled into the lot of the shooting range, he could hear the unmistakable popping of a handgun.

He parked beside Bobby's pickup, got out. Aside from another, newer pickup, the lot was empty. It was an outdoor range, with a shack for an office and a covered wooden platform that looked out on a long stretch of bare ground. At the end of the range were bulldozed mounds of dirt high enough to catch stray bullets. Beyond them were woods. He walked toward the sound of the shots.

Bobby had the firing platform to himself. He stood at a table behind the railing, the Glock in a two-handed grip, squeezing off shots, taking his time. Brass clattered onto the walkway and the smell of cordite was sharp in the air.

He fired twice more and the slide locked back empty. He ejected the clip, set the gun on the table.

"What's that come out to?" Harry said as he stepped up onto the platform. "About fifty cents a bullet?"

Bobby looked at him. "More like seventy-five. I'm just finishing up. How'd you find me?"

"I called the boatyard and they told me you'd left early."

On the table was another full clip, a leather handgun case, and a plastic spackle container, the bottom of which was already lined with spent shell casings.

"I had some comp time coming. I wanted a chance to get away, think for a little while."

He took the full magazine, slid it into the grip until it seated. He thumbed off the slide lock, and the mechanism slid forward and chambered a round. He held the gun out, butt first.

"No, thanks," Harry said.

Bobby stepped up to the railing, the gun in his right hand. He braced his wrist with his left hand, aimed at the man-sized paper target mounted on a pole about twenty-five yards away. Harry stepped back as he began to fire. The gun jumped in his hand, the crack loud and flat in the air. A casing flew between them.

Harry couldn't see where the shot had gone. Bobby steadied off, closed one eye, and squeezed again. This time the bullet nicked the top right edge of the target.

"It pulls high and to the right a little," Bobby said. "Like I said, it's light, so it kicks."

He fired three more times in quick succession, the bullets

marching across the target from right to left. Gray smoke drifted around him. He paused again, adjusting his aim, and then began to fire steadily at one-second intervals, the gun rising in his hand, the sound of the shots echoing back at them from the wall of dirt. Star-shaped holes ran in a diagonal pattern across the center of the target.

"Not bad," Harry said.

He counted seven shots before the slide locked back. Bobby ejected the clip, cleared the breech, set the gun on the table.

"I had a little luck today," he said.

"How's that?"

Bobby put the gun in the case, the two empty clips in an inner side pouch.

"Guy I know, I did some work on his boat on the side. He's owed me money since January. I called him yesterday and he managed to come across with some of it today. Fifteen hundred."

"That's good."

Bobby knelt and began to pick up shell casings from the walkway. He dropped them clinking into the bucket.

"And I went to the bank this morning too, cashed in a CD. Took a hit on it, but that's another two thousand. So I've got thirty-five hundred I can give him right away."

"That's a start. I'll make the call, set it up."

"You don't need to do that. Christ, I can take him the goddamn money."

"Better if it's me. Right now he's a little nervous, and that's to our advantage. I'm an unknown quantity to him, so he'll want to be careful."

Bobby tucked the gun case beneath his arm, picked up the bucket.

"You sure about that?"

Harry nodded.

They went to the office, where a half door opened onto the walkway. Bobby nodded to the old man inside, who handed him a clipboard, a ballpoint pen attached to it with string. On the wall behind the old man, Harry could see boxes of ammunition stacked on shelves, orange ear protectors hanging from nails. Bobby signed out, handed back the clipboard. They went down the steps to the parking lot.

"So why'd you come out here?" Bobby said.

He unlocked the tool chest welded to the bed of his pickup, set the gun case and bucket inside.

"I had some luck this morning too," Harry said.

Bobby locked the chest again.

"What do you mean?"

Harry took a thick bank envelope from the back pocket of his jeans, held it out.

"What's this?" Bobby said.

"It's not much, but along with what you already raised, it should keep him quiet for a while. Consider it a loan. You can pay me back when all this gets settled."

Bobby took the envelope, opened the end flap. He looked at the hundred-dollar bills inside.

"Take it," Harry said. "If you don't want to tell Janine about it, then don't. I'm sure you're good for it."

"How much is in here?"

"Five thousand."

"I can't take this."

"Yes, you can."

"I'm the one who screwed up, not you."

"Did I say otherwise?"

Bobby leaned against the tailgate, closed the flap of the envelope.

"Five is too much," he said.

"I can afford it."

"That's not what I mean."

"I don't want to get into this with you, Bobby. Take the money. If you want to thank me, do it by getting this business straightened out before someone gets foolish. For Janine's sake if nothing else."

Bobby tapped the envelope against his knee, looked at it again.

"You'll get this back," he said.

"I know."

Bobby looked away, squinting in the sun.

"But that's not the only reason I came out," Harry said. "Some new information turned up that you should know about."

"What kind?"

Harry told him about the photos, about Andelli and Dunleavy. When he was done, Bobby took a long breath, let it out, and stared into the distance.

"This just gets worse and worse, doesn't it?" he said.

"You needed to know."

"So how does this affect me?"

"Maybe not at all. I'm not telling you this to scare you."

"I'm not scared. Just pissed. Pissed at Fallon, pissed at myself. You know this Dunleavy?"

"By reputation mostly. We met once or twice. He chose to stay on the road as a trooper. Our paths didn't cross much."

"And what was his reputation?"

"Bad."

"Meaning what?"

"He was the kind of trooper who specialized in stopping people for DWB."

"DWB?"

"Driving While Black. When that whole racial-profiling issue broke a few years back, he was at the center of it. He already had half a dozen lawsuits against him for excessive force. Then he ended up in a shooting incident, down in Cocaine Alley."

"Where?"

"Cocaine Alley. That's what we called that stretch of Turnpike through Camden County. We used to catch a lot of drugs in motor vehicle stops there, people driving up from Florida with garbage bags full of pot in their trunk, that sort of thing. He worked that area for a long time, made a lot of arrests."

"What happened?"

"One night he pulled over this van, two black guys in it. He later said he stopped them because they were driving erratically, but I don't think anyone believed that. The way he told it, when he went up to the window, the driver reached beneath the seat, as if going for a weapon. He opened fire, killed the driver, wounded the passenger and a ten-year-old girl who was sleeping in the backseat."

"Jesus."

"There was no gun anywhere, but there was cocaine in the van—two kilos. But when the passenger—the driver's brother—came to trial, he testified there was another kilo that Dunleavy took out of the van before he called EMS."

"Was it true?"

"Probably. Regardless, the brother had a good lawyer. The case was dismissed on the grounds it was a bad stop. A week later Dunleavy was charged with aggravated manslaughter."

"I can guess how that came out."

"The jury ruled it self-defense, justifiable homicide, that he was in fear of his life, whether there was an actual weapon or not. But he didn't make out as well in the internal review. There'd already been rumors that he was stealing from drug dealers he'd stopped, taking their stash and letting them go. He didn't have much support in house. They gave him a choice: quit or face departmental charges. He quit."

"And now he's working for Fallon."

"Apparently."

Bobby looked down, scuffed at the ground with his heel.

"What do you think we should do?" he said.

"Stick to our plan. Fallon wouldn't bother Andelli with a problem like this, it would make him look bad. But just in case there is something in the works, we should stop it short. Giving him this money will help."

"In the works? What's that supposed to mean?"

Harry didn't answer.

Bobby looked away again.

"Eight grand," he said, after a moment. "It's not much, is it?"

"It's enough for now. He's just going to have to wait for the rest."

"Yeah, but will he?"

"He'll have to," Harry said. "He has no choice."

That night, he sat at his kitchen table, counting out the money Bobby had given him. It was mostly hundreds and fifties, with only a few twenties thrown in. He added it to his own five thousand, then divided the total into three piles, wrapped each with a wide rubber band.

He'd stopped on the way home from Bobby's and bought a package of heavy-duty four-by-ten manila envelopes. He slid the money into one, licked the flap, and sealed it. The phone on the wall began to ring.

He looked at it, then at the clock above the sink. Ten forty-five. He waited. It rang again, loud in the empty house. He got up from the table just as the answering machine on the counter clicked on. He punched it off, lifted the receiver.

"Hello?"

"You were in the phone book," she said.

Her voice was deeper than he'd known it, rough-edged, with the harshness of cigarettes.

"Yes," he said.

"It's funny. I never thought to look until today. I've been back here for almost seven months now and I never thought to look."

"I never left."

"It was a shock, seeing you like that."

"For me too."

"I knew he was meeting someone there, but he didn't tell me who."

"You haven't changed much."

"You're being nice, but you're lying. It's been nearly eighteen years. A long eighteen years."

"You're his wife."

"Yes."

"How long?"

"Three years now, almost."

"Where did you meet him?"

"In Florida. That's where I was living at the time. He brought me back up here with him."

"Back home."

"It's not home for me anymore, Harry. It hasn't been for a long time."

There was a distant whine of static on the line.

"What's that?" he said.

"I'm on a cell phone. In the garage. It's some kind of interference."

"Why did you call?"

"To say hello. To see how you were. That's all, I guess."

"I'm glad you did."

There was silence on the line and, for a moment, he thought she had hung up.

"I am too," she said finally. And then there was a faint click and she was gone.

SEVEN

He called the Sand Castle at ten-thirty the next morning, left his name and phone number. After he hung up, he made a second cup of coffee, then flipped through the phone book until he found a listing for a J. Cortez in Bradley Beach. He wrote the number and address on the back of an envelope, then tried the number, let it ring a dozen times. There was no answer.

He was on his third cup of coffee when the phone rang.

"Yeah."

"You the guy called, looking for Mr. F.?"

"That's right."

"What can I do for you?"

The man coughed, a deep, wet sound choked with phlegm.

"He and I spoke at the club," Harry said. "He'll know who I am. Tell him I've got something for him. It's ready now."

"The guy from the club. Okay, I'll pass it on. I'm not sure if I can find him right away, though, you know? He's in and out. We'll see what happens."

"Yeah, we will. Just make sure he gets the message." He hung up.

A half hour later, he was watering the flower beds on the side of the house when he heard the phone ring. He shut off the valve, coiled the hose, and went inside.

"Yeah?"

"Okay, here's the deal," the voice said. "He wants to meet with you tomorrow."

"Where?"

"Here at the restaurant. You know where it is?"

"I know. What time?"

"Say, four-thirty. Just come on in. We'll be waiting for you."

"Four-thirty."

"Sharp." The line went dead.

He drove slowly, counting house numbers. It was a street lined with squat, redbrick apartment buildings and two-family houses, far enough from the beach that it might as well have been in another town. Dirty children played on the sidewalk, and all the cars he saw were at least ten years old.

Cortez's apartment was above a garage in a rear yard, at the end of a dirt driveway. He parked the Mustang on the street, walked back. He'd worn a shortsleeved T-shirt, but he could already feel the sweat trickling down his back. As he passed the front house, he caught movement from the corner of his eye. He turned to see a boy of about six watching him from an uncurtained window, expressionless.

The backyard was overgrown, strewn with broken toys. A swing set sagged in one corner of the yard. He looked through the side window of the garage, saw that the inside was cluttered with junk and old furniture. But space had been cleared for a car, and oil stained the concrete floor.

He went up white wooden steps to the apartment, knocked, listened. He shaded his eyes and looked through a window, but the blinds were tightly closed. He knocked again. There was no sound from inside.

"Jimmy's not there, if that's who you're looking for."

He turned. A woman stood at the rear of the main house, holding open the screen door, the boy from the window at her side. Behind her, a dog that was at least half German shepherd was trying to squeeze past her leg. She pushed it back.

He went down the stairs slowly, watching the dog. The woman stamped her foot, drove the dog back, then stepped outside with the boy and shut the screen door behind her. The boy glanced at Harry, then ran past him and clambered up the ladder of the swing set.

Inside, the dog began to bark. It leaped against the screen door, shook it in its frame.

"It's okay," the woman said. "He can't get out. He's just not used to strangers."

She was in her early twenties, a little over five feet tall, with light brown hair cut short, pale blue eyes. She wore cut-off jeans and a man's blue work shirt with the tail out and the sleeves rolled up. She folded her arms over her breasts, watched him.

"I'm sorry to bother you," he said. "My name's Harry Rane. I'm a friend of Jimmy's."

"You looking for him?" Her voice held the rhythms of Appalachia. Child bride transplanted to the Jersey Shore.

"Do you know where he is?"

"He's not here. At least not now. I don't know where he went, either."

"You own this property?"

"Why?"

She was watching him closely, suspicious but maybe intrigued. She met his gaze without looking away, and for the first time he saw the compact toughness there. This was a woman who could hit back if she had to, and would make it count.

"Jimmy's sister asked me to look in on him," he said. "She lives out in Colorado. She hasn't heard from him in a few weeks, couldn't get an answer when she called. So she asked if I'd stop by, see what was the matter."

"You live around here?"

"Colts Neck."

"You rich?"

He smiled. "No."

"Live out there you must have some money."

"It's an old farmhouse my grandparents owned. They left it to me."

"What's his sister's name?"

"Andrea," he said. She seemed to register the moment's hesitation.

"And you two are friends?"

"All the way back to high school," he lied. "Red Bank Catholic."

She scratched an elbow, looked past him at the garage, as if she were considering everything he'd said, turning it over to find the falseness in it. He waited.

"Well, like I said, he's not here. And he hasn't been for a while. He may have moved out, for all I know."

"Why do you say that?"

"He hasn't been around in close to a month. The mail was piling up, so I started to take it in. People around here, if they know you're away, they'll break in, rob you blind. It's bad up here. It's not like home."

"Where's home."

"West Virginia."

"That's beautiful country down there."

"I guess. But it's nowhere you'd want to spend your life."

He smiled at that, liking her more now, sensing the intelligence beneath the pose.

"How long have you been out here?"

She unfolded her arms, put her hands in her back pockets.

"Three years now. But we've only been in this place"—she nodded back at the house—"for about nine months."

"You know Jimmy well?"

"He was living there when we moved in. I know him to say hello to and all that but . . . it's not like we socialized."

"Is your husband home?"

She brought her left hand around so he could see there was no ring.

"So you don't own the property?"

"No. I rent. We all rent around here."

The dog had stopped barking but was watching him

intently through the screen door. He could hear a television on somewhere inside.

"Miss . . ."

"Pettimore."

"Miss Pettimore, do you mind if I have a look in the garage?"

"Go ahead. It's unlocked. There's some things of ours in there, but mostly it's Jimmy's stuff. God knows what all's in there."

She looked back at the house.

"If there's something you need to do . . ." he said.

"It's the baby. I put her to bed right before you got here. I don't like to leave her alone for this long without looking in on her."

"Go on," he said. "Don't worry, I won't take anything."

She gave that a small smile, started back to the house. He watched her hips as she walked, knew she was aware of his eyes on her. He felt something stir inside him, something gone for a long time.

He went over to the garage door, twisted the handle, and heaved until the door rattled up on its tracks. Inside, an old washer and dryer, edges eaten through with rust, were shoved against one cinder-block wall. A child's plastic wading pool, a hole in its side, was propped against the other. He knelt and touched the oil stains on the concrete. One of them was still wet.

He found a rag on a shelf, wiped his fingers, and looked around. There was a battered kitchen table against the far wall. On it were half a dozen cardboard boxes sealed with masking tape. He took out his pen knife, sliced through the tape on one box, and pulled the flaps back to reveal a set of cheap dishes packed in newspaper. The next box contained glasses, packed the same way. A third held clothes.

He heard the screen door shut as she came back out. He resealed the flaps as best he could, folded the knife, and put it away. When he turned, she was standing at the entrance to the garage.

"Find anything?" she said.

"Nothing that helps."

She nodded at the washer and dryer. "I tried to haul them out myself once, but they were too heavy. And I just can't see paying someone to do it. Terry—that's my husband, ex-husband now—wanted to clean all this out, build a work-shop. I guess he just never got around to it. Like everything else in his life."

"He lived here with you?"

"For a while."

"He know Jimmy?"

"Not hardly. I don't think they liked each other very much."

"Why not?"

"Terry was the jealous type. Not that he had any reason to be."

"What do you mean?"

"Jimmy's one of those boys who act like they've got the world wired. Some girls go for that, I guess. I didn't."

"Has your ex-husband been around lately?"

"He comes by every week or so, to see the baby. And he gets Terry Jr. every other weekend. A boy needs his father, after all, even if his parents can't get along. God knows we couldn't, no matter how much we tried."

"So you last saw Jimmy when?"

"End of June?" She scratched her collarbone beneath the shirt. "Three weeks, at least."

"Well, Miss Pettimore, I'll be honest."

"Lynn."

"Lynn. Jimmy's sister is worried about him. It isn't normal for her not to hear from him for this long."

"I can understand that. If he were my brother . . ."

"You wouldn't happen to have a key to his apartment, would you? For emergencies?"

She tilted her head.

"I don't think I could do that," she said. "I mean, he's gone and all, but still, it wouldn't be right."

"You can come with me if you like. I just want to take a

quick look around, see if there's any clue where he might have gone. And . . . you never know."

"You mean he might still be up there? Sick or something?"

"I doubt it. But when I call his sister back, I want to be able to tell her that for sure."

"But I heard him leave that night. In the car."

"When was this?"

"About three weeks ago, like I said. It was maybe two o'-clock in the morning. I hadn't seen him for a week or so, then one night I was up late with the baby and I heard the car pulling out. He was in a hurry, I guess, or drunk or something."

"What makes you think that?"

"Look what he did to the door."

She pointed and, for the first time, he saw the scrape on the garage's wooden doorframe at about knee height.

"He hit that going out," she said. "There's no way he couldn't have noticed it. I heard it in the house. He didn't even stop to look."

He knelt, examined the scrape. There were blue flecks of paint driven into the splintered wood.

"What kind of car was it?" he said.

"I don't know cars that well. A Chevy maybe. It was old and banged up, I can tell you that. Big and noisy, like it needed a muffler. That's what I heard first."

"Do you think I could have a look in that apartment? It would only take a minute. His sister would be grateful."

She folded her lower lip between her teeth.

"That wasn't very nice of him," she said. "Take off like that, leave her worrying."

"No, it wasn't."

She watched him for a moment.

"Hang on," she said.

As she walked back to the house, he heard chains creak and he turned. Terry Jr. sat on a swing, scuffing his heels in the dirt, watching him. Harry smiled and the boy stared back at him, his expression unchanged.

When she came out of the house, there was another brief

struggle with the dog. She pushed it back inside, shut the screen door. He met her at the bottom of the stairs, and she handed him a single key on a paper clip.

"You know, you're pretty good at this, for someone who's just doing a favor for a friend," she said.

"If you'd told me to leave, I would have."

"I know."

"You must fool a lot of people yourself. With that act."

"Act?"

"Never mind," he said. "Let's go."

As they went up the stairs, their shoulders brushed. He caught a faint whiff of perfume.

"It works in both locks, I think," she said.

He unlocked the doorknob, then the dead bolt.

"Let me go in first," he said. "And give me a minute."

He turned the knob, pushed the door open with his fingertips, sniffed, then stepped into the dimness of a kitchen. The air inside was hot and oppressive. All the blinds were closed, and dust moved in shafts of light around their edges. The sink was filled with dishes.

There was a phone on the wall but no answering machine. Beyond the kitchen was a small living room with a love seat, a recliner, a TV and a VCR on a stand. The VCR's clock was flashing 12:00. A battered air conditioner sat silent in one window.

He heard her come into the kitchen.

"Well?" she said.

"Hold on."

There was a single short hallway off the living room. He walked past a bathroom and into a room with an unmade bed, a scratched dresser, and a cheap stereo with turntable. There was a poster for a boxing match on one wall, a framed Harley-Davidson print on another. There was no sign of a woman's touch anywhere. He wondered if his own bedroom would look the same to a stranger.

"It's okay," he called out. "It's empty."

He looked in the bedroom closet. Work shirts, a leather

jacket, and a single suit hung there. He went to the dresser, opened drawers. There were clothes in all of them.

She came into the bedroom.

"I guess he did leave, after all," she said. "It would have been awful if he'd hurt himself on something in here. I don't think I could have handled that."

He squatted beside the bed, looked beneath it. There was a suitcase there. He dragged it out. It was cheap, vinyl over cardboard, and the latches were dusty. He popped them open. There was nothing inside.

"Maybe he had another one," she said. "Or one of those overnight bags."

"Maybe."

He shoved the suitcase back under the bed, dusted himself off. She unlocked one of the bedroom windows and pushed up on it until it opened. A breeze blew through the apartment. Outside, birds were singing.

He went into the tiny bathroom, tugged aside the plastic shower curtain. The sink and tub were rust-stained but clean. The medicine cabinet held a disposable razor, toothpaste, a can of shaving cream, and three condoms in foil wrappers. In a wicker basket beside the toilet was a *Racing Form* from May and a *Rolling Stone* and a *Penthouse* that were both a year old.

That was the whole of the apartment. He went back into the living room, felt the depression settling around him.

On top of the VCR was a videocassette in a brown plastic case. He opened it. Inside was an adult film and a yellow rental receipt from a video store. It was dated June 28. Four weeks ago.

"He never returned this," he said.

"What?" she called from the bedroom.

He put the tape back. She came into the living room, went to the window beside the love seat.

"Have you seen enough?" she said.

She undid the latch, pushed up on the sash, but it wouldn't give. He came up behind her, saw the thin sheen of perspiration on the back of her neck, smelled her perfume.

"Hold on," he said.

He reached above her, his chest touching her shoulders. She didn't move away. He pushed up on the sash with both hands until it slid open.

"There," he said and stepped back. She turned to face him, only inches between them. The room felt tiny, airless.

Without thinking, he touched her forehead, pushed a lock of hair away from her eyes. She looked up at him and he leaned close, gently kissed the side of her neck. When he drew back, she caught his hand.

Outside, Terry Jr. was singing a nonsense song, accompanied by the squeaking of the swing.

"What about the baby?" Harry said.

"She's sleeping. She'll be all right."

She smiled, bit the edge of her lip.

"Lock the door," he said.

Later, he went naked into the bathroom, urinated into the toilet, dropped the condom in, and flushed. He looked at himself in the mirror, turned on the faucet, and palmed cold water into his face. He wanted a drink. He wanted to be gone from there.

When he went back in, she was still in bed. She stretched her arms above her head, then sat up, the sheet slipping away from her. She got her panties and cutoffs from the floor, wriggled into them without leaving the bed.

"God knows what you must think about me," she said. "I'm not like this."

He pulled on his jeans, saw that she was looking at his scar.

"An accident," he said, "at work."

"It must have been a pretty bad one."

"It was."

She gestured at her shirt. He handed it to her, watched her finish dressing.

"Do you think we should call the police?" she said. "About Jimmy being missing? Wouldn't his sister want you to?"

"At some point, maybe." He sat on the edge of the bed to pull on his boots. "But we'll give it some time first. I'm going to look around a little more, see if I can turn him up. If I can't, I'll call her and ask what she wants to do."

She sat beside him, put an arm across his bare shoulders, and kissed the side of his face.

"I'm glad you wore that thing for me," she said. "Some men won't. I don't know why. There're enough babies in this world already without somebody to love them."

She got up and went down the hall to the bathroom, closed the door. He pulled on the T-shirt, went out into the living room. The VCR blinked at him. He had the feeling that, whatever happened, Jimmy was never coming back here.

When she came out of the bathroom, her hair was still damp with sweat, her face flushed.

"I hope he doesn't get back and wonder why his bed is messier than when he left," she said.

"I wouldn't worry about it."

She stood on tiptoes, gave him a quick kiss on the lips.

"I'm going to leave the windows open a little while," she said. "Let some fresh air in here."

They went out onto the steps and she locked the door behind them. Terry Jr. was gone from the swings.

"The mail you saved for him," he said. "Do you have it handy?"

"The mail?"

"It might be helpful. There may be some sort of indication as to where he went."

"I don't know if I should let . . ."

"I want to be able to tell Andrea everything I can."

She looked at him, considering.

"Come on, then," she said.

He followed her to the house. When she opened the screen door, the dog came scrabbling along the kitchen floor toward him. She slapped it sharply on the snout, and it whimpered and backed away. She pushed open the door, let it run out into the backyard.

In the living room, Terry Jr. sat on the arm of an old, overstuffed couch, watching cartoons, swinging his legs.

"Hi," Harry said.

The boy ignored him. His heels thudded on the couch.

"This way," she said. "I keep it in here."

There was a small table in the hallway leading to the front door. She opened a drawer and started to pull out envelopes. Upstairs, a baby began to cry.

"I threw all the junk mail out," she said. "Everything else is here. You'll have to look yourself. I'll be back." She went up the stairs.

He flipped through the pile. About a dozen envelopes, mostly bills—cable, phone, electric. Credit card solicitations. No personal letters. He folded the envelope with the phone bill in half and slipped it into his back pocket.

She came back down cradling the baby, its crying now reduced to moist sobs.

"Anything interesting?" she asked.

"No. Bills mainly."

She gently bounced the baby. "This is Lee Ann," she said. "Say hello, Lee Ann."

The baby turned away from him, buried her face in her mother's shoulder, gripped her collar.

"She's shy," she said. She cooed to the baby, then shifted it to her other side. "You know, I don't remember seeing any letters in there from Colorado. Isn't that where you said his sister lived? Why didn't she write if she was worried about him?"

"He never was very good at answering letters. She figured it would be quicker if I stopped by."

The baby began to gurgle. Lynn took a corner of her shirt and wiped its mouth. He looked at them, searching for the words.

"Can I call you?" he said.

"If you want to." She pulled the baby close, kissed its forehead.

"I want to."

Outside the kitchen door, the dog began to bark.

He leaned to kiss her brow and she tilted her lips to meet him instead. As they kissed, the baby extended a tiny hand, touched his face.

Driving home, he stopped at a liquor store in Neptune and bought two bottles of wine. He knew he'd need them.

He locked the bottles in the trunk, then went across the street to a coffee shop and got change for a dollar from the cashier. She pointed him to a phone booth by the kitchen entrance. He called Ray at his office.

"You still have a Red Line to DMV?" he asked.

"Don't use it much, but I still pay for it. What are you looking for?"

He gave him Cortez's name and address. "Car make, model, license number," he said. "Anything that DMV has in their computer that might help."

"If I do you this favor, you promise to tell me what's going on at some point?"

"I promise. I know it's hard to believe, but right now you know almost as much as I do."

"You're right, it is hard to believe. Give me a few minutes. What number are you at?"

"It's a pay phone. There's no number on it."

"Call me back in ten minutes."

Harry gave him twelve, drank a cup of coffee at the counter. He borrowed a stub of pencil from the waitress, got a white paper napkin from the dispenser, wrote down the information Ray gave him.

After he hung up, he pulled a tattered directory from the shelf beneath the phone. He paged through it, found a listing for a Pettimore, L., at the right address. He wrote down the number, looked at it for a long moment.

He imagined calling her. He wondered what he'd say.

EIGHT

When he got home, Janine's blue Subaru was parked in front of the barn. She was sitting on the picnic table in his side yard, palms against the wood, shoulders forward, watching him. She wore jeans and a black jersey with a white 12 on it.

He parked alongside the Subaru, got out.

"What's wrong?" he said.

She shook her head, hopped down from the table.

"Nothing. I had to run some errands in Freehold, so I thought I'd come by, say hello."

"I don't know if I believe that," he said. "But come on inside."

In the kitchen, he got two small plastic bottles of Evian from the refrigerator, held one out. She took it.

"Are you okay?" she said.

"What do you mean?"

"You look a little down."

He shrugged, opened the Evian.

She looked around.

"New floor in here," she said. "Or new linoleum."

"Both. The old wood rotted straight through, I had to rip it all out. First time you've been up here in a while, isn't it?"

"Yes. It's amazing, all this time and it still looks like no one lives here."

"I'd give you a tour, but I gave the maid the year off. Let's go out on the porch. It's cooler."

Outside, he let her take the rocker, sat on the top step near her feet, facing her. He sipped water.

"How do you feel?" he said.

"Fine, so far. Fat."

"I can't tell."

"Give it a month."

She leaned forward, elbows on her knees, the bottle in both hands. She scraped at the wet label with a thumbnail.

"I did have another reason for stopping by," she said.

"I guessed."

"I wanted a chance to talk with you when Bobby wasn't around."

He drank water, waited.

"Bobby's good at a lot of things, but he's a bad liar," she said. "And I guess he's smart enough to know when not to even try. He told me what you gave him."

"It was a loan. That's all."

"I'm not sure whether to be grateful or angry."

"Why would you be angry?"

"This is our mess, Harry. Not yours. And that's a lot of money."

"That's a matter of perspective, isn't it? I've got this house, this land, and the money that went along with it. None of which I worked a day for. And a pension on top of that. I can afford it."

"That's not the point."

"All of a sudden I feel like I should be defending myself, and I don't know why."

"That other night, after you left. I was up a long time thinking."

"About?"

"About pulling you into this."

"Nobody did any pulling."

"Maybe not, but now you're in it, aren't you? And I'm worried that you're in it more than either of you are telling me."

He put down the bottle.

"Bobby screwed up," he said. "I'm sure if he could go

back in time, he'd do things differently. But right now he's in a jam, and I might be able to help him get out of it. It would be hard to turn away from that."

"It's you I'm worried about."

He leaned back against the railing, looked up at her.

"I know," he said. "But you don't need to be."

"You've been through a lot."

He looked off across the yard, watched a rabbit nose through the grass beneath the willows.

"I've known Bobby a long time," he said.

"I know."

"Longer than I've known anyone else in my life. Anyone."

She didn't respond.

"He crossed a line with this thing, a big one. But I have no desire to see him get screwed over as a result, either, especially by people like those. He made a mistake and he realizes that. You guys have been together for, what, fifteen years?"

"Sixteen next month."

"And you've got the baby to think about as well now. You don't need this hanging over you. Now, I can rag on Bobby for being a screwup, walk away from him, or I can do my best to help him out. And I can help him, it's in my power. One mistake shouldn't doom people for life. That's not fair, either."

"I guess what it comes down to is I'm scared. By this whole thing."

"I know."

"And angry too. If he had come to me first . . ."

"You'd have told him not to do it."

"Absolutely."

"That's why he didn't. He knew what you'd say."

"Then why did he go through with it?"

"He told me you needed the money."

"Of course, we needed the money. We *always* need the money. But not like this. Jesus, Harry, he's pushing forty. He's going to be a father. He's not a kid anymore. This isn't a game."

"He knows that."

"And when it comes to money, there are things we could do. My parents . . ."

"I doubt Bobby would have gone for that."

". . . or worse comes to worst, we could go down to North Carolina and live with my sister. There were other options."

"Maybe he wanted to be the one to provide, no matter what it took."

"Excuse me, Harry, but that's male bullshit."

"Maybe."

"It is. And maybe I'm not being fair to him, I don't know. But when I think about it, this whole thing just makes me so goddamn mad. Mad that he would get involved with someone like that, even madder that he would endanger what we've got. It feels like we've worked so hard for so long, and he's risking it all. And now you're in it as well."

"Slow down," he said. "What's going on in your relationship is between you two. But this issue right now, it's a money question, that's all. It can be dealt with. I already talked to Fallon."

"You did? What did he say?"

"Not a lot. But I think we can deal with him, if that's what you're asking. We already have some money to give him. It will keep him quiet long enough for Bobby to work on the rest."

"You sound sure of that."

"For Fallon to do anything else would be counterproductive at this point. And whatever he is, he's no fool. He wants his money, that's all."

"You're trying to make me feel better," she said. "But I don't know if you believe all this yourself."

She sipped water, watched him. They sat in silence for a moment.

"Forgive me for saying this, Harry. But you know what I think?"

"What?"

"It's not just Bobby, is it?"

"What do you mean?"

"You don't have a family of your own anymore. So you're trying to protect ours."

He looked away. A light wind had sprung up, stirring the willows. The rabbit was gone.

"And bless you for that," she said. "But you can't solve all our problems. You shouldn't try to."

"I'm not."

"There's something else about Bobby too. The way he is; he always thought he could lean out over the edge as far as he wanted, that somebody would always be there to pull him back. He's been that way since he was a kid. It used to be me he relied on, to catch him before he fell."

"I know."

"This time it's you."

He had no answer for that.

Later, after she left, he brought the bottles in from the trunk, put them in the refrigerator. But he didn't open them.

Around eleven, he took the Mustang keys, went out to the car. The restlessness was on him, a feeling he couldn't name or satisfy. He headed east on 537, dark fields stretching away on both sides. He noticed a slight roughness to the engine, an erratic cough in the exhaust. When he reached Tinton Falls the streets narrowed and the farms gave way to houses with warm second-floor lights, the occasional blue glow of a television in a downstairs window.

He picked up Route 36, drove east to the ocean, pushing fifty, the wind whipping through the car. He thought of Lynn Pettimore and her two children, of the emptiness of Jimmy's apartment. He thought of Cristina and Fallon, of his bulk on her, moving in the dark.

The Sand Castle was a sprawling two-story restaurant on the inlet in Manasquan. Nestled in the shadow of a highway bridge, it sat on a pier that extended out over the water and into the sunlight. On the far end of the pier were tables beneath umbrellas. Though the tables were empty, Harry could see gulls perched on the railings as if waiting for the diners to return. Gray wooden steps stretched from the gravel parking lot to the front door.

There was a two-lane access ramp that curved down to the restaurant from the bridge, the only way in and out. Just before the turnoff was a small strip mall with a pizza parlor, video store, and Laundromat. From where he'd parked alongside the Laundromat, he had an unobstructed view of the ramp and restaurant. He looked at his watch. Three-thirty.

He took the field glasses from the seat beside him. They were hard green plastic, made for jungle use, and he'd paid $200 for them at an army surplus store ten years ago. He took off his sunglasses, hung them on the rearview mirror, and brought the binoculars up. The restaurant sharpened into view as he focused.

The outside was decorated with fishing nets, life preservers, buoys, and fake harpoons—Shore tourist-trap kitsch. He scanned the front of the restaurant, saw the CLOSED sign on the glass door. Through the wide windows he could see empty tables set for dinner.

There were only four cars in the lot, a black Jeep Wrangler, a ten-year-old Plymouth with a Rutgers sticker in the rear window, a tiny Geo Metro, and a dark blue BMW with its top down. It was either the same car he'd parked alongside at the country club or its twin. No Lexus.

He opened the glove box, rooted under papers until he felt the smooth, pocket-sized can of CS spray. He set it on the console, then reached under his seat and drew out the manila envelope full of money. He put it on the passenger seat, picked up the glasses again.

At ten to four, a maroon Buick with New York plates drove past him, turned down the ramp, and pulled into the restaurant lot. Two men got out. The driver was in his mid-forties, heavy, dark haired, with broad shoulders and a distended gut. He wore a sport jacket over a polo shirt, had a cigarette dangling from his lips.

The passenger was twenty years younger and a hundred

pounds lighter, with brush-cut black hair and a feral face. He wore a dark suit jacket over an open shirt, matching pants. Harry could see the glint of a gold chain around his neck.

They stood outside the car for a few moments, talking. Then the heavy man took a final drag on his cigarette, flung it away, put his fist to his mouth, and coughed. They went up the steps and into the restaurant.

Fuck this, Harry thought.

He waited for another twenty minutes. No more cars arrived. He got out of the Mustang, went to a phone booth outside the pizza place, and dialed the restaurant number.

"Hello?"

"Let me talk to Fallon."

"Who?"

"Don't fuck with me. If he's there, put him on."

"Who's this?"

"You've got three seconds."

"Maybe you didn't hear me. I asked who this is."

Harry hung up.

He went back to the car, started the engine. As he began to back up, he saw the door to the restaurant swing wide, thrust open by an unseen arm. He braked, waited.

When she came out, her copper hair flashed in the sun. She wore a sleeveless floral print dress, her hair tied in a single elaborate braid that fell down her back. She paused at the door, put on a pair of tortoiseshell sunglasses, then started down the steps. He watched her walk to the BMW, get behind the wheel.

He shifted into neutral. She pulled out of the lot, came up the access ramp faster than she should have. At the top, she turned left, drove past the strip mall. For an instant, he thought he saw her head turn toward him.

He watched as she went up to the next light, stopped briefly at the red signal, and then turned right.

It would be foolish to follow her. At the speed she was going, she would be out of sight before he could even make the light. There was no sense in it. No sense at all.

He reversed the Mustang in a wide arc, knocked the stick

into first. He waited for a break in the traffic, then bumped over the curb and into the street, hit the gas. There was a squeal of brakes behind him, an angry horn. He ignored it, ground the gears into second, signaled, and hit the light just as it flashed from yellow to red. He checked for cross traffic, then turned right, foot on the gas again. Far ahead, he saw the BMW brake, turn left onto a side street. He sped after it.

There was a condominium complex on the right side of the street, a supermarket on the left. He braked for a car turning right out of the complex, then passed it, swung back into the right lane. There was no oncoming traffic, so when he reached the side street he turned left without slowing, his tires squealing, the needle at forty, not wanting to lose sight of her. He shifted into third, hit the gas, and saw then that it wasn't a side street, it was a cul-de-sac—less than a hundred feet of blacktop that ended against a knee-high guardrail. Fifty feet ahead of him, the BMW was sideways across the road, halfway through a three-point turn.

He stood on the brake, yanked the wheel to the right, downshifting at the same time. The Mustang coughed, jerked, and stalled. The front tires hit the curb, climbed slowly, and rolled back down.

She calmly finished her turn, then pulled up so that their driver's side doors were parallel. She looked across at him, smiling faintly, her eyes unreadable behind the sunglasses.

"Why don't you park that thing," she said.

He did, backed up snug against the curb, shut off the ignition, and looked across at her.

"Get in," she said.

They were driving north along the ocean, the wind blowing around them. Bicyclists raced along the shoulder of the road. The manila envelope lay on the floor at his feet.

Up close, he could see the changes in her. She was too thin, her bones close to the skin, and even though she wore sunglasses, he could see the tight wrinkles of skin around her eyes. But the spray of freckles on her shoulders and collarbone was as he remembered it. Her skin was smooth and slightly tan, and her perfume had the faint scent of lilacs.

"You're staring," she said.

It was the first either of them had spoken since he'd gotten into the car.

"I'm sorry," he said.

"I thought that was you. I wasn't sure. I had decided to go back and check, and the next thing I knew, you came whipping around that corner behind me."

"I recognized you right away. I was afraid I was going to lose you."

"What were you doing back there?"

"I was supposed to meet your husband."

"At the Sand Castle? He wasn't there."

"I figured."

"He's up in North Jersey all day. Are you the reason the manager was in such a hurry for me to finish my lunch and leave?"

"Probably."

"What's in the envelope?"

"Money."

"How much?"

"Eighty-five hundred dollars."

She looked at him.

"Whose?"

"Your husband's now."

"Then I probably don't want to know about it. Light me a cigarette, will you? I don't want to run over anyone."

There was a brown leather cigarette case on the console. He opened it, took out a pack of Marlboro Lights and a bright silver lighter. He got one of the cigarettes going, read the inscription on the lighter. Engraved there was an Irish Claddagh symbol—clasped hands within a circle of intricate hearts—and the words, "To Cristina, My Angel—E."

"Take one for yourself," she said. "You still smoke, don't you?"

"No. I quit."

"Smart. I wish I could."

"Have you tried?"

"A couple of times. Once almost for good, but I always go back."

He handed the cigarette to her.

"How is it," she said, "that we don't see each other for all these years and then run into each other twice in one week?"

"I don't know. Fate?"

"I don't believe in it. Tell me, what went on between you and Lester at the club?"

"He grabbed me. We got into a tussle and he fell."

"That doesn't sound like you. You were the calmest person I'd ever met. What happened?"

"People change."

"He was insane afterward. He wanted to kill you. He was back there, you know, at the restaurant."

"I figured that too."

They drove on, past beachside snack bars and a miniature golf course.

"How come you're not married anymore?"

He looked at her. She pointed at his left hand.

"There's an outline where your ring was. Divorced? Or just pretending?"

"Widowed."

She grew quiet.

"I'm sorry."

"It's all right."

"How long ago?"

"Two years."

"What happened?"

"Cancer."

"Forgive me. I didn't mean to pry."

"You're not prying."

He shifted in the leather seat, looked around. "Nice car," he said.

"A birthday present. Last year. You still a motorhead?"

"Not as much as I used to be. Where are we going?"

She signaled, slowed. "Here."

Ahead on the wide shoulder was a truck selling Italian ices. She pulled smoothly off the road and parked behind it.

"I want one of those," she said. "Cherry, if they have it."

He looked at her, got out of the car. The truck's chimes were playing softly, a children's tune. He found some crumpled singles in his jeans pocket, went up to the truck, and ordered two small cherry ices. He saw her get out, walk over to the hurricane fencing that bordered the beach. There was a volleyball game in progress beyond, teenagers in bathing suits racing back and forth, sprawling in the sand, laughing.

The ices came in white paper cups. He paid, pulled napkins from the dispenser, and carried them over to her.

"Thanks," she said, taking the ice. A soft breeze moved her hair, pinned two strands of it to her cheek. She pushed them away with a finger. They walked back to the car.

"Funny, isn't it?" she said.

"What?"

She leaned against the fender.

"People who haven't seen each other in twenty years. When they finally do, they don't have much to say to each other."

"It's been a long time. It's only natural."

She nibbled at the ice, looked off at the volleyball game.

"So much has happened," she said. "I don't know where to start."

A thin line of red juice ran from her lips.

"What are you smiling at?" she said.

"Nothing."

"Napkin."

He gave her one and she wiped the juice from her chin. He slurped some of his own ice, felt the cold run up through his teeth, plant a needle of headache in his skull.

"Well," she said, "at least you're not fat and bald."

"Not yet."

"And getting you to talk about yourself is still like pulling teeth. How well do you know my husband?"

"Not very. I met him for the first time that day at the club."

"So why are you giving him money?"

"It's a long story. The money belonged to someone else. I was just handing it over."

"Should I ask what it's for?"

"You can, but I won't tell you. He might."

"I doubt it. And I won't ask. Is there a message that goes with it? Or do I just hand it to him and say, 'Here, honey, someone gave this to me today for you'?"

"The money is the message. He's expecting it."

"It's always money, isn't it?"

"What do you mean?"

"Never mind."

She started around to the driver's side.

"Come on," she said. "I'll take you back to your car."

She got behind the wheel, started the engine. He waited a moment, then got in beside her, pulled the door shut. She signaled, craned her head to look for a break in the traffic.

"It wasn't the money," he said.

She pulled back out onto the road, accelerated.

"That's not why I followed you."

She turned to him.

"Then why did you?"

"Because I wanted to see you, talk with you. And I meant what I said on the phone. You haven't changed much."

She turned away.

"But I have," she said. "In ways I couldn't even begin to tell you."

She drove another block, made a U-turn in the parking lot of a 7-Eleven, and started back the way they'd come.

They finished their ices on the ride back, neither of them speaking. When they got to the cul-de-sac, she pulled up alongside the Mustang.

"You can leave the envelope," she said. "I'll give it to him. Don't worry."

"I'm not worried."

He got out of the car and looked down at her. She took off her sunglasses, turned to face him. Her green eyes were wet and he could clearly see the patch of gold in her left iris.

"Call me," he said.

She turned away, shook her head. "I don't think that's a good idea."

He stepped back. She U-turned, cutting the wheel to clear the opposite curb, then headed back to the cross street. He watched her go.

When he got in the Mustang, he realized he was still carrying the crumpled, red-stained cup.

He took it home with him.

The phone rang. He stirred in his sleep. On the second ring, he reached, fumbled the receiver to his ear.

"Yeah."

"What are you trying to pull?"

He looked at the clock radio on the nightstand. Two A.M. He shifted the phone to his other hand.

"You there?" the voice said. "You hear me, you fuck?"

"Who is this?"

"You know who this is. Let me tell you something. If you're pulling something funny, or if you're even thinking about it, you've got shit for brains."

"Fallon."

"Who do you think?"

"Why are you calling me?"

"You were supposed to come to the restaurant. You've got a lot of fucking nerve, following my wife like that."

"Is that what all this is about?"

"You want to be a smartass? Fuck with me and see where it gets you. You understand what I'm saying?"

"I understand."

"Then what do you have to say for yourself?"

"Just this, I guess. Did you get the money?"

"Yeah, I got the money."

"Then go fuck yourself," Harry said and hung up.

He pulled the plug from the back of the phone, let it drop to the floor. He rolled over, pulled the pillow to him and, within five minutes, was asleep again.

NINE

He woke the next morning with the vague sense of having set something in motion, of purpose. It felt good.

After he showered and ate, he found Cortez's phone bill, slit the flap of the envelope with his pen knife. He saved the pages with the outgoing calls, threw everything else away.

There were about twenty calls listed, most of them local, but there were a half dozen to a number with a 609 area code—South Jersey. He remembered what Bobby had said about Jimmy's biker friends. There was a single call to Denver on June 16 and no calls at all after June 28. He circled the long-distance numbers with a pen.

There was no answer at the Denver number and no machine. He called Denver information and asked for listings for Cortez, on the off chance the sister was unmarried or had kept her maiden name. He got ten numbers back from the irritated operator, one for an A. Cortez that matched the number on the bill.

He left the other numbers for later, found the coffee shop napkin. He copied the information he'd gotten from Ray onto a yellow legal pad. There had been only one vehicle registered in Cortez's name, a blue 1990 Monte Carlo, license number TFW-456. The registration was up for renewal next month.

He looked at Lynn Pettimore's number. After a long moment, he picked up the phone again, keyed in the number. It rang six times and then a male voice, irritable, answered. Harry set the receiver back in the cradle.

He spent the rest of the afternoon under the hood of the Mustang, his *Chilton's Guide,* pages spotted with dark fingerprints, open on the fender. He replaced the spark plugs and points, started the engine. Listening closely, he adjusted the idle setting on the carburetor, turning the tiny screw that regulated the air-to-fuel ratio until the roughness in the engine noise was gone. Then he shut the hood, put away his tools, and went for a test-drive.

He headed west on 537 to Route 9, then turned north. He worked smoothly through the gears until the needle was trembling at seventy-five. Stopped at a light, he heard an engine racing and turned to his left to see a teenager in an old Mercury Cougar alongside him. The car was painted a metal-flake blue and had oversized rear tires. The kid looked over at him, teased the gas so that the Cougar seemed to strain forward. The kid gestured up at the light and Harry nodded.

Harry shifted into first, pushed in the clutch, gave it gas, the 289's rumble growing into a roar. The kid revved his own engine in answer, looked up at the light. When it switched to green, the kid popped the clutch, shot off the line, rear tires squealing, raising smoke. Harry watched him go, took his foot off the gas, and waited until the SUV behind him beeped its horn before he started across the intersection.

The Cougar was already out of sight. He wondered how far the driver had gone before he'd realized he was alone. *Adios, kid,* he thought. *Don't kill yourself.* He U-turned at the next jug handle, headed home.

He was in the kitchen, washing the rest of the engine grease from his hands, when the phone rang. He dried his hands on a dish towel, picked up the receiver.

"For somebody who gives my husband money," she said, "you sure seem to make him mad."

He leaned back against the counter.

"I guess it wasn't enough."

"With him, it never is. Are you all right?"

"What do you mean?"

"When I told him about running into you yesterday, it really set him off. He got angrier than he'd been in a long time."

"I know. He called me last night."

"I overheard. His end of it, at least."

"Would your husband happen to be in the room there with you now?"

"No. He's over at the restaurant. He'll be back in a little while."

"What can I do for you?"

"I was just wondering. Do you need me to make any other mysterious deliveries for you, or are you planning to handle it yourself from here on?"

"I'm not sure," he said slowly. "Maybe it's something worth talking about."

"Maybe it is," she said.

There was a steady wind out of the northeast and, even though the day was warm, it was chilly here at the top of the hill. They were standing on the stone parapet outside the Twin Lights, the pair of century-old brownstone lighthouses rising fortresslike behind them. She'd gotten a waist-length black leather jacket from the BMW and put it on over her chamois blouse, zipped it against the wind. Her hair was loose and moved in the breeze.

He leaned against the parapet's waist-high wall. Below was a steep drop through trees and brush as the hill sloped down to the Navesink River. He looked toward the ocean. In the hazy distance to the north, out past Sandy Hook and the long stretch of New York Bay, he could see the silhouette of the Verrazano Bridge, Brooklyn beyond.

"I remember the first time we were ever up here," she said.

He nodded. They had sneaked in here often at night, after the park gates were closed, to look out at the lights of New York. On clear nights, they could see all the way to Coney Island, the glow of the Ferris wheel lighting up the sky. A month before she left, they had made love here, on the soft grass of the north side of the hill. He remembered rolling over to look up at a sky full of stars, his breath still heavy, and seeing the blink-quick path of a meteor out over the ocean.

"Tell me about your wife," she said.

"What do you want to know?"

"How old was she when she got sick?"

"Thirty-four."

"Was it sudden?"

"I came home one night, late, found her on the kitchen floor. She was semiconscious, couldn't speak. I had no idea what had happened. I called nine one one and we got her to the hospital."

There were about a dozen tourists around, taking photos of the view or picnicking on the grass. A sudden shift in wind snatched napkins and paper plates, sent them scudding along the ground, owners in pursuit.

"Had she been sick at all? Any symptoms before that?"

He shook his head. "If so, she never let on."

"What happened at the hospital?"

"Our doctor met us there. After a while, when they had her stabilized, she was able to talk a little bit. She said she'd gone into the kitchen to answer the phone and the last thing she remembered was the smell of burning wires."

"Wires?"

"The doctor told me later that stroke victims often smell burning wires just before the attack. When they started running down the list of what it could be, a stroke was the best-case scenario."

"What did they do?"

"Ran a CAT scan. She was conscious mostly by then, scared. That's when they found it."

"A tumor?"

He put his thumb and index finger together in a circle. "About this big. They couldn't believe she'd been walking around with it, not been affected. They decided to go in right away, get as much of it as possible. She was in surgery sixteen hours. When it was over, the surgeon told me they'd gotten all they could. The way the tumor was placed . . . well, there wasn't a lot they could do."

"Does it bother you to talk about this?"

"Not too much anymore."

"What happened after the operation?"

"She was in the hospital about two months. They started the chemo there. They sent her home because there wasn't much else they could do for her. We were living in Metuchen at the time. I rented a hospital bed, set it up downstairs. I took some time off from work, hired a visiting nurse. We kept up the chemo. She had good days and bad days."

"Was she aware of what was going on?"

"Most of the time. During those first few months she could talk more or less, though sometimes she had trouble stringing her thoughts together. Later on, she couldn't talk at all. I just did whatever I could to keep her comfortable."

"You never had any children?"

"No. We'd been talking about it. But the time just never seemed right. Then she got sick and suddenly there was no more time."

"How long was it? Between when she went home and . . ."

"She died?"

"Yes."

"Eight months."

"That's so quick."

"It didn't seem that way. Toward the end, she was hallucinating. She was in pain a lot of the time, so we had a morphine drip hooked up. Even with that, it got pretty bad."

"I'm sorry."

"It's me who should be apologizing. You don't need to hear all this."

She hooked her elbow in his. "Come on," she said. "Let's walk."

They started back toward the lighthouses.

"After you left," he said, "I used to come up here sometimes on my own. I still do every once in a while."

They walked out onto the picnic area. There was an

unoccupied redwood table and a pair of benches in the shade of a sycamore tree.

"You were upset," he said. "The other day. When you dropped me off."

She leaned against the table.

"I guess I was thinking about all the things that had happened since I left."

"So why did you call me?"

"Like I said. I wanted to make sure you were all right."

"That's why you called yesterday. How about today?"

"Do I need a reason?"

"No."

"You think too much, Harry. You always did. It's not a good thing."

"Maybe you're right."

"Tell me, how did you end up a cop? It's the last thing I would have expected from you."

"I was with the state police. It's a little different."

"How long?"

"Twelve years, give or take a couple months."

"What did you do there?"

"When I quit, I was a detective with the Major Crimes Unit. We handled high-profile cases, helped out local police on homicide investigations when they requested it. That sort of thing."

"You didn't drive around, give people tickets?"

"I did for a while. All troopers do. Four years of that and I was promoted to road detective. Did that for two years and then put in for MCU."

"Why'd you leave?"

"I had an accident."

"A car accident?"

He shook his head. "I was shot."

She straightened. "What happened?"

"It wasn't long after Melissa died. Coming home one night, I stopped a car that was driving erratically. When I went up to the window, a woman shot me."

"Why?"

"We never found out. She panicked, maybe they had something in the car. I don't know. The driver got away."

"Where were you shot?"

He touched his stomach. "It went in the front and out the back and managed not to hit any major organs along the way: I was in the hospital for a while. But that was two years ago now."

"What happened to the woman?"

"She died."

"How?"

"I shot her."

She watched him, said nothing.

"I could have gone back," he said. "But I didn't."

"Why not?"

"My grandmother had left me a house and some money, enough to get by for a while. After Melissa died, I decided I needed a change. I sold the house in Metuchen, moved out to Colts Neck. I'd only been there about a month when I got hurt. When the time came to go back, I couldn't do it. So I took a partial pension instead, handed in my papers."

"What have you been doing since?"

"Not much. This and that."

The wind moved the branches above their heads. They watched a young couple head back to the parking lot, a boy of about four or five between them. They each held one of his hands.

"It's getting late," she said. "I should get going."

"Is he home?"

"He will be."

"I can't see it."

"What?"

"You and him."

She looked at him, then turned away.

"I have to go," she said.

They walked side by side to the parking lot. When they reached the BMW, she got out her keys, slid behind the wheel. He closed the door for her, stood there with his hands still on it.

"You never asked," he said. "About the money."

"Does it concern me?"

"I guess not."

"Then that's why I didn't ask."

She started the engine and a bell began to ding inside the car. She looked over at where the Mustang was parked.

"Reliving your teenage years?" she said.

"I was four when that car came out."

"It's you."

"We'll go for a ride sometime."

She smiled at that. "Maybe."

She pulled on her seat belt, put the car in gear. The bell stopped. She looked up at him, held his gaze.

"So," he said. "I'll see you around. Maybe."

"You never know."

He stepped away as she backed out. He watched her drive past the gate, saw the sun flare in her hair for just an instant before the car vanished down the narrow, sloping road that led back down the hill.

TEN

The bundle of money sailed through the air, landed on the coffee table, and slid to the edge. He caught it before it went over.

"You're not going to believe this," Bobby said. He took another bundle from the purse-sized canvas bank bag, tossed it after the first. "Fifteen grand," he said. "Not bad for two days' work."

They were in Bobby's living room, the afternoon sun streaming through the windows. Harry sat straddling a kitchen chair. He picked up the second bundle, thumbed it, saw mostly new bills. The stacks were bound with thick brown rubber bands.

"What did you do?" he said.

"What didn't I do." Bobby put the bag on the table, dropped down on the couch. "Five of that is from cash advances on our credit cards. We'll be paying interest on it until the fucking cows come home. But at least I don't have to worry about Citibank sending someone around to break my kneecaps."

He picked up the guitar from where it leaned against the wall.

"And the rest?" Harry said.

Bobby strummed a minor chord with his thumb.

"I called in a couple favors. Got a two-week advance at work and a loan from my boss. He wasn't happy about it, but

I'd agreed to help crew his boat when he takes it down to Lauderdale this fall, so he didn't want to blow that. And he knows that if it comes down to it, I can work for free for the next six months and it's no skin off his ass."

"He ask what it was for?"

"Yeah, and I lied. But the real indignity"—he pointed at the money—"is that six of that is from Janine's father."

"I didn't think you two spoke."

"We don't. But it turns out Janine talked to him last week. I had no idea. If I had, I probably would have said no."

"Pride is maybe not the most useful quality right now."

"He came through, I'll give him that. And she managed to get it out of him without telling him what it was for, either. That's the amazing part."

"Almost twenty-four grand. Halfway there."

"I've got a few moves left too. I think I might be able to come up with some more before too long."

"Maybe you didn't need my help after all."

"No, I did. You helped me get my head on straight about this. Once I got my mind around the idea of actually having to pay him, I started figuring out ways to make it work. I guess I needed that kick in the ass."

"So the light at the end of the tunnel's getting brighter?"

"So bright I need shades. How are we going to do it this time?"

"I'll leave that up to him. I'll contact him, let him name a time and place. He won't have expected this much so soon."

"You trust him?"

"That's a question you should have asked yourself a while back, isn't it?"

"I mean now. You've met with him, talked to him. Do you trust him?"

"Not much. But he wants his money, I can tell you that. He'll do whatever it takes to make sure he gets it, even if that means doing nothing. He's had a taste now, he won't spit the hook."

"Let's hope. So tell me about Jimmy's apartment."

"Not much to tell. When he left, he left in a hurry. Most, if not all, of his clothes are still there."

"You had a good look around?"

"As much as I could. There's nothing there that helps."

"That's too bad. I was hoping you might find something to help make sense out of all this."

"Just this: No one else had been through that apartment before me, I'm pretty sure of that. If somebody took him off and they knew where he lived, chances are they would have gone back and torn the place apart to see what they could find. There was no sign anybody had been there."

"So he ran out on me?"

"Looks that way, yeah. There aren't too many other ways to read it."

"You think he went to his sister's?"

"It's possible. I'll check into it, see what I can find out. But in the meantime, we need to get our priorities straight."

"Meaning?"

"The issue here is getting Fallon his money, not if Jimmy screwed you or not. Your house is on fire, forget about looking for the match."

"You don't see it the way I do. He was my friend. I trusted him."

"You want to know what happened, I understand that. But it's time to cut your losses. You told me this was a one-shot deal. . . ."

"It was."

"Then write it off as experience. If he does come back—a big if—the best thing you could do is pretend you don't know him. There could be things going on here you're not even aware of. You don't know what people he's been dealing with or what he's done in the interim. Could be he's already attracted police attention, or even the DEA, if he's traveling around trying to unload a kilo of heroin. They could be after him already for something else. You have no way of knowing."

"Or they could be after me."

"I doubt it at this point. You'd know it if they were. It could be that if they do nail him for something, he might try to sell you out. But then it's only his word against yours. There's no evidence. It'll never fly."

"I hope you're right."

"You've got a chance to reverse this situation here, break clean. You get involved with Cortez again—in any capacity—and all bets are off. You pop up at a DEA surveillance or on a wiretap talking about all this, and boom. Even if you never get convicted—even if the case is so weak it doesn't stand a chance of going to trial—they'll take everything you own. The cars, the boat. They'll seize all your assets, lock up your bank account so you can't get near it. In the meantime, some lawyer's going to be bleeding you dry the entire time."

"I get the idea."

Harry opened the bank bag, put the cash inside. Bobby watched him.

"We're just going to hand that over to him," he said. "It almost doesn't seem right."

Harry zipped the bag shut.

"Right has got nothing to do with it," he said.

At noon the next day, he called the Sand Castle, left a message and his number. Thirty minutes later his phone rang.

"It's been a while, Sergeant Rane. You probably don't even remember me."

"I remember you, Mickey. I heard you were back up here."

"Hard to believe, isn't it? Couldn't keep away."

"What can I do for you?"

"I'm returning your call. Sounds like things got screwed up the other day."

"He was supposed to meet me there. He didn't show. That's why I didn't go in."

"I don't blame you. He got tied up at the last minute, had to send someone else. I talked to him, though, calmed him down. He understands. He's sorry about the way things happened. I'm sure he'd like to tell you that himself."

"You have a message for me?"

"He wants to talk with you, informally. Get to meet you, smooth some things out so there's no more misunderstandings."

"We've already met."

"I heard about that. But things are a little different now. He knows you're on the level. I told him I knew you, that we had worked together."

"I wouldn't put it that way."

"Close enough though, right? We wore the same uniform. You can't put that kind of thing behind you. And we were too good for it, the both of us. We were better than the job."

"Where does he want to meet?"

"He's got tickets for the fights tomorrow night in Asbury, at the old Convention Hall on the boardwalk. He's checking out some Mex kid he's thinking about putting some money into. There'll be a ticket in your name at the box office. Get there say nine or so, we'll see how this kid does, then relax a little bit, have a drink. You can talk to the man right there, work all this out. Can you swing that?"

"Nine. I'll be there."

"And remember, this is just friendly. To talk, nothing else. So don't bring anything. We'll set up a time to take care of business later."

"All right."

"One other thing, Harry. This is just for you. So come alone."

"What are you worried about?"

Dunleavy laughed. "Worried? Lighten up, Harry. You take things too seriously. He wants to talk, get a couple things settled, get to know you a little. That's all."

"Okay."

"Then we'll see you there. Looking forward to it."

ELEVEN

Convention Hall was a flat-topped concrete building that loomed over the desolate north end of the Asbury Park boardwalk. It stretched out over the beach on pilings, its big windows throwing light onto the sand. It had been built in the 1920s, when Asbury was one of the most popular tourist destinations on the East Coast. Harry's mother had often talked of attending dance marathons there during World War II, when the town was full of British sailors on R&R, billeted in the hotels along the beach.

Those hotels were long gone now, and the hall's fortunes had faded with the city's. Despite a partial restoration a few years back, paint still peeled from the outside walls and cracks webbed the highest windows.

There was a single ticket in his name at the box office. He gave it to the elderly man working one of the three doors, took the torn stub that was handed back, and went through into the hall.

The ring was set up in the center of the floor, with rows of metal folding chairs on all four sides. The chairs in the first five rows on each side were painted red, the others were a uniform gray. Wooden seats rose off the floor on all sides, climbing bleacherlike to the high windows.

The seats around the ring were mostly occupied, but the bleachers were less than half full. Old chandeliers hung from the high ceiling, cigarette smoke gathering around them.

The walls were lined with peeling bas-reliefs on sea themes: shells and mermaids, fin-tailed cherubs. A half-visible King Neptune looked down from high on the far wall.

In the ring, two black men circled each other, popping off jabs but not doing much damage. They clinched and the referee broke them up just as the bell rang to end the round. They retreated to their corners and were met with a chorus of boos from ringside.

He looked at his ticket stub. His seat was off the floor on the right side of the ring, halfway up. As he started up the concrete steps, watching for row numbers, he heard the next round begin. Most of the faces in the crowd were black or Hispanic. They ignored him as he went past, found his row. The seats around his were empty.

In the ring, things were picking up. The bigger fighter was moving with renewed energy, tagging his opponent with jabs, then following through with solid rights. A buzz of approval ran through the crowd.

He scanned the floor seats, saw Fallon in a red chair, two rows back from the ring. Beside him sat Mickey Dunleavy, elbows on his knees, watching the action. He looked heavier than Harry remembered, his dark suit stretched tight across wide shoulders. He said something to Fallon and then sat back, pulled a pack of cigarettes from his jacket pocket. There was no sign of Wiley.

The smaller fighter was in trouble now, losing his bearings, circling into punches instead of away from them. When the bell rang, he walked slowly back to his corner and collapsed on his stool, chest heaving. The referee leaned over him while the cornermen swabbed him down. On the other side of the ring, his opponent was on his feet, pacing, waiting for the bell.

The referee turned away, shook his head sharply. There were more boos from the crowd, and a plastic water bottle sailed through the air and skittered across the canvas. The referee swept it away with his foot, crossed the ring, and caught the winner's forearm, raised it high.

From behind Harry, a voice said, "What a couple of pussies."

He swiveled. Two rows behind him was the younger of the two men he'd seen go into the Sand Castle that day. He wore a yellow Fila warm-up suit over a white T-shirt, and his high-top basketball shoes were propped on the seat in front of him.

"He asked me to come up, keep you company," he said. "Make sure you didn't get lost."

Harry looked him over, then turned back to the ring. There were two new fighters in there now, both Hispanic. One was short, dark, and heavily muscled, with a broad Indian face. The other was thinner, lighter skinned, Puerto Rican maybe, with smooth, almost pretty features. They met in the center of the ring, touched gloves, and went back to their corners.

"It's the Mexican kid he came to see," Warm-up Suit said. "We'll go down after it's over."

The bell rang and the two fighters came out. The good-looking one was moving fast. He stretched out his left glove as if measuring distance, keeping the other man at bay. He shuffled his feet, hot-dogging it, and the Mexican stepped in and hit him a solid shot beneath the left elbow.

A cry went up from the crowd, but the light-skinned fighter covered up, took the follow-up blows on his elbows and forearms, stealing time to catch his breath. Then he peeked out, flashed a jab that hit the Mexican above the right eye and snapped his head back. He tried to close, but the Mexican swung wildly at him with both arms, angry. They clinched, staggered around the ring as one until the referee broke them up.

At ringside, Fallon and Dunleavy were in conference, heads together.

The bell rang for the second round and the two fighters came out strong, the light-skinned one firing lefts. The Mexican took a couple in the head, then waded in, started to work the body again. But the other fighter danced away, used his longer reach to land a solid shot on the Mexican's left ear. A chant came up from the ringside seats: "NAN-do! NAN-do! NAN-do!"

Nando acknowledged them with a quick shuffle, stung the Mexican with another jab, and then walked right into a body shot that doubled him. They tangled again, clinched, Nando sucking wind. But when they broke, he managed to tag the Mexican solidly on the jaw, sending him stumbling back.

Nando closed then, hurt but working through it, looking for the openings. The Mexican bulled in again but Nando kept him at arm's length, popping jabs, every third one followed by a solid right.

The Mexican was bleeding from his left eyebrow now. He planted his feet, head down, threw big, slow blows that bruised arms and elbows but didn't get through. By the time the bell rang, the cut was bleeding freely. He slumped onto his stool and his cornermen worked at the cut, swabbed blood from his eye.

"That's it," Warm-Up Suit said. "I think Pancho there lost his chance."

But when the bell rang, the Mexican was up and moving, head down as if he intended to force the other fighter out of the ring with his body alone. Most of the ringside crowd were on their feet now. Fallon and Dunleavy sat impassive.

The Mexican pushed forward, bracing his feet, throwing blows that would have ended the fight if they had connected. But Nando hung back, reading the distance. He made the mangled eyebrow his target, fired shots into it whenever he could, then danced away. The Mexican plodded on, as if walking through mud, and Nando set him up with a left jab, then hammered him with a right. Sweat, blood, and spittle flew. The Mexican took one drunken step in the wrong direction and Nando hit him three times in quick succession. The Mexican sat down hard on the canvas, a look of confusion on his face, and the crowd roared.

"That's it for the beaner," Warm-Up Suit said.

And it was. He made it back up and to his corner, but when the bell rang for the next round, he stayed there. Nando leaped into the air and his cornermen crawled through the ropes to join him in the ring. They had to hold him still long enough for the referee to come over and raise his glove.

Harry stood, heard the seat behind him flip up as Warm-Up Suit did the same. Harry made his way to the aisle, started down the concrete steps, not waiting for him. Below, he saw Dunleavy and Fallon already out of their seats, coming toward him. He met them on the floor.

"How are you, Harry?" Dunleavy said, putting his hand out.

He was a full head taller than Harry and heavier. He wore a suit jacket and white shirt, but no tie. His short black hair was showing gray on the sides and his face was ruddier, but his eyes were the same dull gray Harry remembered. His grip was strong.

"Mickey," he said.

"That was a sad-ass performance to have to watch," Fallon said. He was dressed the same way he had been at the country club, this time all in black. "Sorry to put you through it. Let's go get a drink. They got a bar set up outside."

They went through a side door and out onto a roped-off area of the boardwalk. There was a minibar and a handful of tables with wooden chairs set up, but only one was occupied: two young black men nursing bottles of Heineken. The pair watched them until Dunleavy met their eyes, then they looked away.

"Let's sit down," Fallon said.

The night had chilled slightly and a light fog hung over the water. The fast-food stands and fortune-telling booths that lined the boardwalk were all dark and shuttered, some for good. The only sounds out here were the waves rolling up the beach and the muffled noise of the crowd inside. The air smelled of salt water and creosote.

Fallon dragged a chair out, turned to Warm-Up Suit.

"Tommy," he said, "do me a favor, will you? Go see if you can find Saba. He'll be looking for me. Tell him I'll catch up with him later. We'll talk about the kid."

Dunleavy sat down. Tommy looked at him, then back at Fallon.

"Eddie," he said, his voice tight. "I think we got a misunderstanding here."

Fallon sat down, signaled to the middle-aged black woman standing alongside the bar. Harry remained standing.

"What do you mean?" Fallon said, touching himself for a cigarette.

"If you don't want me around while you talk, just say it," Tommy said. "You don't need to come up with some bullshit errand for me. That's an insult."

Fallon found his pack, took it out.

"What bullshit?" he said. "The guy's going to be looking for me. I don't want him coming out and bothering us when we're talking, that's all. Relax."

He took out his lighter, got the Kool lit.

Tommy looked at him, chewed his lower lip. "One of these days, Eddie," he said, "we got to talk about some things. I think you're a little confused about the situation."

The waitress came over to take their order and Tommy looked at her, then started back toward the hall, walking slowly. Harry pulled out a chair, sat down.

"You shouldn't bust his balls like that," Dunleavy said. "He's a good kid."

"What a hothead," Fallon said. "You see that look? Like he wanted to take a swing at me?"

"You should show a little more respect," Dunleavy said. "Humor the kid. He's a hard worker."

"Maybe so, but I feel like he's in my face every time I turn around."

Fallon ordered bottles of Lowenbrau. Out beyond the jetty, Harry could see the lights of fishing boats in the darkness.

"This is better," Fallon said. "It's hard to concentrate with fifteen hundred screaming spics around you."

Dunleavy turned to Harry. "What's it been?" he said. "Six years?"

"About that."

The waitress brought their beer and glasses. Fallon gave her a twenty, told her to keep the change. He poured beer into his glass.

"This guy Saba," he said. "He's trying to get me to put some money into this stable of fighters he's bringing up. The Mexican was supposed to be his star."

"Looked like he ran out of steam," Harry said.

"Ran out of heart, more like it," Dunleavy said. He sat back, tipped his bottle into the glass. His wrist was thick, vein-roped. "None of it counts if you can't go the distance."

Fallon shifted in his seat, looked uncomfortable, a flash of irritation on his face.

"Excuse me for a minute here," he said. He stood up. "I'll be right back. Give you guys a chance to talk about old times."

As Fallon went back inside the hall, Harry looked over to see the two black men watching them again. They wore FUBU satin jackets and cargo pants, braided gold around their necks. The one on the right wore a diamond-studded cross on a silver chain that hung halfway down his chest.

"Prostate trouble," Dunleavy said. "Guy can't go a half hour without having to take a piss. He's getting to be like an old woman."

Dunleavy looked older, harder than the last time Harry had seen him. The lines around his eyes were cut deeper and there was a fleshiness to him that hadn't been there before. He still radiated strength, but the aura of health was gone.

"Kind of a surprise, isn't it?" Dunleavy said. "Running into each other like this?"

Harry poured his own beer, stopped when the glass was half full.

"How's the stomach?"

"Fine, now."

"I caught one in the arm once." Dunleavy touched the fleshy part of his arm over the left elbow. "Chasing a stolen car on the Turnpike. They ditched it, ran. When I went after them, one of them turned and started popping off at me with this little twenty-five he had. I was so charged up I didn't even realize he'd tagged me. The piece of shit jammed and he was still trying to clear it when I put six in him. You got yours too, I heard."

Harry didn't answer.

"Twenty years ago—hell, ten—you would have gotten a medal for it."

"Maybe not."

"They turn on you quick, don't they? You make the job your life, and the next thing you know they come down on you for doing it too well. I went through the same thing."

Harry drank some of the beer. Fallon came back to the table, sat down.

"It's amazing," he said. "There's a mosaic on the wall in the men's room, looks like fucking Michelangelo painted it, but half the pissers are broken."

"What'd you expect?" Dunleavy said.

"I tell you, though," Fallon said, "This used to be some place. When I was growing up they had shows here all the time. Hendrix, the Stones. Even the Beatles. And before that it was Ella Fitzgerald, Frank Sinatra, Tommy Dorsey, they all played here. Now it's a place where niggers and spics pay twenty dollars a pop to watch other niggers and spics pound the crap out of each other. I guess it's—what do they call it?—cathartic."

Harry looked past Dunleavy's shoulder to where the black men sat, listening to them. He wondered if Fallon was unaware of their presence or just didn't care.

"So let's talk," Harry said.

"Okay." Fallon settled back. "First, let me say I had no idea you two knew each other. We didn't exactly get off on the right foot. I'm sorry about what happened at the club."

"That Lester should cut down on his steroid intake," Dunleavy said. "He didn't know what he was getting into."

"But you know how it is," Fallon said to Harry. "When you're in my position, somebody's always trying to get one over on you. At the time I didn't know you. You came out of nowhere, you understand what I'm saying?"

"You still don't know me."

"Maybe not. But Mickey filled me in. He told me you were a stand-up guy. If he'd been at the club that day, everything would have gone differently. But what's past is past."

"Okay," Harry said.

"So you met my wife?"

Harry looked into his eyes, saw no reaction there.

"Only briefly," he said. He lifted his glass.

"What did you think?"

He shrugged. "A beautiful woman."

"Yeah, God bless America, right? An old guy like me. We've been married close to three years already, she tell you that?"

"No, we didn't talk much."

"Three years. Why she stays with me, sometimes I don't know. A high-maintenance woman, you know what I mean? I have to keep my eye on her all the time."

"How's that?"

"Oh, I don't mean she fools around on me or anything. It's just that she likes to test me every once in a while. We were out in Vegas last month and she must have dropped ten grand of my money. You should see that woman bet. Never a thought to it, never a plan. Always the hunch, the feeling. The risk doesn't matter to her. But that's how women are, right?"

"I guess."

"She used to live around here, years ago. But I met her down in Florida, working in a restaurant, believe it or not. Girl with a college education. She'd gotten hooked up with the guy that ran the place."

"What happened?"

"It was just like in the movies. Love at first sight. I used to come into the restaurant sometimes, flirt with her, you know, all that stuff. Then we got to talking a little. This guy she was with at the time, he was a jerk-off. A drinker, a doper, out of control, running the business into the ground, stealing out of the register with both hands. She was looking to get out, but he wouldn't let her go, you know? He was stupid."

"Stupid?"

"There's times you should fight to protect something, and

there's times when you should step aside and let things take their course. This guy didn't know which was which."

"So you swept her off her feet?"

"Like I said, this guy, he didn't know it was time to let go. For him it was already a lost cause, he just wouldn't accept it. He should have walked away, counted himself lucky that a loser like him ever knew a woman like that at all. But he couldn't. So he got hurt—and why? Because he was stupid. No other reason. What was going to happen was inevitable."

"How did she feel about that?"

"To tell the truth, I don't know that she ever knew the whole story. But what's done is done. It was natural selection. Darwin. No woman ever got wet over a man because he was a nice guy. It doesn't work that way."

Harry sat back.

"I'm sorry I got her involved in this," he said. "It was just the way things worked out."

"Like I said, past is past. What's important is what happens now. Mickey tells me you have something for me."

"Not a lot. But something. More than last time."

"It's always been my feeling that, in business, it's good faith that counts most. That's what's important. A couple bucks here, a couple bucks there, it all balances out in the end. What matters is how you treat the people you do business with."

Harry nodded.

"You're a smart guy, Harry. I sensed that when we met, even before Mickey told me about you. I think we may be able to wrap this up today, if we're lucky. I'd like to see that. And you and your buddy, I'm sure you'd like the same thing."

"That's why I'm here."

A pager went off, a shrill insistent beep.

"It's me," Dunleavy said. He twisted, pulled the pager from his belt, looked at the number.

"There a phone around here?"

"Down in the lobby," Fallon said. "There's a couple of

booths there if somebody hasn't ripped the phones out to sell them."

"I'll be back in a minute." He got up from the table.

Fallon gestured at his back as he walked away. "That's a good man there. He caught a bad break, that trouble with those niggers. He didn't deserve it."

Harry lifted his glass.

"I was out before that happened."

"A real shame that was. That's a guy who'd give his left nut for you if you asked. Whenever he's taking care of something, I don't have to worry about it. It's as good as done. That's why, after he told me about you, I knew we could do business, settle this thing."

"We knew each other briefly. But I can't say we were friends."

"But you don't have to be beer-drinking buddies, playing cards on Friday, slapping each other on the back to know what's what, right? Sometimes you meet a man and you know him right away. Sometimes you know a man twenty years and then he goes and does something that proves he was a stranger all along."

"I guess that's true."

"Hey, believe me, I know. I've seen it. You can love and trust someone like a brother and the next thing you know, he turns around and tries to fuck you. And it's usually because someone's waving something green at him. But when you're on your deathbed, do you wish you had more money, more cars, a bigger house? No. You wish you still had the friends you lost along the way. That's the tragedy of it. Because then it's too late.

"So I know what you're going through here, Harry, getting involved for your friend and all. I understand it and I admire it. That's why I asked Mickey to set this thing up. I don't want our misunderstandings to go any farther. I was angry when I called you, but I was out of line, I admit it. Whatever was said that night between us is forgotten. All right?"

"Forgotten."

"Good. Now that's what I mean about acting in good faith. That tells me everything I need to know about you."

Dunleavy came back, sat down, poured the rest of his beer into the glass.

"You find it?" Fallon said.

"Yeah."

"We're wrapping up here," Fallon said. "We were just working out some details." He turned back to Harry.

"So let's do it this way," he said. "Whatever it is you have that belongs to me, hold on to it for a while. Knowing you've got it is good enough."

"What do you mean?"

"Keep it for now. You brought something to the table. Now it's my turn. I'm willing to accept that this whole thing was an unfortunate accident, that your friend trusted someone he shouldn't have. It happens.

"So I'll tell you what I'm going to do. We'll make it forty and call it quits. You already gave me eight and a half. Give me the other thirty-one and change and that's it, debt's closed as far as I'm concerned. That's forty paid on fifty, more like sixty if you were adding in interest. So an even forty and we finish this once and for all, lick our wounds, and walk away. I'll chalk the rest up to experience, the price of doing business. How's that sound?"

Harry gave that a moment, sipped beer, conscious of both of them watching him.

"Well?" Fallon said.

"I'll pass that on to him. What kind of time frame are we looking at?"

Fallon shrugged. "Hey, I'm not a bank. Or a mortgage company that's going to come and take everything and leave some family out on the street. This is business. These things happen. But I'm not a fool, you know? Best intentions and all, people can get a little lazy if they're not motivated. The clearer things are between us, the better for everybody."

"How long?"

"Let's say a week. No, ten days. Take ten days. From today."

"That's not enough time."

"Look at it this way, with whatever you've got for me now, you're probably about halfway there already, right?"

"I had fifteen to give you. You're talking about raising another sixteen in ten days. That's too much money and too little time."

"Well, that's my offer. I think it's more than fair. Ten days. If we have to negotiate further on details, we'll do that. But understand, Harry, this is going on a month. I've been very patient up to now. If Mickey hadn't vouched for you, we wouldn't even be having this conversation."

"It could be a problem. I'd have to talk to Bobby."

"Go ahead. Call him from here if you want to. But I have to tell you, this is a limited-time offer. Just like on TV. I want to put this matter to rest. I don't even want to think about it anymore. When you walk out of here, I want this thing to be settled."

Harry looked at him, scratched his elbow.

"It's not much time," he said.

Fallon sat back, watched him.

"Make the call," he said. "See what he says."

"I don't need to."

Fallon smiled, leaned forward. He put his hand across the table. Harry took it.

"I'm going to be out of town for a few days, beginning tomorrow," Fallon said. "I have to go up to Boston to settle some things. Mick will be with me. When I get back, we'll hook up, work out the details. Are we agreed?"

Harry nodded.

"See? That was easy." He looked from Harry to Dunleavy. "You were right."

Harry stood up.

"When it's all together, I'll call the restaurant," he said. "We can set up a time and place."

"However you want to do it," Fallon said. "I'll leave it to you."

"Hang on," Dunleavy said, getting up. "I'll walk you out."

"Send Tommy back if you see him," Fallon said. "I'll buy him a drink."

"So," Dunleavy said as they started back toward the hall. "Miss the job?"

"Not too much these days."

As they passed the table with the two black men, one of them mumbled something. Dunleavy stopped, turned toward them, smiling. They watched him, hard-eyed. They were in their late twenties, cold, confident. The one with the thug cross had pushed his chair back slightly from the table.

"Excuse me," Dunleavy said. "I should apologize. My friend back there doesn't always realize what he's saying. But he doesn't mean anything by it."

Harry looked around. The waitress was alone behind the minibar, watching them. Fallon had his back to them, oblivious.

"What I'd like to do," Dunleavy said, "is buy you two a drink."

"Just go about your business, man," the one on the left said, low, almost a whisper.

"Nah, I insist," Dunleavy said. "It would make me feel better. What you guys got there, Heineken? I'll get you two more. Unless you'd prefer a couple of 40s, some of that malt shit you people drink."

"Mother*fuck*," Cross said and started to get up.

Dunleavy was still smiling when he kicked the edge of the table hard. It caught the rising man in the stomach, sent him backward along with the chair. The table crashed down onto its side, the second man trying to get clear, getting his legs tangled in his own chair. The Heineken bottles hit the boardwalk, spraying foam.

Harry watched as if frozen, everything moving fast but in sharp focus. Cross kicked the table away, rolled onto all fours and reached for one of the Heineken bottles. As he got his fingers around it, Dunleavy stepped around the table, raised his knee high, and brought his foot down hard on the man's hand.

The bottle exploded with a flat pop, and when Cross drew his hand back, there were shards of green glass embedded in his palm. He reeled back onto his knees, cradling his hand, and Dunleavy heel-kicked him in the face.

It was over as quickly as that. Harry was stepping in, reaching for Dunleavy's sleeve, but Cross was already falling back limp, his nose flat and bloody, his eyes half open. He rolled onto his side and a cell phone fell from his pocket and clattered onto the boardwalk.

Dunleavy turned toward the second man, who was still on the ground. He gestured at him to get up. The man looked up at him, then slumped back into a sitting position, shook his head.

Dunleavy caught the edge of the table, righted it.

"You should have taken the drink," he said.

He stepped on the cell phone, crushed it, then kicked the pieces off the boardwalk and onto the sand.

"I hate those things," he said.

He turned to face the waitress, who was still behind the bar.

"You get out of here," she said. "You get out of here now."

He turned back to the second man. Fallon had turned his chair around, was watching them.

"You want her to call the police?" Dunleavy said to the man. "Get a cop here?"

He shook his head again.

"What?" Dunleavy said.

"No, man." He looked at the waitress. "No police."

"You get out of here," she said again.

The unconscious man groaned, shifted slightly.

"Hope he had his tetanus shot," Dunleavy said.

He turned to Harry. "Come on, let's go."

Harry stayed where he was.

Dunleavy looked at him. "That bother you?"

"Was it necessary?"

"He dealt the hand."

They watched each other. After a moment, Dunleavy

seemed to relax, the smile creeping back over his face. He stepped aside, gestured as if to let Harry go by.

"We'll have to get together someday," he said. "Talk about old days. With no distractions."

"Maybe. But like I said, I don't think much about the old days. There's a lot I'd like to forget."

Dunleavy almost laughed. "Wouldn't we all?"

Harry went past him, back into the hall and the crowd noise. Two fighters clinched in the ring, heads together, arms moving weakly. Harry started for the lobby and then turned and looked back out the door he'd come through. On the boardwalk, the waitress was kneeling alongside the unconscious man. Beside her, ignoring them, Dunleavy stood with his hands on his hips, watching Harry.

Harry turned, headed for the doors that led to the lobby. Behind him, he heard the crowd roar, heard the hard slap of leather against flesh. He didn't look back.

TWELVE

He stood on the floating dock, watched Bobby bring the runabout in off the river. It was a low, fast boat with a single outboard engine, fiberglass body gleaming in the late morning sun. Bobby waved, throttled back, the exhaust chugging. He steered carefully, slid the boat in against the plastic fenders, killed the engine. He caught the line Harry tossed, fixed it around a cleat, then flung the noosed stern rope onto the dock. Harry slipped it around a piling, reached down to give Bobby a hand up. The dock moved beneath them.

"Yours?" Harry said.

"Yeah, right. Owner's picking her up today. I replaced the fuel pump, blew out the lines. I wanted to take her out, see how she ran before he came to get her. You're not here to look at boats, I guess."

"Got five minutes?"

"Yeah. Let's go back to the office. I need to drop off this key."

They went up weathered stairs onto the main landing.

"I'll wait here," Harry said.

Bobby crossed the parking lot to the single-story office, went inside. Harry watched a trio of shirtless men, burned red by the sun, using electric sanders to scrape the underside of a cabin cruiser careened in the dry dock.

"Okay," Bobby said when he came back out. They walked toward the river's edge, away from the sound of the sanders. Harry could see new homes being built on the other side, could hear the drone of power saws. A jet skier went past, the craft thumping in the water, spray flying around him. Harry waited until the roar of the engine had died away.

"Good news," he said. "Bad news."

"Good news first. I don't get enough."

"I talked to Fallon."

"You give him the money?"

"No, I still have it. He just wanted to talk this time. He asked me to hold on to it."

"And?"

"He's willing to cut you a break, shave ten grand from what you owe him."

"Why?"

"If I had to guess, I'd say he's tired of this. It's too much bullshit and he has more important irons in the fire. He wants done with it."

"That makes two of us."

"He says he'll take forty on the fifty. Since we've already given him eight five, that means thirty-one five, minus the fifteen you raised already."

"So sixteen more and we're quits?"

"That's what he says."

"Well, hell. We can do that. What's the bad news?"

"He wants it in ten days."

"Son of a bitch."

"I told him yes."

"Oh, boy."

"It's too good an offer to let pass. We bite the bullet, raise the final sixteen, get it over with. Go on with our lives."

"There you go with that 'we' shit again."

Bobby went over to where the water lapped against pilings. Harry followed him, saw the bloom of Portuguese man-of-wars just below the surface. Bobby bent, scooped up a handful of pebbles.

"I'll help you in any way I can with the money," Harry said.

"I don't want that."

"You said you had more moves you could make."

"A few. But sixteen K in ten days. I don't know if I have that many."

"Do what you can. If there's anyone who owes you favors, now's the time to cash them in. I'll come up with the balance, you can take it as a loan."

"You've given me enough already."

"Don't be stubborn. There's a window of opportunity here we have to take advantage of. We hold up our end, and two weeks from now this whole thing is nothing but a bad memory."

"There's a certain appeal to that, I guess."

"Do whatever you need to do. Let's make this happen."

Bobby side-armed pebbles into the water. The man-of-wars fluttered in protest, moved on. After a moment, he looked back at Harry.

"What can I say? This is it, isn't it, what they call a 'threshold moment'?"

"I guess so."

"Then I'd better step through, huh?"

"It's your call."

He tossed the last of the stones into the water.

"Let's do it," he said.

Around nine, he poured himself a glass of wine, took it outside. He sat on the back steps, looked up at the sprawling star field, listened to the low bellow of bullfrogs from the creek that bordered the backyard. The wine had the faint taste of cork and there were brown flecks of it floating on the surface. He dabbed them with a finger, scraped them against the lip of the glass, and flicked them away.

A gentle breeze rustled through the willows beyond the creek. He thought about taking the Mustang out, making a run up the turnpike. A good forty-five minutes up to the George Washington Bridge, forty-five back. Time to think.

He went back inside, put the half-full glass on the kitchen

counter. He had just taken the keys from the hook on the wall when he heard the sound of tires on the gravel driveway.

He put the keys back, moved into the dark living room. Headlights played across the side of the house, threw a shadow pattern of venetian blinds against the living room wall. He went to the window near the fireplace, eased open the curtain, pushed aside the blinds with a finger.

In the glow from the security light on the barn, he saw the BMW roll into the side yard, park near the picnic table. The headlights winked out.

He stepped away from the window, heard a car door open and shut. He waited, heard footsteps on the front porch. Then, from the door, the softest of knocks.

Later, they lay in bed, slick with sweat, the fan turning slowly above them. The glow of the barn light came in a faint wash through the windows.

He was drifting in and out of sleep, his arm thrown across her warmth. He felt her slide out from under him, heard the bed creak. There were footsteps in the hallway, then the sound of water running in the bathroom.

He rolled on to his back, stretched, the taste of her still strong on his lips. He sat back against the headboard, took the wineglass from the nightstand.

She came back into the room and he watched her move around, naked in the shadows. She picked up her denim skirt from the floor, got her cigarette case from the pocket.

"There's an ashtray in the nightstand," he said.

"For company?"

"If so, it's wishful thinking on my part. I can't remember the last time someone used it."

She sat on the edge of the bed, took out the ashtray.

"Are you surprised I'm here?" she said. She took out a cigarette, lit it, set the ashtray beside her.

"The way the last few days have gone, nothing surprises me."

"I stopped twice on the way over," she said, "and thought about turning around, going back."

"I'm glad you didn't."

He touched the fall of her hair, traced the bumps of her spine with his fingers. She shivered.

"Your hands are smooth," she said. "For someone who lives on a farm."

"There is no farm anymore. Just the house. And I was never a farmer."

He ran a thumb along the curve of her right breast. Her nipple was pale pink against the milk-whiteness of her skin.

"You're bigger," he said.

"It was Edward's idea. I'm still not sure how I feel about it."

His thumb slid over the nipple, felt it harden.

"I'd almost forgotten," he said.

"What?"

"How beautiful you are. When I saw you at the club that day, it took my breath away."

"I'm not seventeen anymore."

"Neither am I."

She took the glass from him, drank.

"Were you planning on getting loaded by yourself tonight?" she said.

"Thinking about it. It's a problem sometimes, drinking alone. I have to be careful."

She put the glass on the nightstand, sat back against the pillows, hugged her knees. He touched her leg, slid his palm down the outside of her thigh. He had a sudden vision of the first time they'd made love all those years ago. Of the way she'd looked into his eyes as he entered her, never looked away.

"I didn't think I'd ever see you again," he said. "I thought you were gone forever."

She blew a thin stream of smoke toward the fan. It dissipated in the moving air, vanished.

"Tell me what happened," he said.

She looked at him.

"After you left," he said.

She tapped ash from the cigarette.

"We went back to Ohio. I had an aunt there, so we stayed with her at first. After a while, my mother came back out. I finished high school there."

"You went to college."

"How did you know?"

"Your husband."

"Junior college at first. But I wasn't very serious about it, I guess. I worked, took some classes, did some modeling. When I finally had enough credits, I applied at a small school outside Dayton. I was more amazed than anyone when I got in."

"What did you study?"

"Education. I wanted to work with children, teach elementary school. Things never worked out, I guess."

"Why not?"

"It's a long story."

"Did you graduate?"

She shook her head.

"Are your parents still out there?"

"My aunt moved to Arizona about ten years ago. My mother lives with her." She took a long drag on the cigarette. "My stepfather's dead."

"I'm sorry."

"Don't be."

"Your husband told me he met you in Florida. Said you were with someone there."

"That was Garry. He wasn't very good for me, I'm afraid." She blew out smoke. "One of a long line. Present company excluded."

He moved his hand across the softness of her stomach, felt her tighten.

"No children," he said.

"I can't. That operation."

She put her hand over his, held it.

"The way my life has been, maybe it's a good thing," she said.

She put her cigarette in the ashtray, caught a strand of his chest hair, tugged on it. Her hand moved down until she touched his scar, traced it with a fingertip.

"Did it hurt?" she said.

"At the time."

"But no more?"

"No more."

"Good."

Her hand moved lower. He felt himself stir as she closed her fingers around him. She stroked gently and he hardened in her grasp.

"Enough about the past," she said. "There's nothing anyone can do about it, anyway. Are you glad I'm here?"

"More than I could ever tell you."

"Then let's just concentrate on now."

She put the ashtray beside the glass, rolled toward him. When they kissed he could taste the tang of smoke in her mouth. She straddled him, put her palms on his chest, sat up. He ran his hands over her buttocks, up her rib cage. He cupped her breasts, felt her nipples grow hard against his palms. Her hair spilled down over her pale shoulders.

"And just think," he said. "All I had to do was give you an envelope full of money and buy you a cherry ice."

"Money, it's very overrated, trust me."

"I do."

She took him in her hand again, guided him inside her. He closed his eyes as he slid home, enveloped in her warmth. He started to speak, to tell her how he felt, but she laid a finger on his lips. They moved together slowly in the darkness, the pressure building within him. When it broke finally, deep in her heat, he pulled her to him, buried his face in the lilac smell of her neck, her hair, felt the water well up in his eyes. He held her tightly, felt something give way inside of him, like an old and useless structure that had outlived its purpose, crumbling slowly and finally into dust.

• • •

When he awoke, the room was still dark. She was out of bed, getting dressed by the windows. Her clothes whispered as they moved on her body.

"You can turn on the light," he said.

She zipped her skirt.

"I wasn't running out on you. I would have woken you before I left."

"I know."

She put a hand against the wall for balance, slipped on her shoes.

"When's he coming home?" he asked.

"Monday night. His flight gets in around eleven."

"How do you know he didn't call you tonight?"

"I don't know all of what he does when he goes up there. Whatever it is, I'm sure he isn't thinking about me."

She moved away from the windows and into darkness. He saw the flare of her lighter, smelled the smoke.

The bed creaked as she sat down. He found her hand. His fingers traced her wedding band, felt the trio of tiny diamonds inlaid there.

"Should I not have worn that?" she said.

"It doesn't matter."

"It's been so long since I've taken it off. They'll probably have to take my finger with it when it goes."

" 'When' it goes?"

She took her hand away. Her cigarette glowed in the darkness.

After a moment, he said, "I'm worried."

"About what?"

"That I'm going to wake up tomorrow and find this was all a dream."

She touched the back of his hand with the tip of the cigarette. He yanked it away.

"There," she said. "Now you'll know it wasn't a dream."

"Thanks." He rubbed at the burn. "You could have sent flowers."

"What's life without pain?"

She set the cigarette in the ashtray, took his hand again.

"You're wondering what I'm doing here, aren't you? I can see the wheels turning. You can't figure me out, can you?"

"Well . . ."

"I'm here because I want to be here. Isn't that enough? You didn't have to answer the door, you know."

"You drove all the way out here. It was the only gentlemanly thing to do."

"There it is. You were just being a gentleman. Leave it at that."

"All right."

"Like I said, Harry, you think too much. Sometimes you just have to let things be."

He touched her leg, felt her warmth. She put her hand over his.

"You look like an angel there in the dark," he said.

"You're sweet. You always were. How did you ever get involved with my husband?"

"I didn't. A friend of mine did. Like I said, I never met your husband before that time at the club."

"Who's your friend?"

"Bobby Fox."

She looked at him.

"From high school?"

He nodded.

"I remember him. You two are still friends?"

"Yes."

"And he owed Edward money?"

"Owes. That was the first payment. He was involved in a deal that fell through. Your husband is putting pressure on him to hold up his part of it. I'm trying to help him out."

"Do I need to know anything else about this deal?"

"Probably not. It's got nothing to do with this, with us. I hope to have the whole thing resolved in a week or so."

"Good."

She took a final drag on the cigarette, put it out in the ashtray.

"It'll be light soon," she said. "I have to go."

"Is there anyone else at your house?"

"Is there anyone waiting up for me? No."

"What about Wiley?"

"What about him?"

"Is he around?"

"No, he doesn't live with us, thank God. It's bad enough having him hanging around all day. But to tell the truth, I'm almost happy to see him lately, as opposed to the alternative."

"What do you mean?"

"There's another man works for Edward now. He started about two months ago."

"Mickey Dunleavy?"

"You know him?"

"He used to be with the state police too. We met again yesterday."

"Small world," she said. "Or small state."

"Seems that way sometimes."

"I'm not sure what his deal is exactly. He seems to be doing some of the things Lester used to do, but Edward treats him differently, with more respect. I don't like him."

She stood up. He held onto her hand.

"I have to go," she said.

"I'll walk you out."

"Don't bother. I'll find my way. I'll lock the door behind me."

"Kiss me."

She leaned down, touched her lips quickly to his. He tried to pull her down, but she laughed, put a hand against his chest and pushed gently until he let go.

"Enough," she said. "I wrote down my phone number."

"On the bathroom mirror? With lipstick?"

"On a piece of paper, with a pen. It's under the ashtray. That's my cell phone. I keep it in the car most of the time, but it's the safest way to call me. I'm the only one who answers it."

"All right."

"But in the meantime, it might be better if I just called you instead."

"Does this mean I'm going to see you again?"

"What do you think?"

She moved away from the bed. He heard keys jingle.

"Be careful," he said.

She stopped in the doorway, looked back at him.

"You be careful yourself," she said and was gone.

He slipped out of the sheets, walked naked to the open window. He heard the front door open and shut, then, a few moments later, the BMW growl into life. As she K-turned in the side yard, her headlights streamed across the house, the open barn and the Mustang parked inside. Shadows raced across the bedroom.

He watched her taillights creep down the slope of his driveway. To the east, the dawn was a purple glow low on the horizon. He closed his eyes and smelled the air, the night, the woods, the last traces of lilac on his skin. When he opened his eyes again, the lights were gone.

THIRTEEN

Harry sat across from Janine on the redwood deck, a citronella candle burning on the table between them. Even in the noon heat, the mosquitoes were out in force.

Bobby came out through the sliding glass door carrying a pair of Coronas, set them on the table. He went over to the gas grill, used a metal spatula to flip the hamburgers that sizzled there.

"What I still don't understand," he said, "is why he would even consider taking a ten-grand loss."

Harry took one of the beers. It was ice-cold and sweated in his grip. He waited for Bobby to sit down.

"A couple of reasons, I'd guess," he said. "Maybe he's thinking you won't be able to get the money together anyway, so this way he can at least say he gave you every reasonable opportunity. Maybe he's got something else lined up, some business thing that's demanding his attention, and he wants to be done with this. There's a lot of possible explanations. But in the meantime, I think we have to take him at his word."

"Sixteen five. You're a pretty good negotiator."

"It was his idea."

"You should let me call my sister," Janine said. "She and Rich might be able to lend us something toward it, maybe most of it."

"And want to know what it was for," Bobby said.

"Does it matter what anybody thinks about us, as long as we get out from under this?"

"Either way," Harry said, "we should get cracking. Ten days isn't long."

"You've done enough," Bobby said. "The money's my responsibility now."

"I'll see it through. In the meantime, I want to poke around a little more into this Cortez business."

"What's the point now?"

"I've been giving it some thought. Something doesn't feel right. I want to call his sister, sound her out a little bit. For all we know, he's been out there the entire time."

"If so, he flew," Bobby said. "Or took a bus or something. That car was a piece of shit. It wouldn't have made the trip."

"So he left the car somewhere. The airport, maybe. Say he did the deal, stashed some of the money here, took some with him—I doubt if he'd try to bring it all on the plane. Or he took a bus or a train and is holed up somewhere with a suitcase full of cash. It's worth looking into."

"You're acting optimistic all of a sudden."

"Who knows, I might be able to shake a little loose, help you get back some of what you're giving Fallon. It's worth a shot."

"I thought you said it was a lost cause."

"Maybe not."

Bobby thought that over for a moment, then raised his beer.

"Here's to sixteen grand," he said. "Sixteen grand we can do."

They clinked bottles.

"And here's to old business," Harry said. "And the end of it."

"There's so much," she said. "That I haven't told you."

He was sitting in the sand at her feet, squinting out at the ocean. Out over the water a Cessna, engine droning, was towing a Coppertone banner across the sky.

He put a hand over her bare foot.

"Take your time," he said.

She was in a beach chair, an oversized umbrella stuck into the sand behind them. They'd chosen Ocean Grove because it was the least crowded of the nearby beaches and it was unlikely they'd run into anyone she knew. It was a Methodist-founded town, one-mile square, with a large population of retirees and senior citizens, so the beach was filled with young children and their grandparents. Inflatable toys and plastic buckets littered the sand.

"It didn't seem like the summer would ever come this year," she said. "It felt like February was going to last forever. All those gray days, the snow. Like it would never end."

"Everything ends," he said. "But everything comes back too."

"What were you? The philosopher cop?"

He turned to look at her. She wore a white one-piece bathing suit that clung to her body, and her exposed skin was slick with tanning oil. He looked back at the water, watched a gull dive-bomb a wavetop and come away with something squirming in its bill.

She touched his hair, tucked a lock of it behind his ear.

"I always had such great memories," she said. "Of the beach. Of living around here. I wish I could have stayed."

He rubbed her foot, touched the rose tattoo just above her right ankle, traced the design with his finger.

"The other night," he said, "when I told you I was sorry your stepfather had died. You said 'don't be.' "

She was silent for a moment.

"He was a bad man," she said. "A bad father." Another pause. "There are things I never told you about him."

A sudden gust of wind swept along the beach. The umbrella trembled. She dug into the canvas beach bag at her side, came up with her cigarette case and lighter. She got a cigarette between her lips, turned away from the wind and lit it.

"You don't have to talk about this if you don't want to," he said. "Ever."

"No, it's better this way, out in the sun like this." She blew out smoke, taking her time, gathering her thoughts. "My mother married Vic when I was thirteen, after she and my father got divorced. You know all that."

He nodded.

"When I was fifteen—had just turned fifteen—a boy asked me to the junior prom. His name was Billy Stokes. He hadn't said a word to me the entire school year until that day. He was sixteen and he was cute, he played baseball, and all the girls wanted to go out with him. I remember, when he asked me, he seemed more scared than I was.

"At first I didn't want to tell anyone about it. You know the way you feel sometimes, as if talking about something would keep it from happening? That's the way I felt. But I couldn't think of anything else for the rest of the day, couldn't concentrate on any of my classes.

"I went home that afternoon and told my mother. I was nervous. I couldn't sit still, couldn't eat. Vic was out. He was a guard at the county jail in Ashland. When he worked a middle shift, he always went out afterward, so he didn't get home until after I'd gone to bed. I used to hear them arguing at night, and it would wake me up. My bedroom was on the second floor, but their voices would come right up through the heat vents, so I could hear every word they were saying. It was like they were in the room with me. I used to wrap my pillow around my head to shut them out."

He moved his hand to her foot again, rubbed his thumb into the bunched muscle of her instep. She bit the edge of a fingernail, watched a fishing boat cruising slowly offshore, its wake lapping the jetties.

"I think my mother was almost as excited about it as I was," she said. "The prom was only two weeks away at that point, I think. Most of the girls already had their dresses. It's funny how that silly stuff can mean so much to you at that age. She told me she would take me out that weekend to find a new dress, just for the prom. You would have thought I was getting married.

"So I went to bed that night—Vic still wasn't home—and

I was so nervous, so excited, so . . . I guess, happy, that I couldn't sleep. So after my mother went to bed, I snuck back downstairs with my pillow and a blanket and lay on the couch to watch television. I don't know why I'm telling you this."

"Go on."

"I fell asleep on the couch. When I woke up—I have no idea what time it was—Vic was there, sitting alongside me. He was drunk, I could smell it, and he had lifted up the blanket so he could touch me. That's what woke me up."

She dragged on the cigarette, blew smoke into the breeze.

"He was gentle at first. That's what fooled me. I wasn't used to him being gentle. He was just smiling the whole time, in a silly way, a stupid way. The way a drunk does. He had one hand up under my nightgown, touching my legs, my knees. I was scared, but I didn't know what to do. He told me to be quiet, not to wake my mother, but the whole time he kept touching me.

"I was a virgin, of course. But I knew what was going on, and I knew it was wrong. And then he put his fingers inside me and it hurt. A lot. I started to cry then, told him to stop. He got rougher, told me I'd been teasing him, that I deserved this. I guess on one level I must have believed him. He said he'd tell my mother about it, say I'd started it, unless I made him feel good. He said if I did he would leave me alone after that. Pleasant story, isn't it?"

"I'm sorry."

"You haven't heard the best part. I started to do what he asked me to do, to make him go away. That's when my mother came downstairs and found us. She didn't say a word. I thought she would scream at him, hit him, throw him out of the house. But she didn't say anything. She just went back upstairs. She didn't say anything about it the next day, either.

"He never touched me again, though, so maybe she threatened him or whatever, I don't know. But we never mentioned the prom again, either, or the dress. The next time I saw Billy Stokes I avoided him. He cornered me one day finally and I told him that I couldn't go with him, but I never told him why. Poor Billy. He thought he'd done something wrong.

"It wasn't long after that we moved out here. It was like we were always running. I don't know from what. Now that my mother's in Arizona, we talk on the phone maybe once a year, if that. We've never talked about that night, ever."

He gently squeezed her foot.

"You're only the third person I've ever told that story to."

"Who were the others?"

"My first roommate in college. And a therapist I was seeing for a while a year or so ago. I never told Edward."

"Why not?"

"He wouldn't understand."

"Do you love him?"

"You've asked me that before."

"Do you?"

"I don't know. I used to. When I was in Florida, it seemed like things were falling apart around me again. I was drinking too much. I met this guy, Garry, who ran a restaurant in Boca. He hired me to keep the books, manage the place with him. He was dealing coke on the side, so he used to give me a little now and then, to keep me going. We got married in Miami, but to tell you the truth, I don't even remember much of it. It was just easier to stay drunk and stoned."

"What do you mean?"

"I didn't love him. He was just . . . an escape, I guess. I'd wanted to be married and now I was. He'd slept with every waitress in the place, and he didn't stop after we got married, either. I tried not to make a big deal about it—maybe I didn't even really care that much—but after a while he wasn't even trying to hide it from me anymore."

"And then Fallon came along?"

"I guess I thought Edward was going to be the one to take me away from all that. To protect me and take the place of everyone who didn't. What a laugh. See what I got out of that year of therapy? An explanation for why I'm fucked up and a prescription for Valium."

She dropped her cigarette, pushed sand onto it with her foot.

"You got a divorce."

"An annulment. Edward saw to it. I had almost no money of my own, and Garry swore if I left he wouldn't give me a penny. He even threatened to hire someone to hurt me, cut my face, if I hired a lawyer. I was scared of him. Edward took care of all that, and then I didn't have to be scared anymore."

"What went wrong?"

"I'm not sure. I was a basket case when we met. He got me healthy again. He was good for me for a while. And I was good for him too. That's what he told me. Now, I don't know. I'm useful to him in some ways, I guess."

"Useful?"

"He puts things in my name sometimes. Loans he takes out, things he buys. The house is in my name, the cars too. It makes things easier for him."

"He must trust you."

"I signed a prenup. I would never get anything besides what he wanted to give me. He has lawyers that would see to that. And I understand that, I accept it. You're not that different, you know. The two of you."

"How's that?"

"You're both strong—or you try to be. It's very important to you, isn't it, being strong? Being in control of the situation."

"Sometimes. Not always. That bothers you?"

"No, I like it. That's why I was attracted to him once upon a time. Maybe that's why I'm attracted to you now."

The breeze off the ocean cooled. The shadow of a cloud passed over the sand.

"It's getting cold," she said. "I think I want to go back."

They got slowly to their feet, brushed sand off, began to gather towels. He pulled on his T-shirt, slipped his feet into sandals. She shook out the blanket and folded it while he cranked the umbrella closed and pulled the shaft from the sand. She stowed the towels in the beach bag, tucked the strap over her shoulder, put on her sunglasses. By the time he got the beach chair folded, she was halfway to the boardwalk.

He caught up with her at the BMW. They stowed the umbrella and chair in the trunk, and he leaned against the fender to towel sand from his legs.

"I'll drive you to your car," she said.

"It's only three blocks. I'll walk."

She'd taken an oversized tan work shirt from the trunk and pulled it on over her bathing suit.

"Thank you," she said.

He got the last of the sand from his calves, looked at her. "For what?"

"For being here when I came back."

She leaned close, kissed him lightly on the lips. Then she turned quickly, shut the trunk, got the keys from the beach bag.

He was still standing there, the towel over his shoulder, when she drove away.

FOURTEEN

By the time he got home, the temperature had dropped another ten degrees and the willows were swaying in the wind. Rain spotted the windshield as he parked in the side yard. Thunder echoed in the distance.

He showered and dressed, the wind howling around the house. He tuned the kitchen radio to an all-news AM station for the weather report, but static was already choking the weak signal. He turned it off just as thunder cracked with a force that shook the windows. The real rain followed, drumming on the house like fast-approaching footsteps. Through the kitchen window, he saw a finger of lightning split the gun-gray sky.

He paced the house, listening to the rain, until the restlessness got to him. Then he found the legal pad on which he'd written the make and license number of Cortez's car, tore off the sheet, grabbed his leather jacket and keys, and headed out into the storm.

Traffic was slow on the Turnpike and the Mustang crawled along, headlights on, wipers thumping frantically, defroster on full blast. The rain was coming down in sheets now, bouncing high off the roadway. A bus returning from Atlantic City, going too fast for the weather, changed lanes in front of him, sprayed water across his windshield.

Past Linden, the low clouds hid the tops of the refinery exhaust stacks, the burn-off flames producing a hell glow that lit the grayness from within. As he got closer to Newark Airport, he saw a pair of disembodied lights in the clouds ahead. They grew brighter and, gradually, an airliner took shape, emerging slow and ghostlike from the overcast.

He got off at Exit 14 and followed the signs to the airport, winding his way through four different cloverleafs before coming out into the terminal area. He drove slowly, watched for the entrance to the long-term parking lots.

Lot D was the first. He steered into the entrance, got his ticket from the machine, and waited for the gate to lift. How many vehicles would be in this lot alone? Ten thousand, twenty thousand?

He took the sheet of legal paper from his jacket pocket and turned down the first row of cars.

Forty-five minutes later, he estimated he had driven past more than a thousand vehicles of one type or another. He had found six Monte Carlos with New Jersey plates and paint jobs dark enough to be worth getting out of the car to take a closer look at.

A half hour after that, he'd found three more. Only one of them was blue, and it had New York plates. This time he didn't get out.

He reached the end of a row and turned down the next, the beginnings of a sinus headache taking shape behind his eyes. He felt fragmented, off-center, as if he had forgotten something.

Halfway down the row, he spotted a new Dodge minivan, its rear license plate hanging askew. It was held by only one bolt, as if the other had vibrated loose and fallen off.

He braked, looked at the van for a long moment, then swung the Mustang around and headed back the way he'd come.

It took him fifteen minutes to find the Monte Carlo with New York plates again. He pulled the Mustang up behind it, took the already wet collapsible umbrella from the passenger side floor. He got out, popped open the umbrella, the rain thwocking against the stretched vinyl. There, low on the Monte Carlo's right front fender, was a foot-long scrape where the metal had been pushed in, the paint marred.

He peered through the passenger's side window. There was trash on the floors, newspapers and empty fast-food bags. There was a faint fishlike smell in the air. Sticking out from beneath the passenger seat was a piece of tan metal that could have been the edge of a license plate.

He walked around the car, the scent stronger now. There was no front plate at all. He went around to look more closely at the rear plate, knelt down, holding the umbrella above him.

The smell seeping from the trunk rocked him back on his heels. He sat down on the wet pavement and backed away, gagging—but not before he saw the looseness of the bolts that held the rear plate, the fresh screwdriver scratches on the metal.

He got to his feet, dropped the umbrella, leaned against the Mustang, and vomited onto the blacktop.

He sat in the back of the Port Authority police car, looking out at the rain, which had slackened to a steady drizzle. From the front passenger seat, Ray swiveled around and held out a pack of Lucky Strikes. Harry shook his head.

"Sorry," Ray said. "Forgot. Mind if I do?"

"Go ahead."

"I'll take one of those," the PA cop behind the wheel said. He was in his late thirties and at least fifty pounds overweight.

Ray and the driver lit up, Ray cracking his window to let the smoke out. The car filled with it anyway, and Harry felt his eyes water. There was no window button in the back.

They were parked near the Monte Carlo, a state police car and another Port Authority cruiser drawn up at angles in front of them. Blue, red, and yellow lights swept the glistening rows of parked cars. One of the uniformed state cops, in a blue rain slicker with a plastic protector over his hat, was kneeling on the front seat of the Monte Carlo, going through the glove box. The other was standing alongside the car, talking to a pair of PA cops. No one seemed very concerned.

"Thanks for coming," Harry said.

"I would say thanks for calling me," Ray said, "but I'd be lying."

"I thought it might make things go smoother if you were here, simplify it a little bit."

"If this is what I think it is, I don't see 'simple' being an operative word here." He blew a plume of smoke through the crack in the window.

Another car drew up to their left and parked, a dark green Ford Crown Victoria with state government plates.

"That Wesniak?" Harry said.

"Yeah," Ray said. "Let's go." He popped his door open.

Two men had gotten out of the Ford and were huddling with the other cops. One of the newcomers was tall and young, in uniform, wearing a blue rain slicker with orange lining, no hat. The other was older, with close-cropped steel-gray hair, hands in the pockets of his dark trench coat.

Ray walked over, Harry following.

"Hello, Bernie," Ray said. "Glad to see you guys here."

The man in the trench coat turned. He was in his early fifties, shorter than Harry, with sharp blue eyes. He slowly extended his hand.

"Hello, Raymond," he said. "I heard you were out here."

They shook. He looked at Harry, nodded.

"How are you, Rane?"

"Lieutenant," Harry said.

Wesniak looked him over. "Been a long time," he said.

"It has."

"You're the one called this in?"

Harry nodded.

"Tell me what happened."

"I was looking for a car." He pointed at the Monte Carlo.

"I was trying to find the owner, thought he might have taken a flight out, so I decided to look here first. It was a total fluke that I came across it."

"Why were you looking?"

"The owner is a man named James Cortez. He's been missing for close to a month. He works with some friends of mine. People were starting to get worried about him."

Wesniak frowned. "Anyone report him missing?"

"Not yet."

"They couldn't have been too worried, then."

Harry shrugged.

"So you just decided to look for him on your own?"

"He owed a friend of mine some money. I figured it was worth a shot, drive up here, take a look around."

"Good guess on your part. You tell all this to the Port Authority officers?"

"Yes."

Wesniak looked at the Monte Carlo. "Well, we might as well see what we've got here. You two know Lou Eagleman?" He gestured at his driver, who nodded. Harry had never seen him before.

"All right, let's go, Lou."

Eagleman took a pair of work gloves from the pocket of his slicker. He unlocked the trunk of the Ford, opened it. He pulled on the gloves, rooted around in the trunk and brought out a long metal rod and a mallet. One of the other troopers came over to help. The fat PA cop got out of the car to watch.

Eagleman took a white painter's mask from the trunk, handed another to the trooper along with a second pair of gloves. They adjusted the masks to cover their mouths and noses, then carried the tools over to the Monte Carlo.

"Rain's keeping the smell down today," Wesniak said. "But the way the weather's been lately, I'm surprised no one called this in sooner."

The trooper set the pointed tip of the rod against the keyhole of the trunk, held it in place. Eagleman lifted the mallet, gave the flared head of the rod a solid whack. The tip punched through the keyhole and into the mechanism. The trooper twisted the rod, pulled it back out of the hole, and the trunk lid rose slowly. Both of them stepped away.

"Whew," one of the PA cops said. "That's ripe."

The smell wafted out of the gaping trunk like a cloud. Wesniak took out a handkerchief, held it over his nose and mouth, and moved closer to take a look.

"Fifth one this year," the fat PA cop said.

Harry moved closer to the Monte Carlo, held his breath.

"Let's get a mobile crime scene lab and a camera down here," Wesniak said to Eagleman. "I want to get some video before anything gets moved."

Harry looked over Wesniak's shoulder. All he could see in the shadows of the trunk were indefinite shapes beneath a green army blanket. He followed the outline of the blanket until he saw something sticking out from beneath one edge. After a moment, he realized he was looking at a pair of swollen, blackened hands, tied together at the wrists.

"Twins," Eagleman said.

Harry looked at him.

"Twins. There's two of them in there."

"Nobody touch anything," Wesniak said. "All we're going to do now is wait."

The fat PA cop snorted, scaled his cigarette away onto the wet blacktop.

"Guess they missed their flight," he said.

FIFTEEN

Later, in the close warmth of the port authority office at the main terminal, he drank coffee at a metal table and told his story again, this time to a bored PA lieutenant and a uniformed trooper who took notes on a legal pad. Wesniak stood with his back to the rain-streaked window, watching Harry the entire time.

The PA lieutenant's name was Doyle. He asked Harry to spell Cortez's name. Then he turned to Wesniak.

"That's the name on the registration too."

Wesniak said to Harry, "Any idea who the other one might be?"

"None. I didn't even know Cortez that well."

Wesniak looked at one of the other troopers. "You check them for ID?"

The trooper shook his head. "Lieutenant, they were practically turning to liquid in there. I figured I'd let the ME's guys do that."

"What about you, Ray?" Wesniak said. "Any idea what went on here?"

"Not a clue. All I know so far is what Harry told me. But if that's Cortez in that trunk, it looks like someone got mighty pissed at him."

A knock sounded at the door and Eagleman came in, shaking rain from his slicker.

"ME's done," he said. "They've taken the bodies and a wrecker's on its way. Silverstone took a preliminary look."

"And?" Wesniak said.

Eagleman caught sight of the coffee maker on the other side of the room, went over and took a Styrofoam cup from the stack.

"Two males," he said as he poured. "Damn, this stuff is hot. Mid- to late thirties, maybe; he says it's hard to tell. Caucasian or Hispanic. Both of them tied up, put in the trunk face to face. At least two each in the back of the head. Not much blood around, so Silverstone thinks they were killed somewhere else, then dumped in the trunk and driven here. Looks like typical wiseguy shit. Anybody got any real sugar?"

Doyle opened his pencil drawer, fished out two white packets and tossed them onto the blotter.

"Thanks," Eagleman said. "I hate this NutraSweet crap." He shook the packets, ripped them open and poured their contents into his coffee. "Nothing else in the car to indicate what went on. No casings. They'll fingerprint the whole thing, let the drug dogs take a shot at it."

"They have wallets?" Doyle asked.

"Yeah, in the trunk. Looks like somebody went through them, then tossed them in with them. No IDs or credit cards. A couple family photos in one, some rubbers in the other. No driver's licenses. I don't envy whoever has to print them. They were coming apart like Thanksgiving turkeys."

Wesniak stood, took his trench coat down from a peg on the wall.

"Harry, I'm sure you know the drill in these cases," he said. "I'm going to need to talk to you again, soon. You know this Cortez by sight? Well enough to identify him?"

Harry shook his head. "I was mainly just looking for the car."

Wesniak watched him, pulled on the coat.

"Then I guess there's nothing we can do until the ME gets through," he said. "Gentlemen, we'll talk again."

Wesniak and Eagleman left the room. Doyle picked up the phone.

"I'll take you back to your car," Ray said.

They got up, nodded at the others, went out into the corridor.

"I'm not happy," Ray said. "But I'm sure you guessed that already."

They went out the front door into the rain. The green Ford was waiting at the curb, engine running. The passenger window slid down and Wesniak gestured to them.

Harry went over, leaned in the window.

"Being that you are both former law enforcement professionals," Wesniak said, "I don't really need to tell you what a piss-poor story that was you gave me in there, do I?"

"What do you mean?" Harry said. He was aware of Ray close behind him.

Wesniak looked out through the windshield.

"Just doing a favor for a friend. Don't even know the individual you're looking for. Wouldn't recognize him if you saw him. If we hadn't been in mixed company, things would have gone different. You'd be in the back of this car right now. But the last thing I need is some PA cop telling people that an ex-trooper is being questioned in a pair of homicides."

Harry waited. Wesniak took a business card from his inside jacket pocket, held it through the window.

"I want you to call me tomorrow at that number," he said. "I'll be expecting it. Are we understood on that?"

Harry nodded. The window slid up again and the Ford pulled away from the curb.

Harry looked at the card, put it in his jacket pocket.

"Well," Ray said, "I think we can safely say things have taken a turn for the worse."

Harry looked at him.

"He won't let go," Ray said, "until he figures out where you fit into all this. You know that, don't you? Right now he's confused. And so am I. After you get your car, meet me at my office. We need to talk about some things."

• • •

Forty minutes later, they were sitting in Ray's office, rain blowing against the windows. Ray laced his fingers behind his head, tilted back in his chair.

"Okay," he said. "I'm listening."

Harry told him everything. When he got to the part about Cristina, Ray leaned forward on his chair, elbows on his knees, hands loosely clasped between them.

When Harry was done, Ray sat back. The chair creaked under him.

"That's all of it?" he said.

"Everything."

Ray nodded. "Well, I guess I've only got one question for you, then. What the *fuck* were you thinking?"

"What do you mean?"

"Trying to help out your friend I can understand, even if he was dealing. But the rest of it . . ."

"I don't know that I was thinking much at all. I was going with what felt right at the time. I guess I was making an effort *not* to think about it too much."

" 'Think a little less, live a little more'?"

"Something like that."

"Famous last words. They sound great in a courtroom. 'Well, Your Honor, the incident in question just happened to coincide with the time that I decided to stop thinking so much.' "

Harry stood, wandered over to the window, watched the traffic crawl by below.

"You're the one who told me I needed to 'reengage,' remember?"

"That's not quite what I meant."

"No? It was part of it. And you were right. I felt like my life was slipping away, and there wasn't anything I could do about it. It was a relief to stop thinking about things for a while, to just go with something."

"Couldn't you have been shagging some waitress somewhere instead? I mean, considering the risk you're putting yourself at, is it worth it?"

"I lost her once, Ray. I don't want to lose her again."

"Jesus, I can't believe I'm hearing this from you. Mr. Logic. Mr. Don't-Do-Anything-Until-You've-Figured-out-All-the-Angles. What was this, your fall from grace?"

"Maybe."

"Well, you picked a hell of a time to stop being yourself."

"Did I? Maybe when all this started I was just bored. Maybe that's why I agreed to help Bobby in the first place. Maybe I was just tired of watching the world go around without me. But I'll tell you something, Ray. This woman, she is worth it."

"Worth what? Winding up in Raritan Bay with a couple of twenty-two longs in the back of your head?"

"He's a scumbag."

"Since when is that your concern? She stays with him, doesn't she?"

"She has her reasons."

"If she didn't want to be with him, she'd walk."

"It's not that easy. He wouldn't let her."

"So what makes you think he's going to let her leave with you?"

"He might not have a choice."

"You're gone," Ray said. "You're lost. I can see it in your eyes. You can't even hear what you're saying. And maybe you weren't paying attention back there when they popped that trunk, but . . ."

"I don't think Fallon had anything to do with that. I think something else was going on."

"Even so. Even if we forget about Fallon and what he does for a living, and whether or not he was involved in this, the fact remains this woman is still his wife. Not his squeeze, not his mistress, not some go-go dancer he bangs on the side. His *wife*."

"That's why I told you all this. As a precaution. I wanted you to know what was going on, in case anything happened."

"Not much consolation to me, is it? You're on pretty shaky ground here, partner, and you seem awful calm about it."

"You're anticipating the worst."

"You should be too."

"It could work out."

"Yeah, and it could get you killed too. If I had to bet, I'd go with the second scenario. And there's another complication."

"What's that?"

"Wesniak. In case you forgot, he led the drive to get Dunleavy shitcanned. He's the one who made it happen. He's gonna love it if he finds out the two of you are mixed up in this thing together."

"Coincidence."

"Tell that to him. What are you going to do now?"

"Check on some things. I'll call Wesniak tomorrow. Anything you can find out from the ME in the meantime would be helpful."

"Why did I know that was coming? Maybe you can ask Wesniak when you talk to him. I'm sure he'll be happy to provide you with as much information as he can."

"I told you I'd fill you in on all of this, Ray. And I have. But I still need your help."

"What you're going to end up needing is a lawyer, and maybe a twenty-four-hour bodyguard. Helping a friend out is one thing, Harry. But if you're in any way involved with the person who whacked those two guys, or even if you know who might have been responsible and aren't telling, then that's a different story."

"I've been straight with you, Ray. Right down the line."

"Then I hope it stays that way, for both our sakes."

Ray stood up. "Call me tomorrow," he said. "I'll see if there's anything new from the ME. Either way, stay in touch. Let me know that you're still alive, at least. I don't like this situation at all."

Harry put out his hand. They shook.

"I hope to Christ you know what you're doing," Ray said.

Harry tried to smile. "So do I."

• • •

Clouds filled the sky and no moon. The bedroom window was open, but no breeze came through. The night air was thick and still, the only sound in the room the fan whispering softly above them.

"I saw two dead men today," he said. "I saw their bodies."

She raised her head from his shoulder.

"I can't get them out of my mind."

She sat up and moved away from him. The edge of the sheet slid off her breasts. "What are you talking about?"

"I was looking for someone. I had a description of his car. I found it today at the airport. There were two bodies in the trunk."

"You're serious."

"Yes."

"Did you call the police? Did anyone else see them?"

"Anyone and everyone. State police, Port Authority cops."

"Port Authority?"

"They're the ones responsible for the airports. Case like this, they have to get involved. But the state police are leading the investigation. It's their show."

She caught the sheet, pulled it up again, studied him.

"This person you were looking for. Did he have anything to do with your friend Bobby?"

"Yeah, he did."

"And this involves Edward?"

"Maybe not."

"The one you were looking for . . ."

"Was he one of the bodies? I don't know. Probably. They have to do postmortems, get IDs."

"This happened today?"

"This afternoon, after I left you. I decided to look for the car, figured I'd give the airport a shot first. I guess you could say I got lucky."

"My God."

He sat up, propped the pillow behind him. She was watching him.

"You're not telling me the truth, are you?" she said.

"About what?"

"You say this might not have anything to do with Edward. But you think it does, don't you?"

"I don't know. Maybe."

"You think it does. That's why you brought it up."

She shrugged the sheet off, got out of bed. He watched her move naked down the hall to the bathroom. He heard water running. After a few moments, she came back in and began to dress.

"What's wrong?" he said.

"What's wrong?" She pulled on her jeans. "Why is it that every time we're together it comes back to this?"

"To what?"

"Edward. It's always about him, isn't it? Tell me, Harry, what is it you want from me? Do you want me to go and talk to him about your friend?"

"No."

"You want me to ask him about those two dead men? Is that why you told me this? Is that what's going on between us?"

"That's not why I told you."

"You don't get it, do you, Harry? I'm with you because I want to be away from him. From what he does. From the people he has around him."

"Then why don't you leave him?"

"And move in with you? Is that your idea of a solution?"

"You could do anything," he said. "Anything you wanted."

She finished dressing, tucked the tail of her sweater into her jeans.

"You think so? Do you actually believe it would be that simple?" Her voice softened. "Sometimes, Harry, I think you really don't understand things very well at all."

"I'm sorry."

"Forget it."

She picked up her shoes.

"I'm sorry about what happened today," she said. "I'm sorry you had to be the one who found those men. But that has nothing to do with me."

"I know."

"I hope you and your friend work things out."

"Don't leave like this."

"It's late."

"Stay here."

"I have to get back. I might not be able to call you for a couple of days. Maybe longer."

"I love you," he said.

"What?" She stopped in the doorway.

"I said I love you."

She stood there, watching him.

"Your timing's a little off," she said.

"Stay here tonight."

"You don't understand, do you, Harry? You really don't."

She turned away and went down the hall into darkness. He heard her footsteps on the stairs, heard the front door open. He could not move.

SIXTEEN

His sleep that night was fitful, his dreams dark. Bloated corpses reached for him, took his hand, and drew him into darkness.

He got up a little after six, the sour taste of the dreams forcing him into the day. He showered and dressed, then paced downstairs, drinking coffee, until it was late enough to start making calls.

He called Bobby's house a little after eight and Janine answered. When Bobby picked up the phone his voice was thick with sleep.

"We need to talk," Harry said. "Today."

"What happened?"

"I found the car."

"Jimmy's?"

"Yes."

"Where?"

"At the airport. There were two bodies in the trunk."

Silence on the line.

"There's a chance it's not him," Harry said. "But I wouldn't put money on it. If he ripped you off, he didn't make it very far afterward."

"Oh, Christ."

"We'll know for certain soon. There are police all over this, but I've kept you out of it so far. You know where Pratt's is in Asbury?"

"Yeah."

"Meet me there this afternoon, say four-thirty. I might know more by then. We need to talk in person. Phones are no good."

"Jesus . . . I can't believe this."

"Believe it," Harry said.

For lunch, he made a bacon and lettuce sandwich, carried it out onto the front porch. He could get only half of it down, so he broke up the rest and tossed it onto the grass. Birds circled, swooped and landed, snatched up pieces, and flew away.

When the phone rang he brushed crumbs from his pants, went inside. It was Ray.

"Tell me something I want to hear," Harry said.

"How about some preliminary autopsy results?"

"That's quick."

"Wesniak put a rush on it. He had them in there at six-thirty this morning. Toxicology report's still pending and the prints aren't back from AFIS yet. But they know a little."

"What?"

"Two males, both of them bound. Each shot twice in the back of the head."

"Was it Cortez?"

"Looks like it, but they haven't gotten his dental records yet. They're trying to find a next of kin."

"He has a sister in Denver. She's listed under Cortez, first initial A."

"I'll pass that along."

"What about the other one?"

"Hector Ramirez. That name ring a bell? His fingerprints were on file in Trenton. A biker, used to ride with the Pagans when they were still going strong. Now he lives—lived—down in South Jersey, Mays Landing or some place like that, I didn't write it down. He was Cortez's cousin."

"They know that for sure?"

"They've already been in touch with Ramirez's mother,

lives in Philly. She hadn't seen him in a month. Where do you think he fits in here?"

"I don't know. I've never heard of him. He might have been the buyer, or Cortez may have taken him along for backup. Or it might be something else altogether. Did they find the slugs?"

"All four of them. Thirty-eights. Burns on the back of the head, so it was probably point-blank range. Professional."

"What else?"

"Traces of white powder in the trunk. On Ramirez too. They haven't finished the tests, but chances are it will turn out to be heroin or cocaine. So they had the merchandise on them at some point."

"And somebody took it away from them."

"Looks like. They're tearing the car apart now. The phony plates were old, hadn't been registered in years. Someone must have had them lying around somewhere."

"Will you hear if they turn up anything more?"

"Will I hear? Probably. Will you hear? Only if I tell you. But what you should be worrying about is what you're going to tell Wesniak. You talk to him yet?"

"No, I was planning to call later."

"Do it. His pushing through these autopsies like this isn't good news."

"Why's that?"

"Because it means he's taking a personal interest in the case. At some point he's going to want to know for certain where you figure into this, and the smoke you floated his way yesterday isn't going to be enough."

"Have you heard from him?"

"No, and I don't want to, because I have the feeling he's going to ask me questions I can't answer."

"I'll call."

"Do that. You wrongfoot him again and he's going to think you're more involved then you are, and he's not going to let it go."

"I guessed as much. He had the look."

"You used to have that look too, Harry."

"Maybe I did," he said. "A hundred years ago."

"Good of you to call," Wesniak said.

"No problem. But I'm afraid I'm not going to be much help to you."

"Well, you never know. That was a bad situation yesterday, you were a little shook up, I know. And there were other agencies present, so I can understand why maybe you were reluctant to get more involved. But you've got to look at it from my point of view as the investigating officer."

"Everything I told you yesterday was true."

"So what were you leaving out?"

He got up from the kitchen table, went over to lean against the counter, taking his time. He switched the phone to his other hand, looked out into the backyard.

"I wouldn't hold back anything that I thought was relevant to your investigation. The job's tough enough as it is, I know."

"Glad to hear you feel that way."

"And I don't know anything about those two bodies or how they got there."

"What do you know?"

"Not much beyond what I told you. Cortez owed a friend of mine some money for some work he'd done. Three weeks went by and he hadn't seen or heard from him. Nobody else had either."

"How much money?"

"Not much."

"How much?"

Harry drew a slow breath before going on. "Five hundred dollars."

"What kind of work?"

"Engine work. On his car. He was as concerned about what happened to Cortez as he was about getting the money. They were friends."

"So you offered to help out?"

"Yes. I stopped by Cortez's apartment, but he wasn't there and the car was gone. I had the license number and the description, so for the hell of it I thought I'd run up to the airport, look around. Like I said, it was a fluke."

"You knew Cortez previous to this?"

"Barely. I may have run into him once or twice, but I don't think I could pick him out in a crowd."

"And this friend? What's his name?"

"He has nothing to do with any of this, trust me on that. He's got enough problems in his life already. I don't want to get him mixed up in this if it can be avoided."

"Might be it can't."

"He's not involved. Take my word."

"I guess I will. For now. But we're taking jurisdiction on this case, you know that, don't you?"

"I guessed."

"And if we find out anything I don't like, or that suggests there's more to this than you're telling me, then I'm going to have to come back at you."

"I understand."

"So if there's anything you're leaving out, or anything you know that might steer us in the right direction, now's the time to tell me."

"There's nothing."

"Okay, then, we'll leave it at that, see where the road takes us."

"You know how to reach me. If there's anything I can do for you, I will."

"That's good to hear," Wesniak said. "Because the feel I'm getting on this, we'll need all the help we can get."

Pratt's was across from the boardwalk, the only open business on a four-block stretch of Ocean Avenue. Years ago, the city had turned over the waterfront rights to a single developer, and most of the existing businesses had relocated, anticipating the seizing of their property by eminent domain. But the developer had gone belly up a few months into the project, and now the rights were so tied up in litigation that no one could come in to finish the job. It had left this whole side of the city a ghost town.

He parked at the curb behind Bobby's truck, slid the Club over the steering wheel and locked it in place. The other buildings on the block were shuttered, their walls covered with gang graffiti. There was broken glass in the gutters, and the wind blew trash along the wide street.

Across the intersection he could see the crumbling blue-green facade of the Palace Amusements building, the grinning ten-foot-high face on its north wall smiling out on empty streets and vacant lots. The arcade entrances were covered with plywood; broken neon tubing hung from the walls. He thought of the hours he had spent there as a kid, playing pinball, firing the real .22s in the shooting gallery, riding the bumper cars. It hurt to look at it now.

The door to Pratt's was propped open with a cinder block. It was a low-ceilinged place with wide windows, a half dozen booths against one wall and a single pool table in the back. Three old men were drinking at the bar, nursing glasses of beer and looking out the dirty windows as if there were something out there only they could see. The bartender was in his sixties and his hands shook as he drew change from the cash register.

Bobby was alone in one of the booths, a bottle of Heineken, a box of Marlboros, and a half-filled ashtray in front of him.

Harry slid in across from him.

"Hey," he said.

Bobby was unshaven, circles under his eyes. Half the Heineken label had been peeled away. Wet, rolled-up pieces of it were piled alongside the ashtray.

"Hey." He tapped ash off his cigarette.

Harry nodded at the bottle. "How many of those have you had?"

"Not enough."

Harry felt a flash of irritation, said nothing.

"Was it him?"

"They're still checking dental records, but it looks like it, yeah."

Bobby brought the bottle to his lips, then set it back down without drinking.

"A cousin of his was in the car too," Harry said, watching for a reaction. "Hector Ramirez. It looks like they were both killed at the same time. Did you know him?"

"Met him once. Jimmy introduced us."

"Was he one of the bikers Jimmy was selling to?"

"I don't know that for certain."

He started to raise the bottle again and Harry took it from his hand.

"What the fuck?" Bobby said.

Harry set down the bottle.

"Tell me what you do know for certain."

"Back off."

"Quit fucking around, Bobby. We're in this deep now. I need to know that you've told me everything there is to tell."

Bobby sat back, closed his eyes, and began to rub at a spot above his left eyebrow.

"Talk to me," Harry said.

"Hell, it could be he was the one, I don't know. And that's the God's honest. Like I said, Jimmy didn't tell me any more than I needed to know—and I didn't ask. He told me Hector was a biker, knew a lot of people, but that was it. There was no reason to bring his name up to you."

"Mistake."

"Maybe."

"Could be Hector had friends who knew about the deal. Maybe he was selling to them. Maybe they decided they didn't have to pay."

"Doesn't matter much now, though, does it?" He stubbed out his cigarette. "Did they find anything else?"

"Like drugs? Or a suitcase full of cash? No. Whoever

took them off got the money or the package or both, depending on what side of the deal he caught them on. There were traces of powder in the car. My bet is Jimmy was selling to Hector, or to Hector's friends. Someone knew about it, tracked them, was there when they made the transfer. Popped both and walked away with the money and the drugs."

Bobby didn't say anything. A salt breeze came through the open door, riffled a pile of cocktail napkins on the bar. He looked out the window at the empty street.

"My fault too," he said finally. "I helped set it up, but it was Jimmy took the risk."

"If you'd gone along, you'd be in that trunk too. They were adults, they knew what they were getting into. They knew better than you did. How are you making out with the rest of the money?"

"Janine's sister and her husband agreed to give us ten. They're wiring it tomorrow. I'm working on the rest."

"Good. After we get it together I want you and Janine to think about going away for a little while."

"Why?"

"Because I don't know who killed Jimmy and his cousin. The state police don't either. But they're looking, and they're asking questions. It would be safer for you not to be here, on both counts. Your name hasn't come up yet, but it might. I'd like to get you clear at least until I settle this thing with Fallon."

"I thought it was already settled. We pay him and that's it."

"I want to be careful. Where does Janine's sister live?"

"North Carolina."

"Can you go down there for a while?"

"Probably."

"You have any time coming at work?"

"Enough."

"Then do what you need to do to work things out. It'll be best for everyone."

"It's amazing, isn't it?"

"What?"

"It took me thirty-nine years to fuck up like this. But when I did, I sure did it big time."

"Help me out, Bobby. Call the sister. Take Janine and get away for a while."

"Things will never be the same, will they?"

"What do you mean?"

Bobby lifted the bottle.

"Between you and me," he said. "After what I did. This situation I created."

"We've been over this before, slick." He eased out of the booth. "Make that call."

"Never the same."

Harry tapped his knuckles lightly on the tabletop, started for the door, and went out into the brightness of the day.

At a quarter to ten that night, he was standing at an open phone booth, the ocean at his back. He fed coins into the slot, punched in the number. The line rang once, twice. He waited. On the fifth ring she answered.

"I need to see you," he said.

A pause. "Where are you?"

"On the boardwalk, in Spring Lake. There's a bandshell here. They have concerts sometimes. Do you know where it is?"

"Yes, but . . ."

"Come get me." He hung up before she could answer.

The boardwalk crowd had thinned, the families gone home. It was mostly couples now, hand in hand, joggers, an occasional teenager on a bicycle. He walked past the empty bandshell, put his elbows on the railing, and looked out at the ocean. To the north, the moon was partially hidden by clouds. The wind off the water smelled of wildness, of the sea and the night.

After a while he heard footsteps behind him, smelled her perfume, felt her shoulder against his.

"You must be out of your mind," she said.

"Maybe I am."

"Do you have any idea how risky this is, meeting here?"

"When's he get back?"

"His flight's due in at eleven. They'll be back here by twelve or so."

"That's still two hours."

"I need to be home. If the plane's delayed or if there's a problem, he'll call. He'll wonder if I'm not there."

"You think he suspects?"

"He always suspects. But up to now, he never had a reason to."

A jogger lumbered past them, sneakers clomping on the boardwalk. Harry watched him go. Farther down, a single figure stood at the railing, looking out at the water, smoking.

"I'm sorry about last night," he said.

"Are you?"

"Yes. There were things going on I couldn't quite figure out. I guess I felt a little lost. I didn't mean to hurt you."

"And have you figured anything out since then?"

"No, but I know enough not to involve you in things that have nothing to do with you. I'm sorry about that. I wanted you to stay last night."

"I wanted to."

"This business with your husband, it ends this week. Then I'm done with it, it's over. I'm going to go away for a while. I want you to come with me."

She looked out at the ocean.

"I've got nothing here holding me," he said. "No job, no family. I want you to leave with me and not come back. No matter what happens between us, never come back."

"Just like that?"

"If you want to, yes. Just like that."

"Is that what you want?"

"Yes."

She slipped her arm through his, held it tight.

"I need time," she said. "To think."

"You've got it. As much as you need."

"I have to go. He might call."

She released his arm, kissed the side of his face.

"I'll see you soon," she said. "I promise."

He listened to her steps as she walked away. He looked back out at the ocean. The clouds had parted now, the moon lighting a silver path along the water.

He went back to the Mustang and drove north along the beach, past bandstands and boardwalks and amusement piers, one town fading into the next. He felt as if he were driving toward the moon, following its path in the sky. The night filled the car, bringing with it the smell of creosote from the piers, the tang of salt air. He wanted to drive forever, until there was nothing left but the road beneath him and the moon on the water.

SEVENTEEN

Money and guns," Bobby said. "they make the world go 'round."

He unsnapped his denim jacket, took out a thick manila envelope, set it on Harry's kitchen table.

"I don't know about the guns," Harry said, "but let's have a look at the money."

He picked up the envelope.

Bobby pulled out a chair, sat down.

"Rich and Jennifer came through," he said. "They wired the ten this morning."

Harry took out a single thick bundle of cash, bound with rubber bands. He thumbed through it, saw that the bills were mostly hundreds.

"I sold some equipment that I had in storage too. A pair of compressors, a depth finder. Four grand total. That's in there too. Only three and a half left to raise."

"I'll loan it to you. I want to get this over with as soon as possible."

"You afford that?"

"I'll add it to your tab."

"It might turn out to be a long-term tab by the time I get out from under."

"I'll live with it. Wait here a minute."

Harry went upstairs, got the bank bag with the fifteen thousand from the nightstand drawer. He brought it back down, unzipped it, shook out the bills. He added the new bundle to the pile, counted through the whole thing.

"Janine's going down to North Carolina for a while," Bobby said. "I made the plane reservations. She leaves tomorrow night."

"What about you?"

"After Fallon gets the money, I'll fly down and meet her. I'm sticking around till then."

"No need for that. Go with her."

"Can't do it, Har. I can't just take off and leave you to clean up this mess. I told her I'd follow as soon as I could."

"Go with her. I mean that. It's best for everyone if you get out of here as soon as possible."

"I don't—"

"Don't fight me on this, Bobby. Janine's going to need you. She know about Cortez?"

"I had to tell her."

"And?"

"And she's scared."

"And how do you think she'll feel down there, with you alone up here? Think about it."

"I was thinking about you."

"Don't. It'll be easier for me if you're gone, believe me. If you're up here, it's one more thing I've got to worry about."

"When you put it like that . . ."

"Go. Do you have your ticket yet?"

"Not yet. Janine has hers. But all it'll take is a phone call."

"How long were you planning on staying?"

"Depends. I've got two weeks off from work. That's the most I can stretch it. If I come back at all."

"What do you mean?"

"I've been thinking a lot lately—even before all this—that it might be time to move on, get out of Jersey."

"How's Janine feel about it?"

"She's for it. Especially with the baby coming. While we're down there I'm going to look around a little, see what the economy's like. Cost of living is cheaper, at least. It might be easier to start over."

"Sounds like a good idea."

"Something else too. This thing with Jimmy, it's . . . I feel like I'm responsible. Staying around here, knowing that . . . I don't think I could do it."

"The only person responsible for Jimmy's death was the one who killed him."

"Maybe so, but I tell you, Harry, this whole situation has made me think a lot about where I was headed."

"How so?"

"Dicking around, day after day, not caring what I was doing or where I was going. If it wasn't for Janine, I'd be a fucking ghost. Until we got married, I'd never lived in the same place for more than a year, never had the same job for more than six months. Janine's spent our whole marriage trying to help me grow up, you know? And I've been dragging my feet the entire time. Getting involved with Jimmy, with Fallon. That was all part of it."

"I thought you told me it was the money."

"That too. But it wasn't the main thing. You want to know the truth? It felt good. When I went in on this with Jimmy, when we turned over that money, it was the most exciting thing I'd done in years. It sounds fucked up, but it's true. Getting involved with this, it made me feel . . . younger, I guess. Thing is, after what's happened, I feel older than ever."

"You made a mistake. Put it behind you."

"Is it that easy? It's funny, almost. It's like you stumble along, never knowing just where it is you're going. Like you're ignorant of yourself, of what you're doing, of the life you're leading. Then suddenly you get this moment of clarity. The whole thing—your life, your past, everything—comes into focus. And you know something? It's those moments of clarity that put a gun in your hand."

"You raised the money. You did the best you could. Once I turn it over to Fallon, that part of your life is over. You can do anything you want after that."

He put the money into the bag, zipped it shut. Bobby pointed at it.

"Do you know what that is?" he said. "That's not a debt. That's ransom money."

"How's that?"

"Ransom money for my fucked-up life. I'm not paying it to Fallon because I owe it to him, I'm paying so that I can start again. But it takes more than money to start a new life, Harry. It takes luck. And you're either born with it or you're not."

"Bullshit."

"You look at it differently, I know. People make their own luck and all that, that's the way you think. But maybe some of us are born into a hole. And we try and try to crawl out and we stand on anyone we can, but we still can't do it. And you know why? Because the hole, that's where we belong. And the only thing to look forward to is the day somebody finally gets around to shoveling the dirt in."

"Shoot," the voice on the phone said.

"This is Harry Rane. You remember me?"

"Rane, sure."

"You know why I'm calling?"

"Yeah, I think so."

"Tell Fallon I'm ready to close the deal. He'll understand."

"Sure. You're ready to close a deal, I'll tell him. I don't know if I'm going to see him, though. You know, he don't exactly come in every day, so . . ."

"Are you finished?"

"What?"

"Are you finished fucking with me? Because, to tell the truth, it's getting a little old. Make sure he gets that message today. He knows how to get hold of me. I'll let him decide how he wants to handle it."

"Hey, *rilassare,* eh? Of course I'll give him the message. Did I say I wouldn't?"

"He has my number," Harry said and hung up.

• • •

For dinner, he cooked ground beef in a skillet. He pushed it onto a plate, took a Corona from the refrigerator, and brought everything into the living room. He ate at the coffee table, watching the news, his concentration drifting. He could smell lilacs.

He had just finished eating when the phone rang. He caught it on the third ring.

"Ahead of schedule," Mickey Dunleavy said.

"Things fell together. We can wrap this up whenever he's ready."

"Good. I've already talked to him. He appreciates the way you handled this. He asked me to thank you personally for helping to work things out."

"When and where?"

"How about tomorrow night?"

"Where?"

"You know the Rip Tide?"

"In Sayreville?"

"That's it."

"Why all the way up there?"

"He's going to be in North Jersey all day. It'll be easier to meet there. There's an office in the back, you can both have some privacy. Get there around closing time, one-thirty or so. They'll let you in."

"That's late."

"He's going to the races. Meadowlands traffic and all, we won't be out of there till eleven or so. Then we have to make one other stop. Trust me, if he could make it any earlier, he would."

"I don't know."

"Listen, if it's really bothering you, I'll tell him no go, we'll pick some other place. It's all the same to me. He thought you wanted to wrap this up as quickly as possible. But if you say no, then it's no."

He gave that a moment and then said, "Never mind. I'll be there."

"Your friend coming?"

"No."

"Whatever. Eddie said he's welcome if you want to bring him along. We'll all sit down, have a drink, shake hands on the whole thing. If it turns out you can't make it, call back, let us know. We'll make alternate arrangements."

"No need. I'll be there."

"And Harry?"

"Yeah?"

"Trust me on this. You've got nothing to worry about."

He called Bobby later that night.

"Got your ticket?"

"There's no arguing with you about this, is there?"

"No. Did you get it?"

"I got it. We're on the same flight. Newark to Charlotte, seven-thirty. A friend of Janine's is driving us to the airport."

"Good. I talked to Fallon's people. We're setting something up."

"When?"

"Soon. We haven't worked out all the details yet."

"I guess I shouldn't ask for a receipt."

"I'll bring it up if you want me to."

"Never mind. He doesn't have much of a sense of humor. You want the Glock?"

"No. When we do meet, they're likely to check me for a wire. If I have a weapon, they'll just take it away. It won't do any good and it might piss them off. A gun's the last thing I need."

"Okay, slick, you're calling the play. Let me know what you need from me."

"I just need you and Janine to be somewhere other than here."

"You got that. Although I'm still having a problem with it."

"Don't. Call me when you get settled and I'll let you know what's going on."

"I will. And Har . . ."

"Yeah?"

"Thanks. I mean that. We need to have a few drinks and talk about this some night. After it's over."

"Count on it," Harry said.

EIGHTEEN

He woke sweating, pushed the sheets from his legs. He stumbled into the bathroom and showered with the water on full cold, felt himself begin to waken.

When he was done, he put on gym shorts and a T-shirt and went into the backyard. He stretched out on the grass and did push-ups, three sets of twenty-five, sweat pouring from his body. Sit-ups came next, two sets of forty, until the muscles in his stomach were knotted and aching, the blood singing in his ears.

He went back inside, still breathing heavily, dialed Cristina's cell phone, let it ring twice, and hung up. Five minutes later she called back.

"Beach day," he said.

"I have things to do."

"Bag them. Let's go."

"Where?"

"Anywhere you like. Ocean Grove?"

"No. Closer, I think. Avon maybe. What time?"

"It's noon now. I have to make a trip to the bank, but I can be there by one-thirty. Can you?"

"I think so."

"Where is he?"

"He left a little while ago for North Jersey. I think for the day."

"Dunleavy go with him?"

"He drove. They took Lester too. I'm alone here except for the maid."

"Then what are you waiting for?"

"Meet me on the beach, near the lifeguard tower. That way neither of us has to wait around on the boardwalk. Anywhere near the tower, I'll find you."

"Wear a bikini this time."

"I thought the idea was not to call attention to ourselves?"

"I don't care. Wear it anyway."

"Maybe you need to take a cold shower."

"I did."

"Then take another."

"I can't. There's no more cold water. Why are you still on the phone?"

"You're dangerous, you know that? Sometimes I think you really don't care."

"You holding that against me? I thought women liked spontaneity."

"Spontaneity is one thing. But you scare me. Sometimes you're all wrapped up and supercautious, other times you act like you're out of your mind. You swing from one extreme to the other."

"Is that the way it seems?"

"That's the way it is. You just can't see it."

"It's my nature," he said. "I can't help it. I'll see you there."

She wore the bikini after all.

"You're late," she said.

He sat in the sand beside her chair.

"Hello to you too," he said. "You look beautiful. Black suits you. How's the water?"

"Haven't been in yet. I was waiting for you."

He pulled off his sneakers, put his watch and keys inside them, tugged his T-shirt over his head. She touched the back of his neck, rubbed the muscles there. He kissed the outside of her thigh, flicked his tongue against it. Her skin was warm and salty.

"You're giving me goose bumps," she said.

"Good."

"Your neck's stiff."

"That's not all."

"Don't be crude."

He leaned forward, letting her knead the muscles in his neck and shoulders. He felt the tension draining out of him.

"It's all set up," he said. "Tonight. Then it's over."

She took her hand away.

"I wanted you to know that." He turned to look at her. "After tonight, it's through."

"Are you meeting him?"

"At the Rip Tide. I give him what Bobby owes him, we shake hands, and that's it."

"What about those two men? The ones you found?"

"They're not my responsibility. It's being investigated. It doesn't concern me anymore."

"What does this mean for us?"

"It means that, from now on, what happens between us is just that. There are no other factors."

She put her hand back on his shoulder.

"Think about what we talked about," he said. "About going away. After tonight I have no reason to stay. We could go anywhere we wanted. You could pick a place."

"And then what? After we go, what happens then?"

"Then we'll decide."

"Right now I want to swim. Come in with me."

He stood, put out his hand, and helped her up. They walked together to the water, the sand hot beneath their feet.

He waded out until the surf was chest deep, then dove. He moved underwater, pumping his legs, until he felt the burning in his lungs. When he broke the surface, she was ahead of him, swimming with a strong and steady stroke. He followed her.

They swam out past the breakers. When he stopped and looked around, they were alone. The water was calmer out here, lifting them on gentle swells. She rolled onto her back, floated, and he treaded water beside her.

"You're a good swimmer," he said. "Better than you used to be."

She suddenly dove beneath him, and he felt her brush against his leg. She surfaced a few feet away.

"Do you think we're out too far?" she said. "Is it dangerous?"

He shook his head. She swam slowly toward him, came in close, and put her arms around his neck, her lips over his. He kissed her, tasting her tongue, and her legs swung up to lock around his hips. He kicked slowly, keeping them afloat.

She nodded back toward the beach.

"Can they see us?" she said.

"Maybe."

The water gently raised and lowered them. He shifted so that his back was toward the beach, let his hands slide over her buttocks.

"I wore the bikini," she said.

"I noticed."

"Do you like it?"

"Very much. Pull down your top."

"What?"

"Pull down your top. Just a little."

She hesitated a moment, then peeled a strap from her shoulder. The bikini top slid off her left breast, exposing the pebble-hard nipple. He took it into his mouth. She tightened her legs around him.

"We could drown out here," she said.

He took his mouth away, gave the nipple a last flick with his tongue, felt her shudder. He eased her breast back into the cup and she tugged the strap into place. The nipple poked stiffly through the material.

"You're hard, aren't you?" she said. Her hand slid down the front of his cutoffs.

He nodded, slipped a hand beneath the elastic of her bikini bottom, cupped soft flesh.

"We could do it," she said. "Right here. No one would know." She kissed him again, unsnapped the button on his cutoffs, tugged at the zipper.

The lifeguard's whistle screeched.

He swiveled to look back at the beach. The lifeguard was standing on the tower, gesturing to someone swimming too close to the jetty, far to their right.

Behind him there was splashing. He turned to see two boys, about ten years old, kicking their way toward them, trying to maneuver Styrofoam bodyboards past the breakers.

She smiled, let her legs drop.

"Maybe next time," she said.

She kicked away from him, almost laughing now, and began to swim back toward shore. He fumbled with the snap of his cutoffs, trying to tread water, feeling foolish, watching her as she swam away.

Spring Lake was old money, Irish money. The streets were lined with elms and hundred-year-old houses, some with low stone walls bordering their property. Fallon's house was newer, two stories, white with mahogany shutters. A wide driveway led to an attached two-car garage. The lawn was a lush green despite the heat of the last few weeks. Sprinklers circled slowly, the water making rainbows in the sun.

She pulled the BMW into the driveway, shifted into neutral, engine running.

"I don't think this is a good idea," she said.

"You sure the maid's left?"

"She parks on the street when she's here. Her car's gone."

"You have nosy neighbors?"

"I don't even know their names."

"Let's go inside."

There was a garage door opener hooked to her visor. She thumbed the button.

"You *are* crazy," she said.

The door rolled up and she pulled in, shut off the engine. The door began to close behind them, darkening the garage. They got out of the car and she used a key to unlock the connecting door to the house.

"This way."

He followed her through the door and into a wide, white kitchen. There were two ovens, two refrigerators, a microwave mounted beneath oak cabinets. Every surface was spotless.

"Looks just like my kitchen," he said.

"Edward bought most of this stuff after I moved in. I guess he thought it would impress me. I should have told him the truth, that I didn't know how to cook."

They walked through the kitchen into an adjoining dining area, then down three steps into a sunken living room laid with deep red pile carpet. Central air-conditioning hummed around him. Against one wall was an entertainment center with a large screen TV, VCR, and stereo system. Curtained French doors led onto a flagstoned back patio.

He went over to the TV. There were four videocassettes on top of the cabinet. One was a store-bought women's exercise tape, the others were in black plastic cases, unmarked.

"Surveillance tapes," she said. "From the restaurant and the club. He tapes everything to see if anyone's stealing from him, then watches them here. It's his idea of an evening of light entertainment."

He followed her back into the kitchen. She took a carafe of ice water from one of the refrigerators, poured a glassful. She drank from it, handed it to him.

"Well, this is it," she said. "This is where I lead my life of luxury and leisure. Is there anything else you want to see?"

"What's upstairs?"

"More rooms. Why? Are you planning on coming back later tonight to rob the place?"

"You never know."

"Well, come on upstairs. You can prowl around while I shower."

He followed her up carpeted stairs to a long hallway. Half a dozen doors opened off the corridor. The one at the far end was shut.

"What's that?" he said.

"His office. He always keeps it locked when he's not in the house. I don't even have a key."

"How does the maid get in there?"

"Once a week he lets her in, but he watches her the whole time, as if she were going to steal one of the paperweights from his desk or something."

He looked into the first room they passed. There were two single beds, both neatly made. The room looked spartan, unlived in.

"Guest room," she said. "But since we never have guests, it's kind of a joke. I think Edward hoped that, after we got settled here, the girls would come to stay with him."

"The girls?"

"He has two daughters from his first marriage. Fifteen and sixteen. They live with their mother up in Short Hills. But they don't want anything to do with him, or me for that matter. They think I'm after his money."

She led him into the master bedroom. It was the size of his own living room and kitchen combined. A door near the bed opened onto a small bathroom.

"I'm going to take a shower," she said. "Make yourself at home."

She went into the bathroom and shut the door behind her. After a few moments, he heard the shower come on.

He looked around the room. The bed was king-sized, with dark satin sheets and half a dozen pillows. An oak armoire took up one wall, horse-racing prints lined the others.

He moved to the right side of the bed, opened the nightstand drawer. Inside was a racing program, folded open along the spine, the names of horses circled in red. Underneath it was a gold cigarette case and matching lighter, an issue of *Playboy,* a pair of bifocals.

He shut the drawer and went around to the nightstand on the other side of the bed. The drawer there held three packs of Marlboro Lights, two of them half empty, a small black address book, and a plastic container of Vaseline. Near the back of the drawer was a small battery-powered vibrator.

He put everything back, shut the drawer, looked around the room a final time. Then he went to the bathroom door, tried the knob. It was unlocked.

When he pushed open the door, steam rushed out to meet him. He stepped inside, saw a shower stall big enough for four people, her blurred shape visible through the pebbled glass. The counters were marble, the fixtures gold-plated. One entire wall was mirrored, the surface fogged with steam.

He shut the door behind him, locked it, took off his sneakers and T-shirt, undid his cutoffs and let them fall. He slid open the shower door.

"I thought you got lost," she said.

He stepped in and she turned her face up to the water, eyes closed, shampoo lather running down her back and buttocks. He fitted himself to her, reached around to cup her slick breasts. She moved against him.

"Let's clean you off," she said. She stepped away to let him get under the water, took a bar of soap from the rack, and began to lather his back, then his chest and stomach. She moved lower to his hardness.

"Rinse," she said.

He turned into the spray, did as he was told. After a minute she reached around him, shut the water off.

"Out," she said.

She opened the shower door, stepped out onto the bathmat, got a thick towel from the counter, and began to dry herself. He followed her, his legs shaking, took the towel from her.

"Let me," he said.

He dried her first, then himself. When he was done he took her hand, tried to lead her into the bedroom.

"No."

She took back the towel, used it to clear a wide spot in the mirrored wall, then spread it out on the counter.

"In here," she said. "In front of the mirror."

She faced him, put the heels of her hands on the counter and hopped up, pushing things aside to make room. A bottle of perfume broke in the sink. The smell of lilacs wafted around them.

"Like this," she said. "So I can watch."

NINETEEN

It took him a little more than a half hour to get to the Rip Tide, driving north on Route Nine all the way. The night was hot and the wind had died. The strip malls and stores he passed were dark and silent.

He'd dressed in jeans, a black T-shirt, and a thin black windbreaker, and he was sweating lightly inside his clothes. The bank bag was beneath the seat, tucked into the springs.

When he saw the floodlit sign for the club, he moved into the right lane and slowed. The building was set back from the road, a one-story cinder-block structure embroidered with neon. He could hear the thump of music from inside.

He drove past, went up a half mile, took a jug handle, and swung around onto the southbound side of the highway. There was a darkened strip mall on the right; almost directly across from the club. He pulled in, steered the Mustang around so it faced the road, then cut the lights and the engine. He looked at his watch: twelve-thirty.

He took the field glasses from the seat beside him. There was a half-filled blacktop parking lot alongside the club, lit by two pole lamps. In their glow he could see Fallon's Lexus parked nose first against the side of the building. Beside it was the maroon Buick he'd seen at the Sand Castle.

While he watched, the door of the club opened and a group of young people spilled out, drunk and laughing, the music following them. They split up into pairs and trios, went to their cars, peeled rubber leaving the lot.

He waited, watched people leave the club in couples and groups, saw a fight broken up by bystanders, the combatants dragged off by friends. At one-fifteen, the music stopped.

One-thirty came and went. Ten minutes later, there were only three cars left in the lot, the Lexus, the Buick, and a black Jeep Wrangler, the same one he'd seen in the Sand Castle lot that day. The floodlights beneath the sign winked out, the neon flickered and faded.

He started the engine, pulled onto the highway. He had to go a quarter mile south before he could turn around again. He steered into the lot, his headlights sweeping the building and the cars parked against it.

He circled the lot, pointed his lights down the alleyway behind the building. There was a Dumpster there, stacked cases of bottles. A rear fire door was propped open.

He backed into a spot on the far side of the lot, shut off the engine and lights. From the glove box, he took a small notebook and a stub of pencil, wrote down the license numbers of the Jeep and the Buick. He touched the can of CS spray on the console, decided against it. The notebook went back in the glove box.

He opened the door, reached beneath the seat, and tugged out the bank bag. He slid it into his windbreaker as he got out of the car, zipped up to hold it in place, and shut the door with his hip. As he started across the parking lot, a car flew by on the highway, laughter spilling from its open windows.

The heavy glass door was unlocked. He stepped through into a dim mirrored foyer, empty except for a cigarette machine. Beyond was the brightly lit main room, chairs upended on the bar, a wall of metal legs. A doorway to the right led onto the dance floor, a wide room with mirrored walls and tables on one side.

He went in. Two men in suits sat across from each other at a table toward the back. One of them was Tommy from Convention Hall. He lifted his chin at Harry, and the other man swiveled in his chair. It was the heavy man he'd seen outside the Sand Castle. Harry walked toward them.

The heavy one coughed, dug in his jacket pocket, and came up with a pack of cigarettes. He lit one without taking his eyes off Harry, then clicked the lighter shut and dropped it on the table. He pointed the cigarette at the back wall.

Harry looked, saw the door there marked PRIVATE. Beside it, the DJ's booth was silent and empty.

He nodded, headed for it, feeling their eyes on him. The door opened into a wide, concrete-floored storage area. Cases of beer lined one wall. On the other, a door marked OFFICE was partially open, a TV on inside.

Wiley came in through the fire door. He looked at Harry, turned slowly, and spat outside.

"He's here," he said toward the office.

They watched each other. Wiley broke eye contact first, hoisted a case of empty beer bottles from against the wall, and lugged them into the alley. Demoted, Harry thought, and not happy about it.

The office door opened wide and Mickey Dunleavy was standing there, smiling.

"Harry," he said. "Come on inside. Have a seat."

Harry followed him in. Filing cabinets lined one wall, on top of them a small TV was tuned to a boxing match. Fallon sat behind a battered wooden desk, holding a carton of take-out Chinese food, idly prodding at its contents with a plastic fork. He wore a dress shirt, tie undone, suit jacket hung on the wall behind him. There were other food cartons on the desk, a bottle of Chivas Regal, and a cheap white Polaroid camera.

Dunleavy sat down in a chair near the door, crossed his legs. He gestured at a leather couch against the far wall.

"Go ahead," Fallon said without looking up. "Sit down." He took a remote control off the desk top, pointed it at the TV, and the screen went dark.

"What's it like outside?" Dunleavy said.

"Hot," Harry said. He stayed where he was.

"Supposed to get a hell of a storm later."

Fallon put the carton on the desk, pushed it away.

"Who can eat this shit?" he said. "Nigger food. Did you ever notice that every nigger neighborhood has a half-dozen Chinese take-out joints?"

"They like the spare ribs," Dunleavy said.

Fallon opened the Chivas, splashed scotch into a square glass.

"I've got it," Harry said.

Fallon looked at him. He swished the scotch in the glass, drank some.

"That's Harry," Dunleavy said. "Always business first." He uncrossed his legs, stood up. "Do me a favor, will you, Har? Go over there and put your hands on top of that cabinet? Just for a minute."

"What's this?"

"Relax." Dunleavy touched him lightly in the small of the back. "This is what I do now, remember? Don't be offended."

He had expected it, but it still felt wrong. He didn't move.

"Come on, Harry, you understand. Let's get this over with."

He went to the cabinet, raised his hands to shoulder height. Dunleavy patted him down quickly, unzipped the windbreaker, and took out the bag. He set it atop the cabinet, then crouched and ran his hands up and down Harry's legs. He slapped his ankles, then straightened up, took the bank bag, and set it on the desk.

"Close the door," Fallon said.

Dunleavy shut the door quietly, then sat back down. Harry turned to face them.

Fallon nodded at the bag. "How much?"

"All of it," Harry said. "Thirty-one five. Count it and see."

"I will. I will definitely do that."

Harry turned to Dunleavy.

"Is there a problem here?"

Dunleavy shrugged, half smiled, crossed his legs again.

Fallon unzipped the bag, spilled the bundles onto the desk.

"Thirty-one five," he said. "Not much, is it? We do that much business here on a good weekend."

"It's what we agreed on."

"I know what we agreed on."

Fallon pushed the bundles around the desk with a finger, drank from the glass again.

"The thing is," he said, "the more I think about it, the more I'm reminded of all the time my money was tied up. And then I start to think that maybe some interest is in order."

"We had a deal. No one said anything about interest."

"Maybe not. But as I was waiting all this time for this piddling thirty K, I was starting to feel like I was being taken advantage of."

"What's this all about?"

"You tell me."

He looked from Dunleavy to the door, then back to Fallon.

"Okay, I'll tell you. There's your money. It's what we agreed on. We're done."

Fallon stood. He put the bundles back into the bank bag one by one.

"There's a lot of things you can do to a man," he said. He zipped the bag shut. "You can hurt him physically. You can humiliate him. You can take away whatever it is that he cares about. But the worst thing you can do is treat him like a fool and expect him to like it."

"What are you talking about?"

Fallon started around the desk.

"It's impossible to keep a secret from me, you know that? I've got too many friends, too many people I've done favors for. Too many people who owe me."

"Sit down," Harry said.

"What I have, I worked for. And I did what was necessary to keep it. No one ever gave me anything. And no one's going to take anything away from me either."

Harry looked at Dunleavy, still sitting, relaxed. He turned back to Fallon.

"You've got your money. What you do now is your business. I'm going home."

Dunleavy laughed, uncrossed his legs. When he started out of the chair, Harry turned and drove a straight punch at his face, his whole body behind it.

Dunleavy was off balance, half standing, an easy target. But he pushed the chair over as he rose, got the room he needed, swiveled, and Harry saw it was too late to stop. His fist met nothing but air and then his momentum carried him forward and something hit him hard in the lower ribs, bent him. Dunleavy's left elbow drove toward him in a blur, snapped his head back, and sent sparks dancing along the edges of his vision.

He tried to back away, get his hands up, and then another sharp pain in his ribs took his breath away. He started to go down and Dunleavy caught him, spun him, drove him fast and hard into the door, face first. He rebounded, felt himself falling, but Dunleavy had his left arm twisted behind his back, holding him up. He slammed him into the door again, pinned him there.

"Whoa, boy," Dunleavy said. "That wasn't very nice, was it?"

He tried to suck in air, his left cheek against the door, heat spreading through his locked elbow. He could taste blood. Dunleavy grabbed his hair, yanked his head back so that he couldn't gain any leverage. He looked up at the stained tiles of the drop ceiling.

"Break it," Fallon said.

He put a knee against the door, tried to push away, and Dunleavy twisted the arm higher. The pain brought him onto his toes. Dunleavy leaned into him.

"There's a lesson for you here, partner," he said softly. "Never swing on someone unless you're sure you can take him out."

"Do it," Fallon said.

Dunleavy let go of his hair. Harry felt him shift his grip, one hand around his wrist, the other at the elbow.

"Mickey . . ." he started to say, and then the elbow went up, hard, and a feeling like electricity surged through his arm. Water rushed into his eyes.

"That's my interest," Fallon said.

Harry squeezed his eyes shut, drew deep breaths. Slowly, Dunleavy eased the pressure on his arm. It felt loose, limp.

"Turn him around," Fallon said. "Hold him up."

Dunleavy wheeled him around. He tried to pull away, and Dunleavy twisted his arm again as if he were wringing a towel. The pain ripped the breath out of him. His knees sagged.

"I should have done that myself," Fallon said. He pulled the tie from around his neck, began to wrap it around the knuckles of his right hand. Harry watched as he moved closer. "Hold him good."

He put the fingertips of his left hand on Harry's chest, as if measuring the distance.

"That was for interfering in my business," he said. "This is for my wife."

His fist blurred in the air. Harry felt his nose give way, the pain a sunburst behind his eyes. They fell back against the door with the force of it, Dunleavy still holding him tight. Harry kicked out instinctively, aiming for the groin, but Fallon stepped inside it, caught the kick on his thigh. He cursed, drew back, and Harry spit blood at him, saw it spot his shirt.

The fist filled his vision again. His head snapped to the side and he felt something wet leave his mouth and fly off. The lights in the room dimmed.

"Break your hand like that," Dunleavy said.

"Let him go."

Dunleavy pushed him away and Harry took two lunging steps and went down, cold concrete under him. He fell onto his side, saw Fallon above him, shaking his right hand, flexing the fingers. Fallon drew a deep breath and Harry saw what was coming, but not quick enough, and the toe of the shoe hit him hard above the left eye. He tried to cover up, to protect his head, but his left arm wouldn't respond. The second kick, solid into the midsection, stole his breath. Hot fluid rose in his mouth and spilled from his lips. He tried to curl up, take the kicks on his arms, his elbows, his legs, but Fallon was aiming them now, taking his time, and the hard heels and toes were getting through, thumping into his sides, his armpits, the sides of his face. He pulled his knees toward his head, and finally the blows slowed and stopped.

He could hear heavy breathing above him. Fallon spit and Harry felt the wetness on his face.

"You go near her again and I'll cut your fucking throat. Do you understand?"

Harry opened his mouth, gulped air. Fallon kicked him again in the ribs, weaker this time.

"And I'll do your friend and his cunt wife for the hell of it. Do you understand? Answer me, you fuck."

Harry coughed, trying to clear the fluid from his throat.

"Take the pictures," Fallon said.

Harry was aware of Dunleavy beside him. There was a flash that blinded him, then a whir. He tried to bring his right hand up to cover his face, but Fallon put a foot on his wrist, pinned it against the concrete. The camera flashed and whirred twice more, and the rest of the room seemed to grow dim around it.

"Get a couple more," Fallon said.

More flashes. Fallon took his foot away.

"Now get the fuck out," he said.

Harry tried to move, slowly. He looked back toward the door.

"Out," Fallon said.

He pushed the floor away, crabbed toward the door, the sides of his boots slipping on the smooth concrete. He heard Dunleavy's voice.

"Think about what I said, Eddie. Come all this way, we might as well finish it."

He pushed closer to the door, looked up and saw a pattern of tiny blood droplets across the wood.

"That piece of shit's not worth it," Fallon said.

Dunleavy's feet moved aside. The door opened wide.

He was getting air now, but every breath brought pain. He slid over the bump of the doorway and into the outer room, the floor seeming to tilt away beneath him. There was a drain in the center of it and he took that as his target, crawled toward it. Then there were legs in front of him, barring his way. He looked up, saw Wiley standing there.

"Hey, *poliziotto*," a familiar voice said from behind him. "You're a mess."

He turned and the heavy man was there, Tommy alongside him.

Wiley leaned down, caught his right wrist, slid his other hand beneath his left arm.

"Come on." he said. "Get up."

He didn't have the strength to pull away. He got his feet under him and Wiley helped him up, slowly. He couldn't see from his left eye, and his right was blurring in and out of focus. He leaned against Wiley until he was steady.

"Having a hard time standing up straight, huh?" Wiley said.

He looked at the open fire door, the alley beyond. He took a step toward it, wobbled. Wiley caught the sleeve of his windbreaker, held him up.

"Where you think you're going?" he said.

Harry pulled away, felt the hand catch his jacket again.

"Turn around. Look at me."

He tried to lunge toward the door, but his legs were loose, drunken.

"Look at me."

He turned then, saw the fist rising toward him. But he never felt it.

TWENTY

The thunder woke him. He felt it in the ground beneath him, more vibration than sound. There was a drop of wetness on his face, thick and warm as crankcase oil, then another. A second rumble of thunder, closer now, more drops. He blinked, opened his eyes.

He was on hard blacktop, the bulk of a car in front of him. It took him a moment to realize it was the Mustang. He rolled onto his side, triggered a spasm of pain that forced him to lie still again until it faded. His left arm was limp beneath him.

Thunder cracked, almost directly above him now, and the rain came down. He rolled onto his stomach, got his knees under him. He put his right hand against the car, waited like that, the rain bouncing off his hunched shoulders, until the world stopped spinning.

He slowly got to his feet, using the side of the car for support. Rain was moving in sheets across the parking lot now, illuminated by the pole lamps. The club was dark.

He slid around to the driver's side, pulled the keys from his jeans pocket, dropped them. When he bent to pick them up, a wave of nausea rolled through him. His stomach clenched and he threw up, thin and watery, onto the blacktop. He got the keys, straightened, saw the spiderweb crack in the driver's side window, the dent in the door, a footprint in the center of it.

He fumbled the door open, slumped into the seat, had to reach across with his right hand to close the door, lock it. After three tries, he got the key into the ignition, started the engine.

Twice on the way, he felt himself losing consciousness, the lights of oncoming traffic blurring in front of him. Each time horns blared and he had to drag the wheel back to the right.

When he got off Route Nine, he drove slowly, looking at street signs. He got lost twice before he found the right one. He pulled into Ray's driveway, saw his Toyota Camry parked nose first against the garage door. He shut off the engine, closed his eyes, and felt himself drift. He woke with his head against the steering wheel, Ray standing outside in the rain, tapping on the window.

Harry tried to smile. He unlocked the door, felt it pulled open, and then he tumbled sideways out of the car. Ray caught him, lowered him to the ground. There was no pain now, no nausea. He looked up into the falling rain, felt it on his face. He closed his eyes.

The nurse's name was Elita. He read her name tag as she leaned over to check the IV needle on the back of his right hand. She was thirtyish, Hispanic, and pretty. She smelled of sandalwood. He tried to tell her this, but his throat was too dry, his lips too swollen.

"Try not to move around too much," she said, "or you'll pull the needle out. I'll be back in a little while to give you something to help you sleep."

Locked in silence, he nodded, watched her walk away, then looked out the window. A gray morning outside, rain still streaking the glass.

"You look like hell," Ray said from his chair at the foot of the bed. "Not that you were ever pretty."

His face felt swollen, hard. The cast lay like a dead weight across his stomach, thick plaster that reached almost to his wrist. He touched his nose with his right hand, careful not to dislodge the needle. His nostrils were packed with cotton, a strip of heavy surgical tape across the bridge.

"You scared the shit out of us," Ray said. "Edda thought you were dead."

Harry gestured at the plastic glass of water on the rolling table beside the bed. Ray got up and brought it to him. He sucked on the straw, cool liquid filling his mouth. He coughed once, water dribbling onto his chin, and Ray took the glass away.

"You're lucky they had a room open," he said, "or you'd still be down in the ward sleeping in the hall. It took a while, but I managed to talk them into moving you."

"Thanks." His voice was hoarse, low. He leaned toward the glass, sipped more water, felt it soothe his throat.

"Where am I?" he managed.

"St. Peter's in New Brunswick. It was closest."

"I don't . . ." he said and coughed.

"Easy." Ray brought the glass closer and he drank again, waited a moment before speaking.

"I don't have any insurance."

"All full-time employees of RW Security get a benefits package, including hospitalization. You've been one for about four hours now. And when you get out of here, I've got a private doctor for the follow-ups."

"I'm causing you a lot of trouble."

"You'll be out tomorrow. They just want to keep you for the night for observation, do a couple more tests, a CAT scan." He dragged his chair over, sat down. "You want the full damage report?"

"Yeah."

"You've got a dislocated elbow, which you probably already know. Plus a broken nose and a mild concussion. A lot of bruises too, but it doesn't look like there's any internal damage. If you start pissing blood, let somebody know."

"I will."

"So are you going to tell me what happened?"

"I delivered the rest of the money to Fallon last night. It was a setup."

"Where?"

"Club he owns in Sayreville."

"You went alone?"

"Yeah."

"Stupid."

"Maybe."

"You should have called me."

"There was no reason to. We'd worked it all out."

"I can see that. Was Fallon there?"

He nodded.

"Who else?"

"Wiley, Dunleavy. Two others. Andelli's people, maybe. I'd seen them before."

"Those two get in on it?"

"Not while I was conscious, at least."

"You're lucky you're not in a coma. Or dead. I think we need to get some other people involved here."

"No."

"Then you better come up with a story to tell the resident who treated you, because he's going to want one, and I'm not much for lying. He wanted to call the New Brunswick cops when we got here, but I put him off until I could talk to you."

"Tell him I fell down the stairs."

"Original."

He held out the glass again and Harry raised himself enough to reach the straw. He drained the water, settled back against the pillows.

"You should get some rest now," Ray said. "I'll see if I can find that nurse."

Harry nodded, eyelids fluttering, sleepy. He felt as if he were sinking deeper into the bed.

Ray stopped at the door, turned.

"I don't know if it means anything to you," he said. "But I want you to know that, one way or another, this gets squared. There's no way it doesn't. Whether it's by me or by the locals, it gets squared. Bet on it."

They let him out the next afternoon. The CAT scan results had been negative. There was no skull fracture, no buildup of blood around his brain.

In the end, he didn't even need a story. By the time they processed him out, the resident who'd treated him was nowhere to be found, and the one who'd taken his place had only the mildest interest in Harry's condition. He wrote him a prescription for Percocet and told him to make an appointment with his own doctor as soon as possible.

A male nurse's aide wheeled him through the electronic doors to the curb, where Ray's Toyota was waiting. The rain was gone, the day bright. But Harry felt cold, as if he had carried a chill with him from inside the hospital.

He wore the T-shirt and jeans Ray had brought him from the house, carried his torn and bloody clothes in a plastic bag on his lap. His cast was nestled in a light blue nylon sling with Velcro snaps. They'd taken the cotton from his nostrils, but the tape remained, an X across the bridge of his nose. On the left side of his mouth, two molars were loose. When he probed them with his tongue, it sent a dull ache through his jaw.

Ray opened the passenger side door. Harry thanked the aide and climbed out of the wheelchair, waved Ray away. He eased into the passenger seat, wincing at the pain in his ribs. He put the plastic bag on the floor, pulled the door shut.

"I won't ask how you feel," Ray said as he got behind the wheel.

"Good."

Neither of them spoke again until they were on the Parkway, heading south.

"I called that number you gave me," Ray said. "She answered the phone, sounded all right. But I took a drive out there anyway, parked on the street, watched the house. She went out about ten this morning, with Fallon, in a Lexus. Some big guy was driving, not Dunleavy."

"How did she look?"

"She's not exactly my type."

"That's not what I meant."

"Relax. Fine as far as I could tell. I got a pretty good look through the binoculars, and she seemed to be all right. No marks on her that I could see. I guess Fallon took it all out on you."

"He took pictures of me afterward."

"For what?"

"To show her, I guess."

Ray said quietly, "Son of a bitch."

They drove in silence for a few moments.

"I can swing by there again tonight if you want. Follow them if they go anywhere, try to get a closer look."

Harry shook his head, powered down the window to feel the breeze on his face.

After a while, Ray said, "Let me know how you want to handle this."

"What do you mean?"

"You know goddamn well what I mean. You say the word. I'll back you up any way you want."

Harry watched the traffic.

"I'm not sure if I've quite figured it out myself yet," he said. "I might ask you to do me a couple of favors later in the week. We'll see what happens."

"It's your call. But don't cut me out of this now. You did it before and look what it got you, a busted elbow and a broken nose. I don't have that many friends that I can allow this kind of shit to go on."

"I'll take care of it."

"Somebody will. No way in hell this goes unanswered."

They rode in silence again. Ray watched him out of the corner of his eye.

"You okay, partner?"

Harry looked out the window, breathed in.

"No," he said.

• • •

They parked in Harry's side yard. The door to the barn was pulled shut.

"Your car's in there," Ray said. "I had it driven back. Let's go inside and get you settled."

In the kitchen, the red light of the answering machine was flashing insistently.

"Think you'll be able to get around all right?" Ray said.

"Yeah, good enough. It's my arm that's broken, not my legs."

"If I were you, I wouldn't be driving anywhere anytime soon. At least not until you've had a day or so to rest. If you think of anything you need, or there's any place you want to go, give me a call. I'm not that far away."

"Thanks. I've put you through enough already, I think."

"Come outside with me for a minute. I've got something for you."

Harry followed him out to the Toyota. Ray opened the trunk, shifted things around inside, took out a gray plastic case.

"It would make me feel a lot better if you took this," he said.

Ray undid latches and opened the case. Inside, on gray packing foam, was a Smith and Wesson .38 with a two-inch barrel and mother-of-pearl grips. Ray picked it up.

"Can't hit shit with it at over twenty feet," he said. "But it has a lot of punch up close."

He popped open the empty cylinder, held out the gun. Harry took it, felt its weight.

"Easy to maneuver with one hand," Ray said. "No slide to work. And it'll stop anything you point it at. Here."

Ray reached into a jacket pocket, came out with a baggie filled with shells, short stubby .38s with blue tips.

"Glaser Safetys," he said. "Teflon-tipped. Hit 'em anywhere and that's all she wrote. There's twelve of them in here. They're illegal, but I don't have to tell you that."

Harry snapped the cylinder shut, turned the gun over in his hand.

"You think I've lost it," he said.

"Lost what?"

"My edge, my confidence. My balls. You think having a gun around will make me feel better, give me a psychological advantage."

Ray shrugged.

Harry looked at the .38, tucked it into his sling, saw it stayed there without sliding out.

"Thanks," he said.

"It's clean. But unlicensed. So if you have to use it, throw it in the river afterward. Do whatever you have to do, just don't get caught with it."

"I'll keep that in mind."

Ray closed the case, replaced it in the trunk, and shut the lid. He put out his hand and Harry took it.

"Remember what I said in the car," Ray said.

Harry nodded, held his grip.

"Call me anytime, day or night," Ray said. "If I'm not there, leave a message. Home or office, it doesn't matter. You're not alone in this."

"Thanks. I know that."

"*Vaya con dios*, partner. Don't forget who your friends are."

TWENTY-ONE

He slept twelve hours that night, woke dry mouthed and aching, the noon sun high in the sky.

He showered carefully, holding the cast outside the curtain to keep it dry. He toweled off as best he could, looked at himself in the mirror. Both his eyes were still blackened, the color fading to a sickly yellow. A scab bisected his left eyebrow, and there was a plum-colored bruise on his right side, red scrapes on his chest and arms.

He fought his way into a short-sleeved sweatshirt and jeans, then attached the Velcro strips of the sling behind his neck, pulled it around him like a bra, and nestled the cast into it. His elbow throbbed with a dull, wet ache.

In the kitchen, he scrambled eggs and made instant coffee. He drank as much as he could, but the hot liquid sent waves of pain through his loose teeth. He ate half the eggs, threw the rest away.

There'd been three messages on his answering machine when he got home from the hospital, the first from Bobby, leaving his number in North Carolina, the other two from Wesniak. He played the messages back again, wrote down Bobby's number, reset the tape.

After a while, he went out to the barn, wrestled the door open one-handed. Sunlight flooded the interior, illuminating dust motes in the air.

The driver's side window of the Mustang was cracked through, sagging. The dent in the door was deep enough that it would need to be pulled and compounded. Someone had raked a key or knife along the side of the car as well. There were deep gouges in the paint, stretching from the door to the left rear quarter panel.

He opened the passenger side door, popped the glove box. The notebook was still there. He took it with him back to the house.

He waited, listening to Muzak, while the receptionist connected him.

When Ray came on the line, Harry said, "Favor time."

"That didn't take long."

"I've got two vehicles and plate numbers. I'm looking for registration, addresses, et cetera."

"Hang on a second." Then, "Go."

He read him the numbers and descriptions.

"I'll get back to you," Ray said. "May take a while, things are hopping here today."

"No rush."

"How are you feeling?"

"Better than yesterday. Worse than tomorrow."

"That's about as well as can be expected, I guess. Anything else I can get you?"

"A bottle of scotch and a fistful of Percocet."

"Better hold off on the scotch for a while. You can get the Percocet through normal channels. I'll call back."

He was sitting on the porch, his feet propped on the railing, when the dark green Crown Victoria came up the driveway. Eagleman was at the wheel, Wesniak beside him. They pulled into the side yard, got out, both wearing suits and sunglasses. He raised a hand to them, let his feet come down.

He stood up as they came across the lawn. Wesniak

stopped at the porch steps, looked up at him. He took off his sunglasses, folded them and tucked them into a pocket, slowly shook his head.

"I got your messages," Harry said. "I just haven't had a chance to get back to you."

"I was worried something had happened to you. Looks like it did."

"Come on inside."

They followed him into the living room. Eagleman was chewing a toothpick, studying him.

"Looks like somebody punched your ticket," he said.

"I got mugged."

Eagleman grunted, a noise with no meaning.

"Where?" Wesniak said.

"Brooklyn. My car broke down. I was walking to a gas station and I got jumped."

"They catch the guy?"

"No."

"Hell of a thing," Wesniak said. "Mind if we have a seat?"

He pulled up a chair, sat down. Eagleman stayed by the door.

"You're in bad shape," Wesniak said. "Was there more than one?"

"Yeah."

"You file a police report?"

"No."

"Why not?"

He sat on the couch, winced at the pain in his ribs.

"No point. They would have been long gone."

"They get much?"

"My wallet. About fifty dollars."

"Why they decide to beat up on you like that?"

"I don't know. They didn't explain themselves."

"Hell of a thing," Wesniak said again. "Reason we're here, we were just having lunch down the road, thought we'd drop by, save you a call. Or a trip. From the looks of you, that was probably a good idea."

"I was going to call you today. I've been pretty busy."

"I can see that. You know, it's been a while since I've been out here. I grew up in this part of the county, you know that?"

"No."

"My father had a chicken farm in Manalapan, not far from here. I close my eyes and I can still smell it. They sold it all back in the sixties. Part of that land is where the high school is now."

"Progress."

"I guess. But it's hard to even recognize anything around here these days. All these rich people from New York coming down, buying up all the land, building those big ugly houses. New Jersey peckerwoods like us are an endangered species."

"What can I do for you?"

"Well, I'd been thinking a lot since the last time we talked. About this whole Cortez business. I get the sense it's just the tip of the iceberg."

"How's that?"

"I don't know exactly. I just can't shake the feeling there's something going on here I'm not seeing. Like it's right in front of my face, but I'm missing it. That's why I wanted to go over your story again, maybe find something I missed the first time."

"There's nothing more than what I told you. In fact, I'm surprised you're taking such an interest. It's a drug killing, isn't it? Hardly what you'd call a redball."

"Yeah, I know. Not that unusual, is it, this sort of thing? People get greedy, stupid. It's a dangerous business by nature. Sooner or later they all get what's coming to them."

"Usually."

"That's right. Usually. Not always."

"So what's bothering you?"

"Well . . ." He sat back. "This bit about looking for Cortez. About his owing a friend of yours some money for engine work. Timing's odd, isn't it, that all this happened just before someone decided to take him out?"

"Maybe not. Maybe Cortez owed a lot of people money."

"Could be. The last time we talked, you were reluctant to give me the name of this friend, the one you were doing the favor for. Has that changed?"

"No. Like I said, he's not involved."

"Then, there's my problem."

Harry looked at him, leaned forward.

"I don't know about the timing," he said. "But my looking for Cortez had nothing to do with drugs. Or anything else that may have been behind the deaths of those two men."

"How can you be sure? Maybe your friend didn't tell you the whole story. Maybe it was more than five hundred dollars."

Harry shook his head.

"I want to believe you, Harry, I do. After all, if you—or this friend of yours—were involved in Cortez's drug dealing, I have to think you would have come up with a better story at the airport. Or more likely, you never would have called it in in the first place."

"Probably."

"There you go. So, on one level, I have to think what you're telling me is mostly the truth. On the other, I still have this feeling there are things you're not telling me at all, either to protect someone or to cover yourself. Is that the case?"

"No."

Wesniak nodded. "It's good to hear you say that. And I do understand you might have a perfectly good reason, in your mind, for keeping something from me. But I guarantee you, whatever logic you're using, it's a mistake. The sooner you realize that, the better for all of us."

"If you think I can tell you anything that's going to break this case for you, you're wrong. I don't know who killed Jimmy Cortez and his cousin. I don't know who they were selling drugs to or buying drugs from, if that's what they were doing."

"All the more reason you should tell us who this friend is, so we can talk to him and rule both of you out. Believe me,

I'd like to forget all about your involvement in this. But right now, you're the only string I have to pull on. I'm not about to let go."

"I found the car. By accident. That's all. If you're trying to build something else out of that, you're wasting your time. If I had anything to do with those two bodies . . ."

"No one said you did."

". . . I wouldn't have been anywhere near that airport. And I certainly wouldn't have involved the police in it."

"Or Ray Washington."

"Especially Ray."

"Good point. Which leads me to something else I wanted to say. Ray was a good investigator, a real pro. He had his troubles with the organization, and I'm sure a lot of it had to do with the color of his skin, but he never let it affect his work. He broke a lot of cases in Major Crimes. You did too. No one respects him more than me. But he's not a cop anymore. And neither are you. Don't forget that. This case, it's my problem now, and I have to take it by the numbers. It doesn't matter if I want to cut someone a break or not. So all I can do is encourage you to do the smart thing."

"Which is?"

"Come clean. Everything. You're a good man who's had some tough breaks—your wife, the shooting. Anything you or Ray got involved with here, I'm sure you had a reason for it. But the more I know, the more I can help look out for your interests."

"Ray had nothing to do with any of this."

"I'm not saying he did, I'm not saying he didn't. I'm just telling you what my situation is. I'm in the dark right now, and that's not a place I like to be. And when I'm there, I can't help anyone else. I have to prioritize. And if you won't cooperate with me, then your priority gets lower and lower."

"I haven't asked for your help. In any way."

"True, but that could change. Whatever's going on here, it's not over. And looking at you, I'd say the situation's deteriorating."

"What happened to me had nothing to do with Cortez."

"Okay, you got mugged. Happens all the time. Even to ex-cops. But look after yourself, because we'll be talking again. I could arrest you right now, you know, take you out to Trenton, force you to make bond. It wouldn't hold up, but it would ruin your week."

"Why don't you?"

"Two reasons. Number one, I don't think you're the bad guy here, even if you are holding out on me. Do you know what number two is?"

"You realize it'll be a waste of time?"

Wesniak smiled, shook his head. "Your time, not mine. It wouldn't bother me at all. No, the second reason is the simpler one: professional courtesy. Don't mistake it for anything else."

"I won't."

"I'm glad to hear that." He got to his feet. "There now, I've said my piece and I've heard your side of it, as far as that goes. So I really have only one other thing to say."

He moved toward the door.

"And that is that I hope you'll reconsider. And I hope you'll do it for the reasons we talked about. If you don't, I guess I'll just have to live with that. But you'll have to live with it too. You've got one week."

"What?"

"One week to give me that name. Seven days from today. If I don't hear from you by then, we'll be coming back, and we won't be leaving alone."

Eagleman opened the door.

"That's not a threat," Wesniak said, "that's reality. You're involved in this, Harry, one way or another. And now so am I. Pick your side."

"Got a pen?" Ray asked.

Harry shifted the phone to his left ear, held it there with his shoulder.

"Hold on a sec."

He sat down at the kitchen table, pulled the notebook

toward him and flipped to a fresh page, picked up the stub of pencil.

"Ready."

He wrote as he listened. The Jeep was registered to Lester James Wiley at an address in Manasquan. The Buick was owned by a company called Christo Waste Hauling on Richmond Parkway in Staten Island.

"I'm guessing what this is about," Ray said, "but don't do anything until we've had a chance to talk about it, okay? Promise me that."

"I'm just getting some information together. I'm in no shape to be doing much of anything else just yet."

"It feels different, doesn't it?"

"What?"

"When you're a civilian. You know what I'm talking about."

He didn't say anything for a moment.

"I don't know. Maybe. I'd been away from the job so long . . . I guess maybe I started to look at things differently."

"And then all this shit happened and now you feel like you're right back in it, but it's not the same anymore, is it?"

"No, it's not."

"Why do you think I applied for my license after sitting on my ass at my brother-in-law's mortgage company for a year? I missed it. I missed the Life."

"I left the job because I was sick of it. Why would I miss it?"

"Because you know too much. You've seen the world the way it really is, the way it operates. And it's a scary place when you don't have the badge or the gun or the attitude anymore. But you can't go back to pretending it's some other way."

"When you look at it like that, it's not much of a world, is it?"

"Maybe not. But it's ours."

Later, he dragged the phone book from a drawer, found numbers for a rental car agency and a cab company in

Freehold. He made two phone calls, then tore the page from the notebook and went out onto the porch to wait. He sat there, looked at the names and addresses he'd written down.

It was a start.

TWENTY-TWO

The next morning, he called the number Bobby had left him. A man answered and asked him to hang on. A few moments later, Bobby came on the line.

"It's done," Harry said.

"I was starting to get worried about you, slick. You weren't calling me back. Are you all right?"

"I got busy. How's everything down there?"

"Fine. We're fine. What happened? You give him the money?"

"Yeah, I gave it to him. We're settled. But it's best if you stay down there a while."

"I was planning on it. Then it's over?"

"It's over. You're quits with him."

"Hard to believe, after all this."

"Believe it."

"And everything went okay?"

"Everything's fine. I can't talk much now. I just wanted to let you know it was done. I'll call you later in the week, update you on what's going on."

"What do you mean?"

"There's still a couple things I want to look into."

"I thought you said it was over?"

"It is," he said. "For you."

• • •

At noon, he was parked a half block from her house, beneath a stand of trees on the opposite side of the street. The driveway was empty, the garage door closed.

The car he'd rented was a midnight blue two-door Saturn with tinted windows. He wore sunglasses and a baseball cap, had tilted the seat back enough so that he was low in the car but could still watch the house.

He took off the glasses and looked at himself in the rearview mirror. The bruises below his eyes had lost their purple sheen, the swelling gone for good. He'd taken the tape from his nose, but the flesh there was still red, slightly puffy. Whenever he touched it he felt a warm flow of pain back through his sinuses.

At ten after one, Wiley's Jeep turned down the street. Harry sank lower as it went past him and pulled up into the driveway. Wiley got out, went to the front door, rang the bell. After a moment, the door opened and he went in.

He'd brought the notebook and a pen from the house. He opened the notebook on his leg, braced his cast across the top of the pad, and wrote.

> *C:*
> *I am all right. I need to know that you are. Be very careful. Call me if you can, but don't take any chances. I will reach you somehow.*

He left it unsigned, tore the page from the book, folded it, and slipped it into his shirt pocket.

At one-thirty, the garage door started to roll up. The Lexus backed out past the Jeep, and he could see the BMW parked inside. When the Lexus pulled onto the street, he could see Dunleavy at the wheel, Fallon beside him, the backseat empty. Neither of them looked at the Saturn as they drove past. The garage door rolled shut again.

He started the engine, drove three blocks, and found a pay phone at a gas station. He dialed her cell phone, let it ring four times, and then a computer-generated voice mail message picked up. He clicked off.

There was a mall about ten minutes away. He went to four stores before he found what he was looking for, a brown leather cigarette case that looked enough like hers to pass a quick inspection. He stopped at a 7-Eleven, bought a pack of Marlboro Lights, opened it, and took three of them out. He rolled the note into a tube, slid it down into the pack.

He drove back to the house, parked beneath the same trees. The Jeep was still there. He got out of the car, crossed the street. There was a loose, shoulder-high hedge separating Fallon's property from the house next door. He stepped over a stone wall and moved along the hedge until he reached the garage, then pushed through an opening to the other side. He waited there, out of sight of both houses, listening. Then he turned the corner of the garage, looked into the backyard.

The French doors were closed, but the curtains in one of them were pulled aside. It would have to do. He lobbed the cigarette case so that it fell short of the door, landing on the flagstones in full view.

He moved back around the garage, pushed through the hedge again. Somewhere inside the neighbor's house, a dog began to bark. He crossed the stone wall and walked back to his car.

At ten P.M., the phone rang.

"Harry?"

"Where are you calling from?"

"A pay phone. I snuck out. He's down at the restaurant. Lester's here but he's sound asleep on the couch."

"Be careful. You got my note?"

"Yes. Lester saw the case, brought it in. He thought it was mine."

"Are you okay?"

"Edward showed me pictures . . ."

"It looked worse than it is. I'm all right."

"Oh, God, I'm so sorry."

He could hear the tears in her voice.

"Has he hurt you?" he said.

"What happened to you? Have you been to a doctor? Are you all right?"

"I'm fine. You didn't answer me. Has he hurt you?"

"It's you I'm worried about, Harry. Those photos . . . It looked like they'd killed you."

"They didn't. You should get back to the house."

"Edward took my cell phone. I don't know where it is. Whenever he goes out, he has Lester here watching me. I don't know what to do or what . . ."

"Get hold of yourself."

"How did he know?"

"I'm not sure. Maybe he had someone following you. I don't know."

"Oh, God. I should never have brought you into this. I should never have . . ."

"Stop it. Has he threatened you?"

"No. He just said I should forget about you because you weren't coming back, that you'd learned your lesson. What did he mean? What did he do to you?"

"Don't worry about that for now. Go back to the house. I'll explain everything later. What's important now is that he thinks I'm out of your life. Let him keep thinking that. I'll get a message to you somehow."

"Harry, I love you."

It took him by surprise.

"I love you," he said. "And don't worry. I'm not going anywhere."

TWENTY-THREE

Wiley's house was a bungalow in a neighborhood of bungalows, a quarter mile from the ocean. Harry had driven past it twice earlier that day to get a feel for the surrounding area. Summer rentals mostly, long blocks of sandy yards and no trees.

Wiley's Jeep had been in the driveway the first time he'd driven by, was gone the second. At nine P.M., he'd used a pay phone to call the Rip Tide, asked for him. When Wiley came on the line, he'd punched numbers in at random and hung up. Now, four hours later, the driveway was still empty, the house dark.

He turned down a side street, parked behind an abandoned bait shop he'd seen earlier. The windows were boarded, the lot dark. He got out of the car, locked it, walked back through the silent neighborhood.

He cut through two backyards, ducked under a clothesline hung with swimsuits and towels, came up behind Wiley's house. There were two windows back there, both about a foot over his head. He reached up to the first one, felt the heavy glass of a storm window. The second held an air conditioner. The bedroom.

He circled the house. On the north side, toward the front, was another window. When he reached, he felt screen beneath his fingers.

He took a red recycling bucket from the side of the house,

overturned it beneath the window, and climbed up. He was looking into a living room, lit only by the glow of the streetlight. He could see a couch, a coffee table, a TV, a short hallway that led into the kitchen. The kitchen table had been pushed against the wall to make room for a weight bench. There was a fully loaded barbell on the bench, scattered weights on the floor around it. Beyond was the open bedroom door.

He took out his pocket knife, thumbed open the blade, and sliced two small holes in the screen above where he estimated the thumb pushes would be. He put the knife away, worked fingers inside one hole, pulled the thumb push until the spring released, then did the other. With the screen loose in the frame, he tilted it, slid the tabs from the runners, and eased it out of the window toward him. He lowered it until it was only inches above the ground, then let it drop almost silently.

With his fingertips, he gripped the sash, pulled it down and shut. It slid easily in its frame, would open just as easily when he pushed up.

He climbed down, carried the screen and the bucket to the rear of the house, set them in the shadows. There was a small, prefab toolshed in the next yard, a pile of stacked cinder blocks behind it. It was as good a place as any. He climbed up on the cinder blocks, his back against the rear of the shed. He could hear big band music playing softly from an open window in the house next door. He closed his eyes and sat back to wait.

The girl couldn't have been more than twenty. Bottle-blonde, tight jeans, purple blouse. He watched her walk carefully on high heels from the Jeep to the side door of the house, Wiley close behind her. He put an arm around her shoulder, whispered something, and she giggled as he unlocked the door and led her in.

He looked at his watch; one forty-five. The houses on

both sides were dark. He slid from the cinder blocks, dusted off his jeans. Lights went on in the bungalow.

He took the .38 out of his sling, stuck it deep in his right front pocket so that it wouldn't fall out. He undid the sling's Velcro snaps, slipped it off, and set it atop the cinder blocks. He could move better without it.

Voices inside now, the girl's laughter. He decided to give them ten minutes to get comfortable. After a while, the kitchen light went out, the bedroom light on. To the east, a shooting star streaked across the sky and was gone.

He got the recycling bucket from the back of the house, brought it around to the dark living room window. He put his hand flat on the glass, pushed, felt the window glide upward. He could hear voices then, Wiley's low and slow, the girl's higher, not laughing anymore. He climbed up on the bucket, slid the sash higher.

A bed creaked. He heard the girl say something in complaint but couldn't make out the words. Then came the sound of a brief, compressed struggle, contained as soon as it began. The girl's voice again, meeker this time, then the sharp smack of a hand against flesh, and she was silent.

He braced his cast on the sill for balance, hoisted one leg in. He hung there for a moment, the other leg waving in the air, then drew himself in, holding tight to the windowsill. He went in silently, felt the floor beneath his feet. The light wash from the open bedroom door lit up half the kitchen, cast shadows on the linoleum. He heard Wiley moan softly, his breath quicken. The girl was whimpering now.

He moved into the kitchen. Wiley had the girl on her knees in the bedroom, his fist twisted in her hair, his shirt off, pants down at his ankles. The girl was half naked, blouse and bra on the floor, her palms against the sculpted muscles of his thighs, trying to push him away. He held her there, his hips moving, eyes closed. As his thrusts increased, she tried to twist away, and he pulled up hard on her hair. Her hands dropped to her sides and she stopped fighting. Harry could see the tears on her cheeks.

There was a door to his left, the bathroom. He stepped in, saw the gray fuse box on the wall beside the door. The moonlight coming through the window was bright enough that he could read the labeled switches. He found the one marked BEDROOM.

Wiley was moaning louder now, a slow hitched-breath rhythm, an unmistakable primal sound. As it gained momentum, neared its peak, he switched off the breaker.

Silence and darkness. Then the sound of a struggle, a clumsy fall. The girl came through the moonlit kitchen, half running, half stumbling. He stepped out of the bathroom, saw Wiley coming after her, one hand holding up his pants.

"Back here, bitch!"

Wiley never saw him. Harry stepped forward, braced his legs, raised the cast over his right shoulder, and swung it hard.

It took Wiley full across the face. His legs shot out from under him and he went down hard on the linoleum. Harry stepped in, kicked him sharply in the lower ribs on the right side, his weight behind it. Wiley's breath exploded out of him and he rolled onto his side, his mouth wide as he fought for air.

Harry turned to see the girl watching, frozen, from the living room.

"It's okay," he said to her, pulling the handcuffs from his belt. "It's all right."

He swung one cuff open, slapped it over Wiley's thick right wrist, and locked it. He dragged him two feet across the floor, ratcheted the other end around a front leg of the weight bench. Wiley's face was covered with blood, black in the moonlight.

Harry stepped back, breathing heavily, the pain sharp in his arm. He stepped around Wiley and went into the bedroom, got the girl's blouse and bra. He brought them out to where she stood trembling in the living room, her arms crossed to hide her breasts. Her face was streaked black with mascara.

"Are you all right?" he said.

She backed away from him. He set the clothes on the arm of the couch.

"Go ahead," he said. "Get dressed. He's not going to hurt you."

In the kitchen, Wiley moaned. Handcuffs rattled on the bench leg.

Harry found the wall switch, turned on the kitchen light. Wiley had raised himself into a sitting position alongside the bench. His nose was red and flattened, a bubble of blood in one nostril, blood spotting his chest.

"Sorry to interrupt your date," Harry said.

Wiley spit blood, tried to roll onto his knees. Harry took a step forward, raised a boot. Wiley sank back down.

"Sit there. Don't move. We've got some things to talk about."

He went back into the living room. The girl had her bra on, was turning her blouse right side out.

"Don't look at me," she said.

He got Kleenex from the bathroom, carried them out to her. She had the blouse on, was fumbling with the buttons. Two of them were missing and the discovery bought a fresh round of tears.

He handed her the tissues, stood back. She turned away, wiped at tears and ruined mascara, blew her nose.

"What's your name?" he said.

She ignored him, began to button the blouse as best she could.

"Where do you live? Do you have enough money to get a cab home?"

She turned to him. "Who are you? Are you a cop?"

"No."

"What are you doing here?"

"Let's just say . . ."

"I want to call the police."

"You can if you want to. The phone's in the kitchen."

She looked in there, then back at him. For the first time, he saw the faint red imprint of a palm across her left cheek.

"I want to get out of here," she said.

"I'll call you a cab. It's late, though, it might take awhile."

"I want to get out of here right now."

He pulled the Saturn key chain from his left jeans pocket. He saw her eyes drop, knew she was looking at the butt of the .38.

"My car's parked nearby," he said. "Here's the key, you can wait there. I'll be out soon and I'll drive you home." He held it out.

"Are you going to kill him?"

He didn't answer.

"Are you?"

"What you want to do now is up to you."

She took the key.

"Go out to the street, make a right, walk a block, and then make another right. There's a building there, used to be a bait shop. The sign's still there. You can't miss it. There's a blue Saturn parked behind the shop. When you get to the car, stay there. Lock the doors. Don't come back."

Wiley was sitting up, watching her.

"Go on," Harry said.

She went to the front door, pulled at the locks, got it open.

"Cunt!" Wiley called out.

She went out and Harry closed and locked the door behind her. Then he moved to the window he'd come through, slid it closed. He went back into the kitchen.

"Couldn't resist that last remark, could you?" he said.

Wiley spit a clot of blood onto the floor at Harry's feet.

"Time to talk," Harry said.

"Get fucked."

"You're making this easier."

He caught one of Wiley's loose pants legs, yanked on it. Wiley tried to hold on to the waist, but Harry had the pants down his legs and off in three pulls. Wiley wore no underwear and his testicles and penis were tight and shrunken. He shifted his legs to cover himself.

Harry tossed the pants into a corner, dragged a kitchen

chair away from the wall, sat down, still breathing heavily, his arm throbbing within the cast.

"Here we are," he said.

"I ain't saying shit to you."

"You're all hormones and no brains, Lester. That's the problem. You can't see what's going on here."

"Unlock these handcuffs and we'll see what's going on."

"Is that what you want?"

"You act tough now. You weren't so tough that other night, were you?"

He stood up, dug into his jeans pocket, came up with the handcuff key, bounced it off Wiley's chest. It skittered on the floor.

"Go ahead. Unlock them. Come get me."

Wiley looked at the key.

"Do it. Go on."

He waited. Wiley didn't move. Harry leaned over, picked up the key, and pocketed it again.

"Then shut the fuck up," he said.

He went into the bathroom and looked at his cast. There were thin cracks along the forearm and the plaster was smeared with blood. The pain was like heat in the bone.

He yanked aside the shower curtain and pulled it out of the bathtub, plastic rings popping off. He found the rubber plug and fit it into the drain, then twisted the cold faucet. Rust-brown water streamed into the tub, then cleared. Above the sound of the water, he heard the creak of the weight bench.

He opened the medicine cabinet, looking for aspirin. Inside were prescription bottles, toothpaste, a disposable razor, and a tube of ointment, nothing else. When he shut the door, plaster dust drifted from the bottom of the cabinet. He looked down and saw there was already a thin film of it on top of the toilet tank and on the floor behind.

He opened the cabinet again, put his fingers against the inside wall, and pushed. It rocked slightly.

He went back into the kitchen. Wiley was crouched

beside the weight bench, trying to get enough leverage to lift it and slide the cuff off the leg. He got the leg about an inch off the floor, but the end was flared and the cuff wouldn't clear it.

"Hey," Harry said.

The leg came down with a crash.

"Where's a screwdriver?"

"What?"

"Screwdriver. You deaf?"

Wiley looked at him.

He tried the drawers near the sink. In the third one down he found a long-handled screwdriver mixed in with a tray of silverware. Wiley was watching him now, the weight bench forgotten.

He went back into the bathroom, took out the contents of the medicine cabinet and set them on the floor, then used the tip of the screwdriver to pry the bottom edge of the cabinet from the wall. It came out easily.

He shut the cabinet door, then used the screwdriver on the edges. When a full two inches of the cabinet was out of the wall, he put down the screwdriver, got his fingers under the bottom edge, and tugged. The cabinet came out all at once. He pinned it against the wall with his shoulder to keep it from falling, then lowered it to the floor beside the toilet. Plaster dust floated around him.

He looked into the hole. About a foot down inside the wall there was a small blue knapsack wedged against one of the joists.

He pulled it out, raising more dust in the process. The bag swung heavily. He set it on the closed toilet seat, worked the zipper up and around. Inside was a package about the size of a hardcover book, wrapped in brown butcher's paper sealed with strips of white tape. He set it on the sink, took out his pocket knife, and sliced through the tape. Beneath the paper was aluminum foil. He peeled it away and inside were individually sealed glassine bags of white powder, maybe twenty in all.

The auxiliary drain began to work noisily as the tub filled. He twisted the faucet off, went back into the kitchen, tossed the screwdriver on the counter.

"Going into business on your own, Lester? That's about a half a pound of skag you got in there."

"I don't know what you're talking about."

"Some things are starting to make sense now."

He reached into his back pocket, pulled loose the can of CS spray. Wiley saw it, tried to get to his feet, hauling the weight bench with him, and Harry gave him two solid blasts in the face from about a foot away. He cried out, folded, and Harry got a knee in his back, pinned him to the floor. He shoved the canister back in his pocket, took out the key, and unlocked the cuff from the bench leg. He managed to pin Wiley's arms behind him, got the loose cuff around his left wrist, locked it shut, then took hold of the short chain and hauled him across the linoleum and into the bathroom, panting with the effort.

He got Wiley to the tub, heaved up on the chain, and pushed him forward so that the rim of the tub hit him across the chest.

"Go on. Get your face in the water."

He pushed Wiley's face down, then let go. Wiley kicked out, his heel thumping into the base of the toilet, but his struggles slowed as the water cooled the burning in his eyes.

Wiley kept his face there until Harry pulled back on the chain. He slumped down the outside of the tub, his back against the porcelain. Water splashed over the rim and onto the floor. His eyes were still slits, the flesh around them puffy, but he could see now. His chest was heaving.

Harry took out the .38, moved the knapsack to the floor, and sat on the toilet seat facing him. A thin trickle of blood still oozed from Wiley's left nostril and his eyes were a bright red. All the fight was gone.

"I'm about done here," Harry said. "The only question is what kind of shape you're in when I leave."

Wiley blinked water from his eyes, watched him.

"You know why I filled the tub?"

Wiley coughed pink phlegm, spit it away. He shifted against the tub, skin squeaking on the porcelain.

"If I put you facedown in the water and shoot you in the back of the head, it won't make much of a mess at all. And chances are I'll be able to recover the bullet and take it with me. Then I can throw some of this smack around, put a twenty-dollar bill in your mouth and, as far as the cops are concerned, it's an open-and-shut case. Six months from now, no one will remember who you were, or care."

Wiley let his chin drop to his chest as if exhausted, shut his eyes. Harry touched the muzzle to the center of Wiley's forehead.

"Look at me. Look at my arm, my face. You think I won't pull the trigger on you?"

Wiley looked up through half-closed eyes.

"I had nothing to do with that."

"Bullshit."

"That was between you and Eddie."

"You took your shot when you got the chance, though, didn't you?"

He thumbed the hammer back to half-cock.

"This . . ." Wiley started. "This is all Eddie. It's his thing now. I never wanted anything to do with it."

"How did he know?"

"About what?"

"About me."

"He had me watching her when he wasn't around. He thought she was acting funny, so he asked me to stick close to her. Then one day I followed her to the beach. It didn't take long to figure out what was going on."

"So you're the one who told him?"

"That's what he was paying me for, man."

"Did he hurt her?"

"I don't think so. I don't know. She didn't look it. Fuck, I don't know what's going on with him anymore. He doesn't tell me anything."

He took away the gun.

"That night at the Rip Tide. Who were the other two?"

"I don't know their last names."

"Tell me what you know."

"The fat one, his name is Vince. The other one's Tommy. They've been hanging around the restaurant for a couple of months, walk around like they own the fucking place."

"Dunleavy know them?"

"Yeah, he knows them. He wanted to handle things differently."

"What do you mean?"

"He told Eddie they should just clip you, then and there. He said it would be a mistake to fuck with you and leave you walking around."

"He was right. What did Fallon say?"

"He wanted to teach you a lesson. He said you weren't a cop anymore, you didn't have any connections. There was nothing to worry about."

"Tell me about Bobby Fox and Jimmy Cortez."

"Eddie doesn't tell me his business. I just go where he wants me to and do what he says. I watch his back when he needs it. That's all."

"I don't believe you. You were around. You must have seen them, heard them being talked about. You must have known what this situation was all about in the first place."

"It was about money. What else is there?"

"Tell me what happened."

"I don't know."

"Lester, I'm trying to be patient. There's enough shit in that knapsack to light up half the junkies in New Jersey for weeks. Don't tell me you didn't know what was going on."

"That's Eddie's stuff. I was keeping it for him."

"You're a fucking liar. And I'm starting to feel like I'm wasting my time."

He snicked the hammer back to full cock.

"Man, be careful with that thing."

"Turn around."

"What?"

"I said turn around."

He stood, caught the handcuff chain with his left hand, pulled it so that Wiley was facing the tub again.

"Put your face down there."

"Don't do this."

"You think I'm fucking with you? Put your face down there."

He pressed the muzzle of the .38 behind Wiley's left ear.

"Please," Wiley said.

"Do it."

He leaned forward so that the tip of his nose touched the water.

"Look at the water. Don't turn around."

Wiley was shaking now, softly. His lips were moving without sound, and tears dropped from his cheeks into the pink water.

"Talk to me," Harry said.

"Please." He tried to raise his head. Harry pushed it back down with the gun.

"It could all end just like this, Lester. Right now. It's up to you."

Wiley shut his eyes tight.

"Cortez," he said. "Eddie knew him from around. He'd moved some stuff for him before."

"Go on."

"Eddie wanted him to take more, a whole key, but he said he couldn't afford it."

He eased up on the gun. "Where was he getting it from?"

"Man, I don't know that."

"Guess."

"He was spending a lot of time with people up in North Jersey. Maybe he was getting it from them."

"Mob guys?"

"What do you think?"

"Paulie Andelli's crew?"

"I got nothing to do with that shit. That's all Eddie."

"What about Bobby Fox?"

"This Cortez told Eddie that if he could get a partner, he'd take him up on the deal. Then he brought this Fox guy around. They'd come up with the front money, but Eddie saw through him right away."

"What do you mean?"

"Man, he had no fucking idea what he was getting into. He was in way over his head. You could spot it from a mile away."

He took away the gun.

"How many people was Fallon dealing to?"

"Four, five. I don't know. Cortez and that other guy just happened to be in the right place at the right time or Eddie wouldn't have gone near them. But he had more shit than he knew what to do with. He needed help moving it."

"When did Dunleavy get involved?"

"A few months back. You gotta understand, Eddie doesn't tell me much anymore. After Mickey showed up, it was like I became the fucking delivery boy or something."

"Who killed Jimmy Cortez?"

"I don't know, man. I swear to Christ I don't know."

Harry sat back down.

"That knapsack in the wall," he said.

"I never even wanted that shit here. Eddie gave it to me to move about three weeks ago. I sold a little of it, but it's tough. There's a glut now, or people are doing other things. I don't know what the fuck I'm going to do with it. I ain't no fucking dealer. He was trying to make me one."

Harry pointed the .38 at the floor, uncocked it, stood.

"Sit up," he said.

Wiley turned away from the water, slipped back against the side of the tub.

"Okay," Harry said. "Here's the deal. You just retired from the bodyguard and surveillance business. Pack up your Jeep tonight and get the hell out of here. Get as far away from Fallon as you can and stay there."

"Man, what are you talking about?"

"Just what I said. Things are going to hit the fan here, Lester. You want to catch your share of the shit? I'll make sure it happens."

"I can't just take off, leave with that stuff here."

"Don't worry about the drugs, Lester, worry about your life. This is the last time we have this conversation. If I have to deal with you again, you won't even see it coming. But if you want to guarantee yourself a federal trafficking beef, stick around. You'll go down with Fallon as sure as shit. Either way, you're fucked. Get used to it."

"None of this was my idea, man."

"This chance might not come again, Lester. There's going to be so much trouble for Fallon in the next few days he's not going to have the time or resources to send someone after your sorry ass. He'll have other things on his mind."

"That's what you're telling me, but you don't know that. Eddie's different now. He's not like he used to be. He'd have me taken out in a second if he thought I ripped him off. Dunleavy would do it for him."

"Then go somewhere he can't find you. And forget about the package. I'm taking it."

"What?"

"If I let you keep it, you'll sell it or give it back to Fallon. You'll do anything you have to do to square the books with him. I don't want that. I want you far away and not even thinking about coming back. It's a second chance, Lester. Not many people get one. Take it."

"Nowhere's far enough. If he finds me, he'll kill me."

"That's the risk you'll take. But any way you look at it, your life here is done. Accept that fact and you might get out of this alive."

He tucked the .38 back into his pocket. Wiley watched him from the floor. "Stay there," Harry said.

He took everything into the kitchen, rewrapped the package and resealed the tape ends. He put it back in the knapsack, zipped it closed, then got the handcuff key and went back to the bathroom.

"Part of you is going to want to get on that phone as soon as I leave," he said. "Call Fallon and tell him what happened, plead for mercy. If that happens, I promise you you'll be dead or in jail before the week's out. I can't afford to have you around. You're a loose end. And I'll do whatever I need to do to get you out of the picture. Do you understand?"

Wiley looked at the floor, nodded.

"Turn around."

He swiveled slowly on his knees to face the tub. Harry unlocked the cuffs, took them off. They left deep red welts.

He tucked the cuffs into his back pocket. Wiley sat up, began to rub his wrists.

"It may not seem like much of a chance," Harry said, "but it's more than Jimmy Cortez got. Keep that in mind."

"Just get out of here, man. Just leave me the fuck alone."

"Like I said, Lester, it's your choice. I'll deal with it either way."

He left him there, got the knapsack, and let himself out the side door. At the toolshed, he put the sling back on, slung the knapsack over his shoulder. His arm felt as if it were on fire.

The moonlit streets were silent as he walked back to the car. When he got close, he saw it was empty.

"Hey," a voice said softly.

He turned. The girl stepped out from the shadows at the side of the building.

They faced each other for a moment, and then he raised his right hand. The key chain flashed in the moonlight. He caught it, opened the trunk, dropped the knapsack inside, shut it.

He unlocked the passenger side door for her. She got in, leaned over and popped the lock on his side. He took the .38 out of his pocket before climbing behind the wheel.

"Open the glove compartment," he said.

She looked at the gun.

"Did you kill him?"

"No."

He held the gun at an angle, showed her the empty chambers.

"It's not loaded," she said.

"That's right."

She opened the glove box. He put the gun inside, closed it, started the car.

"Why did you go in there with an unloaded gun?" she said.

"Because I was afraid I might kill him."

"What if he had his own?"

"That was the chance I took. Where are we going?"

"I live in Toms River."

"I don't know that area too well. You'll have to give me directions once we get down there."

He turned on the lights and backed out into the street. For the first five minutes, they drove in silence.

"Thank you," she said.

"For what?"

"For getting me out of there. And for not killing him."

"Would it have bothered you if I had? After what happened?"

"If you had, it wouldn't have been for me. It would have been for whatever was going on between the two of you."

"That's right."

"But I would have blamed myself when I found out about it."

"Maybe you blame yourself for too much."

She was quiet until they got on to the highway, heading south.

"I would have done almost anything he wanted," she said. "He didn't have to treat me like that."

She rolled the window down halfway, let in the warm night air.

"You never told me your name," he said.

"Ally. My name's Ally."

"It's nice to meet you, Ally. I wish it were under better circumstances."

"What's yours?"

"Harry."

"Harry, nothing around here looks familiar."

"What do you mean?"

"I'm not sure if I know how to get home from here."

"Neither am I," he said.

TWENTY-FOUR

The next morning he got a pry bar from the barn, carried the knapsack out to the woods. He leapt the creek carefully, made his way through the willows. When he was about two hundred yards from the house, he found the blackberry tangle that was his landmark. He stood in one spot and turned slowly, watching the ground, until he spotted the cement well cap, half hidden in the undergrowth.

He dropped the knapsack and squatted. Using the pry bar, he tore away vines, then wedged the forked end below the lip of the cap. The concrete grated as he pushed on the bar. When the cap shifted slightly, he sat down in the dirt and used his boot heels to push it away from the opening.

The well had been dry for as long as he could remember. Much of it was caved in now and it was only ten feet at its deepest. Bricks from the shaft wall littered the dirt below.

He lay flat on the ground and reached in. When his fingers found the loose bricks in the wall, he began to pull them out one by one and stack them beside him. By the fourth brick, he'd exposed the hollow space he knew was there, a natural cubbyhole formed by a rock shelf. He lowered the knapsack in and pushed it through. When it was wedged tight, he replaced the bricks.

When he was finished, he stood and brushed himself off, then pushed and prodded the well cap back into place with his feet. He picked up the pry bar and headed back to the house.

"Talk to me," Ray said. "Reconstruct."

Harry sat back in the chair, adjusted his sling. Ray had his feet up on the desk, the window behind him open to the sounds of traffic. It felt like old times.

"Eddie Fallon sells drugs," Harry said.

"Surprise."

"More than we thought. He played around a little in the past, a deal here, a deal there. Then earlier this year he met Paulie Andelli and friends."

"A real entrepreneur, this Fallon. Go on."

"He makes a few small deals, moving stuff through the clubs, people he knows. Everybody makes out. Eventually Andelli starts putting pressure on him to stop fooling around, move into the big leagues. So he does, little by little."

"You know all this for a fact?"

"Some of it. The rest isn't hard to figure out. It all falls into place."

"Okay, what then?"

"Fallon's torn. Both the clubs and the restaurant are losing money, so what he's bringing in on the side is a big help. But now suddenly he's moving with a different class of people. He's not a big fish in a small pond anymore. He has to keep watching his back. So Andelli introduces him to Dunleavy."

"You're losing me. Dunleavy was in with the Scarpettis?"

"Maybe. They had to at least know who he was, his background."

"Wesniak would have an aneurysm if he heard all this. You think Dunleavy was with them when he was still a trooper?"

"Who knows? My guess is he knew a couple of them. After he got back from Florida, could be he offered them his services. Maybe he knew some wise guys down there, gave him an introduction. But there are a lot of crews that got burned in the past by an ex-cop who, it turned out, wasn't so ex after all. So maybe they kept him around and steered him Fallon's way, to see what happened."

"I'm sure he passed the test with flying colors," Ray said.

"Yeah, but for Dunleavy, working for Fallon is just another step on the ladder. He's proving to Andelli and the rest of the Scarpettis that he's fit for better things. He's smarter than Fallon—and tougher—and they both know it."

"So Fallon's in bed with the Eye-Ties and he hires Dunleavy at their suggestion?"

"Looks like it."

"That sounds like a foolish position to be in. For Fallon, I mean."

"Thing of it is, now he's connected. If he needs help, if he needs some muscle, all he has to do is make a phone call. Andelli sends a couple people down and at the same time they keep an eye on Paulie's interests, let him know what their new friend is doing, who he's talking to."

"Those names you gave me on the phone this morning. Were they the ones at the Rip Tide?"

"Yeah."

"Well, let's take a look." Ray picked up a sheaf of faxes, took a pair of reading glasses from his shirt pocket, put them on.

"Between the first names you gave me and the registration of that Buick, my friend at OC was able to come up with a couple probables. No pictures, though, so we won't know for sure."

"Let's hear it."

"Vincent Perna, known as 'Vincent the Bear,' also known as 'Big Vince'—I love this shit—also known as 'The "V,"' Forty-eight years old, did three years in Rahway in the seventies for a truck hijacking at Port Newark. He's been with Paulie's crew since he got out of prison. A handful of arrests since, no convictions."

"How about the other one?"

"Thomas Anthony Rego, otherwise known as 'Tommy T.' Twenty-six. Two arrests, one in 1994 for drunken driving, one in 1996 for aggravated assault and terroristic threats. No convictions. He and Perna are both on the books as employees of Christo Waste Hauling."

"Andelli's ambassadors to the private sector," Harry said. "Keeping an eye on their new partner."

"That's what I'd guess. Paulie's not stupid, he knows he's at risk dealing with someone like Fallon. Loan-sharking, gambling, is one thing. Moving weight through an amateur is another. That's thirty years in Marion on a federal pop, maybe more. It's got to make him nervous."

"Maybe he's not so smart after all."

"Dope has always been Paulie's thing—heroin, coke, whatever. It shifts. Whatever's making money at a particular time, Paulie's there. But when the Scarpettis were around, they always kept him in the back room, even though he was making them rich. Now, with the brothers out of the picture . . ."

"The back-room business is in the front room."

"Practically out in the street. Paulie's experience is paying off. He has a taste for the business and he's not going to let anyone scare him away from it. But I'm betting he has a short reign."

"Why?"

"Anybody who lets himself be photographed hugging somebody he's selling drugs to isn't going to be around very long. There are too many people watching him, waiting for him to fuck up. In the meantime, of course, he's making money hand over fist."

"That's what he needed Fallon for, I guess. A new outlet."

"More than that. With somebody like Fallon, who's a halfway legitimate businessman, it opens up other avenues of opportunity. They can move cash into the clubs and the restaurant, launder money back and forth. A man like Fallon would be very attractive to somebody like Paulie Andelli. They're made for each other. Fallon gets a steady supply of cash and a little muscle behind him. Andelli gets an outlet for his drugs and a place to hide the profits. Everybody makes out."

"Until Andelli starts pushing Fallon to move more stuff than he can handle."

"I think that's where your friend came in. You want to tell me what happened there?"

"Bobby's broke. He's barely getting by on what he makes. He finds out his wife's pregnant and he's worried whether or not they can afford it. Then somebody he works with comes to him with a deal: help him raise some front money, get a big payday at the back end."

"Cortez?"

"They'd done some business in the past, little stuff. But Cortez was the one with the connections. He was the one who was hooked up with Fallon. Then, one day, Fallon wants Cortez to up the ante. He wants him to take a lot at once, a whole kilo."

"The pressure from Paulie is rolling downhill."

"So he goes to Bobby, who starts to think that maybe it's not such a bad idea. He can make this one deal, earn enough money to start over."

"I've heard that before."

"In the meantime, Cortez has worked out a way to get rid of the whole thing at once, through a cousin who's a biker. They come up with the front money, give it to Fallon, get the smack. Then Cortez and his cousin wind up in a car trunk."

"Bikers?"

"Maybe. Could be them, could be somebody else who realized he was dealing with a bunch of fuckups who were in over their heads. Bobby and Jimmy were easy targets. Anybody could have taken them off."

"So your friend gets left holding the bag?"

"Suddenly he's out his front money, he's lost the dope, and he owes Fallon the balance, which he most definitely does not have."

"Is that what all this was about? From the beginning?"

Harry nodded.

"I hate to say it, Harry . . ."

"I know, I know."

". . . but he had it coming. He's a *dope* dealer, for Christ's sake. First time, last time, doesn't matter. He's a dealer."

"I couldn't leave him in that situation if there was something I could do to help him."

"You should have cut him loose, let him solve his own problems."

"Maybe. But I couldn't."

"And look where it got you."

"We all make our decisions," Harry said. "For better or worse. Then we figure out ways to live with them."

"Sometimes we don't get the luxury."

"The luxury?"

"Of living with them."

Harry shrugged. There was nothing to say to that.

TWENTY-FIVE

On the way home, he stopped at a pay phone, called Wiley's number. On the sixth ring, a voice that wasn't Wiley's said, "Yeah?" He hung up.

A full moon that night and no sleep. He tossed and turned, the ache in his arm weak but constant. He thought about the Percocet in the medicine cabinet.

When pale light filled the windows, he wrote off the night as a lost cause. He pushed away the sheets and lay there, listening to the fan creak above him, the singing of the birds outside. He could smell her perfume, taste her on his lips. He rose, tired and aching and hopeful, to meet the day.

He spent the morning and afternoon in a post-insomnia fog. Around three, he went into the backyard and did one-armed push-ups in the grass, trying to clear his head. But the movement only made him dizzy and, after the fifth one, he lost his balance and fell painfully onto his left arm. He rolled onto his back, looked up at the sky, feeling his heart thumping in his chest.

By dusk, his arm was throbbing with a deep, damp pain that seemed to stretch to his shoulder. He finished the TV dinner he'd heated up, went up to the bathroom, and got the bottle of Percocet from the medicine cabinet. He took it downstairs, broke a tablet in half, washed it down with a glass of tap water.

Stretched out on the couch, the TV on, he thought about the heroin in the well shaft, why he had taken it and what he would do with it now. In the back of his mind, he had considered it a bargaining chip, a trade-off to help get Cristina clear, to force Fallon to choose one or the other. But it felt strange having it here, in this place. And he knew there was no way he could turn it over to Wesniak without raising more questions than he wanted to answer.

He thought about just slicing open the bags, shaking them empty into the well, then putting the hose in there, running the water and leaving it on. Washing it all away forever.

Halfway through the national news, he was drifting, his limbs heavy, his eyelids fluttering. Vaguely aware of the remote control slipping from his fingers, he closed his eyes and let the waves take him.

The sound of footsteps on the porch.

He woke instantly, instinctively. The room was dark except for the TV's blue glow. A shadow passed by the front window.

He sat up slowly, reached over to the end table, and slid open the drawer. The .38 was there, loaded now. He took it out, eased off the safety. The remote fell from his lap, clattered to the floor.

There was a loose floorboard on the porch, directly in front of the door, and he heard it creak now. He got up, the .38 at his side. There were two hard raps at the door.

He crossed to the side window and parted the curtains. In the light from the barn, he saw a red El Camino parked in the driveway.

Another knock, then a familiar voice called, "Harry, you there?"

He put the .38 in the sling, went to the door, unlocked and opened it. Bobby was standing on the porch.

"Hey, slick," Bobby said, and then he saw the sling and cast. "What the fuck . . ."

"Come on in. Don't stand there on the porch."

Harry shut and locked the door behind him.

"You shouldn't be up here," he said.

"What happened?"

"It had nothing to do with you. It was a personal beef between me and Fallon. I got stupid."

"Personal beef? What are you talking about?"

"I fucked up. That's all. It's over. Go on, sit down. Let me turn on a light."

Bobby stayed where he was. When Harry switched on the end table lamp, he stepped closer, looked into his face.

"I can still see the bruises," he said. "Tell me what happened."

Harry shut off the TV, sat down in the chair.

"Everything's like I told you on the phone," he said. "We're settled with Fallon. This was something else. Sit down, for Christ's sake."

Bobby hesitated, then perched on the edge of the couch.

"Who did it?"

"Drop it. It's over. What are you doing here?"

"I didn't like the way you sounded on the phone. I thought something was up. I guess I was right."

"You drive that thing all the way up here?"

"It belongs to Rich, my brother-in-law. I couldn't get a flight."

"How long did it take you?"

"About nine hours, straight through. We're not going to talk around this, you know."

"The state police were here yesterday, asking questions. It's not a good thing for you to be around right now."

"Fuck that. What happened?"

Harry didn't answer.

"Was it that woman?"

"Like I said. It had nothing to do with you."

"Then it was that woman?"

"You could say that."

"You were seeing her?"

"Yeah."

"And he found out?"

Harry nodded.

"That son of a bitch."

"Enough. It's over. Everybody's square. Forget about Fallon, forget about Jimmy, forget about this whole mess. What happened to me was my own fault, no one else's."

"Are you still seeing her?"

"Yes."

Bobby shook his head slowly, looked at the floor.

Harry got up, went into the kitchen. He put the .38 in a counter drawer, got two Coronas from the refrigerator. He opened them, brought them back out.

"I wasn't kidding about the state police," he said.

Bobby took a beer.

"Do they know about me?"

"Not yet. And if we play it right, they never will. They'll lose interest in this eventually, if enough time passes without anything new coming up. That's why I wanted you away from here." He sat back down.

"There are some things I need to do," Bobby said. "I have to get some papers from the house, pick up some more clothes."

"You can do all that. But you should get yourself back on the road as soon as possible."

"You're not going to tell me what happened, are you?"

Harry shook his head, drank beer.

"And it's really over?"

"Except for the investigation into Cortez's death. And after they've hit the wall enough times on that, they'll put it on the back burner, shove it into a cold case file. That's how it works."

"I don't know what to tell Janine."

"Don't tell her anything. In a while, when this thing is healed, I'll come down to visit. Like I said, what happened to me was my fault, not yours."

"You expect me to believe that?"

"You should, because it's true. Someday I'll tell you about it. But not tonight."

Bobby drank beer, watched him.

"One of the things I was planning to do was take you out for a drink."

"Not a good idea. It's better if no one sees us out in public together for a while."

"Well, shit . . ." Bobby thought for a minute. "Then the least we can do is get a six-pack, go for a night run, see what's biting. Might be the last time for a while."

"We could do that."

Bobby got up.

"Then come on, slick. Move your ass. The fish are waiting."

They were trolling slowly, two lines out and baited for blues. Bobby was at the wheel. A mile away, the shore was an unbroken string of lights.

"So just what is it you're doing down there?" Harry said.

"Rich is a foreman with a construction crew out of Durham. He's agreed to take me on for a while. The pay's good and there're houses going up all over the place. If you know how to swing a hammer, you can get a job. Everything's new down there. Up here, it's over."

"You might be right."

"That beer cold yet?"

Harry ducked into the cabin, got two Coronas out of the small galley refrigerator. He looked for a bottle opener, opened and closed drawers in the sink unit. In the third one was the Glock, half hidden by a nautical chart. He looked at it, closed the drawer again. In the fourth one, he found an opener.

He popped the caps, carried the beers back up. Bobby took one, drank from it, and nestled the bottle into the cup holder beside him.

"Thanks."

Harry sipped his own beer, looked out the windscreen. Their bow wave was luminous in the moonlight.

"You should stay at the farm tonight," he said. "It'll be better. In the morning we'll go over to the house together, get what you need to get."

"All right."

Bobby took a box of Marlboros from the pocket of his denim jacket. He got one out, lit it, cupping his hand around the lighter. He blew smoke out, the cigarette dangling from his lips, adjusted their course slightly.

"We may need to go farther out." He gestured at the lights of a party boat on the horizon. "They're still moving. When they hit a school, they'll stop. That's how we'll know. When that happens I'll swing around behind them, see what we can get."

He touched the throttle and the noise of the engines changed pitch almost imperceptibly. They chugged on, the lights of the shore at their back now.

"This woman," Bobby said. His face was bathed in the green glow of the instrument panel.

"What about her?"

"You took a lot of chances for her, didn't you?"

Harry didn't answer.

"She worth it?"

"You're the second person to ask me that. Yes, she's worth it."

Bobby nodded. "That's good. She feel the same way about you?"

"I think so."

The party boat had slowed, was looming larger in front of them now, light staining the water around it. Bobby throttled back.

"You have no idea," he said, "about how I feel about what happened. I wouldn't know how to tell you, where to start."

"Ancient history. Forget it."

"You helped me get out of something I had just about given up hope of ever getting out of. I thought it was over, man. I thought I was done."

He exhaled smoke and the wind carried it away.

"If it wasn't for you," Bobby said, "we wouldn't have had this chance, Janine and I."

"You would have done the same for me."

"Would I?"

Harry looked at him.

"Maybe I would have. I hope I would have. But I've been finding out as I get older, man, you never know what you're capable of, do you? What you think, what you want, what you pretend . . . it's all bullshit. You never know what you're going to do until the time comes. And then it's too late."

By midnight, they'd caught six blues. Harry was relegated to watching as Bobby reeled them in, worked the hooks out of their jaws, careful to keep his fingers clear of the sharp ridges of teeth. After he'd put the last fish in the cooler, they heard the party boat start its engines again. It swung south and gained speed, moving away from them, running lights glowing fainter in the darkness.

"They'll give it a few more hours," Bobby said. "See if they can get on top of another school. But we've got more than enough here. We'll cook a couple tomorrow and you can put the rest in your freezer."

Bobby started the engine, asked Harry to take the wheel, and then brought in all four lines, stowed the poles. When he was done, he got two more beers from the cabin, put one on the engine housing beside Harry.

"It's the little things you miss," he said. He took a swig of beer. "The things you take for granted, until they're gone. Like this."

Harry pointed them toward the lights of the shore, spray breaking over the bow. He saw the first of the channel buoys, steered toward it, taking them home.

At the marina, Bobby locked up the boat and they carried the cooler to the El Camino, stowed it in the bed. Harry could feel the fatigue catching up with him as they drove home on Route 33, heading west. He leaned against the door, felt himself drifting off. Bobby drove in silence, the radio on low, and Harry rolled down the window, hoping the night air would keep him awake.

He was still drifting in the valley between sleep and waking when Bobby turned into the driveway and up the gravel slope. He steered into the side yard, the headlights flashing across the Saturn and the barn beyond.

"You look like you're about done," Bobby said. "Go on inside. I'll get the cooler."

He shut off the engine, killed the headlights. Harry realized then that the yard was pitch black. The security light above the barn was out.

The gun came through the open window, touched the side of his head.

"Get out of the car," Vincent Perna said.

TWENTY-SIX

Harry didn't move. he turned to Bobby, saw a figure beyond him, another gun. Bobby's hands were flat and motionless on top of the wheel.

"Come on," Perna said. He reached in with his other hand, tugged up on the stem of the lock, pulled the door open. The interior light flashed on.

"Let's go, assholes," the figure outside Bobby's window said.

Perna backed away from the car, gun still up, as Harry pushed the door wide, swung his legs out. He stepped out of the car, right hand up. He heard Bobby's door open behind him.

"In the house," Perna said, gesturing with the gun. Harry saw it was a Ruger automatic, a nine-millimeter. He started around the front of the El Camino, saw that Bobby was out of the car as well, Tommy Rego behind him. He wore the same yellow warm-up suit Harry had seen him in at the boxing match.

Perna's gun touched the small of his back.

"Walk," he said.

The four of them started toward the house. As they neared the porch, the living room lights went on.

"You first," Perna said, and Harry went up the steps. The front door was ajar. Perna shouldered him through it and into the living room.

Dunleavy stood in front of the fireplace, arms folded. He wore a gray sport jacket and black slacks, and Harry could see the edge of the holster on his right hip. In the center of the floor was a ladderback chair that belonged in the kitchen.

"I thought we were going to end up waiting here all night," Dunleavy said.

Perna touched him with the gun again.

"Go sit on the couch," he said.

He did as he was told, saw Bobby come in behind him, hands up, face drained of blood. Rego held a long-barreled Colt revolver with a ventilated rib pointed at his spine.

"You're Fox, aren't you?" Dunleavy said. "Lucky coincidence. I don't think we've met. Your timing ain't worth shit, though."

"What do you want?" Bobby said.

"Shut the fuck up," Rego said.

"What do I want?" Dunleavy said. "Nothing from you, ace. You just happen to be in the wrong place at the wrong time."

Perna closed the front door, leaned against it. Tucked into his waistband was the butt-end of a pistol with mother-of-pearl grips. Ray's .38.

Dunleavy pointed at the kitchen chair.

"Over there," he said, and Rego gave Bobby an open-handed push that propelled him forward. He caught his balance, turned quickly. Rego pointed the Colt at his face, barely three feet separating them.

"Try it," Rego said. "Go ahead."

Bobby lowered his hands, backed up until his thighs touched the chair. He sat down slowly.

Harry looked around. Rego was about six feet from him, Perna farther away. There was no way he could move from the couch without both of them having time to fire.

"I want to make one thing clear," Dunleavy said. "I don't give a shit about your banging Fallon's wife. In fact, nobody does, except Fallon. But business, that's something different."

"I paid you," Bobby said.

Dunleavy looked at him, smiled, and shook his head.

"You didn't pay me, ace. It wasn't my dope you were selling."

"Harry's got nothing to do with this."

"Oh, no?" Dunleavy said. "Pretty hard to buy that at this point."

Harry looked at Bobby, met his glance, kept his own expression blank, willing him to calm down.

"I wasn't sure how to play this until now," Dunleavy said. "To make this happen with the minimal fuss. But I feel like there's an opportunity here I should take advantage of. Tommy, do me a favor? Look around, see if you can find some tape or something. Electrician's tape is fine, anything that's strong."

Rego nodded, went into the kitchen.

"You know, Harry," Dunleavy said, "I was hoping we weren't going to run into each other again. But you just couldn't leave it alone, could you?"

"What is it you want?"

Rego came back out with a roll of duct tape. Dunleavy gestured at Bobby.

Rego put the Colt on the mantelpiece. Dunleavy dug into his pants pocket, came up with a small penknife. Rego held up his hand, caught it. He went behind the chair, started peeling away a strip of tape.

"Don't do anything stupid," Harry said. "Nobody has to get hurt here. Just tell me what you want." Knowing what the answer was.

Dunleavy swept back the edge of his jacket, took a snub-nosed .38 with walnut grips from the holster. He opened the cylinder, shook the shells into his left palm. He dropped them into his jacket pocket, held up a single shell between thumb and forefinger. He slid it into a chamber, spun the cylinder and closed it.

"I just want to make sure we're properly motivated here," he said.

"If it's more money you want—" Bobby said.

"Shut up," Rego said. "Hold still."

He began to tape Bobby's right wrist to the chair arm, passing the roll under and over. After four loops, the silver swathes reached almost to his elbow. Rego opened the penknife, sawed through the tape, patted down the end, and started on the other arm.

"Legs too, I think," Dunleavy said.

Rego cut off longer strips, the noise of the unreeling tape loud in the room. He bound Bobby's feet to the chair legs, then stepped away.

"One more piece," Dunleavy said. He held up his left hand, finger and thumb about four inches apart. Rego cut another strip.

"Just stick it on the back of the chair for now."

Rego put the roll of tape on the mantelpiece, picked up the Colt again.

"It's getting late," Perna said. "Let's cut the bullshit and wrap this up."

"Exactly what I'm doing," Dunleavy said. He put the .38 back in its holster, went over to stand behind Bobby's chair.

"I can get more money," Bobby said. "It'll take a couple of days but I can get it."

Dunleavy ignored him.

"We ran into your buddy Wiley a little earlier tonight," he said to Harry.

"That so?" Harry said.

"Yeah. He didn't show up for work today. We had to go looking for him. Wasn't home, either, and his suitcase and some of his clothes were gone. Didn't look good."

"What's that got to do with me?"

"You want to play this out, huh? Okay, we'll play."

He pulled the strip of tape from the back of the chair.

"Turns out he'd tried to blow town. What he should have done was haul ass and not look back. Sounds easy enough, doesn't it? But some people are just born fuckups, I guess. Nothing you can do for them. It's their destiny."

He reached around with his left hand, cupped Bobby's jaw. Bobby twisted his head away, but Dunleavy pulled it back, held it there. Harry felt himself inching forward on the couch, tasted the beer and bile rising inside him.

"Stay there," Perna said. The muzzle of the Ruger lifted slightly.

"Relax," Dunleavy said and slapped the tape over Bobby's lips, pressed it into place, let go of his jaw. Bobby began to thrash, cracked the back of his head on the chair. The legs squealed on the hardwood floor. Dunleavy held the chair in place with both hands to keep it from going over.

Bobby's face was reddening, panic and anger bright in his eyes. Dunleavy put a hand on his shoulder as if to calm him.

"Problem was," he said, "Wiley had a package that didn't belong to him, something he hadn't paid for yet. So we look all over. No sign of it. But I have a hunch he'll be back, so we stick around. Come six o'clock, who comes walking through the door? Turns out he had an airline ticket to Los Angeles, but his flight wasn't until nine that night. First one he could get. So instead of sitting tight in the airport waiting for the plane, like he should have, he decides to make a last trip home for something he forgot. You know what it was? A high school football trophy. Can you believe that? That's what I mean about some people being born fuckups. But not you, Harry, right?"

"Why are you telling me this?"

"The point of this story, if you haven't already guessed, is that Wiley told us you slapped him around, took the package from him, and told him to get out of town."

"He told you he gave me something?"

" 'Took' was the way he put it. Might be he was lying. If so, I have to give him credit, because he stuck to his story. And we didn't make it easy on him. The other possibility, of course, is that all three of you were in this together. Personally, I doubt it. I can't see you hooking up with a numbnuts like Wiley. But the thing is, either way, it leads back to you. Now, we could spend the next hour and a half tearing your house apart, or you could just tell us where it is and save everybody—including yourself—a lot of aggravation."

"What is it I'm supposed to have?"

"Wrong answer."

He looked at Rego. "Tommy, one more thing. Go upstairs, get me a pillowcase from the bed?"

"What for?"

"You'll see."

Harry heard his footsteps on the stairs. After a few minutes, he came clumping back down with a white pillowcase.

"Thanks." Dunleavy took the pillowcase and looked back at Harry.

"You have a pretty good idea what's going to happen here, don't you?" he said.

Harry didn't answer.

"Okay, then," Dunleavy said. "Your way."

He shook the pillowcase open. Bobby was craning his neck, trying to see what was happening behind him, when Dunleavy worked the pillowcase over his head. Bobby began to thrash again, the front chair legs lifting off the floor, then coming down hard. Dunleavy held the chair still, took the .38 back out. He held it near Bobby's right ear, muzzle pointing at the floor, thumbed the hammer back until it locked.

"Can you hear that?" he said to Bobby. "You know what that is?"

He touched the muzzle to the pillowcase and Bobby twisted his head away. Dunleavy put his left hand on his shoulder, squeezed it reassuringly.

"I know what you're thinking, Harry," he said. "You're thinking, 'I'm dead anyway, why give him the satisfaction?' Right? And that's pretty good logic, I guess, but it's selfish too. You're not thinking about your buddy here."

He brushed the muzzle of the .38 along the side of Bobby's head, stopped where the temple would be.

"And believe me," he said, "you can spare him an awful lot of anxiety."

He squeezed the trigger and the hammer fell. The click of the empty chamber was loud in the room.

No one moved or spoke. Dunleavy took the gun away.

"Have to admit, I cheated there," he said. "I knew it was an empty chamber. Next time I promise not to look."

Acid sourness rushed into Harry's throat. He swallowed. "Go fuck yourself," he said.

Perna laughed. Dunleavy raised an eyebrow.

"Maybe we're not communicating," he said. "If that's the case, it's a shame. Because we've got all night. We could take our time doing you both, then go on and find it on our own anyway."

"What makes you think it's here, whatever it is?"

"Don't disappoint me. We know it's here. You haven't had time to sell it or move it anywhere except somewhere close. Don't wrack your brains trying to come up with an out here, Harry. You don't have a lot of options."

He eased back the hammer of the .38 again, touched the muzzle to the rear of Bobby's head. Rego moved away a step, out of the line of fire.

"Trust me, Harry," Dunleavy said. "If there's a bullet in here, at this range, this is a sight you don't want to see."

"Stop it," Harry said. "Let him go."

"No chance. Tell me where it is."

"It's not in the house. I hid it."

"Bullshit," Dunleavy said and squeezed the trigger. The gun clicked empty.

Bobby doubled in his chair as much as the tape would allow. Rego let out his breath.

"That time," Dunleavy said, "I didn't know."

He cocked the gun again.

"I hid it in the woods, in an old well. I can take you there. Let him go."

"Why should I believe you?"

"I'll take you there."

Dunleavy smiled, put the .38 to Bobby's head again.

"Maybe he's telling the truth," Rego said.

Dunleavy pulled the trigger.

Empty chamber.

"Goddamn you," Harry said.

Bobby's right leg began to vibrate. A wet stain blossomed in the crotch of his jeans, spread down his left thigh.

"Stop this," Harry said. "I'll get it for you. It's in an old well, about two hundred yards from the house."

"I'll go with him," Perna said.

"No," Dunleavy said. "He stays here."

"It's past the willows. On the other side of the creek. There's a cement well cap there, you can't miss it."

"I'll go," Rego said. Then to Harry: "Tell me exactly where it is."

Harry described the area, the blackberry tangle and the chamber beneath the lip of the well cap.

"Flashlight," Rego said.

"Under the sink. There's a pry bar there too. You'll need it."

Rego went into the kitchen and they heard him rooting through the cabinet. The back door squeaked open.

They waited in silence.

"Go stand by the back door," Dunleavy said to Perna. "Have him call to you if he finds it." He opened the .38, reloaded it with the shells from his jacket pocket.

Perna went into the kitchen. The only sound in the room was Bobby's breathing, loud beneath the pillowcase.

"Now, there," Dunleavy said. "Wasn't that easier?" He held the .38 at his side.

Rego yelled from the backyard, too far away for them to make out.

"He says he found it," Perna called from the kitchen.

"Good," Dunleavy said. He took a step away from the chair. Harry watched him, knew what was coming.

More from Rego.

Perna came back into the living room.

"Got it," he said. "Looks like it's all there."

Dunleavy looked at Perna, then nodded at Harry. He cocked the .38 again, stepped away, and pointed it at the left side of Bobby's head.

"Got a real one for you this time," he said. And pulled the trigger.

Harry heard the shot, saw Bobby's head snap to the side. Perna had the Ruger up, was aiming, and Harry dove from the couch at him. The Ruger went off as Harry slammed into him, his right hand going for the grip of the .38. He batted at the Ruger with his cast and got his finger around the trigger of the .38, squeezing it as he twisted the gun inward. He heard the click of the empty chamber and then Perna pushed him away, trying to bring the Ruger up between them, and Harry squeezed the trigger again and the .38 went off.

He stumbled back, heard cloth rip, and suddenly he was holding the gun and Perna was falling. He turned, raising the .38, pointed it at Dunleavy and squeezed the trigger.

Dunleavy fired first. Harry heard the bullet thrum past him. His own shot blew slate from the mantelpiece. He stepped back, aiming, slipped on something, and sat down hard just as Dunleavy fired again, the bullet passing over his head. He rolled away and Dunleavy adjusted his aim, fired twice more, the shots sounding as one.

Splinters erupted from the floor next to Harry's head, upholstery flew from the arm of the couch. He hooked the coffee table with his legs, toppled it onto its side for cover, and fired twice above it. Dunleavy's answering shot punched a hole through the center of the table and into the floor near Harry's groin. Then came the click of Dunleavy's gun, the hammer falling on the spent chamber.

He kicked the table at Dunleavy's legs, raised the .38. Dunleavy was already at the front door. Harry fired, blew out a window. Then Dunleavy had the door open and was through it, onto the porch and running.

Harry rolled to his feet. He was standing in blood. Perna lay faceup on the floor beside him, a black-and-red hole below his left eye. Harry looked to the kitchen. He tossed away the empty .38, picked up Perna's Ruger. It was slick with blood.

He moved quickly to the hallway between the living

room and kitchen, pressed himself against the wall and raised the Ruger, bracing it against the doorframe. A drop of blood fell from the barrel, spattered the linoleum. He aimed at the open back door.

He heard feet on the steps, then the screen door swung open and Rego filled the doorway. The knapsack hung from his left hand, the Colt in his right. The flashlight was tucked beneath his left arm.

"Stop where you are," Harry said.

Rego looked at him. The screen door thunked shut behind him.

"Put the gun on the counter," Harry said. He could feel his arm start to tremble, steadied it. Rego looked past him into the living room.

"On the counter," Harry said again.

The knapsack began to swing lightly, side to side. And Harry saw then what he was thinking. He'd toss the knapsack to his left as a distraction, then raise and fire the Colt. Harry tightened his grip on the Ruger, centered the front sight on the zipper of Rego's warm-up suit, where the white T-shirt peeked out.

"Don't do it, Tommy," he said.

Rego smiled. "Man," he said. "You don't even know me."

He tossed the knapsack, and the Colt came up and Harry squeezed the Ruger's trigger twice. The Colt went off, wood exploding from the corner of the doorway above Harry's head, showering him with splinters. Rego fell back through the screen door, and the Colt and the flashlight hit the kitchen floor at the same time.

Silence. Acrid gunsmoke hung in the air. Harry slowly left the doorway, Ruger out in front of him, went to the back door.

The screen was stuck open, Rego's right leg keeping it from closing. He was lying on the concrete steps, left leg bent beneath him, eyes open and looking at nothing. The holes in his chest were about four inches apart, just below the collarbone on the left side of his chest. The T-shirt was already turning red.

Harry backed away, kicked the Colt, sent it skittering

across the floor and under the kitchen table. He raced back into the living room. Wind was lifting the curtains on the shattered window. He hit the switch to light up the front yard, kicked the door open, went onto the porch, the Ruger raised.

The yard was empty.

Halfway down the driveway, an engine exploded into life, and a car pulled out from where it had been hidden in the trees. Gravel flew as it swung toward the road, lights off. He sighted down the barrel at the back of the car, fired twice, heard glass break. The car flew down the driveway, bottomed out when it hit the road, turned left, tires squealing.

He lowered the Ruger, went back inside.

The pool of blood around Perna was wider now. He stepped around it, tossed the gun onto the couch, went to Bobby.

He was slumped in the chair, his right foot tapping a staccato rhythm on the floor. The left side of the pillowcase was soaked with blood and there was a burned black hole where the muzzle had made contact. Blood was flowing from beneath the pillowcase, down onto his jacket and shirt, soaking his pants, puddling on the chair. Too much blood.

He gingerly righted Bobby's head, slipped the pillowcase up and off.

Bobby's eyes were open and staring. The left side of his head was a mass of matted hair and torn flesh, the area around the wound already swelling. There were bubbles of blood under his nose.

He knelt beside him, wrenched open his shirt, sending buttons flying. He put his left ear above the heart, listened.

At first he thought it was just his imagination, the confusion of hope. He held his breath and the sound came again, beneath the blood, beneath the flesh. A faint muffled thump.

The fingers of Bobby's right hand spasmed and closed. Harry stood, began to pry the edges of the tape off his face, peeled it away. Bobby's mouth sagged open as if he were about to speak, but only blood came out.

Harry wadded up the pillowcase, held it against the

wound. He cradled him, willing the bleeding to stop, the life force to stay inside. Bobby's right arm began to tremble again, the fingers stretching.

Harry held him tight, rocked him like a crying child, but the soft sobs he heard were his own.

TWENTY-SEVEN

Red, blue and yellow lights circled the walls. The curtains on the shattered window moved in the breeze.

Harry sat on the couch, looked at the chair in the middle of the room, shards of duct tape still hanging from its arms and legs. The back and seat were dark with blood.

The room was full of people who moved around him as if he weren't there. No one spoke to him.

The puddle of blood below Perna's body was now four feet across and drying. Perna's slacks were dyed red from the wound in his thigh, but Harry could see that the shot that killed him had gone through his face and out the back of his head. One of Dunleavy's stray .38 rounds. There was blood on the wall beyond.

After he'd called 911, he'd picked up the knapsack and the flashlight, his hands wet with Bobby's blood, not wanting to leave him but knowing what he had to do. He'd tripped twice in the yard, dropped and almost lost the flashlight, before he found the well cap. It was still ajar, the pry bar beside it. He'd pushed the knapsack into the hole in the shaft wall, shoved the cap back with his feet. Then he'd tossed the flashlight and the pry bar as far as he could into the woods. He was back in the house just as he heard the first sirens.

A plainclothes Monmouth County detective named Nolan was standing by the front door, talking to someone on the porch. After a moment he stepped aside and Wesniak came into the room, Eagleman behind him.

Wesniak looked at Harry, then turned back to Nolan. Eagleman greeted one of the state troopers in the room.

"Two dead, one wounded," Nolan said. "The other one is on the back steps. The injured one's at Centrastate. No word yet."

"How bad?"

"From what I saw, bad."

Wesniak looked at Harry.

"He the shooter?"

"One of them. To judge from what he told us and the way this place is shot to hell, it got pretty hot in here for a while. Looks like self-defense, though."

"Don't say that until you know it. Why isn't he handcuffed?"

Nolan looked at Harry, then back at Wesniak.

"Well, Lieutenant, it looks to me like he's got a broken arm there. And he's the one who suggested I call you in the first place. He said he used to be with your outfit."

"I know who he is. He should be handcuffed."

"I think we're getting into a jurisdictional situation here."

"No, we're not. He's a witness in an ongoing investigation and possibly a murder suspect. When we leave, he's coming with us. I appreciate your help, Detective, but if you don't put handcuffs on him, I will."

Nolan shrugged, turned to two other county detectives who had drifted closer during the conversation.

"Anyone got a pair?"

"Shit," Eagleman said. "I'll do it." He took a pair of silver handcuffs from his belt.

"Stand up," he said.

Harry stood. Eagleman took his left arm, still in the sling, and tried to maneuver it behind him.

"In front," Wesniak said, patient.

Harry put his hands together, felt the cuffs close tightly around his wrists. Metal rubbed against the edge of his cast.

"Sit down," Wesniak said. Then to Nolan: "Let's talk."

Harry settled back on the couch. Nolan looked at him almost apologetically, followed Wesniak into the kitchen.

"Got yourself into it this time," Eagleman said. Harry ignored him.

A county forensics man began taking pictures of Perna's body. The flashes lit up the room.

After a few minutes, Wesniak and Nolan came out of the kitchen. Wesniak waved Harry in.

"Come on," Eagleman said.

Harry stood and Eagleman caught his right elbow, led him past Nolan and into the kitchen. Perna's blood spotted the linoleum, and he could see the sole of Rego's high-top sneaker still holding the screen door open.

Wesniak pulled out a chair from the table, gestured at it. Harry sat down. Eagleman posted himself in the kitchen door, blocking it. He took a wooden match from his shirt pocket, began to chew on it.

Through the window, Harry could see men with flashlights moving around the backyard.

"So this is what it comes down to," Wesniak said. He pulled out another chair, sat down. "You should have taken my advice."

"Yeah," Harry said softly. "Maybe."

Wesniak looked at Eagleman, pointed at the handcuffs. Eagleman came over with the key, unlocked them, and then went back to his station at the door.

Harry rubbed his left wrist.

"I talked to Detective Nolan," Wesniak said. "He told me about the statement you gave. Ordinarily, the county sheriff's department would run the show with an assist from the Colts Neck cops, but I think I've convinced him he'll need our help. He's going to officially request it later today."

"Meaning?"

"Meaning it's me you've got to deal with here. But you shouldn't be too surprised by that, should you?"

Harry shrugged.

"Nolan's a good man, though," Wesniak said. "Thorough.

He ran checks on everybody. They all had IDs on them, which made it easier."

"Have you talked to the hospital?"

"Nolan called a few minutes ago. Your friend's still in surgery. They won't know anything for a while. Do you know who the other two are?"

"Yes."

"Both pretty bad guys, from what we're hearing. How'd you get the drop on them?"

Harry said nothing.

"They're both connected. Did you know that?"

"I guessed."

"Not that I care, but you should be aware of possible repercussions down the line. Now for the most important thing. You told Nolan the other man was Mickey Dunleavy."

"It was. We exchanged fire, I missed. He went out the front. He had a car hidden in the trees, but I didn't get a good look at it. I fired twice, might have taken out a window. Either of you have a cigarette?"

Wesniak looked at him for a moment, then over at Eagleman. He came away from the door, took a pack of Winstons from his shirt pocket, shook one out. Harry took it. Eagleman fished out a lighter, and Harry leaned forward, put the cigarette to his lips, realized his hand was shaking.

He got the cigarette lit and sat back. The smoke was bitter, stale.

"They found a car," Wesniak said. "In Freehold. It had been stolen earlier in the day. Holes in the back window but no blood on the seats. Looks like you didn't get him."

"Too bad."

"I feel the same way. Dunleavy and I, we've got a history."

"I heard. He's an errand boy for the Scarpettis now. Did you know that?"

"There were rumors. We'd been watching him, off and on, to see where he landed. More a personal thing than an official investigation. We'd heard about him and the Scarpettis. We didn't know for sure."

"It's for sure."

"We're looking for him right now. We'll find him. He's the one who shot Fox?"

Harry inhaled smoke. "Yes."

"So I'm guessing that's the friend whose name you wouldn't give us. The one you were protecting."

"Yes."

"Hell of a job protecting him," Eagleman said.

Wesniak shot him a glance that silenced him, turned back to Harry.

"I won't belabor the obvious," he said. "I don't have to tell you that if you had given us his name, we could have done something for him, prevented this from happening."

"Done something? Like what? Arrest him?"

"He'd have been a damn sight better off than he is at the moment. I think we need to get everything out on the table now. Do you want a lawyer?"

"Am I under arrest?"

"Not yet."

"Will I be?"

"Depends on what you tell me."

Harry nodded, took the cigarette from his mouth, looked at it. He let it burn as he talked. He told them about Fallon, about Bobby. He never mentioned Cristina or his visit to Wiley's house or the knapsack.

Wesniak nodded occasionally but said nothing. When Harry was finished, the ash on his cigarette was near the filter.

"So they just showed up here tonight?" Wesniak said. "Out of the blue? Looking for Fox?"

"They were waiting when we got back."

"Why would they want to kill him if he'd already paid them what he owed?"

"I don't know."

"That beating you took. You got that when you delivered the money?"

"Yes."

"Why?"

"To teach me a lesson, I guess, for getting involved."

"What was Rego doing in the backyard?"

"I don't know. Maybe they sent him around to watch the door. I knew he was out there, though. When the shooting started, I guessed he'd come in through the back. I ran to meet him and he threw down on me. I had Perna's gun."

Wesniak nodded, stood up. He stretched, walked to the window, and looked out into the yard.

"Your friend," he said. "He was the beginning of all this?"

"For me."

"You have any dealings with Fallon or any of these people before?"

"Never."

Wesniak rubbed his neck, turned.

"You two go back to the car," he said. "I need to talk to Nolan for a few minutes."

"What about the cuffs?" Eagleman said.

"Leave 'em off."

Harry stood, took a final pull on the cigarette, dropped it in the sink and ran water on it. Eagleman gestured at him, and Harry followed him out of the kitchen. The men in the living room watched as they walked past and out the front door.

There were ten cars parked at various angles on the lawn, most of them with emergency lights flashing on roofs or dashboards. There was a county crime scene van in the side yard, and a technician was dusting the door handles of the El Camino.

Eagleman led him down the driveway, lights reflecting off the sides of the cars. Radios squawked around them. To the east, the sky was purple with the coming dawn.

A half hour later, he sat in a hard plastic chair in a break room Wesniak had commandeered at the State Police barracks in Holmdel. The knees and calves of his jeans were stiff with blood.

There was a refrigerator, microwave, and coffee station on one side of the room. A handwritten note taped to the refrigerator said: CLEAN UP YOUR OWN MESS.

Eagleman sat down across from Harry at a folding table, slid a Styrofoam cup of steaming coffee toward him.

"There's tea there too," Eagleman said. "Help yourself."

"This is fine."

Harry sipped the coffee. It was bitter and burnt, and the milk and sugar did little to conceal a faint chemical taste. He put the cup down and didn't touch it again.

Wesniak came into the room, shut the door behind him. Harry looked up.

"Fox is still in surgery," Wesniak said. "That's all I know. I called that number you gave me in North Carolina, talked to his wife."

"And?"

"She's going to try to get a flight up today. She asked about you."

Wesniak pulled up a chair, sat down.

"I got the impression," he said, "that she wasn't as surprised as she should have been about what happened. Why would that be?"

"She knows he owed people money, that's all. She didn't know what it was for."

"Sure of that?"

"I don't know what he told her or didn't tell her, but that was always my impression."

"I hope she gives us the same story when we talk to her."

"Leave her alone. She's not involved with this at all."

"It seems to me that one of the problems here is that you're always looking out for other people's welfare when you should be worried about your own. Under other circumstances, that quality might be something to be admired. Right now, all it does is make me think you're still not telling me everything."

"You know all there is to know."

"Is that right? You want to tell us why you were sneaking around Cortez's apartment? There's a woman named Pettimore there who's wondering what happened to you. Apparently she was expecting a phone call."

"You dog, you," Eagleman said.

"You talked to her?" Harry said.

"We did," Wesniak said. "I got the sense that she was trying to protect you in some half-assed fashion."

"I was looking for Cortez, just the way I told you. I went by his apartment, she let me in. I didn't find anything. And I didn't tell her anything."

"You miss the job that much?" Wesniak said. "You need to go around playing detective?"

"You find Dunleavy?"

"Still looking. Spring Lake police picked Fallon up about an hour ago at our request. We'll be going down there to talk to him, along with someone from the OC office, try and rattle his cage a little bit. Chances are they won't be able to hold him very long, though. If we find Dunleavy, we'll try and squeeze him on the Fallon angle."

"Never happen."

"We'll see."

"If you want something to nail Dunleavy with, dig those bullets out of my floor."

"What?"

"The bullets from Dunleavy's gun. Match them against the ones you took out of Cortez and his cousin."

"Why should we do that?"

"Because the more I think about it, the more it makes sense. If it wasn't Dunleavy who killed them, it was one of the other two, maybe Rego. Check his gun too. It was the perfect way for Fallon to work it."

"Maybe I'm missing something here."

"It's simple. I should have guessed it from the beginning. Fallon was overextended. He owed people money. So he set up Bobby and Jimmy Cortez. He got them to front him money, then take some heroin off his hands. They set up their own deal to get rid of it, through Cortez's cousin. Fallon had someone—probably Dunleavy—follow Cortez when he met the cousin to make the transfer. Dunleavy took the money and the heroin and killed them both. Then someone got Cortez's car from his house, loaded the bodies in the trunk, and ditched the car so it would look like he left town."

"You have any proof of that?"

Harry shook his head. "But think about it. It's the only way it makes sense. Fallon got his front money, plus the money Dunleavy took off the cousin, plus the heroin, which he could sell again. Then he put the squeeze on Bobby to pay him for the heroin he lost. It would have worked out perfectly. Fallon gets paid three times for one deal, and when it's over he still has the same amount of heroin he started with. Bobby was an amateur, he didn't know what he was doing. It would have been easy."

"It might make sense, but that doesn't make it true."

"Check the bullets."

Wesniak looked at Eagleman. He nodded, got up and left the room.

"Look at it from Fallon's perspective," Harry said. "Bobby and Cortez weren't connected to anyone, neither was the cousin as far as he knew. If somebody killed them both and set up Bobby, no one would come looking to even the score. It was perfect."

"What about the cousin's people? The ones he was buying for? What if they came looking for their money?"

"That was a chance Fallon had to take. But there was nothing that tied him to it, except Bobby. Fallon was twice removed from the deal at that point."

"If we ever go to trial, you'll have to testify about your part in all this."

"I will."

"And these other things you're telling me. If your friend lives through this, if he recovers, we're going to have to act on it."

"He was shot in the head. Even if he lives . . ."

Wesniak nodded, stood up, walked over to the coffee station.

"You could be right about all this," he said. "I say 'could be.' We'll find out soon. In the meantime, you're not going to be charged."

"Why not?"

Wesniak poured coffee.

"As far as the shootings go, it looks like it happened pretty much the way you said. Nolan was right, self-defense is the only way to read it. You were facing armed intruders, and none of the weapons were yours. Strange that Perna would bring two guns with him, though. I wonder why he thought he needed both."

"I don't know. So you're letting me walk out of here just like that?"

"Would you rather I arrest you?"

Harry watched him.

"It's not like I have a lot of choice." He brought the coffee back to the table and sat down. "If we find Dunleavy and he tells us a different story about what happened there, then that's another issue."

"He's long gone by now."

Wesniak sipped the coffee, sniffed at it, pushed it away.

"Maybe, maybe not. But I promise you this: It may take a while, but we'll get him."

"I guess there's always a first time, right?"

"You're tired. It's been a rough night. I've been trying to keep that in mind. But don't say things to me you'll regret later. If I were you, I'd see about getting a place to stay tonight. You won't be able to get back into your house for a couple of days, maybe longer."

"I'll find a place."

"Good." Wesniak stood up. "Lou will drive you back to your house if you want. That way you can at least get your car. I'll call ahead and clear it."

"That's good of you."

"You're something, Harry, you really are. You should be thanking me instead of busting my hump. You're lucky I'm letting you go."

"Why? Because you want me out there on the street until you find Dunleavy? Because you want to make sure you get him this time, the way you didn't the last?"

"That's part of it."

"You were thinking the same way about me when we first met, weren't you? You thought I was like him."

"At first, maybe. I was wrong. Dunleavy is a different story."

"Why?"

"He used to work for me. His father and I came up together. His father was a good trooper. After he died, I helped his son get into the outfit. He told me it was his dream, to follow his old man. But I was wrong. He wasn't like his old man at all."

"You were the one who went after him. When you found out what was going on, that he was robbing drug dealers."

"I had a responsibility. I helped train him."

"You did a good job."

Wesniak moved toward the door.

"Like I said, Harry, you're tired."

"Maybe so, but not too tired to see what's going on."

"And what's that?"

"You want me out there because you hope he'll take another shot at me. You're not arresting me because I'm no good to you in custody. Right now I'm the only connection you've got to Dunleavy, aren't I? You want to use me to get to him."

Wesniak looked at him for a long moment.

"I'm sorry about what happened," he said. "And that's the last time I'm going to say that. But we're through here. You're free to go. If you want, Lou will give you a ride back to your house. If not, you can call a cab. It doesn't matter to me. As far as I'm concerned, Harry, you're on your own."

He turned down Eagleman's offer of a ride back to Colts Neck. Instead, he had him drop him off at an Exxon station on the Parkway. Harry got two dollars in change from the Pakistani attendant, took it to a pay phone near the vending machines. It was full daylight now, but the receiver was still wet with dew.

He fed change into the phone, called information for the hospital number. He got through to the night nursing supervisor, who told him she was about to go off duty but would see what she could find out. He dropped another twenty cents into the phone while he waited. When she came back on the line, she told him Bobby was still in surgery. He thanked her and hung up.

Beside him, the soda machine hummed. He waited a moment, then dropped two quarters into the phone and dialed another number.

She answered on the second ring.

"Are you all right?" he said.

"Harry," she said, the edge of panic in her voice. "What's going on? The police were here. They took Edward. What's happening?"

"I'll tell you everything later. Has Dunleavy been around? Have you seen him?"

"Not for a day or so. Why? Harry, tell me what's going on."

"Your husband sent some people to my house last night."

She was silent.

"Was he home all night?" he said. "Before the police came?"

"Yes, he's been running around here like a crazy man the past two days. He says we're going on a trip. Harry, are you okay? Are you hurt?"

"A trip? Where?"

"I've been trying to call to tell you. He wants to go to Mexico City. He says he knows some people there. He's trying to pretend it's just a vacation, but I know it's not. He says I need to be ready to leave on short notice, but he won't tell me anything else."

"Get a pen," he said. "Write down these numbers."

He waited for her, then gave her Ray's home and office numbers.

"Leave a message at either of those if you need to reach me," he said. "I won't be home for a few days. If he says anything more about going away, or if he tells you when he wants to leave, let me know. I'll be checking in at both those numbers."

"You never answered me. Were you hurt?"

"No. But some other people were. Stay close to the phone."

"There's something you're not telling me, Harry. What is it? Are they arresting Edward?"

"Probably not. And, unless something changes, I don't think they'll be able to keep him from leaving the country, either. He told you he knows people in Mexico City?"

"Some businessman he's dealt with. Some sort of real estate thing. He's been down there before, but he's never taken me with him."

"Does he have enough money to stay down there indefinitely if he needs to?"

"Maybe. I don't know. I've never seen him act like this before. It's like he's scared of something."

"Be careful. And when he gets back from the police station, watch what you say around him."

"I will."

"Those things I told you, about going away, about taking you. They weren't lies."

"I know."

"We can do it."

"Be careful, Harry."

"I will."

"I love you."

After he hung up, he stood there for a while, watching the morning traffic speed by on the Parkway. Above the trees on the other side of the roadway, he could see a pair of hawks circling slowly. One angled down, dipped and dropped into the woods. It rose again a moment later, something trapped in its claws. He watched the hawk until it was out of sight.

He picked up the phone again, dropped in the last of his change, and called Ray.

TWENTY-EIGHT

Ray couldn't sit still. He prowled the emergency room waiting area, flipped through magazines, looked out the window. Harry sat slumped in a plastic chair, watching a television set mounted on the wall. There was a talk show on, the sound turned down.

He thought of the last time he'd waited in an emergency room. Ray had been there that time too, the night of the burning wires. A lifetime ago.

"I hate this," Ray said. "Waiting. Never got used to it."

The double doors that led to the treatment area hissed open. Harry turned to see a woman in her forties come out, black hair shot with gray, wearing green scrubs beneath a white lab coat. She stopped at the reception desk, spoke with the female nurse's aide there, then turned and looked at him. He stood and she motioned to him. Ray stayed where he was, watched them.

"I'm Dr. Stefano," she said, extending her hand. He took it. "You're here about Robert Fox?"

"Yes."

"Let's go inside where we can talk."

He followed her through the doors and into a long cream-colored corridor. A state trooper stood halfway down the hall, drinking from a take-out coffee cup. He looked at Harry without interest.

She led him down a side hall and into an empty cubicle.

"How'd you break that arm?"

"Somebody did it for me."

"He must not have liked you very much."

"He didn't. What can you tell me about Bobby?"

"Have a seat."

"I'm fine."

"Well, I won't mislead you. He's in ICU right now. He's been out of surgery less than an hour. Dr. Greenfeldt, the chief surgeon, did everything he could. There's nothing we can do now except wait and see how he responds."

"How much damage?"

"Difficult to say at this stage. He's still in coma. What happens in the next twelve hours or so will tell us a lot. He's on a respirator and we'll be watching him every minute. Anything else I told you would only be a guess—and I don't like to guess. I'm sorry."

"Can I see him?"

"Maybe later today if we get him stabilized. We'll have to see how it goes."

"I saw what happened to him. I was there."

"So I heard. Then you know how serious his injury is."

"I'd rather hear it from you."

She sat down in a chair, crossed her legs, and began to rub her right knee.

"Obviously, he's had a massive cranial trauma. How much brain damage there is, we don't know yet. We might not for a while. The bullet passed through his cheekbone, soft palate, and jaw. We found it embedded in the neck muscle and were able to remove it. It missed the spinal column by about an inch. There's a lot of tissue damage and swelling of the brain, as you can imagine."

"Is he going to live?"

"I couldn't possibly answer that. You should know better than to ask."

"Try at least."

"Well, let's just say I think there's a chance. I've seen

people come back from head wounds you wouldn't have thought they could survive. I can tell you that if he gets through the next twenty-four hours, there's a good chance he'll have some sort of recovery."

"Can I ask for an off-the-record opinion?"

"You can ask, but at this point I don't have one. We're watching him closely and we're doing everything we can for him. On the positive side—if there is one—I can tell you that the bullet also narrowly missed the carotid artery, so I guess we can be thankful for that. But I'm not trying to get your hopes up here."

"I know that. I appreciate it."

"Now if you'll excuse me, I have to get back to work."

"Can I call later?"

"Sure. Call the emergency room number, ask for me. I'm on duty until ten this morning. If I'm free, I'll talk to you and tell you what I know. But for now . . ."

"I know. Thank you."

"You don't look so well yourself. I can give you a prescription for some mild sleeping pills, if you like. I might have some samples here. It'll help you rest."

He shook his head. She stood up.

"We'll do our best for him," she said. "That's all I can tell you. It might not seem like much, but it's the truth."

He watched her head back down the corridor. He turned and went out through the automatic doors into the waiting room.

Ray was standing by the reception desk, talking to the aide. He turned away from her when he saw Harry.

They went out into the parking lot without speaking. The morning sun glinted off windshields. When they reached the car, Ray unlocked the driver's side door, looked at Harry over the roof.

"Well?" he said. "How is he?"

"He's dying," Harry said.

• • •

There were still about a half dozen cars in his yard, but the crime scene van was gone. Ray parked in the grass. Nolan, looking tired, met them at the door.

"Wesniak called earlier," he said. "I'll have someone go upstairs with you so you can get what you need."

Ray waited on the porch while Harry went inside. Where Perna's body had been, the floor was stained black with blood, and there were holes gouged in the hardwood where bullets had been dug out. Each hole had been circled with chalk and marked by a folded triangle of paper with a number written on it.

With one of the county men following him, he went upstairs, got an overnight bag from the bedroom closet, and began to fill it with clothes. Nolan was standing at the foot of the stairs when he came back down.

"The Saturn's cleared, as far as we're concerned," he said. "You can take it. We'll have to move a couple cars for you to get out."

He nodded, went out onto the porch. Ray was leaning against the railing, arms folded. A Colts Neck cop came out of the house and went past them, climbed into a cruiser parked behind the Saturn. He started the engine and began to back up.

"Are you okay to drive?" Ray said.

"I think so."

"Follow me back to the house. Edda's already left for work by now. You can sack out for a while. You look like you need it."

Harry went to the Saturn and Ray headed back to his car. In the rearview mirror, Harry watched the Colts Neck cop pull the cruiser up on the lawn and wait.

Harry started the engine, shifted into reverse, and K-turned, his fender swinging within a foot of the cruiser's grille. As he pointed the car toward the road, he was aware of people standing out on the porch, watching him.

Leaving his house to strangers, he followed Ray down the driveway. He didn't look back.

• • •

The next afternoon, they sat on a bench at the end of the hospital corridor, six doors down from Bobby's room. Janine's eyes were red and wet. She clutched a crumpled tissue.

"He doesn't even know I'm there," she said. "I touch him and talk to him, but it's like he's a million miles away."

Harry looked off down the hall to the nurses' station. A security guard was leaning against the counter, joking with the woman at the desk. She began to laugh. An aide pushed a gurney by, wheels squeaking.

"You should go see him, Harry. He'd want you to."

He stood, went over to the window, and looked down at the parking lot two stories below.

"He always looked up to you," she said. "He loved you like a brother."

He put his fingertips against the window, felt the coolness of the glass.

"Go see him, Harry."

The door was closed. He pushed against it and it whispered open into a world of dimness.

The shades had been drawn but sunlight crept in around their edges. He walked toward the bed.

Bobby's head was a mass of bandages, with only his right eye and cheekbone exposed. The eye was closed, the face dark and swollen. A corrugated plastic respirator tube emerged from beneath the bandages and ran to a machine next to the bed.

Beneath the covers, his chest rose and fell almost imperceptibly. The monitoring equipment beside the bed pulsed in time.

He pulled up a chair, brought it close to the bed, and sat down. He touched Bobby's right hand, curled his fingers around it. The hand was slack, the palm cool and moist. He squeezed it gently, felt no response. He closed his eyes and rested his forehead against the aluminum restraining rail.

After a while, he felt Janine come into the room behind him. She touched his shoulder, then moved to the other side of the bed. She took Bobby's left hand in both of hers.

He felt a tremor in the hand he held, a twitch of the fingers. At first, he was unsure if it was real or imagined. He held his breath and it came again, like a radio signal fading as it neared its destination.

He looked at Janine.

"I felt it too," she said.

He loosened his grip, waited.

"He knows," she said. "He knows we're here with him. He's trying to tell us that."

She leaned over and softly kissed the bandaged head.

"I'm here, baby," she whispered. "I'd never leave you alone. You know that."

He felt the tremor again. This time he squeezed back, gently.

"He's not going anywhere," Janine said. "He's just resting for now. That's what he wants us to know."

She kissed the bandages again, whispered something into his ear that Harry couldn't hear. When she looked up again, he saw the strength back in her face.

"He's not going to die," she said.

Beside them, the machines pulsed on, like the beating of a fragile but immortal heart.

When visiting hours were over, he drove her back to Monmouth Beach. The house was dusty, the air inside stale. She went around opening windows, letting in the night breeze. He sat at the kitchen table, rubbed his eyes, and felt the fatigue creeping through his muscles.

"I could make something to eat," she said.

He shook his head. "No, thanks."

"I'm not very hungry, either."

She leaned against the counter.

"You can stay here tonight. I'll make up the couch for you. It's too late to drive all the way back to your friend's house."

"I'll stay."

"You look like you're about to fall down."

"I haven't gotten much sleep in the last two days."

"I'll get the things for the couch."

She left the kitchen and he got up and began to pace. He went into the living room, checked the front door locks. She came down the stairs with a comforter, sheet, and pillows.

"It's getting cool tonight," she said. "You might need these."

She set them on the couch.

"It would be strange for me," she said, "sleeping in this house alone, without Bobby. I guess I'll have to get used to it, for a while, at least."

"It's okay. I don't mind staying."

They went back out into the kitchen, sat down.

"It's almost funny," she said. "He always says that he gets into trouble without me around. He can't stand to be alone. I shouldn't have let him come back without me."

She blinked back tears. He reached across the table, caught her hand, squeezed it.

They talked for a while longer, but exhaustion had them both. At a little past eleven, she went up to bed. He made up the couch, stripped off his boots, socks, sling, and sweatshirt, and stretched out on his back. He switched off the lamp, pulled up the comforter, and settled down into darkness.

He woke all at once, not knowing why. The room was still black around him, wind rattling the windows. He raised his wrist until the luminous dial of his watch came into focus. Three-thirty. He felt something pass over him, like the shadow of a cloud moving across the sun on a warm day.

He sat up, let the comforter fall away, held his breath, waiting, listening to the house creak around him.

He sat that way until he felt the sensation lessen and pass. Then he gathered the comforter around him again, put his head back down on the pillow. As he closed his eyes, the phone in the kitchen began to ring.

TWENTY-NINE

The wind blew with fury on the day of the funeral. It whipped through the cemetery like a thing alive, scattering wreaths and floral arrangements and flapping the skirts of the tent over the grave. To the east, the sky was dense and gray, clouds moving slow and steady on the horizon.

He stood behind the last of the dozen or so mourners, wearing a suit jacket he'd borrowed from Ray, the left side draped over his shoulder and sling. Janine and her parents sat alongside the casket, listening to the priest finish his reading. When he was done, the mourners began to file by slowly. Some leaned over to kiss her, grip her hand. Harry stayed where he was.

After the last of the mourners had drifted back to their cars, Janine and her parents sat there for a while, alone. Then she stood and tucked a single flower into one of the handles of the casket. Her father, a thin, white-haired man, rose to stand beside her. Harry began to walk back up the hill to where he'd parked his car, separate from the others.

"Harry."

He stopped, turned.

"Harry, wait."

He watched her come up the hill. She'd worn neither a hat nor a veil, and the wind blew loose strands of hair into her face. She brushed them away from her eyes.

When she reached him, she said nothing for a moment.

He put out his arm and she came into it. He held her tight, felt her tremble against him.

After a few moments, she broke away. Her eyes were red-rimmed but dry.

"You should come by my parents' house. We're having some people over. You can follow the cars."

He shook his head, not trusting himself to speak.

"I know how you feel," she said. "But he's safe now."

He felt the wetness in his eyes, looked into the wind.

"I'll be driving back to North Carolina in a couple of days with my sister. Rich is going to stay up here and settle things with the house. I don't think I can bear to stay around here any longer."

"I understand. You're doing the right thing."

"I've been thinking a lot over the last few days. About what happens now. The only thing I know for sure is that I'll miss him every day for the rest of my life."

"So will I."

"There's only so much you can do for someone you love, Harry. You can't live their lives for them, make their decisions. And you can't change their past. All you can do is love them, be there when they need you. It took me a while to realize that. We do what we can, but it isn't always up to us."

He felt the tears now, tried to hold them back.

"You were there when he needed you, Harry. And you loved him. You don't owe him—or me—anything else."

She looked back down the hill to where her parents were waiting.

"I should go," she said.

She raised up, kissed him lightly on the cheek.

"Take care of yourself, Harry," she said. "Come visit someday if you get a chance. Or just call me, let me know how you're doing."

"I will."

"We both need to look ahead now. Not back. That's what he would want."

He took her hand, squeezed and released it. She started

back down the hill, her steps sure. Her father waited for her beside a limousine, the rear door open.

He wiped his eyes, walked up the slope to where he'd left his car. The green Ford was parked behind it, Wesniak and Eagleman standing alongside, a pair of binoculars on the hood.

He looked at them, got out his keys.

"Nice of you to come by," he said. "You here the whole time? See anybody interesting?"

"No one special," Wesniak said. "But you never can tell. It's always worth taking a look around. Buy you a cup of coffee?"

He shook his head, unlocked the door.

"I don't think so. But, hey, the family are having some people over to their house. Maybe you two could go by there, check IDs or something."

"Hold up a minute."

He opened the door, waited.

"I'm sorry things turned out the way they did."

"You told me."

"Your friend made some bad decisions, but he didn't deserve to go like that. We can do something about it, with your help."

"Is that right?"

"Let's talk, Harry. Get out of this wind a little bit." He opened the back door of the Ford.

"Am I under arrest?"

"Of course not."

"Then I'll pass."

"Jesus Christ," Eagleman said. "Just get in the fucking car."

"Easy," Wesniak said to him.

Harry shut the door of the Saturn.

"Okay, let's talk."

He walked back to the Ford, looked at Eagleman, and slid into the backseat. He had to fight the wind to pull the door shut. Wesniak went around to the other side, got in beside him, closed the door. Eagleman stayed outside.

"We ended on a bad note last time," Wesniak said. "That may have been partially my fault. But I thought you should be kept up to date on some new developments. We've got a lead on Dunleavy."

Harry looked at him. Wind rocked the car.

"A surveillance detail spotted him yesterday in Bloomfield, meeting with Paulie Andelli. Do you know who that is?"

"Yeah."

"He got away. They couldn't follow him without blowing the whole setup. They had to make a choice."

"So they let him go?"

"Like I said, they had to make a choice. But at least we know for sure he's still around."

Harry looked out the window. Down the hill, the casket sat alone beneath the tent. Two men in suits were folding up metal chairs.

"We checked out a condominium he'd been keeping in Wall Township. He's gone, but he couldn't have gotten far yet. We'll get him. And you were right."

"About what?"

"The gun he shot Fox with. It was the same one used to kill Cortez and his cousin. The bullets matched. I'm guessing it happened pretty much the way you said."

"Are you surprised?"

"No. But whether or not we can link all this to Fallon is another question. It'll be easier once we get Dunleavy."

"You couldn't hold Fallon."

"No chance. But we're watching him now, and I imagine he'll be showing signs of stress soon. His life may not be worth a lot in the next few days."

"How's that?"

"Put it together. Fallon was handling something fairly straightforward for Andelli and blew it. He got two of Andelli's people killed and drew so much attention to himself that some of it can't help but slop onto the old man. On top of that, Fallon is an amateur. He's not one of them. Andelli can't trust him if anything happens, because he knows Fallon doesn't have the stones to keep his mouth shut. If Fallon was smart, he'd be knocking on our door right now, pleading for protective custody."

"So Dunleavy went to Andelli to square with him, say it wasn't his fault?"

"That's my guess. He wants them to know it wasn't him who fucked up. Dunleavy's smart enough to know he can't run from those people. I don't know if Fallon is. Either way, I think it's likely someone's going to take a crack at punching your clock before too long. Maybe Dunleavy himself. He's no fool, he knows he has to get back in Andelli's good graces. And the only way to do that is to close this thing out and tie up the loose ends. Right now those loose ends are you and Fallon. Without you two, no one could make a case against Andelli in a million years. How does it feel to be so special?"

"Can't say I like the company."

Wesniak gave a short laugh.

"Still calm and cool, eh? Nothing fazes you. Not even a bunch of hard-case Italians walking around with your name and address? Maybe it's time to think seriously about a new career in Argentina."

"Or come in and help you?"

"Did you hear me ask? I don't remember it if I did. As I said last time, you're on your own."

"Then why'd you come here?"

"Just to pass on some information, make the playing ground a little more level. A final favor for a former brother officer."

"Thanks." Harry reached for the door handle.

"Don't mention it. By the way, you can go back to your house now. It's clear. Oh, and there's one other thing."

"What's that?"

"You know that fellow Wiley, big guy, worked for Fallon?"

"Yeah."

"Well, there must have been some dissension in the ranks. He tried to take off a few days ago, bought a plane ticket for California."

"How do you know that?"

"Because he never made it. They found his Jeep in Brooklyn. It was left in a handicapped zone, so it got towed before anyone had a chance to steal it. The registration and insurance card were in the glove box. He had a suitcase full of clothes in the back. It didn't take a lot of detective work to figure out something had happened."

"Did you find him?"

"Yeah, we did in fact. Behind a tank farm on Staten Island. He took three in the head."

Wesniak touched each temple, then his forehead.

"Very thorough. He was naked, tape on his wrists and ankles—that sound familiar? He had burn marks on his thighs and genitalia. Someone used a cigarette lighter on him.

"The only reason I'm telling you this is to let you know what the situation is here. Face it, life would be a lot easier for Mickey Dunleavy without you around. He has plenty of reasons for wanting you out of the picture."

"How did you know?"

"Know what?"

"That Wiley was going to California."

"Easy. It was on his plane ticket. They came across it during the post. Took a while to piece it together, though."

"What do you mean?"

"The ME found it when he went into the stomach. It was in strips. They made him eat it before they killed him."

He drove out to the marina in Sea Bright where Bobby kept his boat, walked up the dock to where it was moored. Boats rolled and creaked in the wind and he had to time his step off the dock to keep from going into the water.

The cabin door was locked. He opened the sliding door of the compartment beneath the helm, knelt, and reached in. His fingers slid across smooth wood until they touched the leather key case that hung there. He took it out, stood up. There were two keys inside, one for the ignition, a smaller one for the cabin.

When he'd gotten what he'd come for, he locked the boat

again, climbed onto the gunwale, and hopped onto the dock. He took the keys with him.

The Sand Castle was closed, the parking lot empty. He drove around to the side, saw the Lexus parked in back of a Dumpster, out of sight from the street.

He parked, got out of the car. The wind raised grit and dirt from the blacktop and sent it swirling around him. Beyond the seawall, he could see whitecaps on the ocean.

He went up the wooden stairway to the rear deck, took the Glock from his sling. A side door that led onto the deck was propped open. He went to it, listened for a moment, then stepped inside.

Fallon sat alone at a booth against the wall, facing the door. He was counting money, an open strongbox in front of him. The wind followed Harry in, lifted place mats and napkins on empty tables. The only sound was a yard-long lobster tank bubbling along one wall.

"How you doing, Eddie?"

Fallon looked up. He let the bills fall into the box, moved his hand to the folded newspaper beside it.

Harry lifted the Glock, shook his head. "Don't."

Fallon touched the newspaper, slowly drew back his hand.

"What do you want?" he said.

Harry slid into the booth across from him, used the Glock to push aside the paper. Beneath it was a silver automatic, the Star 9 he'd taken off Wiley at the country club.

"Nervous?" he said. "Pretty unusual, isn't it, carrying one of these yourself? Running short of help?"

Fallon took a pack of Kools from the table. He shook one loose, speared his lips with it. He looked pale, tired.

"Say what you came to say," he said. "Or do what you came to do."

"I just got back from burying a friend."

"So?"

Without thinking, he swung the Glock, batted the cigarette out of Fallon's mouth. He leaned forward, pushed the gun into the soft flesh below Fallon's left cheekbone, pinned his head against the back of the booth. His finger slid over the trigger and his mind raced ahead, saw the muzzle flash, the spatter of blood on the wall.

They were frozen like that for a moment.

"You don't have the balls," Fallon said.

Harry took the gun away. The muzzle left a white circle on Fallon's skin. Harry sat back, slowly let out his breath. He was trembling.

"That's the difference between you and me," Fallon said. "When it comes down to it, you can't do what has to be done."

"Where's Dunleavy?"

"I don't know. He doesn't work for me anymore."

"I have news for you. He never did."

He put the Glock on the seat, rubbed his sweat-slick palm on his jeans, picked up the Star 9.

"Is this for me or for him?"

Fallon was silent.

Harry made sure the safety was on, put the automatic in his sling. He pulled the strongbox toward him. Inside were loose twenties and fifties, a petty cash fund, maybe five hundred dollars in all. Below the money were deeds, a liquor license. He closed the lid, pushed the box aside.

"Tell me," Fallon said. "How long?"

Harry looked at him.

"You and her. Was it that day at the country club? Or earlier? How long were you screwing around behind my back?"

"Does it matter?"

"I guess not. But what really gets me, what I can't figure out, is what she sees in a washed-out fuckup like you. Or maybe she's back to her old ways, where she'd suck off anybody in the bar for an eight ball of coke. Is that what it is?"

"Shut up."

"Fuck you. You think I'm going to give her up, just like that? Let her walk away with any jackoff who comes down the line? I've got too much time and money invested in her to let that happen. You want me out of the way, you better pull that trigger now."

"It's not me you should be worried about. Dunleavy went to see Andelli yesterday. He sold you out."

"Is that so?"

"It is. If I had to guess, I'd say he told Paulie it was your fault everything went to shit. Now Dunleavy's in charge of closing the pipeline. Guess who's at the top of the list?"

Fallon took another cigarette from the pack.

"If you have any idea where Dunleavy is," Harry said, "this is the time to tell me."

"What, now you're gonna protect me?"

"You blew your shot at the big time, Eddie. You're out of your league. You always were."

"So I'm not a tough guy like you, that it? I don't go around sticking guns in people's faces, fucking their wives?"

"I don't have people killed, Eddie. I don't con them into selling drugs for me and then have them executed."

"I never conned anybody into anything. Anyone I ever did business with, he came to me, not the other way around."

"What about Wiley?"

"What about him?"

"You sent Dunleavy and the others to see him."

"He was running out on me. He had something that didn't belong to him."

"Turns out he didn't."

Fallon said nothing.

"You weren't a very good boss, Eddie. He looked up to you. He trusted you. You owed him more than that."

"Sometimes things don't go the way you'd like them to."

"Is that what happened at my house?"

Fallon tapped the cigarette on the table. He looked away, then back.

"You think I'm calling the shots now?" he said. "Dunleavy's out of control."

"So it's just tough luck, then, isn't it? Tough luck for everybody. Tough luck for Jimmy Cortez and his cousin. Tough luck for Wiley. Tough luck for Bobby. Now it's tough luck for you."

Fallon put the cigarette in his mouth, picked up his lighter from the table.

"I've got nothing else to say to you," he said. "If you came here to shoot me, then do it. If not, then get the fuck out." The lighter flared.

Harry stood up.

"You're right," he said. "I'm not like you."

He slid out of the booth, engaged the safety, and tucked the Glock into his belt.

"I'm glad I'm not. You're done. You're walking around dead and you don't even know it."

"Get out."

"You're over. Lie down and die."

Harry turned his back on him, started toward the door.

"You want to know who got your friend killed?" Fallon called after him. "Look in the mirror."

THIRTY

He tore the yellow crime scene tape off his porch, let the wind carry it across the yard.

When he opened the door, paper triangles fled across the ruined floor. The bloody chair still sat in the center of the room.

In the kitchen, the answering machine blinked redly at him. He unlocked and opened the back door. The blinds above the sink began to rattle like kazoos.

The message from Ray was an hour old. He called the office number and the receptionist put him through immediately.

"Been trying to reach you all day," Ray said. "I was hoping you'd call in, check your messages. Where are you?"

"Home for now."

"Edda called me about an hour and a half ago. She took a message for you at the house. From a woman. She didn't leave her name, but she said you'd know her from the beach. That make sense?"

"What did she say?"

"Just one word: 'Tonight.' She said you'd know what it meant."

He looked at his watch. It was almost five.

"All this mean anything to you?" Ray asked.

"Yes, it does. That's all she said?"

"That was it. Is there something going on I should know about? Something you need help with?"

"No," Harry said. "I don't think so. Not this time."

He took out the phone book and began calling airlines. There were only two flights from Newark to Mexico City that night: a TWA at six forty-five, an American at ten-fifty, changing in Atlanta. Fallon might use Kennedy, or even LaGuardia, but Newark would be closest, easiest.

He called American back, got a different operator.

"I'm calling to confirm a flight tonight?"

"Your name, sir?"

"Fallon." He spelled it.

"Flight number?"

He gave it to her.

There was a pause, the tapping of computer keys.

"Yes, sir, I have you confirmed on American Flight 1062, leaving Newark tonight at ten-fifty, arriving in Atlanta at one-twenty and then continuing on to Mexico City, with an arrival time of four-thirty A.M. Two passengers traveling first class. Do you need to make a change?"

"No, that's fine, thank you."

He changed clothes, put on jeans and boots, the plan already taking shape in his mind.

It took him ten minutes to find the pry bar in the woods. He levered off the well cap, reached in. The knapsack was still there. He pulled it out, set it beside him. The blood on it had dried to a stiff black stain.

He took the Star 9 from his sling, released the safety. Holding the grip in his left hand, he worked the slide with his right to chamber a shell. Then he changed hands, pointed the gun into the well, turned his head away and fired three times, flat cracks like sticks breaking. He could hear the thump of bullets hitting dirt. Cordite smoke drifted past him.

He put the safety on, then pushed the well cap back into

place. When he was done, he looked at his watch. Six o'clock. Time to move.

He parked beneath the same stand of trees, facing Fallon's house, watched figures move back and forth behind lighted windows. The air was thick with humidity. He had to wipe a sleeve across the inside of the windshield every ten minutes to clear it.

At seven-fifteen, a limousine came slowly up the street, as if the driver were reading house numbers. It passed the Saturn, turned into Fallon's driveway.

He wiped the windshield again. The driver got out, went to the front door. After a few moments, it opened a crack and he spoke to someone inside. The door swung wider and he went in.

Harry pulled the knapsack from beneath the passenger seat, unzipped it, and checked the package inside. He had duct-taped the bags of heroin into a tight bundle smaller than a pound of sugar. Taped in the middle was the loaded Star 9, wiped clean of prints.

The driver came back out, carrying a pair of suitcases. He set them down beside the limo, unlocked the trunk, raised the lid. He stowed the bags inside, moved them around, then went back in the house.

Lights began to go off inside. The driver came back out with two more bags, put them in the trunk, and slammed the lid. He opened the back door, waited there, leaning against the fender.

Fallon and Cristina came out of the house together. She wore the leather jacket, a white blouse, jeans. He had her right elbow in one hand, a leather overnight bag in the other. She was moving slowly, as if half asleep. He led her to the open door of the limo and she seemed to hesitate for a moment until he put a hand on her shoulder to guide her in. She slid inside and he followed, bag in hand. The driver shut the door and got behind the wheel.

The limo backed out of the driveway, thumped into the

street, brake lights flaring. It stopped at the intersection, signaled to turn left.

Harry started the engine. He pushed the knapsack back under the seat, pulled away from the curb, lights off. After the limo turned, he waited a moment, then rolled through the stop sign after it.

There were few cars on the Turnpike, and he kept the limo in sight easily. When it took the off-ramp to the airport, he stayed about four car lengths behind, working gas and brake to keep the distance as they navigated the cloverleafs that led to the terminal area. The limo slowed outside Terminal A, where taxis and cars were lined up at the curb, loading and unloading. The driver double-parked, put on his hazards. Harry cruised past, swung into the entrance for the hourly lot beneath the terminal. He got his ticket from the machine, found an empty spot near a concrete post, backed in, and shut off the engine.

He took out the knapsack, unzipped it, and removed the bundle. It fit inside his sling without showing. He got his sunglasses from the glove box, put them on, and got out of the car. He opened the trunk, took out the black windbreaker, and shrugged it on, the left side draped to hide his cast.

He rode the escalator up to the departure level, watching the crowd. A hundred yards away, he saw Fallon and Cristina come into the terminal, a skycap wheeling their suitcases ahead of them, Fallon still carrying the overnight bag. Cristina stopped short, looked around, and Fallon took her arm, tugged.

Harry looked at the arrival and departure screen on the wall above him. The ten-fifty flight to Mexico City—Gate 33—had been delayed by a half hour. When he looked back, Fallon and Cristina were at the American counter, about ten people already ahead of them in line.

Harry went down the short flight of steps to the gate area. Here the terminal branched off into three wide corridors, the entrance to each blocked by a security checkpoint. Beigejacketed guards checked tickets, then waved people into queues for the metal detectors and X-ray machines. Two PA cops hovered nearby.

He moved as far away from the checkpoints as he could, his back against the wall. After a few minutes, he saw Fallon and Cristina ride the escalator down to the gate area. There were about a dozen people ahead of them, waiting to be processed.

Fallon glanced at his watch, then drew Cristina away from the line. He said something to her and she nodded, looked away, as if distancing herself from what was happening.

Fallon handed her the overnight bag, tucked tickets into his inside jacket pocket. Then he headed toward the rest rooms at the far end of the gate area.

Harry was already moving, walking slowly toward her. She stood in the center of the gate area, bag in hand, looking lost. Out of the corner of his eye, he saw Fallon push open the men's room door and go inside. Cristina turned.

"It's me," he said and caught her arm, still moving.

"What are you—"

He squeezed the inside of her elbow, kept her in motion, guiding her across the floor toward the ladies' room.

"What are you doing?" she said. "He'll be back in a second, he's—"

They reached the ladies' room door and he pushed it open, took them through. Water glistened on the freshly mopped floor, a triangular plastic sign warning of the danger in English and Spanish. Only two of the stalls were occupied. He led her into an empty one, squeezed in behind her, and shut the door, latched it.

"Harry, what are you doing here?" She looked at the cast. "What happened to—"

He pulled her close, kissed her. She let the bag drop, and he held her tight with his right arm, his face buried in her hair.

"It's okay," he said.

When he loosened his grip, she pulled back to look at him. He took the bag from her, set it on the toilet, unzipped it.

"I didn't think you got my message," she said. "I didn't think there was any way you'd know in time."

He rummaged through folded clothes until he found a leather shaving kit, took it out. Not big enough.

"What are you doing?"

He reached in again, came out with a polo sweater. Better. He wrapped the sweater around the shaving kit, wedged them behind the toilet.

"He'll be looking for me," she said.

He took the taped bundle from his sling, pushed it down into the bag, moved clothes around to cover it.

"Tell him you had to go to the bathroom," he said. "You couldn't wait."

He zipped the bag back up, hefted it. It was about the same weight and shape it had been.

"What was that?"

"Something that belongs to your husband. I'm returning it."

He gave her the bag.

"Give it back to him as soon as you walk out of here. If he asks you to carry it, don't. Drop it if you have to, but don't go through the checkpoint with it. Do you understand?"

"What is it? Why do . . ."

"Do you understand?"

"Yes."

"Hang back when you get in line. Let some people get between you and him if possible. Stall any way you can."

"Where will you be?"

"Right behind you. Waiting."

She kissed him quickly again, looked into his face.

"I knew you'd come," she said.

"He'll be wondering where you are. Remember what I said."

He unlatched the stall door and she went out. He pulled the door shut again and waited, counting a full minute. When he left the stall, a middle-aged woman was at the sinks. She frowned at him.

"Sorry," he said. "Men's room was full."

He went to the door and looked out. Fallon and Cristina were in line at the checkpoint, a half dozen people ahead of them. He was carrying the bag.

Harry walked away from the bathrooms toward the far wall. The line moved slowly. Fallon had a hand in the small of Cristina's back and eased her forward every time someone passed through the metal detector.

Fallon showed his tickets to the guard, who looked through them, then waved him forward. He moved up to join a queue of four at the metal detector.

Cristina eased away from the line, bent one knee and began to tug at her shoe.

Fallon didn't notice at first. Two people had moved into line behind him before he turned and saw her. He said something Harry couldn't make out, gestured to her. Now there was no one ahead of him in line. The heavy black woman manning the metal detector waved him up. A teenage girl behind him moved around and past him.

The PA cops were starting to take notice now. Behind Fallon was a Hispanic family with three small children. They flowed around him on both sides.

"Sir," the female guard said, loud enough for Harry to hear, "you're holding up the line."

"Come on," Fallon called to Cristina, irritation in his voice. She ignored him, moved over to the wall and calmly took off her shoe, shook it as if to dislodge something.

"Sir, there are people waiting. Step through, please."

Fallon cursed, moved up. He put his bag on the conveyor belt, walked through the metal detector, turned again on the other side.

The belt came to a juddering halt. Harry saw the red light glow on the machine.

Fallon was looking back at Cristina, unaware of what was going on around him. The man at the X-ray screen gestured toward the black woman. She stepped around to look over his shoulder. The ticket checker joined them. The line behind Fallon grew.

The black woman thumbed up her lapel and spoke into a microphone pinned there. The ticket checker motioned for the rest of the line to stand back. The PA cops were already moving in.

Twenty feet away, Cristina gave Fallon a last look and began to walk back toward the escalator.

He called to her, tried to step back through the metal detector. The black woman reached across and caught his sleeve. He wrenched it away from her, turned, and collided with the first PA cop, who had stepped up to block him. From the terminal came two more cops, walking fast.

Fallon looked around, confused. The first cop turned him, guided him toward the wall. They had his bag open, were taking clothes out.

Cristina crossed the gate area, not hurrying. She walked by Harry without looking at him, got on the escalator, rode slowly up to the main terminal.

He stayed to watch. The PA cop had Fallon against the wall now, away from the other passengers. Fallon pulled loose, red-faced and angry, and the cop shoved him back hard. Handcuffs flashed. The other cops moved in.

Harry stepped away from the wall, walked to the escalator. Three more cops raced down the steps from the terminal. Halfway up, he looked back. Fallon had disappeared in a sea of uniforms.

She was waiting for him near the far doors.

"This way," he said.

They took the escalator down to the garage. He led her to the car, unlocked and opened her door, shut it behind her. He got in, started the engine, and pulled out fast. When he stopped at the gate to pay, he saw three PA police cars in front of the terminal, lights flashing.

He followed the signs to the airport exit. Five minutes later they were back on the turnpike, heading south. He turned to her.

"Did you really?" he said.

She looked at him.

"What?"

"Know I'd come?"

She looked out into the night. "Always."

"How did you know he'd leave me alone with the bag?" she asked.

They were southbound on the Parkway, the traffic sparse.

"I didn't. I took a chance. Until the moment he handed it to you, I wasn't sure what I was going to do."

"What will happen to him?"

"Not much. He'll have a rough night, but his lawyer will have him out by the morning. He'll say he was set up and they'll believe him. No one in his right mind would try to carry that much heroin and a recently fired gun onto a passenger flight, especially these days. But until it gets straightened out, it'll screw up any plans he has for leaving the country."

"Heroin?"

"Like I said, it belonged to him. The gun too."

"He'll think I did it."

"Maybe." He looked at her. "That bother you?"

"No."

She took out her cigarette case.

"I hate flying," she said.

"What?"

"Flying. Planes. I hate them. He knew that, but he didn't care."

He pushed in the dashboard lighter.

"Then you got lucky today," he said.

The lighter popped out. He handed it to her and she lit the cigarette, cracked the window to let the smoke out.

"Did he kill someone?" she said.

"Maybe not personally, but he was responsible for it."

"How many?"

"Four that I know of. There might be more."

She replaced the lighter.

"Four people," she said.

"Yeah."

"Then he deserves whatever happens to him, doesn't he?"

He shrugged. "Don't we all?"

THIRTY-ONE

The motel was in freehold, near an industrial park off Route 33. He filled out the registration card and paid in cash, then drove around the back so the car couldn't be seen from the highway.

They'd stopped quickly at her house and she'd loaded a suitcase while he stayed in the car. He carried it up the concrete stairs to their second-floor motel room, locked and chained the door behind them, drew the drapes.

They took turns in the shower, him first, keeping his cast outside the curtain. When he was done, he dried off, wrapped a towel around his waist, and stretched out on the bed, pillows propped behind him. He turned on the television and surfed until he found the eleven o'clock news.

After a while he heard the water switch off. When she came out of the bathroom, she wore a black silk top that ended just below her breasts, a matching pair of panties. Her hair was slick and dark. She crossed in front of the TV to where her suitcase lay flat on a chair.

"I've got something to show you," she said.

He picked up the remote and switched off the TV, watched her. She opened the suitcase, dug through folded clothes, came out with a black leather fanny pack.

"What's that?" he said.

She tossed it onto the bed. He picked it up. It was

bulging, overstuffed. He unzipped it, saw the bundled bills inside. He thumbed the edges. Hundreds.

"His getaway money," she said. "Or I should say part of it. I'm sure he has more hidden in other places. I knew about this because he went to the bank this morning and got it from a safe-deposit box. He packed it in one of his suitcases, but I took it out and hid it in the bathroom closet."

"Why?"

"I'm not sure. Maybe I thought the more money he had, the farther away he'd take me, and the harder it would be for me to get back. Maybe I just wanted to be able to get my hands on some money quickly if I did come back. He never realized it was gone."

"How much is in here?"

"Twenty-five thousand."

"Son of a bitch."

"What's wrong?"

"He'll come looking for this."

"He'll come looking for *me* anyway, won't he? And the way I see it, it's my money too, especially with everything he's put us through. Three years of my life, eight thousand dollars a year. That's pretty cheap."

"I hope he sees it the same way."

"Some of that is probably what he got from your friend."

He zipped the bag shut, weighed it in his hand, set it on the bed.

"Dirty money," he said.

"Is there any other kind? It's a question of degree, isn't it?"

"Drug money."

"Maybe. Maybe not. What's important is that it's not *his* money anymore."

She sat down on the bed, touched his cast.

"Look at what he did to you," she said. "To us."

He took her hand, drew her down beside him.

"I thought it would give us a start," she said.

"We don't need it."

She put a cool hand on his chest, tucked her head beneath his chin.

They lay like that awhile and she whispered, "It's really happening, isn't it?"

"What?"

"I've left him."

"You could have done it a thousand times."

"Not without you."

He pulled her closer, felt her breathing, slow and steady. He held her as she drifted into sleep.

The next morning he crept out of the room, Cristina still asleep, and stepped into blinding sunshine. He walked to the pay phone by the motel office and called his answering machine. Two hangups, no messages. Then he called Ray's office, got him on the line, and talked for ten minutes.

When he was done, he went back to the room, closed the door quickly so the light wouldn't wake her. She lay curled in the sheets, one bare leg exposed. The smell of her perfume hung in the air.

He sat at the desk, found a piece of motel stationery, wrote her a note, and left it on the nightstand. Then he let himself out again, shut the door quietly behind him.

The Ford station wagon that Ray lent him was ten years old, but it ran as if it were new. The body was dented, the paint faded, but the engine leaped when he stepped on the gas. He parked it outside the room and went in to find her dressed and lying on the bed, watching a soap opera, her suitcase packed and set by the door.

"I woke up and you were gone," she said. "It scared me."

"I had to run some errands. That's why I left you the note. I didn't want to wake you."

She switched off the TV.

"Where are we going?"

"Delaware. Near the water. A friend of mine has a place

there. It's empty. We can lie low for a few days until some of this blows over. We'll be out of the way, but I'll still be able to keep an ear to what's going on back here. Then, after a while, we can decide what we want to do."

"How far is it?"

"About three hours, if we don't hit much traffic."

"Don't you need to go to your house?"

"I already did. I've got a suitcase in the car. We can leave whenever you're ready."

"I guess I'm ready now."

She got up, began to gather her things. He propped open the door with a chair, carried her bag out to the station wagon. She came and stood in the doorway.

"What's that?" she said.

"I had to return the Saturn. A friend lent me this. It's a company car. He uses it for surveillance mostly. Nondescript."

"It's that, all right."

"Wait here. I'm going to go check out, settle the bill."

When he got back to the room she was sitting on the edge of the bed, turning something over in her hands. He stopped in the doorway.

"Second thoughts?" he said.

"Just thoughts."

She got up, went over to the TV, set her wedding ring on top of it. Sunlight glinted off the diamonds.

"Are you sure you want to do that?" he said.

"Yes."

She looked at him.

"Then let's go," he said.

They drove down into South Jersey on the Turnpike, caught the ferry that took them across Delaware Bay to Cape Lewes. Outside Belltown, they stopped for lunch and gas, then picked up Route 24 again, heading south.

After they passed Rehoboth Beach, he looked at the handwritten directions Ray had given him. He turned east and, after twenty minutes, the highway gave way to a two-lane county road with ditches on both sides. They passed the roadside farm market Ray had told him about and started looking for the turnoff.

It was a single-lane road, unpaved, and the station wagon rattled in protest, the suitcases shifting in the back. Fire roads led off into the trees on both sides.

"What are those?" she said.

"In case of forest fires," he said. "It allows them to get trucks out into the middle of the woods."

He slowed to twenty-five, watching carefully now.

"There it is," she said, pointing at a rusty mailbox ahead on the left.

He braked, turned into the narrow, rutted driveway. It led uphill, trees on both sides, and when he reached the top he could see sunlight glinting on the waters of Rehoboth Bay. Then they were over the hill and into a clearing, the house ahead of them.

It was a small two-story structure, faded green with white shutters, in desperate need of a paint job. The grass around it was high, almost hiding the slate path that led to the front door.

He pulled into the side yard, shut off the engine.

"Wait here," he said.

He got out of the car, found the key Ray had given him. He unlocked the front door, went through into a small living room where dust floated in the air, a thin film of it covering the hardwood floor. There was an undersized fireplace in one corner, and the only furniture was a couch and a single chair, both covered with bedsheets.

He walked through into the kitchen. The far wall was floor-to-ceiling windows looking out on a slope of dune grass that ran down to a small scallop of beach. The sun flashed hard off the water.

He checked the upstairs rooms, then went back outside and began to pull suitcases out of the wagon.

"Go on in," he said. "It's home, for a little while, at least."

When he carried in the first bag, she was standing in the

kitchen looking out at the beach, her form silhouetted against the windows.

"It's beautiful," she said.

He came up behind her, slipped his arm around her waist, kissed the back of her head. She took his hand.

"Not exactly a honeymoon cottage," he said, "but I guess it's as close as we'll get for now."

She leaned back against him.

"Now's good," she said. "Don't underestimate now."

"I never do."

THIRTY-TWO

There was no phone in the house, so after they had settled in and unpacked, he drove back to the highway, pulled into the first shopping plaza he came to, a cluster of small stores connected to a Kmart. The lot was full of pickup trucks and older passenger cars, the station wagon unobtrusive.

He called Ray's office from a pay phone outside a liquor store.

"We're here," he said.

"Good. Any trouble finding it?"

"No problem. What's happening back there?"

"Fallon was arraigned this morning in Newark. Possession and intent, gun charges, FAA violations, a whole laundry list. Judge set bond at a hundred thousand, but allowed for the ten percent. Not much when you consider he was about to get on an international flight with a loaded weapon and enough heroin to kill an elephant."

"So he's out?"

"His lawyer had the check in hand."

"I'm betting Wesniak talked to the judge. Who was it?"

"Spero."

"Know him?"

"Not well. Though I wouldn't be surprised if he owes Wesniak a favor or two. They go back."

"My guess is Wesniak told him they need to keep Fallon free in order to nail Dunleavy."

"Makes sense. Or maybe Fallon's thinking about playing ball, coming in himself. Could be that business at the airport pushed him over. I can't believe you pulled off that shit, by the way. How are you two making out down there?"

"Fine."

"Place might be a little musty. We haven't had a chance to get down there yet this summer. But the pantry's full and there's a freezer in the basement. Take what you need."

"Thanks. I appreciate everything you've done for us."

"Forget it. One other thing I should have told you earlier. Unless you had a flat tire, you probably haven't noticed, but there's what you might call an emergency kit in the wagon, in the wheel well below the spare. I put one in all the company cars. I don't think you'll need it, but you should know it's there."

"I'll take a look. Thanks again, Ray. For everything. You came through for us."

"You ever doubt I would?"

Back at the house, he found Cristina in the kitchen. She wore a blue one-piece bathing suit beneath a beach robe.

"Where did you find those?" he said.

"Upstairs in the bedroom. The suit's a little big, but it'll do until I get a new one. Let's go."

"Where?"

She took a brown plastic bottle out of the robe pocket, tossed it. He caught it in front of his chest. Suntan lotion.

"Beach," she said. "Now."

"I don't have a suit."

"Improvise. There's no one around."

Before he could answer, she was out the door.

The sun was so bright on the water that it hurt to look at it for too long. He lay on the blanket, naked, almost dry now. He had gone in up to his waist, keeping the cast out of the water, watched her swim out farther, wishing he could follow her. Now she sat beside him, knees pulled up, her suit dark and wet.

He rolled onto his side, felt the sun begin to loosen the muscles in his neck and shoulders, dissolving the tension that had seemed part of him for so long. He closed his eyes and let the feeling take him.

He woke to the sound of gulls squawking. The sun was lower on the horizon, a coolness in the air. He shifted, saw her propped on one elbow beside him, looking down. She touched his cheek, ran a finger across the line of his jaw.

"I love you," she said.

She leaned down, touched her lips to his. He put his arm around her, pulled her close, rolled onto his knees.

"What are you doing?" she said.

He slipped his cast behind her thighs.

"Don't hurt yourself," she said.

He stood, hauled her up with him. She laughed as he stumbled, got his balance again.

"Don't drop me."

"I won't."

She slipped her arms around his neck, and he carried her up the sand to the house.

Later, while she showered, he went out to the station wagon, opened the tailgate. He peeled back the piece of thin carpeting that covered the wheel well, levered up the spare tire. There was a hard plastic briefcase beneath it. He took it out, let the tire fall.

He set the case on the tailgate, popped the latches. Inside was a lightweight Kevlar vest, folded in half. Beneath it was a small black automatic, a Grendel .380, a backup gun. It was unloaded, but two full eleven-round clips were tucked into a leather pouch beside it. Under that was a white business envelope with four new hundred-dollar bills inside. He put everything back in the case, stowed it beneath the tire again.

It was early evening now, the sun a red ball over the water. He walked around to the back of the house, sat down on the steps. Through the open bathroom window, he could hear the shower running. He looked out at the blood-red water and, for the first time in years, he felt like he was home.

The moon was up over the bay, filling the room with a blue and silver glow. They lay on the big bed with the windows open and the lights out.

"I was going to leave him, you know."

He turned toward her silhouette.

"What you said before, about being able to leave anytime I wanted, I guess that was true. But I was scared of him, of what he might do. Then, about two months ago, I decided I couldn't go on like that anymore. I told him."

"What happened?"

"He pleaded with me. Told me how much I meant to him. Finally, he agreed it might be a good idea to spend a little time apart. He offered to rent me a condo in Brielle. I guess he thought five miles away was far enough."

"You didn't do it?"

"I was going to, and then . . . This is going to sound stupid, but it's true. We were getting ready to go through with it and then all of these other things started to happen—the drugs, the people from North Jersey, Mickey Dunleavy. He wouldn't admit it, but I knew he was in way over his head and there was trouble coming. I didn't love him anymore, but I couldn't run out on him in the middle of all that. Crazy, isn't it?"

"Not really."

"I guess I felt that I owed him something. I don't know why. It's like I told you. He was good for me at first. He was strong and I needed that. But after a while that's all he was—strong. There was nothing else there. He didn't care about me, he just didn't want me to leave. He'd get violent sometimes, unpredictable. It scared me because I never knew what would set him off. It got to the point where being with him was like kissing barbed wire."

"What do you mean?"

"I never knew when I was going to come away with blood on my lips."

They watched the moonlight on the water, and neither of them said a word.

Into their second week they had something of a schedule. They'd get up around eleven, make breakfast, then hit the beach. He'd lie in the sun or wade out into the shallows, watch her swim. Back at the house they'd shower, change, then inevitably end up in the bedroom. After dinner, they'd walk through the woods or along the edge of the bay. Slowly, he felt the last month falling away from him.

That Wednesday, she took a pair of steaks from the basement freezer and set them out to thaw on the kitchen counter. She wore the beach robe and, beneath it, the black one-piece bathing suit he'd taken her to buy.

"Some fresh vegetables would be nice for a change," she said. "Something that hasn't been frozen for six months."

"I'll go up to the stand, see what they've got. What do you want?"

"Anything green. Lettuce, celery. Tomatoes if they have them. I think I can manage to make a salad without ruining it."

"I have to make a call anyway. I'll stop on the way back."

"Beach first."

"I'll meet you there later."

He called Ray from the phone outside the liquor store. He wore cutoff jeans and a T-shirt, sandals he'd found in an upstairs closet. His skin was red and stiff from the sun, and he could feel the heat of the pavement through the soles of the sandals.

"Anything new?" he said.

"Not much. They're still looking for Dunleavy. And Wesniak's looking for you. He stopped by here yesterday. I lied pretty well, told him I had no idea where you were, but I don't think he bought it. You need to talk to him at some point."

"I will. I'll call him. A week or so more down here and we're going to see about making some plans to go away for a while. Not sure where yet. When we get back we have to sort some things out. She needs to talk to a lawyer, settle some issues."

"I can imagine. You should be thinking about that yourself. You might need one."

"I'll take my chances."

"Yeah, I know. You always do."

After he hung up he went into the liquor store, bought a bottle of red wine and a half gallon of spring water. He put the bag in the rear of the wagon, headed back to the house. He drove past the farm stand before he remembered he was supposed to stop, then had to K-turn on the narrow road to go back.

There were only two other cars in the gravel lot. Under the awning, a middle-aged woman was stripping corn husks to check the ears. An elderly black man frowned at her from alongside an ancient register behind a plywood counter.

Harry put tomatoes, peppers, and cucumbers into separate plastic bags, passed on the lettuce, which was already browning around the edges. He brought the bags to the register, saw that the old man had a skin condition that had left the right side of his neck a bright, mottled pink.

Harry handed him a twenty and the old man rang him up.

"Cooking for company, eh?" he said. He put the plastic bags into a single paper sack.

"What do you mean?" Harry said.

"Figured you had visitors, that's all."

He handed Harry his change. "Have a good one."

"Wait a minute." For the first time, it occurred to him what the old man had said. "What do you mean, visitors?"

"None of my business," the old man said and turned away.

"No, hold on," Harry said, and the old man turned to face him again, wary, not coming any closer.

"Please," Harry said. "Tell me. What did you mean?"

The old man shrugged. "Visitors. That road don't go but one place. I see a car head down there, don't come back, I figure you got visitors."

He felt the ground shift slightly beneath his feet.

"How long ago?" he said.

"I don't know. Two, three hours, I guess."

"And you're sure it didn't come back."

"I been here all day, just looking out at that road, and I know it ain't come back. 'Course, they could have taken one of those fire roads when they left, come out near Point Creek."

"What kind of car?"

The old man frowned at him. "You in some kind of trouble?"

He sprinted for the wagon, pulling the keys from his pocket. He heard the old man call after him that he'd left his bag behind. He started the engine, spun the wagon around, spraying dust and gravel as he pulled back onto the road.

It might be nothing, he told himself. Someone who got lost. Or someone heading out into the woods. A ranger or a fire marshal. It could be anything.

He got the wagon up to forty-five, the springs bouncing on the dirt road, twice nearly steering into a ditch. He sideswiped bushes turning into the driveway, gave it gas as he went up the hill and had to brake quickly on the far side as the house loomed up in front of him.

He skidded to a stop in the front yard, turned off the engine, and was out of the car before it stopped rocking.

"Cristina!"

He hit the front door hard, sent it bouncing against the wall. The living room was empty.

He looked quickly in the kitchen, saw the steaks still on the counter, flies buzzing around them. He took the stairs two at a time up to the bedroom. There were clothes scattered on the floor, bureau drawers had been pulled out and emptied. He crouched beside the bed, reached underneath, and dragged out her suitcase, threw it open. The Glock was where he'd left it, folded inside a sweater along with the leather pack. He took it out, checked the clip, then pulled out the pack, unzipped it, saw the bills inside, untouched. Whoever had searched the room had done it quickly.

He went back downstairs, gun in hand, then out the back door. He pounded down the slope to the beach, slipped and almost fell headlong. He saw her towel stretched out on the sand, a bottle of suntan lotion beside it.

Sand had been kicked up around the towel. Her sunglasses lay a few feet away, near the dune grass. He picked them up, saw the footprints in the sand there. Bare feet, small, Cristina's. And around them other prints, bigger ones. Shoes.

He looked out over the water, squinted into the sun.

"Cristina!"

A gull called back from high above him.

He raced back to the house, went from room to room and down into the basement, throwing open doors and calling her name. The house was empty.

Up in the bedroom he dressed quickly—jeans, boots, and sweatshirt. He grabbed the pack, stuffed it inside his sling, and picked up the Glock again. He left the front door unlocked behind him.

THIRTY-THREE

He reached New Jersey at dusk, the gas gauge needle hovering in the red. There were lights on in Fallon's house. He parked across the street, took the Glock from the glove box, got out.

He worked his way around the side of the house, looked in the garage window. The Lexus and BMW were both inside. He went around to the back, saw that one of the French doors leading onto the patio was open, the curtain lifting in the breeze. He went through the door gun first.

The living room was empty. He gave it a long count of ten, listening for any sound in the house, then moved into the hallway. The kitchen was dark, the back door closed and chained.

Upstairs, the hall light was on, open doors on both sides yawning into blackness. The door to Fallon's office was closed. He moved toward it, poking the gun into each room he passed, looking inside. All were empty.

When he got to the office, he switched the gun to his left hand, tried the knob with his right. Unlocked. He put the toe of his boot against the base of the door, pushed.

The door scraped on thick carpet, cold air swirled out. He shouldered it open, stepped through.

Fallon sat in a halo of light at the wide cherrywood desk in the center of the room. He was facedown on the blotter as if sleeping, lit by a single gooseneck lamp. Harry moved closer, saw the blood. It had pooled on the desk, dripped down the front in two rusty streaks.

He could smell him now, despite the air-conditioning. Fallon's left cheek was against the desk, his eyes open and staring at a horse-racing print on the far wall. There were spatters of dried blood and flecks of scalp on the bell of the lamp. He'd been shot at least twice in the back of the head—there were teeth on the blotter, blown out by the bullets' exit. His white linen shirt was stained a deep red.

A fly buzzed in through the open door, flew a slow circle around the desk.

He backed out of the room, left the door open, went into the bathroom and got a hand towel from the rack. He wiped the office doorknob clean, then went back downstairs, trying to remember any surface he'd touched. When he was done, he went out the way he'd come, drove three blocks to the gas station. He dialed 911, gave them the address, and told them what they'd find. When they asked for his name, he hung up.

He drove home to wait.

At eleven o'clock, the phone rang.

He sat at the kitchen table, the Glock in front of him. When the machine started to pick up, he shut it off and brought the receiver to his ear.

"Yeah."

"Hey, sport," Mickey Dunleavy said. "I figured I'd given you enough time to get back. There's somebody here who wants to talk to you."

He heard the receiver being put down, then the sound of traffic in the background. A pay phone. Her voice came on the line, weak and frightened.

"Harry?"

"I'm here."

"Harry, don't let—"

Then she was gone. He heard traffic again. Dunleavy came back on the line.

"Kiss, kiss, smooch, smooch, all that," he said. "I just

wanted to let you know what the deal was, in case you hadn't figured it out. I imagine you had a lot of time to think on your way back."

"I did."

"Good. Then you'll make this easy for both of us. Were you wondering how I found you?"

"Yes."

"To tell the truth, Fallon did most of the work for me. He has a lot of contacts, knows a lot of people. Or should I say knew?"

Harry said nothing.

"I guessed you wouldn't go very far. You'd want to see how this fell out, wouldn't you? So I started hanging around the places you might have gone. I even wasted a whole afternoon parked outside Ray Washington's house. Then I started wondering if he had another place somewhere. That's where Fallon came in. I convinced him to make some calls, do some checking with his real estate connections. He found out about the Delaware house. He was ready to come looking for you himself. I saved him the trouble."

"I know. I saw what you did to him."

"Then you know where we stand. Fallon and I had a long talk before we parted company."

"What do you want?"

"What do *I* want? What do you think I want? I can't even go back to the place I live, get a few things, because there's always some cop parked outside. I've been living in a crackhead motel for almost a week now. You think I'm enjoying it?"

"I'll ask you again."

"I want a lot of things. I want to be able to go back to leading a life. I want your head on a fucking stick. Starting to get the picture?"

"Go on."

"Fallon told me the girl left with something that belonged to him."

"I wouldn't know."

Dunleavy sighed.

"We've gone through this before, haven't we?" he said. "And look what happened then. Well, if you don't know, then maybe I'll ask her again. She wasn't too forthcoming the first time."

"Leave her alone."

"You've got it?"

"I've got it. It isn't much."

"Well, it's more than I have access to right now, sport. The way I look at it, it's the least of what you owe me. By the way, I've got to hand it to you, that was a slick number at the airport. That was Wiley's shit, wasn't it? You managed to hold on to it all this time and then used it to pull that off. I have to admire that, Harry, I really do. It was smart. So don't get stupid now."

"You expect me to believe that if I give you the twenty-five grand you'll walk away and leave us alone?"

"I didn't say that. You give me the twenty-five grand and we'll talk about it. By the way, Fallon said it was thirty."

"He was wrong."

"Maybe so. Three things didn't come out of that bastard's mouth that two weren't lies. But the secret is to know who you can lie to and who you can't. And you're smart enough to know that."

"Am I?"

"I think so. And I also think you're smart enough to do what you're told if you think things will work out for you. So get that twenty-five together—if that's all there is—and in just about"—there was a pause—"one hour, I'm going to call a pay phone in Manasquan. You should be there to answer it."

"I'll need time."

"No time left. Be there or we might not talk again."

"What phone? Where?"

"Outside the Sand Castle. The one facing the parking lot. I'm sure you'll make it in time."

"Then what?"

"Then you listen to what I say and you find out what. We'll take it one step at a time. You just worry about being there."

"One hour is tight."

"Conversation's over, sport. You know the game, you know the stakes, you know the way we play. You're not an amateur. One hour."

THIRTY-FOUR

He parked a few feet from the pay phone, his window open. The Sand Castle was dark. Beneath his sweatshirt, the Kevlar vest itched against his chest. He gripped the wheel, tried to slow his breathing, the dread coalescing like stone in his stomach.

At two minutes after midnight, the phone rang, loud in the empty lot. He got to it on the third ring.

"Yeah?"

Silence at first. Then Dunleavy's voice. "That you, sport?"

"It's me."

"Good. I knew you'd make it in time. You sound like you're out of breath. Ready to wrap this thing up, get me out of your life?"

"Talk."

"There's a building in Asbury Park near the beach, a high-rise they never finished. You know it?"

"Yeah."

"Meet me there in an hour. I'll bring the girl. Sixth floor. I'll be in a position where I can see everything going on for blocks around. If you show up with anyone else, or if anyone even decides to follow you without your knowing it, I'll see him. Do you understand that?"

"Yes."

"And if that happens, everything's off. You find the missus at a later date, very much the worse for wear, I promise you."

"I understand."

"Have the money on you. No trips back to the car, no 'It's near but I have to go get it' bullshit."

"How do I know you won't just kill me and take the money?"

"You don't. That's the chance you're taking, isn't it? Have the money on you."

"I'll have it."

"Because if anything doesn't look right, or if everything doesn't go exactly as I say it should, then I cut my losses and walk. And you find yourself another girlfriend."

"I'll be there."

"One A.M.," Dunleavy said and hung up.

He drove to Asbury, spotted the building from blocks away. Twelve stories high, it had been intended as a beachfront condo complex until the developer went bankrupt two months into construction. Now the concrete shell loomed over a neighborhood of boarded-up stores and empty lots.

He circled the block twice, the second time with his lights off. A chain-link fence surrounded the site, but a half dozen gaping holes had been cut into it. Anything in the building worth stealing would be long gone.

He parked a block away, facing the ocean, and turned off the engine, waited for his heartbeat to slow. Out over the water, he could see the moist poundings of heat lightning on the horizon. Above him the sky was cloudless, the moon bright.

A police car sped by, its lights flashing, heading for some other part of town. As the siren faded, the silence returned. He looked back at the building. The interior was unbroken blackness. If Dunleavy waited there, he waited in darkness.

At twenty minutes to one, he got out of the car. The money pack was tucked into his sling, the Glock in his belt at the small of his back. Inside his cast was a thin-bladed filleting knife he'd taken from Bobby's boat. The wooden handle chafed against the inside of his wrist, but he'd found he could draw the seven-inch blade easily without cutting himself.

In the glow of the street lamps, he walked the perimeter of the fence until he found an opening, then pushed through ragged lips of chain. Glass crunched under his feet. Parked alongside the building was an aluminum trailer that had once been a construction office, its windows now broken, sides covered with graffiti.

He walked toward the dark, doorless tunnel of the front entrance, took out the Glock. Beyond was what would have been the lobby, an expanse of concrete stretching toward a dark stairwell at the far end.

He went slowly up the front steps. Inside, every surface was covered with graffiti, the walls like bone in the moonlight. The floor glittered with broken glass.

He moved silently through the lobby. When he got to the wide concrete stairwell, he stopped, drew four long, slow breaths, trying to calm himself.

He stepped into the stairwell, staying close to the wall, and looked up into darkness. He listened for footsteps, the sound of breathing, heard nothing. He started up the stairs, his sneakers silent on the concrete.

At the second-floor landing, he stopped. Like the lobby, this floor was just a length of concrete with high ceilings and gaps in the walls where the windows would have gone. A salt breeze blew through the room.

The third floor was the same, and the fourth. As he neared the fifth, he heard a rustle on the stairs in front of him. He held his breath, raised the gun.

The seagull broke from its hiding place with a flutter of wings, flew straight at him. He dodged and then it was over his head and past. He watched it fly, wings dirty white in the moonlight. It glided the length of the floor and soared out into open air.

He started up the stairs again.

On the sixth floor, the wind was stronger. He stopped in the doorway. Through the far windows came a flash of heat lightning and the distant rumble of thunder. He waited.

Twenty feet in front of him, a flashlight went on. It blinded him briefly, winked out. Afterimages pulsed in his eyes.

"You're early," Dunleavy said.

Harry turned to his right, the gun along his leg. He heard footsteps on concrete. A silhouette moved past one of the windows.

"Where is she?" he said.

The flashlight clicked on again, its beam illuminating a wide circle of concrete floor. He could see nothing but blackness behind it.

"She's here, don't worry."

The circle of light moved toward him, stopped.

"Turn around, Harry. Face the doorway."

He waited, not moving. At the edge of the light a hand came up. In it was a dark automatic, a silver noise suppressor screwed into the muzzle.

"I could shoot you now, Harry. I could have shot you on the stairs if I'd wanted to. Turn around. I won't ask you again."

"I left the money downstairs. If you kill me now, you'll never find it."

"Relax, Harry. You think I'd do you like that? Pop you from behind? Face the doorway."

In that instant, he considered bringing up the Glock, firing at the light. He could wing him at least, maybe bring him down. But he had no clear target. And Cristina might be in the room beyond.

He turned slowly, looked into the darkness of the stairwell.

"Right there," Dunleavy said.

The flashlight came up and Harry's shadow fell huge against the wall. He felt the cold touch of the suppressor against the back of his neck.

"Take a deep breath," Dunleavy said. "Relax."

The flashlight clicked off. Dunleavy's hand moved on him, slid down his arm and found the Glock, pulled it free from his fingers. Harry let him take it. The hand came back, felt along his chest, reached into the sling and took out the leather pack. He heard it hit the floor.

"Move toward the stairs. Not all the way. Stop there."

He stepped forward, felt the suppressor drop away from his neck.

"Where is she?" he said again.

"Waiting for you."

"Where?"

"Close. Shut up and stand still."

The flashlight went on again, played across the walls. He heard a soft grunt as Dunleavy bent over to pick up the pack. He moved his right hand to his cast, touched the handle of the knife.

He heard the pack being unzipped, tried to guess the distance between them. He began to slide out the knife.

"Looks like twenty-five," Dunleavy said after a moment. "Just like you said. Didn't keep any for yourself now, did you?"

"No."

"Good man. Too honest for that, eh?"

The pack was zipped shut again. He tried to picture what was going on behind him: Dunleavy juggling the gun, the flashlight, and the pack. If he wanted to shoot, he would need one hand for the flashlight, the other for the gun. He'd have to drop the money.

He slipped the knife all the way out, held it in front of him.

"Look at it this way, Harry, you're doing a favor for a brother trooper. You're giving me a new lease on life with this money, believe it or not. Now I can start picking up the pieces, work this thing out. I appreciate that."

Dunleavy was closer now. Shadows shifted on the wall. The flashlight changing hands.

"Sorry things went so wrong between us, sport," Dunleavy said. "But I want you to know it was never personal."

Harry bent his knees slightly, gripped the knife.

"So I'll make it easy on you," Dunleavy said. "Adios, partner."

The pack hit the floor.

Harry spun to his right, crouching, and a petal of fire bloomed in front of him. Then he was lunging, the knife up, and Dunleavy was right there, closer than he had expected, and he thrust, felt the blade meet resistance and push past. A hammer blow to his chest knocked him backward, drove the breath from him. He hit the wall, slid down hard. Another flash of fire and a bullet whined off the wall above him, showered him with dust.

Pressure swelled in his chest, paralyzed his lungs. He rolled onto his stomach, scuttled away from the wall. The flashlight beam jittered back and forth, farther away now. The light swept the floor a final time, and then the flashlight fell and rolled and all was darkness.

Harry lay there for a moment, not moving, silently trying to draw air into his lungs. A bullet pranged off the ceiling, ricocheted across the room. In the distance, a pulse of heat lightning seemed to answer it.

He dragged himself along the floor, trying to put distance between himself and the place Dunleavy had seen him fall. He gulped air, felt it spread into his lungs, the tightness in his chest easing.

Dunleavy's silhouette moved past a window, disappeared again.

Harry pulled up the right cuff of his jeans, clawed at the strip of duct tape above his ankle. He yanked the Grendel free and sat up, leaned against the wall. He thumbed off the safety and pointed the gun into darkness.

From a few feet away came a wet, gagging cough. He aimed at the sound, let his lungs fill with air, felt pain there.

"Throw away your gun, Mickey," he said. "Nobody has to die here."

Shuffling steps, then silence. Heat lightning flashed again.

"Toss the gun, Mickey. We can both walk out of here."

Another wet noise, closer now, to his right. Dunleavy was circling toward the sound of his voice.

He inched to his left, faced a window that framed the moon. Dunleavy would have to pass in front of it to close on him.

The sound of shoes on concrete.

"Stop where you are," Harry said.

He pointed the gun at the moon, heard the faintness of labored breathing not ten feet away. Then closer.

"Don't do it, Mickey."

Closer.

"Don't . . ."

An outline filled the window, blotted out the moon.

Harry fired once, twice, saw the form buckle, straighten. He held the Grendel steady, squeezed the trigger again and again, shell casings flying around him. He didn't count the shots and he didn't take another breath until the slide locked back empty.

The silhouette loomed, wavered, vanished. He heard the heavy fall.

Except for the wind, there was silence.

THIRTY-FIVE

After a while, when he could breathe without pain, he put the Grendel beside him, rolled slowly to his feet. Shell casings clattered from his lap to the floor. He listened for the sound of breathing, movement. There was only the wind.

He began to circle the room, using the wall for support. His foot hit something, sent it spinning away. He got down on his knees and crawled until his fingers closed on hard plastic. The flashlight. He pushed the thumb slide forward, shook the tube, slapped it against his thigh. The light blinked on, cut a tunnel in the darkness.

He stood, moved the arc of light along the floor.

Dunleavy lay faceup near the window, eyes wide, one leg folded beneath him. The handle of the knife stuck out from the left side of his chest near the shoulder. His shirt was soaked with blood, a puddle of it fanning out on the floor around him. His right hand still held the automatic, finger in the trigger guard. The Glock had slid halfway out of his jacket pocket.

Harry bent, touched the side of the neck. No pulse, no flutter, the skin already cooling. He picked up the Glock and stuck it in his belt, turned away from the body, played the light across the rest of the room.

He was alone.

• • •

He searched the building from the top down.

There was no access to the roof, so he started on the twelfth floor. He walked the length of each cavernous room, sweeping the light from one side to the other, calling her name. Every floor was the same, strewn with trash, marked with graffiti, empty.

When he reached street level, he went back outside. He walked around the lot, shining the light into patches of high weeds, checking the recesses behind the precut concrete slabs propped against the building. He felt the panic rising steadily, fought it.

At the trailer he shone the light through the broken window, saw a dented metal desk, stacked milk crates, a seven-year-old calendar on the wall. The beam moved across the floor, illuminated the back of an old couch, the upholstery slashed and bleeding foam.

The door was unlocked. He pushed it open, flashed the beam inside. There was a bundle on the couch, a gray blanket over it. He moved closer and the light caught her wet and frightened eyes.

He knelt beside her, set the flashlight on the floor. She still wore the bathing suit. Her wrists and ankles were bound with clothesline, an X of electrician's tape across her mouth. He peeled away the tape and she gasped for air, coughed. He tried to untie her feet, found he couldn't. He took out his pocket knife, sliced through the line, undid her hands.

"Are you all right?" he said.

He put the knife away, began to massage her wrists.

"I heard shots," she said. "I thought it was him. Coming back."

He shook his head. "He's not coming back."

She was barefoot, so he bundled the blanket around her, gathered her in his arms, lifted. He held her tight as they left the trailer, felt her trembling against him despite the night's warmth.

He carried her through the fence and to the station wagon, got her into the front seat, the blanket around her. He took out the Glock, laid it on the seat.

"I'll be right back," he said.

"Don't . . ."

"Just a few minutes. I promise."

He kissed her forehead, locked her door. He walked back to the site, the left side of his chest throbbing, a deep, slow pain that seemed to worsen with every step.

Back at the trailer, he flashed the light around the office until he found what he wanted, a small, paint-stained drop cloth. He folded it, tucked it under his arm, and carried it back up to the sixth floor.

He shone the light along the concrete until he found the body. Something skittered away at the edge of the light, ran along the bottom of the wall. Rats.

With the flashlight propped on a windowsill, he opened the cloth on the floor. He knelt over Dunleavy, tried not to look at the damage the bullets had done. He took hold of the handle of the knife and slowly began to work it back and forth. It came out wetly and all at once, the blade slick with blood. He dropped it in the center of the cloth.

It took him fifteen minutes to find all the shell casings from the Grendel. There were eleven of them, shorter and stubbier than the ones from Dunleavy's weapon. He found the empty Grendel, put it with the knife, dropped the shell casings beside them. Then he folded up the bundle, tied the edges.

The leather pack lay where Dunleavy had dropped it. He put it in his sling.

He used the flashlight to take a final look around the room. When he was sure he had everything he'd brought with him, he picked up the bundle and headed for the stairs.

He stowed the bundle and the money pack beneath the spare tire, unlocked the driver's side door, and slid behind the wheel. She lay against the passenger door, the blanket tight around her, watching him. He touched her leg.

"Do you need to go to the hospital?"

She shook her head, looked out at the empty boardwalk and the ocean beyond.

"Are you sure?"

"Yes. I want to go home."

"Home?"

"With you."

He started the engine, drove them away from there.

He took her back to the farm, carried her up to the bedroom. When he got her undressed and into bed, he saw that the soles of her feet were cut and bruised. He ran a washcloth under hot water, cleaned them, used tweezers to pick out specks of glass and stone. She winced but didn't cry. When he was done, he swabbed the cuts with iodine, then got her a Percocet from the medicine cabinet, a glass of water. He could already see the fatigue working in her.

"Take this," he said. "It'll help you sleep. I have to go out, but it won't be long. I'll be back as soon as I can."

He went into the bathroom, undid the sling, and peeled off his sweatshirt. There was a indentation in the vest where the bullet had hit him. He unsnapped the Velcro stays, let the vest fall away. The skin on the left side of his chest was purple and swollen, pain radiating from it.

He undressed, splashed water in his face. When he went back, the bedroom was dark. He could hear her snoring softly. He took a T-shirt and another pair of jeans from the bureau, dressed in the hallway. He closed the bedroom door quietly, went downstairs and out into the final hours of the night.

By the time he got the boat out, the first traces of dawn were lightening the sky. He steered toward the horizon glow until he was far enough from shore, then eased back on the throttle, killed the engines and the running lights.

He looked back to the darkness of the shore. There were no other boats in sight. He got the drop cloth from the cabin, spread it open on the starboard engine cover.

The day was coming fast, the dawn a pink and blue bar

on the horizon. He took the Glock from his sling, ejected the clip, and set both on the engine cover. Then he closed his eyes for a moment, felt the wind on his face, the motion of the boat beneath his feet.

He threw the knife first, flung it out as far he could against the wind, saw it drop and vanish beneath the surface. The shell casings came next, side-armed one by one out over the water. Then he field-stripped the Grendel into four parts and tossed them in different directions, heard them splash.

Bobby's Glock was last. He scaled the clip out over the water, then cleared the breech, locked the slide back, and gripped the gun by the barrel. He held it low behind him and turned with the throw, twisting his hip into it as he let go.

The gun soared out against the brightening blue of the sky, like a dark and graceless bird. He watched it fall, its flight over, saw it hit the water and disappear from sight.

There was a Catholic church not far from the marina. He parked on the street, made his way up the wide stone steps. He pulled open the door, stepped through into fragrant coolness.

The church was empty except for a young priest lighting candles in an alcove near the altar. He looked at Harry, nodded, turned back to the flames. The stained-glass windows were glowing with the first full light of day.

Harry looked up the wide aisle to the altar, dipped his fingers into the bowl of holy water. He put one knee to the marble, crossed himself, the movement unpracticed for years but instinctive. He rose and made his way up the aisle, then slipped into one of the long pews. He closed his eyes and rested his forehead on the coolness of wood, feeling the pain in his chest and something deeper too. His lips moved as he tried to remember the words from his childhood.

He found them, as he knew he would. He prayed until the day filled the church and pushed back the shadows around him.

THIRTY-SIX

In that last week of august, the first hurricane of the season formed off South America and slowly made its way up the Atlantic coast. It stalled off Virginia, but the low-pressure front it pushed ahead of it brought the summer to an early end. The temperature dropped twenty-five degrees in two days, the skies turning a slate gray. The surf, kicked up by the storm's death throes, was rough enough that it closed beaches from Cape May to Sandy Hook. It was a good time to leave.

In the end, they decided on a place neither of them had ever been, Captiva Island on the west coast of Florida. He called a realtor and arranged to rent a one-bedroom cottage near the beach for September and October. They would drive down, take their time, make it last.

Their first days at the farm were awkward. She'd chosen not to go to the funeral and, in a mutual but unspoken agreement, they hadn't mentioned Fallon by name again. They were each questioned twice, first by the Spring Lake police, then by the county prosecutor's office, with Wesniak sitting in. The county men made another run at them three days later at the farm, but they stuck to their story. She told them she'd been separated from her husband for a month before his death, had planned to file for divorce. She had no idea who might have killed him.

When their Florida plans were complete, he called

Wesniak, told him they'd be leaving for a while, and that any more questions would have to wait until they got back. Wesniak wasn't happy, but he knew there was nothing he could do to stop them.

The week before they left, he went to the doctor Ray had referred him to. His ribs were bruised but not broken where the bullet had hit him, the discoloration already fading. They took X rays of his arm, and the doctor told him the cast could likely come off in a month or so. That same day, he returned Ray's station wagon and leased a two-year-old Ford Explorer from a dealership in Freehold.

He was sitting at the kitchen table after dinner, a map of Florida in front of him, when she came into the room. She set the leather fanny pack on the map.

"Send it to that woman," she said. "Tell her it's her husband's money. Tell her you got it back somehow."

"Are you sure?"

"Yes."

"You said it was your money too. You said the price was cheap."

"I thought we might need it."

"And now?"

"I don't even want it around."

"I'll write her a letter. We can FedEx it out tomorrow."

"The sooner, the better."

"You know, you may not see that much cash together in the same place again for a long time."

"Send it," she said.

When the phone rang, he was at the kitchen window, watching her throw scraps of bread to the birds in the backyard.

"How's it going?" Wesniak said.

"Well enough, I guess. What can I do for you?"

"Do for me? Nothing. Just checking up on you. You still planning on leaving tomorrow, taking that trip?"

"We're packed."

"Good. I understand the prosecutor's office sent some people over to your house to talk with the widow again."

"Last week."

"Can't blame them. That didn't look good, you know, her moving in with you after her husband got clipped."

"She'd been here almost a month before it happened. She heard about it on the news, like everyone else."

"Like you?"

"Like me."

"I talked to Shandler, the assistant prosecutor. He said, when it came down to it, there was no concrete evidence that either of you had been involved . . ."

"He's right."

". . . and he had nothing at hand that would justify pursuing it further. So I guess things worked out for you after all, didn't they? You got lucky."

"Lucky? I haven't felt that way much lately."

"Depends on how you define the concept, I guess. By the way, they found Dunleavy."

Harry gave that a second.

"Where?"

"In Asbury Park. There's a construction site there, abandoned. They found him a couple days ago. Shot to death. ME thinks he was in there a couple weeks at least. Some crackheads found him. Funny how these things end up, isn't it?"

"What do you mean?"

"I mean it's a hell of a way to go. Not much dignity to it."

"Is there ever?"

"He had a gun. Looks like he got off a few shots at whoever killed him."

"Any idea who the shooter was?"

"Not yet. One thing we did find, though. The gun he had with him is the same one that was used to kill Fallon. The bullets match. So that gets you off the hook, I guess. Makes it all kind of neat."

"Neat? I think you should be talking to Paulie Andelli and his friends, not to me."

"I will be. But I doubt if it'll get me anywhere. If Andelli had Dunleavy whacked, it was the sloppiest job I've seen in years. Dunleavy took half a dozen hits, none of them aimed particularly well. And something tells me if Andelli's crew was responsible, we'd never have found the body."

"Heat of the moment," Harry said. "Exchange of gunfire. Somebody forgot to be professional. It happens."

"Yes, it does. Tell me, how's the widow holding up?"

"As good as could be expected."

"Under the circumstances?"

"Under the circumstances."

"There could be more trouble for you two, you know, when the will comes around."

"She's already talked to an attorney. She doesn't want anything. Whatever's left after lawyers and taxes will go to his daughters. It was her decision."

He watched as she stood up, brushed crumbs from her hands.

"I wish you luck, Harry. I really do."

"Thanks."

"But if you think Andelli and his people are going to forget this ever happened and let you get on with your life, you're mistaken."

"I'll take my chances."

"For them, at the moment, it's back to business as usual. It wouldn't pay to go after you now, you're not a threat. But Andelli won't forget. And some day he's going to be drinking espresso in some social club and he's going to say your name, that's all, and someone's going to get up from the table and make a phone call."

"So put him away in the meantime."

"I'd love to. And I intend to. But if I were you, when I got back from that trip I'd think about relocating. For a while, at least."

"I'll keep that in mind."

"Good. Because I never want to hear your name again, Harry. I don't want to see it in a report on my desk or come across it in the transcript of a wiretap. I don't want to read it in the paper. In fact, I don't even want to see it in the phone book."

She came in the back door, took a pack of cigarettes from the counter. She lit one, watched him.

"I get the message," Harry said.

"Good. It's time to say good-bye, Harry. Let's not meet again."

The phone clicked in his ear. He replaced the receiver.

"Who was that?" she said.

"A friend. I think."

"Is everything okay?"

"Yeah."

"Are you sure?"

"Surer than I've been of anything in a while."

"Well," she said, "I guess that's something."

"From where I'm standing," he said, "it's everything."

The next morning, after breakfast, he stowed their suitcases in the back of the Explorer. They'd woken to the sounds of heavy equipment, and when he'd gone out onto the porch, he'd seen a pair of bulldozers plowing through the trees on the property across the road. Men in yellow hard hats stood around, hands on hips, watching what was going on. He could hear chain saws, the rumble of diesel engines.

When he was done loading the Explorer, he went into the backyard, walked out beneath the trees. The air was cool and sharp, and smelled of the woods. He sat on one of the table-size rocks alongside the creek. After a few minutes, she came outside, called his name. He waited, heard her come up behind him.

"There you are," she said. "I was wondering where you'd gotten to."

She sat beside him.

He picked up a pebble, tossed it into the water.

"I was wondering," he said, "what comes next. After we get back."

"We'll worry about that then."

Something moved beneath the surface of the creek, ripples trailing above it. A cloud shifted and sunlight flashed across the water, formed a rainbow pattern in the spray around the rocks.

"Hours of darkness," he said.

"What?"

"I was thinking last night about that phrase. The hours of darkness. They're just that, aren't they? Hours. They end. Things move on."

She reached over and caught the tips of his fingers, squeezed them.

"We should go," she said.

He nodded. They stood, hand in hand, and began to walk back to the house.

At midnight, they were still on the road.